C000204464

THE OTHER VOICE

THE OTHER VOICE

Scottish Women's Writing since 1808

an anthology edited by

Moira Burgess

POLYGON
Edinburgh

First published in Great Britain in 1987
by Polygon 48 Pleasance, Edinburgh EH8 9TJ

The publisher acknowledges subsidy from the Scottish Arts Council
towards the publication of this volume.

Typeset by EUSPB, 48 Pleasance, Edinburgh EH8 9TJ
Printed and Bound by Billing & Sons Ltd., Worcester

Introduction © Moira Burgess 1987.
"Void of Understanding" by Mary Findlater from *Tales that are Told*; published by kind permission of Methuen & Co. Ltd.
"The Pictures" by Jane Helen Findlater from *A Green Grass Widow*; published by kind permission of John Murray (publishers) Ltd.
"Thievie" by Violet Jacob from *Tales of my Own Country*; published by kind permission of John Murray (publishers) Ltd.
"Captain Pert" by Winifred Duke from *Tales of Hate*; published by kind permission of William Hodge and Co. Ltd.
"Clock-a-doodle-do" by Willa Muir; first published by kind permission of Gavin Muir.
"The Zoo: The Dream" © Catherine Carswell from *Lying Awake*; published by Secker and Warburg.
"The Teeth" © Naomi Mitchison from *Five Men and a Swan*; published by kind permission of Allen and Unwin.
"No Letters Please" © Nancy Brysson Morrison from *Casual Columns: The Glasgow Herald Miscellany*; published by kind permission of George Outram & Co. Ltd.
"The Black Madonna" © Muriel Spark from *The Go-Away Bird*; published by MacMillan and Penguin.
"An Edinburgh Lady" © Joan Lingard from *The Prevailing Wind*; published by Hodder and Stoughton.
"It's My Day for Leaving Home" by Joan Ure; published by kind permisson of the proprietor of Joan Ure's literary estate.
"The Gowk" © Jessie Kesson from *Where The Apple Ripens*; published by kind permission of Chatto & Windus: The Hogarth Press.
"Dorothy Dean" © Dorothy K. Haynes from *Peacocks and Pagodas*; published by Paul Harris.
"Bung" by Margaret Hamilton from *Modern Scottish Short Stories* edited by Urquhart and Gordon; published by Hamish Hamilton, Faber and Faber; published by kind permission of Mrs Nora Hunter.
"The Pedestrian" by Elspeth Davie from *The Night of the Funny Hats*; published by kind permission of Hamish Hamilton.
"The Pigeon" © Eona Macnicol from *A Carver of Coal*; published by kind permission of Ramsey Head Press.
"The Deprived" © Janet Caird from *Scottish Short Stories 1976*; published by kind permission of William Collins Ltd.
"A Bad Year for Trees" © Catherine Lucy Czerkawska; first published in Chapman issues 27-28.
"A Change of Face" © Agnes Owens from *Lean Tales* (co-authors Alasdair Gray, James Kelman); published by kind permission of Jonathan Cape.

British Library Cataloguing in Publication Data
    The Other Voice: Scottish women's writing from 1808.
    1. Short Stories, English—Scottish
    authors 2. short stories, English—
    Women authors 3. English fiction—20th
    century
    I. Burgess, Moira
    823'.01'089287[FS]   PR8676

ISBN 0-948275-39-1
ISBN 0-948275-31-6 Pbk

CONTENTS

INTRODUCTION

Charlotte Bronte wrote of her feelings on finding the manuscript of her sister Emily's verses:

Something more than surprise seized me — a deep conviction that these were not common effusions, nor at all like the poetry women generally write. I thought them condensed and terse, vigorous and genuine . . .

With a further 150 years of evidence to consider, critics and readers (even in Scotland) probably no longer take a simplistic view of 'what women generally write'. Yet conditioning is strong: mention women's writing, and old unworthy suspicions raise their heads. Sentimentality, domestic detail, 'women's stories' — these are some of the spectres waiting to be laid.

The editor of a collection such as this, the first anthology to cover the field of Scottish women's writing from the beginnings to the present day, is in an interesting dilemma: to ignore these suspicions, or to refute them? Perhaps it would be good to present a collection of writing by women which might in every respect have been produced by men. If one could do this, on the other hand, where would be the justification for making a collection of women's writing at all?

To quote again from Charlotte's opinion of Emily's verses:

To my ear, they had also a peculiar music — wild, melancholy, and elevating . . .

I think there is a music, or tone of voice, peculiar to Scottish women's writing, which is clearly heard in most of the pieces in this collection, and it is not a sentimental one. It tends rather to an ironic detachment, particularly perhaps when the writer is observing other women. This may be expected in the moderns like Muriel Spark and Joan Ure, but what about the elegant hatchet-work of Mary Brunton, whose *Self-Control* was published in 1811?

Yet with skilful malice [Lady Pelham] contrived to awaken Laura's natural
bashfulness, by saying, as they were alighting at Mrs Clermont's door,
'Now my dear don't mortify me to-night by any of your Scotch *gaucheries.*
Remember every eye will be turned upon you.'

Certainly this anthology also contains pieces of a different tone,
but their very difference is worth attention. Far from being detached,
Lorna Moon's 'Wantin' a Hand' builds to an outburst of passion that
leaves the reader shaken. Eona Macnicol's 'The Pigeon' displays an
empathy with the central character — a man — which may lead us
to consider the strength of feeling behind much of the work included
here. 'Terse, vigorous and genuine' it is indeed.

When co-editing an anthology of Glasgow short stories* I found
the 'child's eye-view', the more or less nostalgic recall of boyhood,
remarkably prevalent. If there was a similarly recurrent subject
among the candidates for the present anthology, it was probably
the middle-aged to elderly woman. Nostalgia, however, was not
the prevailing mood; see Ferrier's richly comic Lady Maclaughlan,
counterpointed here by Tytler's grimly humorous picture of the Miss
Mackinnons in their ceremonial burning of a disputed will.

But, as we have already hinted, these Scottish women writers do
not confine themselves to the domestic scene, nor exclusively to the
woman's viewpoint. In my short-list of possible selections, it gave me
pause to discover two stories, seventy years apart in date, each having
as the main character a 'natural', or as Jessie Kesson's North-East
community succinctly has it, a 'gowk'. On consideration it seemed
well worthwhile to include both, so telling is the contrast between
them. Mary Findlater's observation of the reluctant young stepmother
in 'Void of Understanding' is a prime example of our
ironic detachment: read the short scene centred on the first wife's
photograph. Mary's stories are, however, more of their time than are
those of her sister Jane, and she hovers, here and there, on the verge
of sentimentality. It was a severe temptation to lose the last sentence
of 'Void of Understanding' in the course of editing, for the greater
good of all. Kesson's Gowk also has an unsympathetic stepmother,
but events take a quite different course. The only similarity lies in
the compassion that illuminates Kesson's tough, economical writing
all the way to her devastating last line.

It was at first our intention to illustrate the development of Scottish
women's writing through short stories, but the purist will observe that
this is not quite the final shape of the book. When one considers early

Scottish women writers of fiction, the name of Susan Ferrier comes at once to mind. Unfortunately for our purposes, neither she nor her near contemporary Mary Brunton, so far as I have discovered, wrote any short stories; they would have been extremely early in the field of Scottish short story writing if they had. It seemed wrong, however, to open our account baldly with Margaret Oliphant, as if her forerunners did not exist. We have therefore included reasonably self-contained extracts from novels by these founding mothers, and indeed pushed the frontier back a little beyond them. Elizabeth Hamilton's *The Cottagers of Glenburnie* (1808) may well have a didactic intent, but throughout its earnest pages humour, sharp observation and that distinctive dry tone of voice are always breaking in.

Apart from these early examples, we have been sparing in our use of extracts. Sarah Tytler is a rather special case; she was a prolific writer of short stories, but those I have been able to trace are hack-work. However, she is — or should be — known for two of her novels, and it seemed only right to include here an extract from one of them.

'The Zoo: The Dream', by Catherine Carswell, was not, apparently, intended as a short story, but its shape and power mark it out as something more than prosaic autobiography. Again, Joan Lingard has not so far written any short stories for adults; but the reader of her novel *The Prevailing Wind* must be struck by the scene between Janet and her mother in chapter 8, a virtuoso passage of perceptive description. Neither of these extracts, in our opinion, would seem out of place if presented in literary periodicals as prose-pieces. We have so presented them here.

In short stories proper there proved to be a rich vein of material to quarry, and for that very reason there is plenty of room for debate about the selection which we have finally made. Why, among Margaret Oliphant's better-known stories, do we include 'The Library Window' in preference to 'The Open Door'? Why 'The Teeth' rather than one of Mitchison's stories of the supernatural — Highland or African — or the chilling 'Remember Me'? Why Haynes's 'Dorothy Dean' rather than 'The Head'? Probably an ideal anthology would include all of these, but in an imperfect world we have capitulated to common sense and pressure of space, and settled on the editor's favourites.

We hope, in any case, that our selection gives an indication of the work of twenty-five Scottish women writers — some famous, some much less well known — whose work can by no means be described as 'women's stories', but equally could never have been written by men.

Thanks are due to librarians in The Mitchell Library, Glasgow; Edinburgh Central Library; and the National Library of Scotland (Lending Services) for help in tracing books, periodicals and information.

* Moira Burgess and Hamish Whyte, eds.: *Streets of Stone* (Salamander Press, 1985)

ELIZABETH HAMILTON

A Sensible Effect on the Nerves

(abridged from *The Cottagers of Glenburnie*)

Mrs Mason, left homeless after a life in domestic service, has come to lodge with her cousin, the well-named Mrs MacClarty.

Mrs Mason retired to her room, under a full conviction, that, in the society of people who so sincerely served and worshipped God, all the materials of happiness would be within her reach.

Her bed appeared so inviting from the delicate whiteness of the linen, that she hastened to enjoy in it the sweets of repose; but no sooner had her head reached the pillow, than she becomes sick, and was so overcome by a feeling of suffocation, that she was obliged to sit up for air. Upon examination, she found that the smell which annoyed her proceeded from new feathers put into the pillow before they had been properly dried, and when they were consequently full of the animal oil, which, when it becomes rancid, sends forth an intolerable effluvia. Having removed the annoyance, and made of her clothes a bundle to support her head, she again composed herself to sleep. But alas, in vain! for the enemy by whom she was now attacked she found to be sworn against sleep. The assault was made by such numbers in all quarters, and carried on with such dexterity by the merciless and agile foe, that, after a few ineffectual attempts at offensive and defensive warfare, she at length resigned herself to absolute despair. The disgusting idea of want of cleanliness, which their presence excited, was yet more insufferable than the piercing of their little fangs. But on recollecting how long the room had been filled with the fleeces, she gladly flattered herself, that they were only accidental guests, and that she might soon be able to effect their banishment.

As day advanced, the enemy retired, and poor Mrs Mason, fatigued and wearied, at length sunk to rest. Happily she was undisturbed by the light; for though her window, which was exactly opposite to the bed, was not shaded by a curtain, the veil of dust which it had contracted in the eighteen years it had stood unwiped, was too thick to permit the rays of the sun to penetrate.

As the clock struck eight, she hastened out of bed, vexed at having lost so much of the day in sleep; and on perceiving, when about half-dressed, that she had in her room neither water nor hand-basin to wash in, she threw on her dimity bed-gown, and went out to the kitchen to procure a supply of these necessary articles.

"Hoot," said Mrs MacClarty, "I fear ye hinna sleepit weel, that he have been sae lang o' rising. It's a lang time since the kettle has been boiling for your breakfast."

"I shall be ready for it very soon," said Mrs Mason; "but I came in search of a basin and water, which Grizzy has forgot to put in my room, and until I wash, I can proceed no farther in dressing myself."

"Dear me," replied Mrs MacClarty, "I'm sure you're weel eneugh. Your hands ha' nae need o' washing, I trow. Ye ne'er do a turn to file them."

"You can't surely be in earnest," replied Mrs Mason. "Do you think I could sit down to breakfast with unwashed hands? I never heard of such a thing, and never saw it done in my life."

"I see nae good o' sic nicety," returned her friend; "but it's easy to gie ye water eneugh, though I'm sure I dinna ken what to put it in, unless ye tak ane o' the porridge plates: or may be the calf's luggie may do better, for it'll gie ye eneugh o' room."

"Your own bason will do better than either," said Mrs Mason. "Give me the loan of it for this morning, and I shall return it immediately, as you must doubtless often want it through the day." "Na, na," returned Mrs MacClarty, "I dinna fash wi' sae mony fykes. There's ay water standing in something or other, for ane to ca' their hands through when they're blacket. The gude-man indeed is a wee conceity like yoursel', an' he coft a brown bason for his shaving in on Saturdays, but it's in use a' the week haddin' milk, or I'm sure ye'd be welcome to it. I sall see an' get it ready for you the morn."

Poor Mrs Mason, on whose nerves the image presented by this description of the alternate uses of the utensil in question, produced a sensible effect, could scarce command voice to thank her cousin for her civil offer. Being, however, under the necessity of chusing for the present, she, without hesitation, preferred the calf's bicker to the porridge plate: and indeed considered the calf as being so much the cleanlier animal than his mistress, that she would in every way have preferred him for an associate.

MARY BRUNTON

A Civilized Kind of Game

(from *Self-Control*)

Laura has long been rejecting the advances of Colonel Hargrave, an unprincipled libertine. Her aunt Lady Pelham and Hargrave's gambler friend Lambert support his cause, and plan to entice Laura to play for high stakes until she is financially and morally indebted to Hargrave. Laura, however, is on principle opposed to gambling.

With her natural singleness of heart, Laura one day mentioned to Lady Pelham the change in Hargrave's behaviour. 'I suppose,' added she smiling, 'that, finding he can make nothing more of me, he is resolved to lay me under obligation by leaving me at peace, having first contrived to make me sensible of its full value.' Lady Pelham was a better dissembler than Colonel Hargrave; and scarcely did a change of colour announce the deception, while, in a tone of assumed anger, she answered by reproaching her niece with having at last accomplished her purpose, and driven her lover to despair. Yet Lady Pelham was aware that Hargrave had not a thought of relinquishing his pursuit. His new-found self-command was merely intended to throw Laura off her guard, that Lady Pelham might have an opportunity of executing a scheme which Lambert had conceived, to entangle Laura beyond the possibility of escape.

Many an action, harmless in itself, is seen, by a discerning bystander, to have in it 'nature that in time will venom breed, though no teeth for the present.' It happened that Lambert, while at Walbourne, had once seen Laura engaged in a party at chess, and her bent brow and flushed cheek, her palpitating bosom, her trembling hand, her eagerness for victory, above all, her pleasure in success, restrained but not concealed, inspired him with an idea that play might be made subservient to the designs of his friend; designs which he was the more disposed to promote, because, for the present, they occupied Hargrave to the exclusion of that folly of which Lambert had so well availed himself.

It was Lambert's proposal that he should himself engage Laura in play; and having won from her, by means which he could always command, that he should transfer the debt to Hargrave. The scheme was seconded by Lady Pelham, and, in part, acquiesced in by Hargrave. But though he could consent to degrade the woman whom he intended for his wife, he could not endure that any other than himself should be the instrument of her degradation; and, sickening at the shackles which the love of gaming had imposed upon himself, he positively refused to accede to that part of the plan, which proposed to make Laura's entanglement with him the branch of a habit previously formed. Besides, the formation of a habit, especially one so contrary to previous bias, was a work of time; and a stratagem of tedious execution did not suit the impatience of Hargrave's temper. He consented, however, to adopt a more summary modification of the same artifice. It was intended that Laura should at first be induced to play for a stake too small to alarm her, yet sufficiently great to make success desirable; that she should at first be allowed to win; that the stake should be increased until she should lose a sum which might incommode her to part with; and then that the stale cheat of gamblers, hope of retrieving her loss, should be pressed on her as a motive for venturing nearer to destruction.

The chief obstacle to the execution of this honourable enterprise lay in the first step, the difficulty of persuading Laura to play for any sum which could be at all important to her. For obviating this, Lady Pelham trusted to the diffidence, the extreme timidity, the abhorrence of notoriety, which nature strengthened by education had made a leading feature in the character of Laura. Her Ladyship determined that the first essay should be made in a large company, in the presence of persons of rank, of fame, of talent, of every qualification which could augment the awe almost amounting to horror, with which Laura shrunk from the gaze of numbers.

Partly from a craving for a confident, partly in hope of securing assistance, Lady Pelham communicated her intention to the honourable Mrs Clermont, a dashing widow of five-and-thirty. The piercing black eyes, the loud voice, the free manner, and good-humoured assurance of this lady, had inspired Laura with a kind of dread, which had not yielded to the advances which the widow condescended to make. Lady Pelham judged it most favourable to her righteous purpose, that the first attempt should be made in the house of Mrs Clermont, rather than in her own; both because that lady's higher circle of acquaintance could command a more imposing assemblage of visitors; and because this arrangement would leave her Ladyship more at liberty to watch the success of her scheme, than she could be where she was necessarily occupied as mistress of the ceremonies.

The appointed evening came, and Lady Pelham, though with the utmost kindness of manner, insisted upon Laura's attendance. Laura would rather have been excused; yet, not to interrupt a humour so harmonious, she consented to go. Lady Pelham was all complacency. She condescended to preside at her niece's toilette, and obliged her to complete her dress by wearing for that evening a superb diamond aigrette, one of the ornaments of her own earlier years. Laura strenuously resisted this addition to her attire, accounting it wholly unsuitable to her situation; but her aunt would take no denial, and the affair was not worthy of a more serious refusal. This important concern adjusted, Lady Pelham viewed her niece with triumphant admiration. She burst forth into praises of her beauty, declaring, that she had never seen her look half so lovely. Yet, with skilful malice, she contrived to awaken Laura's natural bashfulness, by saying, as they were alighting at Mrs Clermont's door, 'Now my dear don't mortify me to-night by any of your Scotch *gaucheries*. Remember every eye will be turned upon you.' 'Heaven forbid,' thought Laura, and timidly followed her aunt to a couch where she took her seat.

For a while Lady Pelham's words seemed prophetic, and Laura could not raise her eyes without meeting the gaze of admiration or of scrutiny; but the rooms began to be crowded by the great and the gay, and Laura was relieved from her vexatious distinction. Lady Pelham did not long suffer her to enjoy her release, but rising, proposed that they should walk. Though Laura felt in her own majestic stature a very unenviable claim to notice, a claim rendered more conspicuous by the contrast offered in the figure of her companion, she could not with politeness refuse to accompany her aunt, and giving Lady Pelham her arm, they began their round.

Laura, little acquainted with the ease which prevails in town parties, could not help wondering at the nonchalance of Mrs Clermont, who, leaving her guests to entertain themselves as they chose, was lounging on a sofa playing piquet with Colonel Hargrave. 'Mrs Clermont at piquet,' said Lady Pelham. 'Come Laura, piquet is the only civilized kind of game you play. You shall take a lesson;' and she led her niece forwards through a circle of misses, who, in hopes of catching the attention of the handsome Colonel Hargrave, were tittering and talking nonsense most laboriously. This action naturally drew the eyes of all upon Laura, and Lady Pelham, who expected to find useful engines in her timidity and embarrassment, did not fail to make her remark the notice which she excited. From this notice Laura would have escaped, by seating herself near Mrs Clermont; but Lady Pelham perceiving her intention, placed herself there without ceremony, so as to occupy the only remaining seats, leaving Laura standing alone, shrinking at the consciousness of her conspicuous situation. No one was near her to whom she could address herself, and her only resource was bending down to overlook Mrs Clermont's game.

She had kept her station long enough to be fully sensible of its awkwardness, when Mrs Clermont, suddenly starting up, exclaimed, 'Bless me! I had quite forgotten that I promised to make a loo-table for the Dutchess. Do, my dear Miss Montreville, take my hand for half an hour.' 'Excuse me, Madam,' said Laura, drawing back, 'I play so ill.' 'Nay, Laura,' interrupted Lady Pelham, 'your teacher is concerned to maintain your skill, and I insist on it that you play admirably.' 'Had not your Ladyship better play?' 'Oh no, my dear; I join the loo-table.' 'Come,' said Mrs Clermont, offering Laura the seat she had just quitted, 'I will take no excuse; so sit down, and success attend you!' The seat presented Laura with an inviting opportunity of turning her back upon her inspectors, she was averse from refusing such a trifling request, and rather willing to give Hargrave a proof that she was not insensible to the late improvement in his behaviour. She therefore quietly took the place assigned her, while the trio exchanged smiles of congratulation on the facility with which she had fallen into the snare.

Something, however, yet remained to be arranged, and Lady Pelham and her hostess still kept their stations by her side. While dividing the cards, Laura recollected having observed that, in town, every game seemed played for money; and she asked her antagonist what was to be the stake. He of course referred that point to her own decision; but Laura, in profound ignorance of the arcana of card-tables, blushed, hesitated, and looked at Lady Pelham and Mrs Clermont for instructions. 'We don't play high in this house, my dear,' said Mrs Clermont, 'Colonel Hargrave and I were only playing guineas.' 'Laura is only a beginner,' said Lady Pelham, 'and perhaps half a guinea' — Laura interrupted her aunt by rising and deliberately collecting the cards, 'Colonel Hargrave will excuse me,' said she. 'That is far too great a stake for me.' 'Don't be absurd, my dear,' said Lady Pelham, touching Laura's sleeve, and affecting to whisper, 'why should not you play as other people do?' Laura not thinking this a proper time to explain her conscientious scruples, merely answered, that she could not afford it; and, more embarrassed than before, would have glided away, but neither of her guards would permit her to pass. 'You need not mind what you stake with Hargrave,' said Lady Pelham apart; 'you play so much better than he that you will infallibly win.' 'That does not at all alter the case,' returned Laura. 'It would be as unpleasant to me to win Colonel Hargrave's money as to lose my own.' 'Whatever stake Miss Montreville chooses must be equally agreeable to me,' said Colonel Hargrave; but Laura observed that the smile which accompanied these words had in it more of sarcasm than of complacency. 'I should be sorry, Sir,' said she, 'that you lowered your play on my account. Perhaps some of these young ladies,' continued she, looking round to the talkative circle behind — 'Be quiet, Laura,' interrupted Lady Pelham, again in an undertone; 'you will make yourself the town-talk with your fooleries.' 'I hope not,' returned Laura, calmly; 'but if I do, there is no help; little inconveniencies must be submitted to for the sake of doing right.' 'Lord, Miss Montreville,' cried Mrs Clermont aloud, 'what odd notions you have! Who would mind playing for half a guinea. It is nothing; absolutely nothing. It would not buy a pocket handkerchief.' It would buy a week's food for a poor family, thought Laura; and she was confirmed in her resolution; but not willing to expose this reason to ridicule, and a little displeased that Mrs Clermont should take the liberty of urging her, she coolly, yet modestly replied, 'That such matters must greatly depend on the opinions and circumstances of the parties concerned, of which they were themselves the best judges.' 'I insist on your playing,' said Lady Pelham, in an angry half-whisper. 'If you will make yourself ridiculous, let it be when I am not by to share in the ridicule.' 'Excuse me, Madam, for to-night,' returned Laura, pleadingly. 'Before another evening I will give you reasons which I am sure will satisfy you.' 'I am sure,' said Hargrave, darting a very significant look towards Laura, 'if Miss Montreville, instead of cards, prefer allowing me to attend her in your absence, I shall gain infinitely by the exchange.' Laura, to whom his glance made this hint very intelligible, reddened; and, saying she would by no means interrupt his amusement, was again turning to seek a substitute among her tittering neighbours, when Mrs Clermont prevented her, by calling out to a lady at a considerable distance. 'My dear Duchess, do have the good ness to come hither, and talk to this whimsical beauty of ours. She is seized with an economical fit, and has taken it into her pretty little head that I am quite a gambler because I fix her stake at half-a-guinea.' 'What may not youth and beauty do!' said her Grace, looking at Laura with a smile half-sly half-insinuating. 'When I was the Miss Montreville of my day, I too might have led the fashion of playing for pence, though now I dare not venture even to countenance it.' The mere circumstance of rank could never discompose Laura; and, rather taking encouragement from the charming though faded countenance of the speaker, she replied, 'But, in consideration of having no pretensions to lead the fashion, may I not claim exemption from following it?' 'Oh, by no means,' said her Grace. 'When once you have entered the world of fashion, you must either be the daring leader or the humble follower. If you choose the first, you must defy the opinions of all other people; and, if the last, you must have a suitable indifference for your own.' 'A gentle intimation,' returned Laura, 'that in the world of fashion I am quite out of place, since nothing but my own opinion is more awful to me than that of others.' 'Miss Montreville,' said Lady Pelham, with an aspect of vinegar, 'we all await your pleasure.' 'Pray, Madam,' answered Laura, 'do not let me detain you a moment; I shall easily dispose of myself.' 'Take up your cards this instant, and let us have no more of these airs,' said Lady Pelham, now without affectation whispering, in order to conceal from her elegant companions the wrath which was, however, distinctly written in her countenance.

It now occurred to Laura as strange, that so much trouble should be taken to prevail upon her to play for more than he inclined. Hargrave, though he had pretended to release her, till kept his seat, and his language had tended rather to embarrass than relieve her. Mrs Clermont had interfered further than Laura thought either necessary or proper; and Lady Pelham wa eager to carry her point. Laura saw that there was something in all this which she did not comprehend; and, looking up to seek an explanation in the faces of her companions, she perceived that the whole trio seemed waiting her decision with looks of various interest. The piercing black eyes of Mrs Clermont were fixed upon her with an expression of sly curiosity. Hargrave hastily withdrew a sidelong glance of anxious expectation; while Lady

Pelham's face was flushed with angry impatience of delay. 'Has your Ladyship any particular reason for wishing that I should play for a higher take than I think right?' said Laura, fixing on her aunt a look of calm scrutiny. Too much out of humour to be completely on her guard. Lady Pelham's colour deepened several shades, while she answered, 'I child! what should make you think so?' 'I don't know,' said Laura. 'People sometimes try to *convince* from mere love of victory, but they seldom take the trouble to *persuade* without some other motive.' 'Any friend,' said Lady Pelham, recollecting herself, 'would find motive enough for what I have done, in the absurd appearance of these littlnesses to the world, and the odium that deservedly falls on a young miser.' 'Nay, Lady Pelham,' said the Duchess, 'this is far too severe. Come,' she added, beckoning to Laura, with a gracious smile, 'you shall sit by me, that I may endeavour to enlarge your conceptions on the subject of card-playing.'

Laura, thus encouraged, instantly begged her aunt's permission topass. Lady Pelham could not decently refusee; and, venting hr rage, bypinching Laura's arm till the blood came, and muttering through her clenchedteeth, 'obstinate wretch,' she suffered her niece to escape. Laura did notdondescend to bestow any notice upon this assault, but, pulling her gloveover her wounded arm, took refuge beside the Duchess.

SUSAN FERRIER
By Express Invitation
(from *Marriage*)

Lady Juliana, whose headstrong romantic marriage has brought her to the wilds of Scotland, goes visiting with her husband's elderly aunts.

The usual salutations were scarcely over, when Miss Grizzy, flying to her little writing-box, pulled out a letter, and, with an air of importance, having enjoined silence, she read as follows:—

"Lochmarlie Castle, March 27, 17—

"Dear Child,

"Sir Sampson's stomach has been as bad as it could well be, but not so bad as your roads — he was shook to a jelly. My petticoat will never do. Mrs M'Hall has had a girl. I wonder what makes people have girls; they never come to good: boys may go to the mischief, and be good for something — if girls go, they're good for nothing I know of. I never saw such roads — I suppose Glenfern means to bury you all in the highway — there are holes enough to make you graves, and stones big enough for coffins. Colonel G—— is dead — he was near a hundred; she is ninety, so their loves have not been nipt in the bud. She is a Portuguese — he married her in India for her money. She was jealous, and fancied every woman in love wid de colonel. Pretty Miss Macdonald staid two days with them. When she was going away, Mrs G—— said to her, 'You will come again when I do ask you; and dat,' stamping her foot, 'will be — never!' Poor thing! I went to visit her last week. She cried like a baby — she was in weeds, and wore the colonel's long *queue* fastened to her widow's cap, and hanging down her back — a fact which can be attested by living witnesses: it was his own hair. She said she had sent for de minister to make her de Protestant, dat she might go to de same place wid de dear good colonel. She is an oddity; — beware of becoming oddities, dear girls, and hanging *queues* to your widow's caps — if ever you have any. I like you all very much, and you must all come and spend Tuesday here — not all, but some of you — you, dear child, and your brother, and a sister, and your pretty niece, and handsome nephew — I love handsome people. Miss M'Kraken has bounced away with her father's footman — I hope he will clean his knives on her. Come early, and come dressed, to your loving friend,

"ISABELLA MACLAUGHLAN"

The letter ended, a volley of applause ensued, which at length gave place to consultation. "Of course we all go — at least as many as the carriage will hold: we have no engagements, and there can be no objections."

Lady Juliana had already frowned a contemptuous refusal, but in due time it was changed to a sullen assent, at the pressing entreaties of her husband, to whom any place was now preferable to home. In truth, the mention of a party had more weight with her than either her husband's wishes or her aunt's remonstrances; and they had assured her, that she should meet with a large assemblage of the very first company at Lochmarlie Castle.

The day appointed for the important visit arrived; and it was arranged that two of the elder ladies, and one of the young ones, should accompany Lady Juliana in her barouche, which Henry was to drive.

At peep of dawn the ladies were astir, and at eight o'clock breakfast was hurried over, that they might begin the preparations necessary for appearing with dignity at the shrine of this their patron saint. At eleven they reappeared in all the majesty of sweeping silk trains and well-powdered toupees. In outward show, Miss Bella was not less elaborate. The united strength and skill of her three aunts and four sisters had evidently been exerted in forcing her hair into every position but that for which nature had intended it; curls stood on end around her forehead, and tresses were dragged up from the roots and formed into a club on the crown: her arms had been strapped back till her elbows met; and her respiration seemed suspended by means of a pink riband of no ordinary strength or doubtful hue — what wine-merchants call a "full body".

Three hours were passed in all the anguish of full-dressed impatience, an anguish in which every female breast must be ready to sympathise. But Lady Juliana sympathised in no one's distresses but her own; and the difference of waiting in high dress or in *déshabille* was a distinction to her inconceivable. But those to whom *to be dressed* is an event, will readily enter into the feelings of the ladies in question, as they sat, walked, wondered, exclaimed, opened windows, wrung their hands, adjusted their dress, &c., &c.-,during the three tedious hours they were doomed to wait the appearance of their niece.

Two o'clock came, and with it Lady Juliana, as if purposely to testify her contempt, in a plain morning dress and mob cap. The sisters looked blank with disappointment; for, having made themselves mistresses of the contents of her ladyship's wardrobe, they had settled amongst themselves that the most suitable dress for the occasion would be black velvet, and accordingly many hints had been given the preceding evening on the virtues of black velvet gowns: they were warm, and not too warm; they were dressy, and not too dressy; Lady Maclaughlan was a great admirer of black velvet gowns; she had one herself with long sleeves, and that buttoned behind; black velvet gowns were very much wore; they knew several ladies who had them; and they were certain there would be nothing else wore amongst the matrons at Lady Maclaughlan's, &c. &c.

Time was, however, too precious to be given either to remonstrance or lamentation. Miss Jacky could only give an angry look, and Miss Grizzy a sorrowful one, as they hurried away to the carriage, uttering exclamations of despair at the lateness of the hour, and the impossibility that any body could have time to dress after getting to Lochmarlie Castle.

The consequence of the delay was, that it was almost dark by the time they reached the place of destination. The carriage drove up to the grand entrance; but neither lights nor servants greeted their arrival, and no answer was returned to the ringing of the bell.

"This is most alarming, I declare!" cried Miss Grizzy.

"It is quite incomprehensible!" observed Miss Jacky. "We had best get out, and try the back door."

The party alighted, and another attack being made upon the rear, it met with better success; for a little boy now presented himself at a narrow opening of the door, and, in a strong Highland accent, demanded "wha ta war seekin'?"

"Lady Maclaughlan, to be sure, Colin," was the reply.

"Weel, weel," still refusing admittance, "but ta leddie's no to be spoken wi' tonight."

"Not to be spoken with!" exclaimed Miss Grizzy, almost sinking to the ground with apprehension. "Good gracious! — I hope! — I declare! — Sir Sampson!" ——

"Oo ay, hur may see Lochmarlie hursel." Then opening the door, he led the way to a small sitting-room, and ushered them into the presence of Sir Sampson, who was reclining in an easy chair, arrayed in a *robe-de-chambre* and night-cap. The opening of the door seemed to have broken his slumber; for, gazing around with a look of stupefaction, he demanded, in a sleepy peevish tone, "who was there?"

"Bless me, Sir Sampson!" exclaimed both spinsters at once, darting forward and seizing a hand; "bless me, don't you know us! — and here is our niece, Lady Juliana."

"My Lady Juliana Douglas!" cried he, with a shriek of horror, sinking again upon his cushions — "I am betrayed — I — Where is my Lady Maclaughlan? — where is Murdoch? — where is — distraction! — this is not to be borne! My Lady Juliana Douglas, the Earl of Courtland's daughter, to be introduced to Lochmarlie Castle in so vile a manner, and myself surprised in so indecorous a situation!" And, his lips quivering with passion, he rang the bell.

The summons was answered by the same attendant that had acted as gentleman usher.

"Where are all my people?" demanded his incensed master.

"Hurs aw awa tull ta Sandy Mor's."

"Where is my lady?"

"Hurs i' ta teach-tap."*

"Where is Murdoch?"

"Hurs helpin' ta leddie i' ta teach-tap."

"Oh, we'll all go upstairs, and see what Lady Maclaughlan and Murdoch are about in the laboratory," said Miss Grizzy. "So, pray just go on with your nap, Sir Sampson; we shall find the way — don't stir:" and, taking Lady Juliana by the hand, away tripped the spinsters in search of their friend. "I cannot conceive the meaning of all this," whispered Miss Grizzy to her sister as they went along. "Something must be wrong; but I said nothing to dear Sir Sampson, his nerves are so easily agitated. But what can be the meaning of all this? I declare it's quite a mystery!"

After ascending several long dark stairs, and following divers windings and turnings, the party at length reached the door of the *sanctum sanctorum* and having gently tapped, the voice of the priestess

* House-top

was heard, in no very encouraging accents, demanding "who was there?"

"It's only us," replied her trembling friend.

"Only us humph! I wonder what fool is called '*only us!*!' Open the door, Philistine, and see what '*only us!*' wants."

The door was opened, and the party entered. The day was closing in, but, by the faint twilight that mingled with the gleams from a smoky smouldering fire, Lady Maclaughlan was dimly discernible, as she stood upon the hearth, watching the contents of an enormous kettle, that emitted both steam and odour. She turned round on the entrance of the party, and regarded the invaders with her usual marble aspect, but without moving either joint or muscle as they drew near.

"I declare — I don't think you know us, Lady Maclaughlan," said Miss Grizzy, in a tone of affected vivacity, with which she strove to conceal her agitation.

"Know you!" repeated the friend — "humph! Who you are, I know very well; but what brings you here, I do *not* know. Do you know yourselves?"

"I declare — I can't conceive —" began Miss Grizzy; but her trepidation arrested her speech, and her sister therefore proceeded —

"Your ladyship's declaration is no less astonishing than incomprehensible. We have waited upon you by your own express invitation on the day appointed by yourself: and we have been received in a manner, I must say, we did not expect, considering this is the first visit of our niece, Lady Juliana Douglas."

"I'll tell you what, girls," replied their friend, as she still stood with her back to the fire, and her hands behind her; "I'll tell you what, you are not yourselves — you are all lost — quite mad — that's all — humph!"

"If that's the case, we cannot be fit company for your ladyship," retorted Miss Jacky, warmly; "and therefore the best thing we can do is to return the way we came: come, Lady Juliana — come, sister."

"I declare, Jacky, the impetuosity of your temper is — I really cannot stand it" — and the gentle Grizzy gave way to a flood of tears.

"You used to be rational, intelligent creatures," resumed her ladyship; "but what has come over you I don't know. You come tumbling in here in the middle of the night — and at the top of the house — nobody knows how — when I never was thinking of you; and because I don't tell a parcel of lies, and pretend I expected you, you are for flying off again —humph! Is this the behaviour of women in their senses? But, since you are here, you may as well sit down, and say what brought you. Get down, Gil Blas — go along, Tom Jones!" addressing two huge cats, who occupied a three-cornered leather chair by the fireside, and who relinquished it with much reluctance.

"How do you do, pretty creature?" kissing Lady Juliana, as she seated her in this cat's cradle. "Now, girls, sit down, and tell what brought you here tonight — humph!"

"Can your ladyship ask such a question, after having formally invited us?" demanded the wrathful Jacky.

"I'll tell you what, girls; you were just as much invited by me to dine here today, as you were appointed to sup with the Grand Seignior — humph!"

"What day of the week does your ladyship call this?" demanded Jacky, with assumed composure.

"I call it Tuesday; but I suppose the Glenfern calendar calls it Thursday: Thursday was the day I invited you to come."

"I'm sure — I'm thankful we've got to the bottom of it at last," cried Miss Grizzy; "I read it, because I am sure I thought you wrote it, Tuesday."

"How could you be such a fool, my love, as to read it any such thing? Even if it had been written Tuesday, you might have had the sense to know it meant Thursday. When did you know me invite anybody for a Tuesday?"

"I declare it's very true; — I certainly ought to have known better. I am quite confounded at my own stupidity; for, as you observe, even though you had said Tuesday, I might have known that you must have meant Thursday — there can be no doubt about that!"

"Well, well, no more about it: since you are here, you must stay here, and you must have something to eat, I suppose. Sir Sampson and I have dined two hours ago; but you shall have your dinner for all that. I must shut shop for this day, it seems, and leave my resuscitating tincture all in the dead-thraw — Methusalem pills quite in their infancy. But there's no help for it: since you are here, you must stay here, and you must be fed and lodged: so get along, girls, get along. Here, Gil Blas — come, Tom Jones." And, preceded by her cats, and followed by her guests, she led the way to the parlour.

MARGARET OLIPHANT

Mrs Merridew's Fortune

CHAPTER I.

There are two houses in my neighbourhood which illustrate so curiously two phases of life, that everybody on the Green, as well as my self, has been led into the habit of classing them together. The first reason of this of course is, that they stand together; the second, that they are as unlike in every way as it is possible to conceive. They are about the same size, with the same aspect, the same green circle of garden surrounding them; and yet as dissimilar as if they had been brought out of two different worlds. They are not on the Green, though they are undeniably a part of Dinglefield, but stand on the Mercot Road, a broad country road with a verdant border of turf and fine trees shadowing over the hedgerows. The Merridews live in the one, and in the other are Mrs Spencer and Lady Isabella. The house of the two ladies is as perfect in all its arrangements as if it were a palace: a silent, soft, fragrant, dainty place, surrounded by lawns like velvet: full of flowers in perfect bloom, the finest kinds, succeeding each other as the seasons change. Even in the autumn, when the winds are blowing, you never see a fallen leaf about, or the least symptom of untidiness. They have enough servants for everything that is wanted, and the servants are as perfect as the flowers — noiseless maids and soft-voiced men. Everything goes like machinery, with an infallible regularity; but like machinery oiled and deadened, which emits or creak nor groan. This is one of the things upon which Mrs Spencer specially prides herself. The two ladies of the house are not related; they are united only by that closest bond of friendship which often, in despite of all popular fallacies, binds two women. Mrs Spencer is very well off; Lady Isabella not so rich. They never make any great demonstration of their attachment for each other, but are as sisters in their house. Yet, perhaps, not precisely as sisters; rather — if the reader will not laugh — like husband and wife.

And just across two green luxuriant hedges, over a lawn which is not like velvet, you come to the Merridews'. It is possible, if you passed it on a summer day, that, notwithstanding the amazing superiority of the other, you would pause longer, and be more amused with a glance into the enclosure of the latter house. The lawn is not the least like velvet; probably it has not been mown for three weeks at least, and the daisies are irrepressible. But there, tumbled down in the midst of it, are a bunch of little children in pinafores — *"all* the little ones," as Janet Merridew, the eldest daughter, expresses herself, with a certain soft exasperation. I would rather not undertake to number them or record their names, but there they are, a knot of rosy, round-limbed, bright-eyed, living things, some dark and some fair, with an amazing impartiality; but all chattering as best they can in nursery language, with rings of baby laughter, and baby quarrels, and musings of infinite solemnity. Once tumbled out here, where no harm can come to them, nobody takes any notice of the little ones. Nurse, sitting by serenely under a tree, works all the morning through, and there is so much going on indoors to occupy the rest.

Mr and Mrs Merridew, I need not add, had a large family — so large that their house overflowed, and when the big boys were at home from school, was scarcely habitable. Janet, indeed, did not hesitate to express her sentiments very plainly on the subject. She was just sixteen, and a good child, but full of the restless longing for something, she did not know what, and visionary discontent with her surroundings, which is not uncommon at her age. She had a way of paying me visits, especially during the holidays, and speaking more frankly on domestic subjects than was at all expedient. She would come in, in summer, with a tap on the glass which always startled me, through the open window, and sink down on a sofa and utter a long sigh of relief. "Oh, Mrs Musgrave!" she would say, "what a good thing you never had any children:" taking off, as she spoke, the large hat which it was one of her grievances to be compelled to wear.

"Is that because you have too many at home?" I said.

"Oh, yes, far too many; fancy, ten! Why should poor papa be burdened with ten of us, and so little money to keep us all on? And then a house gets so untidy with so many about. Mamma does all she can, and I do all I can; but how is it possible to keep it in order? When I look across the hedges to Mrs Spencer and Lady Isabella's, and see everything so nice and so neat, I could die of envy. And you are always so shady, and so cool, and so pleasant here."

"It is easy to be neat and nice when there is nobody to put things out of order," said I; "but when you are as old as I am, Janet, you will get to think that one may buy one's neatness too dear."

"Oh, I delight in it!" cried the girl. "I should like to have everything nice, like you; all the books and papers just where one wants them, and paper-knives on every table, and ink in the ink-bottles, and no dust anywhere. You are not so dreadfully particular as Mrs Spencer and Lady Isabella. I think I should like to see some litter on the carpet or on the lawn now and then for a change. But oh, if you could only see our house! And then our things are so shabby: the drawing-room carpet is all faded with the sun, and mamma will never have the blinds properly pulled down. And Selina, the housemaid, has so much to do. When I scold her, mamma always stops me, and bids me recollect we can't be as nice as you other people, were we to try ever so much. There is much to do in our house. And then those dreadful big boys!

"My dear," said I, "ring the bell, and we will have some tea; and you can tell Jane to bring you some of that strawberry jam you are so fond of — and forget the boys —"

"As if one could," said Janet, "when they are all over the place — into one's very room, if one did not mind; their boots always either dusty or muddy, and oh, the noise they make! Mamma won't make them dress in the evenings, as I am sure she should. How are they ever to learn to behave like Christians, Mrs Musgrave, if they are not obliged to dress and come into the drawing-room at night?"

"I daresay they would run out again and spoil their evening clothes, my dear," I said.

"That is just what mamma says," cried Janet; "but isn't it dreadful to have always to consider everything like that? Poor mamma, too, — often I get quite angry, and then I think — perhaps she would like a house like Mrs Spencer and Lady Isabella's as well as I should, if we had money enough. I suppose in a nice big house with heaps of maids and heaps of money, and everything kept tidy for you, one would not mind even the big boys."

"I think under those circumstances most people would be glad to have them," said I.

"I don't understand how anybody can like boys," said Janet, with reflective yet contemptuous emphasis. "A baby-boy is different. When the are just the age of little Harry, I adore them; but those great long-legged creatures, in their big boots! And yet, when they're nicely dressed in their evening things," she went on, suddenly changing her tone, "and with a flower in their coats — Jack has actually got an evening-coat, Mrs Musgrave, he is so tall for his age, — they look quite nice; they look such gentlemen," Janet concluded, with a little sisterly enthusiasm. "Oh, how dreadful it is to be so poor!"

"I am sure you are very fond of them all the same," said I, "and would break your heart if anything should happen to them."

"Oh, well, of course, now they are there one would not wish anything to happen," said Janet. "What did you say I was to tell Jane, Mrs Musgrave, about the tea? There now! Selina has never the time to be as nice as that, — and Richards, you know, our man — Don't you think, really, it would better to have a nice clean parlourmaid than a man that looks like a cobbler? Mrs Spencer and Lady Isabella are always going on about servants, — that you should send them away directly when they do anything wrong. But, you know, it makes a great difference having a separate servant for everything. Mamma always says, 'They are good to the children, Janet,' or, 'They are so useful and don't mind what they do.' We put up with Selina because, though she's not a good housemaid, she is quite willing to help in the nursery; and we put up with nurse because she gets through so much sewing; and even the cook — Oh, dear, dear! it is so disagreeable, I wish I was —anybody but myself."

Just at that moment my maid ushered in Mrs Merridew, hastily attired in a hat she wore in the garden, and a light shawl wrapped round her. There was an anxious look in her face, which indeed was not very unusual there. She was a little flushed, either by walking in the sunshine or by something on her mind.

"You here, Janet," she said, when she had shaken hands with me, "when you promised me to practise an hour after luncheon? Go, my dear, and do it now."

"It's so hot. I never can play in the middle of the day; and oh, mamma, please it is so pleasant here," pleaded Janet, nestling herself close into the corner of the sofa.

"Let her stay till we have had some tea," I said. "I know she likes my strawberry jam."

Mrs Merridew consented, but with a sigh; and then it was that I saw clearly she must have something on her mind. She did not smile, as usual, with the indulgent mother's smile, half disapproving, yet unwilling to thwart the child. On the contrary, there was a little constraint in her air as she sat down, and Janet's enjoyment of the jam vexed her, and brought a little wrinkle to her brow. "One would think you had not eaten anything all day," she said, with a vexed tone, and evidently was impatient of her daughter's presence, and wished her away.

"Nothing so nice as this," said Janet, with the frank satisfaction of her age; and she went on eating her bread and jam quite composedly, until Mrs Merridew's patience was exhausted.

"I cannot have you stay any longer," she said, at length. "Go and practise now, while there is no one in the house —"

"Oh, mamma!" said Janet, beginning to expostulate; but was stopped short by a look in her mother's eye. Then she gathered herself up reluctantly, and left the paradise of my little tea-table with the jam. She went out pouting, trailing her great hat after her; and had to be stopped as she stepped into the blazing sunshine, and commanded to put it on. "It's only a step," said the provoking girl, pouting more and more. And poor Mrs Merridew looked so worried, and heated, and uncomfortable, as she went out and said a few energetic words to her naughty child. Poor soul! Ten different wills to manage and keep in subjection to her own, besides all the other cares she had upon her shoulders. And that big girl who should have been a help to her, standing pouting and disobedient between the piano she did not care for, and the jam she loved. — Sometimes such a little altercation gives one a glimpse into an entire life.

"She is such a child," Mrs Merridew said, coming in with an apologetic, anxious smile on her face. She had been fretted and vexed, and yet she would not show it to lessen my opinion of her girl. Then she sank down wearily into that corner of the sofa from which Janet had been so unwillingly expelled. "The truth is, I wanted to speak to you," she said, "and could not when she was here. Poor Janet! I am afraid I was cross, but I could not help it. Something has occurred today which has put me out."

"I hope it is something I can help you in," I said.

"That is why I have come: you are always so kind; but it is a strange thing I am going to ask you this time," she said, with a wistful glance at me. "I want to go to town for a day on business of my own; and I want it to be supposed that it is business of yours."

The fact was, it did startle me for the moment — and then I reflected like lightning, so quick was the process (I say this that nobody may think my first feeling hard), what kind of woman she was, and how impossible that she should want to do anything that one need be ashamed of. "That is very simple," I said.

Then she rose hastily and came up to me and gave me a sudden kiss, though she was not a demonstrative woman. "You are always so understanding," she said, with the tears in her eyes; and thus I was committed to stand by her, whatever her difficulty might be.

"But you shan't do it in the dark," she went on; "I am going to tell you all about it. I don't want Mr Merridew to know, and in our house it is quite impossible to keep anything secret. He is on circuit now; but he would hear of 'the day mamma went to town' before he had been five minutes in the house. And so I want you to go with me, you dear soul, and to let me say I went with you."

"That is quite simple," I said again; but I did feel that I should like to know what the object of the expedition was.

"It is a long story," she said, "and I must go back and tell you ever so much about myself before you will understand. I have had the most dreadful temptation put before me today. Oh, such a temptation! Resisting it is like tearing one's heart in two; and yet I know I ought to resist. Think of our large family, and poor Charles's many disappointments, and then, dear Mrs Musgrave, read that."

It was a letter written on a large square sheet of thin paper which she thrust into my hand: one of those letters one knows a mile off, and recognizes as lawyers' letters, painful or pleasant, as the case may be; but more painful than pleasant generally. I read it, and you may judge of my astonishment to find that it ran thus:—

"DEAR MADAM, — We have the pleasure to inform you that our late client, Mr John Babington, deceased on the 10th of May last, has appointed you by his will his residuary legatee. After all his special bequests are paid, including an annuity of a hundred a year to his mother, with remainder to Miss Babington, his only surviving sister, there will remain a sum of about 10,000*l*., at present excellently invested on landed security, and bearing interest at four-and-a-half per cent. By Mr Babington's desire, precautions have been taken to bind it strictly to your separate use, so that you may dispose of it by will or otherwise, according to your pleasure, for which purpose we have accepted the office of your trustees, and will be happy to enter fully into the subject, and put in possession of the legacy, as soon as you can favour us with a private interview.

"We are, Madam, your obedient servants,
"FOGEY, FEATHERHEAD & DOWN."

"A temptation!" I cried; "but, my dear, it is a fortune; and it is
delightful: it will make you quite comfortable. Why, it will be nearly
five hundred a year."

I feel always safe in the way of calculating interest when it is
anything approaching five per cent; five per cent is so easily counted,
and of course four and a half cannot be much different: it took away
my breath.

Mrs Merridew shook her head. "It looks so at the first glance," she
said; "but when you hear my story you will think differently." And
then she made a little uncomfortable pause. "I don't know whether
you ever guessed it," she added, looking down, and doubling a new
hem upon her handkerchief, "but I was not Charles's equal when we
married: perhaps you may have heard — ?"

Of course I had heard: but the expression of her countenance was
such that I put on a look of great amazement, and pretended to be
much astonished, which I could see was a comfort to her mind.

"I am glad of that," she said, "for you know — I could not speak
so plainly to you if I did not feel that, though you are so quiet now,
you must have seen a great deal of the world — you know what a
man is. He may be capable of marrying you, if he loves you, whatever
your condition is — but afterwards he does not like people to know.
I don't mean I was his inferior in education, or anything of that sort,"
she added, looking up at me with a sudden uneasy blush.

"You need not tell me that," I said; and then another uneasiness
took possession of her, lest I should think less highly than was right
of her husband.

"Poor Charles!" she said; "it is scarcely fair to judge him as he is
now. We have had so many cares and disappointments, and he has had
to deny himself so many things — and you may say, here is his wife,
whom he has been so good to, plotting to take away from him what
might give him a little ease. But oh, dear Mrs Musgrave, you must
hear before you judge!"

"I do not judge," I said; "I am sure you must have some very good
reason; tell me what it is."

Then she paused, and gave a long sigh. She must have been about
forty, I think, a comely, simple woman, not in any way a heroine of
romance; and yet she was as interesting to me as if she had been only

23

half the age, and deep in some pretty crisis of romantic distress. I
don't object to the love-stories either: but middle age has its romances
too.

"When I was a girl," said Mrs Merridew, "I went to Babingtons'
as Ellen's governess. She was about fifteen and I was not more than
twenty, and I believe people thought me pretty. You will laugh at me,
but I declare I have always been so busy all my life, that I have never
had any time to think whether it was true: but one thing I know, that
I was a very good governess. I often wish," she added, pausing, with
a half comic look amid her trouble, "that I could find as good a governess as I was, for the girls. There was one brother, John and one
other sister, Matilda; and Mr Merridew was one of the visitors at the
house, and was supposed to be paying *her* attention. I never could see
it, for my part, and Charles declares he never had any such idea; but
they thought so, I know. It is quite a long story. John had just come
home from the University, and was pretending to read for the bar,
and was always about the house; and the end was that he fell in love
with me —"

"Of course," said I.

"I don't know that it was of course. I was so very shy, and dreaded
the sound of my own voice; but he used to come after us everywhere
by way of talking to Ellen, and so got to know me. Poor John! he was
the nicest, faithful fellow — the sort of man one would trust anything to, and believe in, and respect, and be fond of — but not love.
Of course Charles was there too. It went on for about a year, such a
curious, confused, pleasant, painful —— I cannot describe it to you
— but you know what I mean. The Babingtons had always been kind
to me; of course they were angry when they found out about John,
but then when they knew I would not marry him, they were kinder
than ever, and said I had behaved so very well about it. I was a very
lonely poor girl; my mother was dead, and I had nowhere to go; and
instead of sending me away, Mrs Babington sent *him* away — her
own son, which was very good of her, you know. To be sure I was a
good governess, and they never suspected Charles of coming for me,
nor did I. Suddenly, all at once, without the least warning, he found
me by myself one day, and told me. I was a little shocked, thinking of
Matilda Babington; but then he declared he had meant nothing. And
so —— When the Babingtons heard of it, they were all furious; even
Ellen, my pupil, turned against me. They sent me away as if I had done
something wicked. It was very, very hard upon me; but yet I scarcely

wonder, now I think of it. That was why we married so early and so imprudently. Mrs Musgrave, I daresay you have often wondered why it was?"

I had to put on such looks of wonder and satisfied curiosity as I could; for the truth was, I had known the outlines of the story for years, just as every one knows the outlines of every one else's story; especially such parts of it as people might like to be concealed. I cannot understand how anybody, at least in society, or on the verge of society, can for a moment hope to have any secrets. Charles Merridew was a cousin of Mr Justice Merridew, and very well connected, and of course it was known that he married a governess; which was one reason why people were so shy of them at first when they came to the Green.

"I begin to perceive now why this letter should be a temptation to you," I said; "you think Mr Merridew would not like ——"

"Oh, it is not that," she said. "Poor Charles! I don't think he would mind. The world is so hard, and one makes so little head against it. No, it is because of Mrs Babington. I heard she lost all her money some years ago, and was dependent on her son. And what can she do on a hundred a year? A hundred a year! Only think of it, for an old lady always accustomed to have her own way. It is horribly unjust, you know, to take it from her, his mother, who was always so good to him; and to give it to me, whom he has not seen for nearly twenty years, and who gave him a sore heart when he did know me. I could not take advantage of it. It is a great temptation, but it would be a great sin. And that is why," she added, with a sudden flush on her face, looking at me, "I should rather — manage it myself — under cover of you, — and — not let Charles know."

She looked at me, and held me with her eye, demanding of me that I should understand her, and yet defying me to think any the worse of Charles. She was afraid of her husband, — afraid that he would clutch at the money without any consideration of the wrong, — afraid to trust him with the decision. She would have me understand her without words, and yet she would not have me blame Mr Merridew. She insisted on the one and and defied me to the other: an inconsistent, unreasonable woman! But I did my best to look as if I saw, and yet did not see.

"Then you want to see the lawyers?" I said.

"I want to see Mrs Babington," was her answer. "I must go to them and explain. They are proud people, and probably would resist — or they may be otherwise provided for. If that was the case I should not hesitate to take it. Oh, Mrs Musgrave, when I look at all the children, and Janet there murmuring and grumbling, don't you think it wrings my heart to put away this chance of comfort? And poor Charles working himself out. But it could not bring a blessing. It would bring a curse; I cannot take the bread out of the mouth of the old woman who was good to me, even to put it into that of my own child."

And here two tears fell out of Mrs Merridew's eyes. At her age people do not weep abundantly. She gave a little start as they fell, and brushed them off her dress, with, I don't doubt, a sensation of shame. She to cry like a baby, who had so much to do! She left me shortly after, with an engagement to meet at the station for the twelve-o'clock train next day. I was going to town on business, and had asked her to go with me — this was what was to be said to all the world. I explained myself elaborately that very evening to Mrs Spencer and Lady Isabella, when I met them taking their walk after dinner.

"Mrs Merridew is so kind as to go with me," I said; "she knows so much more about business than I do." And I made up my mind that I would go to the Bank and leave my book to be made up, that it might not be quite untrue.

"Fancy Mrs Musgrave having any business!" said Lady Isabella. "Why don't you write to some man, and make him do it, instead of all the trouble of going to town?"

"But Mrs Merridew is going with me, my dear," I said; and nobody doubted that the barrister's wife, with so much experience as she had, and so many things to do, would be an efficient help to me in my little affairs.

CHAPTER II.

THE house we went to was a house in St John's Wood. Everybody knows the kind of place. A garden wall, with lilacs and laburnums, all out of blossom by this time, and beginning to look brown and dusty, waving over it; inside, a little bright surburban garden, full of scarlet geraniums, divided by a white line of pavement, dazzlingly clean, from the door in the wall to the door of the house; and a stand full of more scarlet geraniums in the little square hall. Mrs Merridew became very much agitated as we approached. It was all that I could do to keep her up when we had rung the bell at the door. I think she would have turned and gone back even then had it been possible, but, fortunately, we were admitted without delay.

We were shown into a pretty shady drawing-room, full of old furniture, which looked like the remnants of something greater, and at which she gazed with eyes of almost wild recognition, unconsciously pressing my arm, which she still held. Everything surrounding her woke afresh the tumult of recollections. She was not able to speak when the maid asked our names, and I was about to give them simply, and had already named my own, when she pressed my arm closer to her, and interposed at once, —

"Say two ladies from the country anxious to speak with her about business. She might not — know — our names."

"Is it business about the house, ma'am?" said the maid, with some eagerness.

"Yes, yes; it is about the house," said Mrs Merridew, hastily. And then the door closed, and we sat waiting, listening to the soft subdued sounds in the quiet house, and the rustle of the leaves in the garden. "She must be going to let it," my companion said, hoarsely; and then rose from the chair on which she had placed herself, and began to move about the room with agitation, looking at everything, touching the things with her hands, with now and then a stifled exclamation. "There is where we used to sit, Ellen and I," she said, standing by a sofa, before which a small table was placed, "when there was company in the evenings. And there Matilda — oh, what ghosts there are about! Matilda is married, thank heaven! but if Ellen comes, I shall never be able to face her. Oh, Mrs Musgrave, if you would but speak for me! ——"

At this moment the door was opened. Mrs Merridrew shrank back instinctively, and sat down, resting her hand on the table she had just pointed out to me. The newcomer was a tall full figure, in deep mourning, a handsome woman of five-and-thirty, or thereabouts, with bright hair, which looked all the brighter from comparison with the black depths of her dress, and a colourless clear complexion. All the colour about her was in her hair. Though she had no appearance of unhealthiness, her very lips were pale, and she came in with a noiseless quiet dignity, and the air of one who felt she had pain to encounter, yet felt able to bear it.

"Pardon me for keeping you waiting," she said; and then, with a somewhat startled glance, "I understood you wanted to see — the house."

27

My companion was trembling violently; and I cleared my throat, and tried to clear up my ideas (which was less than easy) to say something in reply. But before I had stammered out half-a-dozen words Mrs Merridew rose, and made one or two uneasy steps towards the stranger.

"Ellen" she cried, "don't you know me?" and stopped there, standing in the centre of the room, holding out appealing hands.

Miss Babington's face changed in the strangest way. I could see that she recognized her in a moment, and then that she pretended to herself not to recognize her. There was the first startled vivid indignant glance, and then a voluntary mist came over her eyes. She gazed at the agitated woman with an obstinately blank gaze, and then turned to me, with a little bow.

"Your friend has the advantage of me," she said; "but you were saying something. I should be glad, if that was what you wanted, to show you over the house."

It would be hard to imagine a more difficult position than that in which I found myself; seated between two people who were thus strangely connected with each other by bonds of mutual injury, and appealed to for something meaningless and tranquilizing, to make the intercourse possible. I did the best I could on the spur of the moment.

"It is not so much the house," I said, "though, if you wish to let it, I have a friend who is looking for a house; but I think there was some other business Mrs Merridew had; something to say ——"

"Mrs Merridew!" said Miss Babington, suffering the light once more to come into her eyes; and then she gave her an indignant look. "I think this might have been spared us at least."

"Ellen," said Mrs Merridew, speaking very low and humbly — "Ellen, I have never done anything to you to make you so hard against me. If I injured your sister, it was unwittingly. She is better off than I am now. You were once fond of me, as I was of you. Why should you have turned so completely against me? I have come in desperation to ask a hearing from you, and from your mother, Ellen. God knows I mean nothing but good. And oh, what have I ever done? — what harm?"

Miss Babington had seated herself, still preserving her air of dignity, but without an invitation by look or gesture to her visitor to be seated; and in the silent room, all so dainty and so sweet with flowers, with the old furniture in it, which reminded her of the past, the culprit of twenty years ago stood pleading between one of those whom she was supposed to have wronged and myself, a most ignorant and uneasy spectator. Twenty years ago! In the meantime youth had passed, and the hard burdens of middle age had come doubled and manifold upon her shoulders. Had she done nothing in the meantime that would tell more heavily against her than that girlish inadvertence of the past? Yet here she stood —not knowing, I believe, for the moment, whether she was the young governess in her first trouble, or the mother of all those children, acquainted with troubles so much more bitter — among the ghosts of the past.

"I would much rather not discuss the question," said Miss Babington, still seated, and struggling hard to preserve her calm. "All the grief and vexation we have owed to you in this house cannot be summed up in a moment. The only policy, I think, is to be silent. Your very presence here is an offence to us. What else could it be?"

"I should never have come," said Mrs Merridew, moved by a natural prick of resentment, "but for what I have just heard —— I should never have returned to ask for pardon where I had done no wrong — had it not been for this — this, that I feel to be unjust. Your poor brother John——"

"Stop!" cried the other, her reserve failing. "Stop, oh! stop, you cruel woman! He was nothing to you but a toy to be played with — but he was my brother, my only brother; and you have made him an undutiful son in his very grave."

The tears were in her eyes, her colourless face had flushed, her soft voice was raised; and Mrs Merridew, still standing, listened to her with looks as agitated — when all at once the door was again opened softly. The aspect of affairs changed in a moment. To my utter amazement, Mrs Merridew, who was standing with her face to the door, made a quick, imperative, familiar gesture to her antagonist, and looked towards an easy-chair which stood near the open window. Miss Babington rose quickly to her feet, and composed herself into a sudden appearance of calm.

"Mamma," she said, going forward to meet the old lady, who came slowly in, "here are some ladies come upon business. This is — Mrs Merridew." She said the name very low, as Mrs Babington made her way to her chair, and Mrs Merridew sank trembling into her seat, unable, I think, to bear up longer. The old lady seated herself before she spoke. She was a little old woman, with a pretty softly-coloured old face, and had the air of having been petted and cared for all her life. The sudden change of her daughter's manner; the accumulation of every kind of convenience and prettiness, as I now remarked, round that chair; the careful way in which it had been placed out of the sun and the draught, yet in the air and in sight of the garden, told a whole history of themselves. And now Mrs Merridew's passionate sense that the alienation of the son's fortune from the mother was a thing impossible, was made clear to me at once.

"Whom did you say, Ellen?" said the old lady, when she was comfortably settled in her chair. "Mrs ———? I never catch names. I hope you explained to the ladies that I am rather infirm, and can't stand. What did you say was your friend's name, my dear?"

Her friend's name! Ellen Babington's face lightened all over as with a pale light of indignation.

"I said — Mrs Merridew," she repeated, with a little emphasis on the name. Then there was a pause; and the culprit who was at the bar trembled visibly, and hid her face in her hands.

"Mrs Merridew! —— Do you mean ——? Turn me round, Ellen, and let me look at her," said the old lady, with a curious catching of her breath.

It was a change which could not be done in a moment. While the daughter turned the mother's chair, poor Mrs Merridew must have gone through the torture of an age; her hands trembled in which she had hidden herself. But as the chair creaked and turned slowly round, and all was silent again, she raised her white face, and uncovered herself, as it were, to meet the inquisitor's eye. It might have been a different woman, so changed was she: her eyes withdrawn into caves, the lines of her mouth drawn down, two hollows clearly marked in her cheeks, and every particle of her usual colour gone. She looked up appalled and overcome, confronting, but not meeting, the keen critical look which old Mrs Babington fixed upon her; and then there was again a pause; and the leaves fluttered outside, and the white curtains within and a gay child's voice, passing in the road without, suddenly fell among us like a bird.

"Ah!" said the old lady, "that creature! Do-you mean to tell me, Ellen, that she has had the assurance to come here? Now look at her and tell me what a man's sense is worth. That woman's face turned my poor boy's head, and drove Charles Merridew out of his wits. Only look at her: is there anything there to turn anybody's head now? She has lost her figure too; but to be sure that is not so wonderful, for she is forty if she is a day. But there are you, my dear, as straight as a rush, and your sister Matilda as well. So that is Janet Singleton, our governess: I wonder what Charles thinks of his bargain now? I never saw a woman so gone off. Oh, Ellen, Ellen, why didn't she come and show herself, such a figure as she is, before my poor dear boy was taken from us? My poor boy! And to think he should have gone to his grave in a delusion about such a creature! Ellen, I would rather now that you sent her away."

"Oh, mamma, don't speak like this," cried Ellen, red with shame and distress; "what is about her figure? if that were all! — but she is going away."

"Yes, yes, send her away," said the old lady. "You liked her once, but I don't suppose even you can think there could be any intercourse now. My son left all his money to her," she added, turning to me — "past his mother and his sister. You will admit that was a strange thing to do. I don't know who the other lady is, Ellen, but I conclude she is a friend of yours. He left everything past us, everything but some poor pittance. Perhaps you may know someone who wants a house in this neighbourhood? It is a very nice little house, and much better furnished than most. I should be very glad to let it, now that I can't afford to occupy it myself, by the year."

"Mamma, the other lady is with Mrs Merridew," said Ellen; "I do not know her ——" and she cast a glance at me, almost appealing to my pity. I rose up, not knowing what to do.

"Perhaps, my dear," I said, I confess with timidity, "we had better go away."

"Unless you will stay to luncheon," said the old lady, "But I forgot — I don't want to look at that woman any more, Ellen. She has done us enough harm to satisfy anyone. Turn me round again to my usual place, and send her away."

Mrs Merridew had risen to her feet, too. She had regained her senses after the first frightful shock. She was still ghastly pale, but she was herself. She went up firmly and swiftly to the old lady, put Ellen aside by a movement which she was unconscious of in her agitation, and replaced the chair in its former place with the air of one to whom such an office was habitual. "You used to say I always did it best," she said. "Oh, is it possible you can have forgotten everything! Did I not give him up when you asked me, and do you think I will take his money now? Oh, never, never! It ought to be yours, and it shall be. Oh, take it back, and forgive me, and say, "God Bless you, once again."

"Eh, what was that you said? Ellen, what does she say?" said the old woman. "I have always heard the Merridews were very poor. Poor

John's fortune will be a godsend to them. Go away! I suppose you mean to mock me after all the rest you have done. I don't understand what you say."

Yet she looked up with a certain eagerness on her pretty old face — a certain sharp look of greed and longing came into the blue eyes, which retained their colour as pure as that of youth. Her daughter towered above her, pale with emotion, but still indignant, yielding not a jot.

"Mamma, pay no attention," she said; "Mrs Merridew may pity us, but what is that? surely we can take back nothing from her hands."

"Pity! I don't see how Janet Merridew can pity *me*. But I should like," Mrs Babington went on, with a little tremble of eagernesss, "to know at least what she means."

"This is what I mean," said Mrs Merridew, sinking on her knees by the old lady's chair: "that I will not take your money. It *is* your money. We are poor, as you say; but we can struggle on as we have done for twenty years; and poor John's money is yours, and not mine. It is not mine. I will not take it. It must have been some mistake. If he had known what he was doing he never would have left it to anyone but you."

"So I think myself," said the old lady, musing; and then was silent, taking no notice of anyone — looking into the air.

"Mamma," said Ellen, behind her chair, "I can work for you, and Matilda will help us. It cannot, be. It may be kind of — her — but it cannot be. Are we to take charity; to live on charity? Mamma, she has no right disturb you ——"

"She is not disturbing me, my dear," said the old lady; "on the contrary. Whatever I might think of her, she used to be a girl of sense. And Matilda always carried things with a very high hand, and I never was fond of her husband. But I am very fond of my house," she added, after a pause; "it is such a nice house, Ellen. I think I should die if we were to leave it. I shall die very soon, most likely, and be a burden on nobody; but still, Ellen, if she meant it, you know ——"

"Mamma, what does it matter what she means? you never can think of accepting charity. It will break my heart."

"That is all very well to say," said Mrs Babington. "But I have lived a great deal longer than you have done, my dear, and I know that hearts are not broken so easily. It would break my heart to leave my nice house. Janet, come here, and look me in the face. I don't think you were true to us in the old times. Matilda did carry things with a very high hand. I told her so at the time, and I have often told her so since; but I don't think you were true to us, all the same."

"I do not know — I did not mean ——" faltered Mrs Merridew, leaning her head on the arm of the old lady's chair.

It was clear to me that the story had two sides, and that my friend was perhaps not so innocent as she had made herself out to be. But there was something very pitiful in the comparison between the passion of anxiety in her half-hidden face, and the calm of the old woman who was thus deciding on her fate.

"My dear, I am afraid you knew," said Mrs Babington. "You accepted my poor boy, and then, when I spoke to you, you gave him up, and took Charles Merridew instead. If I had not interfered, perhaps it would have been better; though, to be sure, I don't know what we should have done with a heap of children. And as for poor John's money, you know you have no more real right to it, no more than that other lady, who never saw him in her life."

"She has the best possible right to it, mamma — he left it to her," said Ellen, anxiously, over her shoulder. "Oh, why did you come here to vex us, when we were not interfering with you? I beg of you not to trouble my mother any more, but go away."

Then there was a moment of hesitation. Mrs Merridew rose slowly from her knees. She turned round to me, not looking me in the face. She said, in a hoarse voice, "Let us go," and made a step towards the door. She was shaking as if she had had a fever; but she was glad. Was that possible? She had delivered her conscience — and now might not she go and keep the money which would make her children happy? But she could not look me in the face. She moved as slowly as a funeral. And yet she would have flown, if she could, to get safely away.

"Janet, my dear," said the old lady, "come back, and let us end our talk."

Mrs Merridew stopped short, with a start, as if a shot had arrested her. This time she looked me full in the face. Her momentary hope was over, and now she felt for the first time the poignancy of the sacrifice which it had been her own will to make.

"Come back, Janet," said Mrs Babington. "As you say, it is not your money. Nothing could make it your money. You were always right-feeling when you were not aggravated. I am much obliged to you, my dear. Come and sit down here, and tell me all about yourself. Now poor John is dead," she went on, falling suddenly into soft weeping, like a child, "we ought to be friends. To think he should die before

me, and I should be heir to my own boy — isn't it sad? And such a
fine young fellow he was! You remember when he came back from the
University? What a nice colour he had! Always so straight and slim,
like a rush. All my children have a good carriage. You have lost your
figure, Janet; and you used to have a nice little figure. When a girl is
so round and plump, she is apt to get stout as she gets older. Look at
Ellen, how nice she is. But then, to be sure, children make a difference.
Sit down by me here, and tell me how many you have. And, Ellen,
send word to the house-agent, and tell him we don't want now to let
the house; and tell Parker to get luncheon ready a little earlier. You
must want something, if you have come from the country. Where are
you living now? and how is Charles Merridew? Dear, dear, to think I
should not have seen either of you for nearly twenty years!"

"But, mamma, surely, surely," cried Ellen Babington, "you don't
think things can be settled like this?"

"Don't speak nonsense, Ellen; everything *is* settled," said the old
lady. "You know I always had the greatest confidence in Janet's good
sense. Now, my dear, hold your tongue. A girl like you has no right to
meddle. I always manage my own business. Go and look after luncheon — that is your affair.

I do not remember ever to have seen a more curious group in my
life. There was the old lady in the centre, quite calm, and sweet, and
pleasant. A tear was still lingering on her eyelash; but it represented
nothing more than a child's transitory grief, and underneath there
was nothing but smiles, and satisfaction, and content. She looked
so pretty, so pleased, so glad to find that her comforts were not to
be impaired, and yet took it all so lightly, as a matter of course, as
completely unconscious of the struggle going on in the mind of her
benefactress as if she had been a creature from a different world. As
for Mrs Merridew, she stood speechless, choked by feelings that were
too bitter and conflicting for words. I am sure that all the advantages
this money could have procured for her children were surging up
before her as she stood and listened. She held her hands helplessly
half stretched out, as if something had been taken out of them. Her
breast heaved with a breath half drawn, which seemed suspended
half way, as if dismay and disappointment hindered its completion. It
was all over then — her sacrifice made and accepted, and no more
about it; and herself sent back to the monotonous struggle of life. On
the other side of the pretty old lady stood Ellen Babington, pale and
miserable, struggling with shame and pride, casting sudden glances at

Mrs Merridew, and then appealing looks at me, who had nothing to do with it.

"Tell her, oh, tell her it can't be!" she cried at last, coming to me. "Tell her the lawyers will not permit it. It cannot be."

"And Mrs Merridew, too, gave me one pitiful look — not repenting, but yet — Then she went forward, and laid her hand upon the old lady's hand, which was like ivory, with all the veins delicately carved upon it.

"Say, God bless us, at least. Say, 'God bless you and children,' once before I go."

"To be sure," said the old lady, cheerfully. "God bless you, my dear, and all the children. Matilda has no children, you know. I should like to see them, if you think it would not be too much for me. But you are not going, Janet, when it is the first time we have met for nearly twenty years?"

"I must go," said Mrs Merridew.

"She could not trust herself to speak, I could see. She put down her face and kissed the ivory hand, and then she turned and went past me to the door, without another word. I think she had forgotten my very existence. When she had reached the door she turned round suddenly, and fixed her eyes upon Ellen. She was going away, having given them back their living, with so much acknowledgement as if she had brought a nosegay. There was in her look a mute remonstrance and appeal and protest. Ellen Babington trembled all over; her lips quivered as if with words which pride or pain would not permit her to say; but she held, with both hands immovable, to the back of her mother's chair, who, for her part, was kissing her hand to the departing visitor. "Good-by; come and see us soon," the old lady was saying cheerfully. And Ellen gazed, and trembled, and said nothing. Thus this strangest of visits came to an end.

She had forgotten me, as I thought; but when I came to her side and put my arm within her reach, she clutched at it and tottered so that it was all I could do to support her. I was very thankful to get her into the cab, for I thought she would have fainted on the way. But yet she roused herself then I told the man to drive back to the station.

"We must go to the lawyers first," she said; and then we turned and drove through the busy London streets, towards the City. The clerks looked nearly baked in the office when we reached it, and the crowd crowded on, indiscriminate and monotonous. One feels one has no right to go to such a place and take any of the air away, of which they have so little. And to think of the sweet air blowing over our lawns and lanes, and all the unoccupied silent shady places we had left behind us! Such vain thoughts were not in Mrs Merridew's head. She was turning over and over instead a very different kind of vision. She was counting up all she had sacrificed, and how little she had got by it; and yet was going to complete the sacrifice, unmoved even by her thoughts.

I confess I was surprised at the tone she took with the lawyer. She said "Mr Merridew and myself" with a composure which made me, who knew Mr Merridew had no hand in it, absolutely speechless. The lawyer remonstrated as he was in duty bound, and spoke about his client's will; but Mrs Merridew made very little account of the will. She quoted her husband with a confidence so assured that even I, though I knew better, began to be persuaded that she had communicated with him. And thus the business was finally settled. She had recovered herself by the time we got into the cab again. It is true that her face was worn and livid with the exertions of the day, but still, pale and weary as she was, she was herself.

"But, my dear," I said, "you quoted Mr Merridew, as if he knew all about it; and what if he should not approve?"

"You must not think I have no confidence in my husband," she said, quickly; "far from that. Perhaps he would not see as I do now. He would think of our own wants first. But if it comes to his ears afterwards, Charles is not the man to disown his wife's actions. Oh, no, no; we have gone through a great deal together, and he would no more bring shame upon me, as if I acted when I had no right to act, — than — I would bring shame upon him; and I think that is as much as could be said."

And then we made our way back to the station; but she said nothing more till we got into the railway-carriage, which was not quite so noisy as our cab.

"It would have been such a thing for us," she said then, half to herself. "Poor Charles! Oh, if I could have said to him, 'Don't be so anxious; here is so much a year for the children.' And Jack should have gone to the university. And there would have been Will's premium at once," (*i.e.* to Mr Willoughby, the engineer.) "The only thing that I am glad of is that they don't know. And then Janet; she breaks my heart when she talks. It is so bad for her, knowing the Fortises and all those girls who have everything that heart can desire. I never had that to worry me when I was young. I was only the governess. Janet's talk will be the worst of all. I could have made the house so nice too, and everything. Well! – but then I never should have had a moment's peace."

"You don't regret?" I said.

"No," said Mrs Merridew, with a long sigh. And then, "Do you think I have been a traitor to the children?" she cried suddenly, "taking away their money from them in the dark? Would Charles think me a traitor, as *they* do? Is it always to be my part? — always to be my part?"

"No, no," I said, soothing her as best I could; but I was very glad to find my pony-carriage at the station, and to drive her home to my house and give her some tea, and strengthen her for her duties. Thus poor John Babington's fortune was disposed of, and no one was the wiser, except, indeed, the old lady and her daughter, who were not likely to talk much on the subject. And Mrs Merridew walked calmly across to her house in the dusk as if this strange episode of agitation and passion had been nothing more than a dream.

CHAPTER III.

We did not meet again for some days after this, and next time I saw her, which was on Sunday at church with her children, it seemed impossible to me to believe in the reality of the strange scene we had so recently passed through together. The calm curtain of ordinary decorums and ordinary friendliness had risen for a moment from Mrs Merridew's unexcited existence, revealing a woman distracted by a primitive sense of justice, rending her own soul, as it were, in sunder, and doing, in spite of herself and all her best instincts, what she felt was right. That she should have any existence separate from her children had never occurred to anybody before. Yet, for one day, I had seen her resist and ignore the claims of her children, and act like an individual being. When I saw her again she was once more the mother and nothing more, casting her eyes over her little flock, cognizant, one could see, of the perfection or imperfection of every fold and line in their dresses, keeping her attention upon each, from little Matty, who was restless and could not be kept quiet, up to Janet who sat demure, and already caught the eye of visitors as one of the prettiest girls of Dinglefield. Mrs Merridew remarked all with a vigilant mother's eye, and as I gazed across at her in her pew, it was all but impossible for me to believe that this was the same woman who had clung so convulsively to my arm, whose face had been so worn and hollowed out with suffering. How could it be the same woman? She who had suffered poor John Babington to love her — and then had cast him off, and married her friend's lover instead; who had established so firm an empire over a man's heart, that, after twenty years, he had remembered her still with such intensity of feeling. How Janet would have opened her big eyes had it been suggested to her that her mother could have any power over men's hearts; or, indeed, could be occupied with anything more touching or important than her children's frocks or her butcher's bills! I fear I did not pay much attention to the service that morning. I could not but gaze at them, and wonder whether, for instance, Mr Merridew himself, who had come back from circuit, and was seated respectably with his family in church, yawning discreetly over Mr Damerel's sermon, remembered anything at all, for his part, of Matilda Babington or her brother. Probably he preferred to ignore the subject altogether — or, perhaps, would laugh with a sense of gratified vanity that there had been a "a row," when the transference of his affections was discovered. And there she sat by his side, who had — had she betrayed his confidence? was she untrue to him in being this time true to her friends? The question bewildered me so that my mind went groping about it and about it. Once, I fear, she had been false to those whose bread she eat, and chosen love instead of friendship. Now was she false to the nearest of ties, the closest of all relationships, sitting calmly there beside him with a secret in her mind of which he knew nothing? "Falsely true!" — was that what the woman was who looked to the outside world a mere pattern of all domestic virtues, without any special interest about her, a wife devoted to her husband's interest, a mother rapt up, as people say, in her children? I could not make up my mind what to think.

"I hope you got through your business comfortably," Mrs Spencer said to me as we walked home from church.

"With Mrs Merridew's assistance," said Lady Isabella, who was rather satirical. And the Merridews heard their own name, and stopped to join in the conversation.

"What is that about my wife?" he said. "Did Mrs Musgrave have Mrs Merridew's assistance about something? I hope it was only shopping.

When you have business you should consult me. She is a goose, and knows nothing about it."

"I don't think she is a goose," said I.

"No, perhaps not in her own way," said the serene husband, laughing; "but every woman is a goose about business — I beg your pardon, ladies, but I assure you I mean it as a compliment. I hate a woman of business. Shopping is quite a different matter," he added, and laughed. Good heavens! if he had only known what a fool he looked, beside the silent woman, who gave me a little warning glance and coloured a little, and turned away her head to speak to little Matty, who was clinging to her skirts. A perfect mother! thinking more (you would have said) of Matty's little frills and Janet's bonnet-strings than of anything else in life.

And that was all about it. The summer went on and turned to autumn and to winter and to spring again, with that serene progression of nature which nothing obstructs: and the children grew, and the Merridews were as poor as ever, managing *à peu près* to make both ends meet, but always just a little short somewhere, with their servants chosen on the same principle of supplementing each other's imperfect service as that Janet had announced to me. For one thing, they kept their servants a long time, which I have noticed is characteristic of households not very rich nor very "particular." When you allow such pleas to tell in favour of an imperfect housemaid as that she is good to the children, or does not mind helping the cook, there is no reason why Mary, if she does not marry in the meantime, should not stay with you a hundred years. And the Merridews' servants accordingly stayed, and looked very friendly at you when you went to call, and did their work not very well, with much supervision and exasperation (respectively) on the part of the mother and daughter. But the family was no poorer, though it was no richer. The only evidence of our expedition to town which I could note was, that it had produced a new pucker on Mrs Merridew's brow. She had looked sufficiently anxious by times before, but the new pucker had something more than anxiety in it. There was a sense of something better that might have been; a sense of something lost, — a suspicion of bitterness. How all this could be expressed by one line on a smooth white forehead I cannot explain; but to me it was so.

Now and then, too, a chance illusion would be made which recalled what had happened still more plainly. For instance, I chanced to be calling one afternoon, when Mr Merridew came home earlier than usual from town. We were sitting over our five-o'clock tea, with a few of the children scrambling about the floor and Janet working in the corner. He took up the ordinary position of a man who has just come home, with his back to the fire, and regarded us with that benevolent contempt which men generally think it right to exhibit to women over their tea; and everything was so ordinary and pleasant, that I for one was taken entirely by surprise, and nearly let fall the cup in my hand when he spoke.

"I don't know whether you saw John Babington's death in *The Times* three or four months ago, Janet," he said, "did you? Why did you never mention it? It is odd that I should not have heard. I met Ellen today coming out of the Amyotts', where I lunched, in such prodigious mourning that I was quite startled. All the world might have been dead to look at her. And do you know she gave me a look as she would have spoken. All that is so long past that it's ridiculous keeping up malice. I wish you would call next time you are in town to ask for the old lady. Poor John's death must have been a sad loss to them. I hear there was some fear that he left his property away from his mother and sister. But it turned out a false report."

I did not dare look at Mrs Merridew to see how she bore it; but her voice replied quitely without any break, as if the conversation was on the most ordinary subject, —

"Where did you manage to get so much news?"

My dear "Oh, from the Amyotts," he said, "who knew all about it. Matilda, you know poor girl," (with that half laugh of odious masculine vanity which I knew in my heart he would be guilty of,) "married a cousin of Amyott's, and is getting on very well, they say. But think over my suggestion, Janet. I think at this distance of time it would be graceful on your part to go and call."

"I cannot think they would like to see me, now," she said in a low voice. Then I ventured to look at her. She was seated in an angular, rigid way, with her shoulders and elbows squared to her work, and the corners of her mouth pursed up, which would have given to any cursory observer the same impression it did to her husband.

"How hard you women are!" he said. "Trust you for never forgiving or forgetting. Poor old lady, I should have thought anybody would have pitied her. But, however, it is none of my business. As for Ellen, she is a very handsome woman, though she is not so young as she once was. I should not wonder if she were to make a good marriage even now. Is it possible, Janet, after being so fond of her — or pretending to be, how can I tell? — that you would not like to say a word to Ellen now?"

"She would not think it kind from me," said Mrs Merridew, still rigid, never raising her eyes from her work.

"I think she would, but at all events you might try," he said. All her answer was to shake her head, and he went away to his dressing-room shrugging his shoulders and nodding his head in bewildered comments to himself on what he considered the hard-heartedness of woman. As for me, I kept looking at her with sympathetic eyes, thinking that at least she would give herself the comfort of a confidential glance. But she did not. It seemed that she was determined to ignore the whole matter, even to me.

"I wish papa would take as much interest in us poor girls at home as he does in people that don't belong to him," said Janet. "Mamma, I never can piece this to make it long enough. It may do for Marian" (who was her next sister), "but it will never do for me."

"You are so easily discouraged," said Mrs Meridew. "Let me look at it. You girls are always making difficulties. Under the flounce, your piecing, as you call it, will never be seen. Those flounces," she added, with a little laugh, which I knew was hysterical, "are blessings to poor folks."

"I am sure I don't think there is anything to laugh at," said poor Janet, almost crying: "when you think of Nelly Fortis and all the other girls, with their nice dresses all new and fresh from the dressmaker's, and no trouble; while I have only mamma's old gown, that she wore when she was twenty, to turn, and patch, and piece, — and not long enough after all!"

"Then you should not grow so," said her mother, "and you ought to be thankful that the old fashion has come in again, and my old gown can be of use." But as she spoke she turned round and gave me a look. The tears were in her eyes, and that pucker, oh, so deeply marked, in her forehead. I felt she would have sobbed had she dared. And then before my eyes, as, I am sure, before hers, there glided a vision of Ellen Babington in her profound mourning, rustling past Mr Merridew on the stairs, with heaps of costly crape, no doubt, and that rich black silk with which people console themselves in their first mourning. How could they take it all without a word? The after-pang that comes almost inevitably at the back of a sacrifice, was tearing Mrs Merridew's heart. I felt it go through my own, and so I knew. She had done it nobly, but he could not forget that she had done it. Does one ever forget?

And then as I went home I fell into a maze again. Had she a right to do it? To sit at table with that unsuspicious man, and put her arm in his, and be at his side continually, and all the time be false to him. Falsely true! I could not get the words out of my mind.

———

CHAPTER IV.

I do not remember how long it was till I saw in *The Times* the intimation of old Mrs Babington's death. I think it must have been about two years: for Janet was eighteen, and less discontented with things in general, besides being a great deal more contented than either her friends or his desired, with the civilities of young Bischam from the Priory, who was always coming over to see his aunt, and always throwing himself in the girl's way. He had nothing except his commission and a hundred and fifty a year which his father allowed him, and she had nothing at all; and, naturally, they took to each other. It is this that makes me recollect what year it was. We had never referred to the matter in our frequent talks, Mrs Merridew and I. But after the intimation in *The Times,* she herself broke the silence. She came to me the very next day. "Did you see it in the papers?" she asked, plunging without preface into the heart of the subject, and I could not pretend not to understand.

"Yes," I said, "I saw it;" and then stopped short, not knowing what to say.

She had been wearing herself in these two years, as all the previous years in which I had known her had not worn her. The pucker was more developed on her forehead; she was less patient and more easily fretted. She had grown thin, and something of a sharp tone had come into her soft motherly voice. By times she would be almost querulous; and nobody but myself knew in the least whence the drop of gall came that had so suddenly shown itself in her nature. She had fretted under her secret, and over her sacrifice, — the sacrifice which had never been taken any notice of, but had been calmly accepted as a right. Now she came to me half wild, with the look of a creature driven to bay.

"It was for her I did it," she said; "she had always been so petted and cared for all her life. She did not know how to deny herself; I did it for her, not for Ellen. Oh, Mrs Musgrave, I cannot tell you how fond I was of that girl! And you saw how she looked at me. Never one word, never even a glance of response: and I suppose now ——"

"My dear," I said, "you cannot tell yet; let us wait and see; now that her mother is gone her heart may have softened. Do not take any steps just yet."

"Steps!" she cried. "What steps can I take now? I have thrown altogether away from me what might have been of such use to the children. I have been false to my own children. Poor John meant it to be of use to us ——"

And then she turned away, wrought to such a point that nothing but tears could relieve her. When she had cried she was better: and went home to all her little monotonous cares again, to think and think, and mingle that drop of gall more and more in the family cup. Mr Merridew was again absent on circuit at this time, which was at once a relief and a trouble to his wife. And everybody remarked the change upon her.

"She is going to have a bad illness," Mrs Spencer said. "Poor thing, I don't wonder, with all those children, and inferior servants, and so much to do. I have seen it coming on for a long time. A serious illness is a dangerous thing at her age. All her strength has been drained out of her; and whether she will be able to resist ——"

"Don't be so funereal," said Lady Isabella; "she has something on her mind."

"I think it is her health," said Mrs Spencer; and we all shook our heads over her altered looks.

I had a further fright, too, some days after, when Janet came to me, looking very pale. She crept in with an air of secrecy which was very strange to the girl. She looked scared, and her hair was pushed up wildly from her forehead, and her light summer dress all dusty and dragging, which was unlike Janet, for she had begun by this time to be tidy, and feel herself a woman. She in came by the window as usual, but closed it after her, though it was very hot. "May I come and speak to you?" she said in a whisper, creeping quite close to my side.

"Of course, my dear; but why do you shut the window?" said I; "we shall be suffocated if you shut out the air."

"It is because it is a secret," she said. "Mrs Musgrave, tell me, is there anything wrong with mamma?"

"Wrong?" I said, turning upon her in dismay.

"I can't help it," cried Janet, bursting into tears. "I don't believe mamma ever did anything wrong. I can't believe it: but there has been a woman questioning me so, I don't know what to think."

"A woman questioning you?"

"Listen," said Janet, hastily. "This is how it was: I was walking down to the Dingle across the fields — oh! Mrs Musgrave dear, don't say anything; it was only poor Willie Bischam, who wanted to say good-by to me — and all at once I saw a tall lady in mourning looking at us as we passed. She came up to us just at the stile at Goodman's farm, and I thought she wanted to ask the way; but instead of that, she stopped me and looked at me. 'I heard you called Janet,' she said; 'I had once a friend who was called Janet, and it is not a common name. Do you live here? is your mother living? and well? and how many children are there? I should like to know if you belong to my old friend.'"

"And what did you say?"

"What could I say, Mrs Musgrave? She did not look cross or disagreeable, and she was a lady. I said who I was, and that mamma was not quite well, and that there were ten of us; and then she began to question me about mamma. Did she go out a great deal; and was she tall or short; and had she pretty eyes 'like mine,' she said; and was her name Janet like mine; and then, when I had answered her as well as I could, she said, 'I was not to say a word to mamma; perhaps it is not the Janet I once knew,' she said; 'don't say anything to her;' and then she went away. I was so frightened, I ran home directly all the way. I knew I might tell you, Mrs Musgrave; it is like something in a book, is it not, when people are trying to find out —— oh, you don't think I can have done any harm to mamma?"

Janet was so much agitated that it was all I could do to quiet her down. "And I never said good-by to poor Willie, after all," she said, with more tears when she had rallied a little. I thought it better she should not tell her mother, though one is very reluctant to say so to a girl; for Willie Bischam was a secret too. But he was going away, poor fellow, and probably nothing would ever come of it. I made a little compromise with my own sense of right.

"Forget it, Janet, and say nothing about it; perhaps it was some one else after all; and if you will promise not to meet Mr Bischam again ——"

"He goes to-night," said Janet, with a rueful look; and thus it was evident that on that point there was nothing more to be said.

This was in the middle of the week, and on Saturday Mr Merridew was expected home. His wife was ill, though she never had been ill before in her life; she had headaches, which were things unknown to her; she was out of temper, and irritable, and wretched. I think she had made certain that Ellen would write, and make some proposal to her; and as the days went on one by one, and no letter came ——— Beside it was just the moment when they had decided against sending Jack to Oxford. To pay Willie's premium and do that at the same time was impossible. Mrs Merridew had struggled long, but at last she was obliged to give in; and Jack was going to his father's office with a heavy heart, poor boy; and his mother was half wild. All might have been so different; and she had sacrificed her boys' interests, and her girls' interests, and her own happiness, all for the selfish comfort of Ellen Babington, who took no notice of her. I began to think she would have a brain-fever if this went on.

She was not at church on Sunday morning, and I went with the children, as soon as service was over, to ask for her. She was lying on the sofa when I went in, and Mr Merridew, who had arrived late on Saturday, was in his dressing-gown, walking about the room. He was tired an irritable with his journey, and his work, and perennial cares. And she, with sacrifice, and her secret, and perennial cares, was like tinder, ready in a moment to catch fire. I know nothing more disagreeable than to go in upon married people when they are in this state of mind, which can neither be ignored, nor concealed.

"I don't understand you, Janet," he was saying, as I entered; "women are vindictive, I know; but at least you may be sorry, as I am, that the poor old lady has died without a word of kindness passing between us: after all, we might be to blame. One changes one's opinions as one gets on in life. With our own children growing up round us, I don't feel quite so sure that we were not to blame."

"*I* have not been to blame," she said, with an emphasis which sounded sullen, and which only I could understand.

"Oh no, of course; you never are," he said, with masculine disdain. "Catch a woman acknowledging herself to be in fault! The sun may go wrong in his course sooner than she. Mrs Musgrave, pray don't go away; you have seen my wife in an unreasonable mood before."

"I am in no unreasonable mood," she cried. "Mrs Musgrave, stay. You know — oh, how am I to go on bearing this, and never answer a word?"

"My dear, don't deceive yourself," he said, with a man's provoking calm; "you answer a great many words. I don't call you at all a meek sufferer. Fortunately the children are out of the way. Confound it, Janet, what do you mean by talking of what you have to bear? I have not been such a harsh husband to you as all that; and when all I asked was that you should make the most innocent advances to a poor old woman who was once very kind to us both ——"

"Charles!" said Mrs Merridew, rising suddenly from her sofa, "I can't bear it any longer. You think me hard, and vindictive, and I don't know what. You, who ought to know me. Look here! I got that letter, you will see be the date, more than two years ago; when you were absent, and I went and saw her: there — there! now I have confessed it; Mrs Musgraves knows —— I have had a secret from you for two years."

It was not a moment for me to interfere. She sat, holding herself hysterically rigid, and upright on the sofa. Whether she had intended to betray herself or not, I cannot tell. She had taken the letter out of her writing-desk, which stood close by; but I don't know whether she had resolved on this step, or whether it was the impulse of the moment. Now that she had done it a dreadful calm of expectation took possession of her. She was afraid. He might turn upon her furious. He might upbraid her with her despoiling her family, deceiving himself, being false, as she had been before. Such a thing was possible. Two souls may live side by side for years, and be as one, and yet have no notion how each will act in any sudden or unusual emergency. He was her husband, and they had no interest, scarcely any thought, that one did not share with the other; and yet she sat gazing at him rigid with terror, not knowing what he might do or say.

He read the letter without a word; then he tossed it upon the table; then he walked all the length of the room, up and down, with his hands thrust very deeply into his pockets; then he took up the letter again. He had a struggle with himself. If he was angry, if he was touched, I cannot tell. His first emotions, whatever they were, he gulped down without a word. Of all sounds to strike into the silence of such a moment, the first thing we heard in our intense listening was the abrupt ring of a short excited laugh.

"How did you venture to take any steps in it without consulting me?" he said.

"I thought — I thought —" she stammered under her breath.

"You thought I might have been tempted by the money," he said, taking another walk through the room, while she sat erect in her terror, afraid of him. It was some time before he spoke again. No doubt he was vexed by her want of trust, and wounded by the long silence. But I have no clue to the thoughts that were passing through his mind. At last he came to a sudden pause before her. "And perhaps you were right, Janet," he said, drawing a long breath. "I am glad now to have been free of the temptation. It was wrong not to tell me — and yet I think you did well."

Mrs Merridew gave a little choked cry, and then she fell back on the sofa, — fell into my arms. I had felt she might do it, so strange was her look, and had placed myself there on purpose. But she had not fainted, as I expected. She lay silent for a moment, with her eyes closed, and then she burst into tears.

I had no right to be there; but they both detained me, both the husband and wife, and I could not get away until she had recovered herself, and it was evident that what had been a tragical barrier between them was now become a matter of business, to be discussed as affecting them both.

"It was quite right the old lady should have it," Mr Merridew said, as he went with me to the door, "quite right. Janet did only what was right; but I now I must take it into my own hands."

"And annul what she has done?" I asked.

"We must consult over that," he said. "Ellen Babington, who has been so ungrateful to my wife, is quite a different person from her mother. But I will do nothing against Mrs Merridew's will"

And so I left them to consult over their own affairs. I had been thrust into it against my own will; but still it was entirely their affair, and no business of mine.

Mrs Spencer and Lady Isabella called to me from their lawn as I went out to ask how Mrs Merridew was, and shook their heads over her.

"She should have the doctor," said Mrs Spencer.

"But the doctor would not pay her bills for her," said Lady Isabella.

And I had to answer meekly, as if I knew nothing about it, "I don't think it is her bills."

This conversation detained me some time from my own house; and when I reached my cottage, my maid stood by the gate, looking out for me, shading her eyes with her hands. It was to tell me there was a lady waiting for me in the drawing-room: "A tall lady in mourning." And in a moment my heart smote me for some hard thoughts, and I knew who my visitor was.

I found her seated by my table, very pale, but quite self-possessed. She rose when I went in, and began to explain.

"You don't know me," she said. "I have no right to come to you; but once you came to —us — with Mrs Merridew. Perhaps you remember me now? I am Ellen Babington, I want to speak to you about — my brother's will. You may have heard that I have just lost ——"

"Yes," I said. "I am very sorry. If there is anything I can do ——"

"You can do all that I want from anyone," she said. "Janet will never believe that I wanted to keep the money — now. I have seen all children today at church; and I think, if she had been there, I should perhaps have been able — but never mind. Tell her I should like — if she would give her daughter Janet something out of the Money — from me. She is a little like what her mother was. I am sure you are kind to them. I don't even know your name —"

"Mrs Musgrave," I said; she gave a little bow. She was very composed, very well-bred, terribly sad; with the look of a woman who had no more to do in the world, and who yet was, heaven help her! in the middle of her life, full of vigour, and capability, and strength.

"Will you tell Janet, please, that it is all settled?" she said; "I mean, not the girl Janet, but her mother. Tell her I have settled everything. I believe she will hear from the lawyers tomorrow; but I could not let it come only from the lawyers. I cannot forgive her, even now. She thinks it is Matilda she has wronged; but it is me she has wronged, taking my brother from me, my only brother, after all these years. But never mind. I kissed the little child instead today — the quiet little one, with the gold hair. I suppose she is the youngest. Tell her I came on purpose to see them before I went away."

"But why send this message through me?" I said: "come and see her. I will take you; it is close by. And the sight of you will do her more good — more good than the money. Come, and let her explain."

I thought she hesitated for a moment, but her only answer was a shake of her head.

"What could she explain?" she cried, with strange impetuosity. "He and I had been together all our lives, and yet all the while he cared nothing for his sister and everything for her. Do you think I can ever forgive her? but I never forgot her. I don't think I ever loved anyone so well in my life."

"Oh, come and tell her so," said I.

Again she shook her head. "I loved her as well as I loved him; and yet I hate her," she said. "But tell her I spoke to her Janet, and I kissed

48

her baby; and that I have arranged everything with the lawyers about poor John's will. I am sure you are a good woman. Will you shake hands with me for the children's sake before I go?"

Her voice went to my heart. I had only seen her once in my life before, but I could not help it. I went up to her and took her two hands, and kissed her; and then she, the stranger, broke down, and put her head on my shoulder and wept. It was only for a moment, but it bound us as if for our lives.

"Where are you going?" I asked, when she went away.

"I am going abroad with some friends," she said hurriedly.

"But you will come to us, my dear, when you come back?"

"Most likely I shall never come back," she said hastily; and then went away alone out of my door, alone across the green, with her veil over her face, and her black dress repulsing the sunshine. One's sympathies move and change about like the winds. I had been so sorry for Mrs Merridew an hour ago; but it was not her I was most sorry for now.

And this was how it all ended. I was always glad that Mrs Merridew had told her husband before the letter came next morning. And they got the money; and John went to the university, and Janet had new dresses and new pleasures, and a ring, of which she was intensely proud, according to Ellen's desire. I daresay Ellen's intention was that something much more important should have been given to the child in her name; but then Ellen Babington, being an unmarried woman, did not know how much a large family costs, nor what urgent occasion there is for every farthing, even with an addition so great as five hundred a year.

I am afraid it did not make Mr Merridew much happier just at first. She wrote letters wildly, far and near, to everybody who could be supposed to know anything about Ellen; and wanted to have her to live with them, and to share the money with her, and I don't know how many other wild fancies. But all that could be found out was that Ellen had gone abroad. And by degrees the signs of this strange tempest began to disappear — smoothed out and filled up as Nature smooths all traces of combat. The scars, heal, new verdure covers the sudden precipice — the old gets assimilated with the new. By degrees an air of superior comfort stole over the house, which was very consolatory. Selina, the housemaid, married, and Richards retired to the inevitable greengrocery. And with a new man and new maids, and so much less difficulty about the bills, it is astonishing how the puckers died away from Mrs Merridew's forehead – first one line went, and then another, and she grew younger in spite of herself. And with everything thus conspiring in her favour, and habit calmly settling to confirm all, is it wonderful if by-and-by she forgot that any wonderful accident had ever happened, and that all had not come in the most natural way, and with the most pleasant consequences in the world?

The other day I saw a chance copy of *Galignani*, which came to me in a parcel from Paris, the marriage of Ellen Babington to a Frenchman there; but that is all we have ever heard of her. Whether it is a good marriage or a bad one I don't know; but I hope, at least, it is better for her than being all alone, as she was when she left my house that day in June, having made her sacrifice in her turn. If things had but taken their natural course, how much unnecessary suffering would have been spared: Mrs Merridew is, perhaps, happier now than she would have been without that five hundred a year — but of course they spend more; and I don't know that they are to call richer on the whole; but for two years she was wretched, sacrificing and grudging the sacrifice, and making herself very unhappy. And though I don't believe Ellen Babington cared for the money, her heart will never be healed of that pang of bitterness which her brother's desertion gave her. His companion for twenty years! and to think his best thoughts should have been given all that time to a woman who had only slighted him, and refused his love. Mrs Merridew did not see the sting of this herself — she thinks it natural. And so I daresay would half the world beside.

MARGARET OLIPHANT

The Library Window
A Story of the Seen and the Unseen

I was not aware at first of the many discussions which had gone on about that window. It was almost opposite one of the windows of the large old-fashioned drawing-room of the house in which I spent that summer, which was of so much importance in my life. Our house and the library were on opposite sides of the broad High Street of St Rule's, which is a fine street, wide and ample, and very quiet, as strangers think who come from noisier places; but in a summer evening there is much coming and and going, and the stillness is full of sound — the sound of footsteps and pleasant voices, softened by the summer air. There are even exceptional moments when it is noisy: the time of the fair, and on Saturday nights sometimes, and when there are excursion trains. Then even the softest sunny air of the evening will not smooth the harsh tones and the stumbling steps; but at these unlovely moments we shut the windows, and even I, who am so fond of that deep recess where I can take refuge from all that is going on inside, and make myself a spectator of all the varied story out of doors, withdraw from my watch-tower. To tell the truth, there never was very much going on inside. The house belonged to my aunt, to whom (she says, Thank God!) nothing ever happens. I believe that many things have happened to her in her time; but that was all over at the period of which I am speaking, and she was old, and very quiet. Her life went on in a routine never broken. She got up at the same hour every day, and did the same things in the same rotation, day by day the same. She said that this was the greatest support in the world, and that routine is a kind of salvation. It may be so; but it is a very dull salvation, and I used to feel that I would rather have incident, whatever kind of incident it might be. But then at that time I was not old, which makes all the difference.

At the time of which I speak the deep recess of the drawing-room window was a great comfort to me. Though she was an old lady (perhaps because she was so old) she was very tolerant, and had a kind of feeling for me. She never said a word, but often gave me a smile when she saw how I had built myself up, with my books and my basket of work. I did very little work, I fear — now and then a few stitches when the spirit moved me, or when I had got well afloat in a dream, and was more tempted to follow it out than to read my book, as sometimes happened. At other times, and if the book were interesting, I used to get through volume after volume sitting there, paying no attention to anybody. And yet I did pay a kind of attention. Aunt Mary's old ladies came in to call, and I heard them talk, though I very seldom listened; but for all that, if they had anything to say that was interesting, it is curious how I found it in my mind afterwards, as if the air had blown it to me. They came and went, and I had the sensation of their old bonnets gliding out and in, and their dresses rustling; and now and then had to jump up and shake hands with someone who knew me, and asked after my papa and mamma. Then Aunt Mary would give me a little smile again, and I slipped back to my window. She never seemed to mind. My mother would not have let me do it, I know. She would have remembered dozens of things there were to do. She would have sent me upstairs to fetch something which I was quite sure she did not want, or downstairs to carry some quite unnecessary message to the housemaid. She liked to keep me running about. Perhaps that was one reason why I was so fond of Aunt Mary's drawing-room, and the deep recess of the window, and the curtains that fell half over it, and the broad window-seat where one could collect so many things without being found fault with for untidiness. Whenever we had anything the matter with us in these days, we were sent to St Rule's to get up our strength. And this was my case at the time of which I am going to speak.

Everybody had said, since ever I learned to speak, that I was fantastic and fanciful and dreamy, and all the other words with which a girl who may happen to like poetry, and to be fond of thinking, is so often made uncomfortable. People don't know what they mean when they say fantastic. It sounds like Madge Wildfire or something of that sort. My mother thought I should always be busy, to keep nonsense out of my head. But really I was not at all fond of nonsense. I was rather serious than otherwise. I would have been no trouble to anybody if I had been left to myself. It was only that I had a sort of second-sight, and was conscious of things to which I paid no attention. Even when reading the most interesting book, the things that were being talked about blew in to me; and I heard what people were saying in the streets as they passed under the window. Aunt Mary always said I could do two or indeed three things at once — both read and listen, and see. I am sure that I did not listen much, and seldom looked out, of set purpose — as some people do who notice what bonnets the ladies in the street have on; but I did hear what I couldn't help hearing, even when I was reading my book, and I did see all sorts of things, though often for a whole half-hour I might never lift my eyes.

This does not explain what I said at the beginning, that there were many discussion about that window. It was, and still is, the last window in the row, of the College Library, which is opposite my aunt's house in the High Street. Yet it is not exactly opposite, but a little to the west, so that I could see it best from the left side of my recess. I took it calmly for granted that it was a window like any other till I first heard the talk about it which was going on in the drawing-room. "Have you ever made up your mind, Mrs Balcarres," said old Mr Pitmilly, "whether that window opposite is a window or no?" He said Mistress Balcarres — and he was always called Mr Pitmilly, Morton: which was the name of his place.

"I am never sure of it, to tell the truth," said Aunt Mary, "all these years."

"Bless me!" said one of the old ladies, "and what window may that be?"

Mr Pitmilly had a way of laughing as he spoke, which did not please me; but it was true that he was not perhaps desirous of pleasing me. He said, "Oh, just the window opposite," with his laugh running through his words; "our friend can never make up her mind about it, though she has been living opposite it since —"

"You need never mind the dare," said another; "the Leebrary window! Dear me, what should it be but a window? up at that height it could not be a door."

"The question is," said my aunt, "if it is a real window with glass in it, or if it is merely painted, or if it once was a window, and has been built up. And the oftener people look at it, the less they are able to say."

"Let me see this window," said old Lady Carnbee, who was very active and strong-minded; and then they all came crowding upon me — three or four old ladies, very eager, and Mr Pitmilly's white hair appearing over their heads, and my aunt sitting quiet and smiling behind.

"I mind the window very well," said Lady Carnbee; "ay; and so do more than me. But in its present appearance it is just like any other window; but has not been cleaned, I should say, in the memory of man."

"I see what ye mean," said one of the others. "It is just a very dead thing without any reflection in it; but I've seen as bad before."

"Ay, it's dead enough," said another, "but that's no rule; for these hizzies of women-servants in this ill age —"

"Nay, the women are well enough," said the softest voice of all, which was Aunt Mary's. "I will never let them this risk their lives cleaning the outside of mine. And there are no women-servants in the Old Library; there is maybe something more in it than that."

They were all pressing into my recess, pressing upon me, a row of old faces, peering into something they could not understand. I had a sense in my mind how curious it was, the wall of old ladies in their old satin gowns all glazed with age. Lady Carnbee with her lace about her head. Nobody was looking at me or thinking of me; but I felt unconsciously the contrast of my youngness to their oldness, and stared at them as they stared over my head at the Library window. I had given it no attention up to this time. I was more taken up with the old ladies than with the thing they were looking at.

"The framework is all right at least, I can see that, and pented black —"

"And the panes are pented black too. It's no window, Mrs Balcarres. It has been filled in, in the days of the window duties you will mind, Leddy Carnbee."

"Mind!" said that oldest lady. "I mind when your mother was marriet, Jeanie; and that's neither the day nor yesterday. But as for the window, it's just a delusion: and that is my opinion of the matter, if you ask me."

"There's a great want of light in that muckle room at the college," said another. "If it was a window, the Leebrary would have more light."

"One thing is clear," said one of the younger ones, "it cannot be a window to see through. It may be filled in or it may be built up, but it is not a window to give light."

"And whoever heard of a window that was to see through?" Lady

Carnbee said. I was fascinated by the look on her face, which was a curious scornful look as of one who knew more than she chose to say: and then my wandering fancy was caught by her hand as she held it up, throwing back the lace that dropped over it. Lady Carnbee's lace was the chief thing about her — heavy black Spanish lace with large flowers. Everything she wore was trimmed with it. A large veil of it hung over her old bonnet. But her hand coming out of this heavy lace was a curious thing to see. She had very long fingers, very taper, which had been much admired in her youth; and her hand was very white, or rather more than white, pale, bleached, and bloodless, with large blue veins standing upon the back; and she wore some fine rings, among others a big diamond in an ugly claw setting. They were too big for her, and were wound round and round with yellow silk to make them keep on: and this little cushion of silk, turned brown with long wearing, had twisted round so that it was more conspicuous than the jewels; while the big diamond blazed underneath in the hollow of her hand, like some dangerous thing hiding and sending out darts of light. The hand, which seemed to come almst to a point, with this strange ornament underneath, clutched at my half-terrified imagination. It too seemed to mean far more than was said. I felt as if it might clutch me with sharp claws,and the lurking, dazzling creature bite — with a sting that would go to the heart.

Presently, however, the circle of old faces broke up, the old ladies returned to their seats, and Mr Pitmilly, small but very erect, stood up in the midst of them, talking with mild authority like a little oracle among the ladies. Only Lady Carnbee always contradicted the neat, little, old gentleman. She gesticulated, when she talked, like a Frenchwoman, and darted forth that hand of hers with the lace hanging over it, so that I always caught a glimpse of the lurking diamond. I thought she looked like a witch among the comfortable little group which gave such attention to everything Mr Pitmilly said.

"For my part, it is my opinion there is no window there at all," he said. "It's very like the thing that's called in scientific language an optical illusion. It arises generally, if I may use such a word in the presence of ladies, from a liver that is not just in the perfitt order and balance that organ demands — and then you will see things — a blue dog, I remember, was the thing in one case, and in another —"

"The man has gane gyte," said Lady Carnbee; "I mind the windows in the Auld Leebrary as long as I mind anything. Is the Leebrary itself an optical illusion too?"

"Na, na," and "No, no," said the old ladies; "a blue dogue would be a strange vagary; but the Library we have all kent from our youth," said one. "And I mind when the Assemblies were held there one year when the Town Hall was building," another said.

"It is just a great divert to me," said Aunt Mary; but what was strange was that she paused there, and said in a low tone, "now": and then went on again, "for whoever comes to my house, there are aye discussions about that window. I have never just made up my mind about it myself. Sometimes I think it's a case of these wicked window duties, as you said, Miss Jeanie, when half the windows in our houses were blocked up to save the tax. And then, I think, it may be due to that blank kind of building like the great new buildings on the Earthen Mound in Edinburgh, where the windows are just ornaments. And then whiles I am sure I can see the glass shining when the sun catches it in the afternoon."

"You could so easily satisfy yourself, Mrs Balcarres, if you were to—"

"Give a laddie a penny to cast a stone, and see what happens," said Lady Carnbee.

"But I am not sure that I have any desire to satisfy myself," Aunt Mary said. And then there was a stir in the room, and I had to come out from my recess and open the door for the old ladies and see them downstairs, as they all went away following one another. Mr Pitmilly gave his arm to Lady Carnbee, though she was always contradicting him; and so the tea-party dispersed. Aunt Mary came to the head of the stairs with her guests in an old-fashioned gracious way, while I went down with them to see that the maid was ready at the door. When I came back Aunt Mary was still standing in the recess looking out. Returning to my seat she said, with a kind of wistful look, "Well, honey: and what is your opinion?"

"I have no opinion. I was reading my book at the time," I said.

"And so you were, honey, and no' very civil; but all the same I ken well you heard every word we said."

II

It was a night in June; dinner was long over, and had it been winter the maids would have been shutting up the house, and my Aunt Mary preparing to go upstairs to her room. But it was still clear daylight, that

daylight out of which the sun has been long gone, and which has no
longer any rose reflections, but all has sunk into a pearly neutral tint
— a light which is daylight yet is not day. We had taken a turn in the
garden after dinner, and now we had returned to what we called our
usual occupations. My aunt was reading. The English post had come
in, and she had got her *Times*, which was her great diversion. The
Scotsman was her morning reading, but she liked her *Times* at night.

As for me, I too was at my usual occupation, which at that time was
doing nothing. I had a book as usual, and was absorbed in it: but I was
conscious of all that was going on all the same. The people strolled along
the broad pavement, making remarks as they passed under the open
window which came up into my story or my dream, and sometimes made
me laugh. The tone and the faint sing-song, or rather chant, of the
accent, which was "a wee Fifish", was novel to me, and associated with
holiday, and pleasant; and sometimes they said to each other something
that was amusing, and often something that suggested a whole story; but
presently they began to drop off, the footsteps slackened, the voices died
away. It was getting late, though the clear soft daylight went on and on.
All through the lingering evening, which seemed to consist of
interminable hours, long but not weary, drawn out as if the spell of the
light and the outdoor life might never end, I had now and then, quite
unawares, cast a glance at the mysterious window which my aunt and
her friends had discussed, as I felt, though I dared not say it even to
myself, rather foolishly. It caught my eye without any intention on my
part, as I paused, as it were, to take breath, in the flowing and current
of undistinguishable thoughts and things from without and within which
carried me along. First it occurred to me, with a little sensation of
discovery, how absurd to say it was not a window, a living window, one
to see through! Why, then, had they never *seen* it, these old folk? I saw
as I looked up suddenly the faint greyness as of visible space within —
a room behind, certainly — dim, as it was natural a room should be on
the other side of the street — quite indefinite: yet so clear that if someone
were to come to the window there would be nothing surprising in it.
For certainly there was a feeling of space behind the panes which these
old half-blind ladies had disputed about whether they were glass or only
fictitious panes marked on the wall. How silly! when eyes that could see
could make it out in a minute. It was only a greyness at present, but it
was unmistakable, a space that went back into gloom, as every room does
when you look into it across a street. There were no curtains to show

whether it was inhabited or not; but a room — oh, as distinctly as ever room was! I was pleased with myself, but said nothing, while Aunt Mary rustled her paper, waiting for a favourable moment to announce a discovery which settled her problem at once. Then I was carried away upon the stream again, and forgot the window, till somebody threw unawares a word from the outer world, "I'm goin' hame; it'll soon be dark." Dark! what was the fool thinking of? it never would be dark if one waited out, wandering in the soft air for hours longer; and then my eyes, acquiring easily that new habit, looked across the way again.

Ah, now! nobody indeed had come to the window; and no light had been lighted, seeing it was still beautiful to read by — a still, clear, colourless light; but the room inside had certainly widened. I could see the grey space and air a little deeper, and a sort of vision, very dim, of a wall, and something against it; something dark, with the blackness that a solid article, however indistinctly seen, takes in the lighter darkness that is only space — a large, black, dark thing coming out into the grey. I looked more intently, and made sure it was a piece of furniture, either a writing-table or perhaps a large bookcase. No doubt it must be the last, since this was part of the old library. I never visited the old College Library, but I had seen such places before, and I could well imagine it to myself. How curious that for all the time these old people had looked at it, they had never seen this before!

It was more silent now, and my eyes, I suppose, had grown dim with gazing, doing my best to make it out, when suddenly Aunt Mary said, "Will you ring the bell, my dear? I must have my lamp."

"Your lamp?" I cried, "when it is still daylight." But then I gave another look at my window, and perceived with a start that the light had indeed changed: for now I saw nothing. It was still light, but there was so much change in the light that my room, with the grey space and the large shadowy bookcase, had gone out, and I saw them no more: for even a Scotch night in June, though it looks as if it would never end, does darken at the last. I had almost cried out, but checked myself, and rang the bell for Aunt Mary, and made up my mind I would say nothing till next morning, when to be sure naturally it would be more clear.

Next morning I rather think I forgot all about it — or was busy: or was more idle than usual: the two things meant nearly the same. At all events I thought no more of the window, though I still sat in my own, opposite to it, but occupied with some other fancy. Aunt Mary's visitors came as usual in the afternoon; but their talk was of other things, and for a day or two nothing at all happened to bring back my thoughts into this channel. It might be nearly a week before the subject came back, and once more it was old Lady Carnbee who set me thinking; not that she said anything upon that particular theme. But she was the last of my aunt's afternoon guests to go away, and when she rose to leave she threw up her hands, with those lively gesticulations which so many old Scotch ladies have. "My faith!" said she, "there is that bairn there still like a dream. Is the creature bewitched, Mary Balcarres? and is she bound to sit there by night and by day for the rest of her days? You should mind that there's things about, uncanny for women of our blood."

I was too much startled at first to recognise that it was of me she was speaking. She was like a figure in a picture, with her pale face the colour of ashes, and the big pattern of the Spanish lace hanging half over it, and her hand held up, with the big diamond blazing at me from the inside of her uplifted palm. It was held up in surprise, but it looked as if it were raised in malediction; and the diamond threw out darts of light and glared and twinkled at me. If it had been in its right place it would not have mattered; but there, in the open of the hand! I started up, half in terror, half in wrath. And then the old lady laughed, and her hand dropped. "I've wakened you to life, and broke the spell," she said, nodding her old head at me, while the large black silk flowers of the lace waved and threatened. And she took my arm to go downstairs, laughing and bidding me be steady, and no' tremble and shake like a broken reed. "You should be as steady as a rock at your age. I was like a young tree," she said, leaning so heavily that my willowy girlish frame quivered — "I was a support to virtue, like Pamela, in my time."

"Aunt Mary, Lady Carnbee is a witch!" I cried, when I came back.

"Is that what you think, honey? well, maybe she once was," said Aunt Mary, whom nothing surprised.

And it was that night once more after dinner, and after the post came in, and the *Times*, that I suddenly saw the Library window again. I had seen it every day — and noticed nothing; but tonight, still in a little tumult of mind over Lady Carnbee and her wicked diamond which wished me harm, and her lace which waved threats and warnings at me, I looked across the street, and there I saw quite plainly the room opposite, far more clear than before. I saw dimly that it must be a large room, and that the big piece of furniture against the wall was a writing-desk. That in a moment, when first my eyes rested upon it, was quite clear: a large old-fashioned escritoire, standing out into the room: and I knew by the shape of it that it had a great many pigeon-holes and little drawers in the back, and a large table for writing. There was one just like it in my father's library at home. It was such a surprise to see it all so clearly that I closed my eyes, for the moment almost giddy, wondering how papa's desk could have come here — and then when I reminded myself that this was nonsense, and that there were many such writing-tables besides papa's, and looked again — lo! it had all become quite vague and indistinct as it was at first; and I saw nothing but the blank window, of which the old ladies could never be certain whether it was filled up to avoid the window-tax, or whether it had ever been a window at all.

This occupied my mind very much, and yet I did not say anything to Aunt Mary. For one thing, I rarely saw anything at all in the early part of the day; but then that is natural; you can never see into a place from outside, whether it is an empty room or a looking-glass, or people's eyes, or anything else that is mysterious, in the day. It has, I suppose, something to do with the light. But in the evening in June in Scotland — then is the time to see. For it is daylight, yet it is not day, and there is a quality in which I cannot describe, it is so clear, as if every object was a reflection of itself.

I used to see more and more of the room as the days went on. The large escritoire stood out more and more into the space: with sometimes white glimmering things, which looked like papers, lying on it: and once or twice I was sure I saw a pile of books on the floor close to the writing-table, as if they had gilding upon them in broken specks, like old books. It was always about the same time when the lads in the street began to call to each other that they were going home, and sometimes a shriller voice would come from one of the doors, bidding somebody to "cry upon the laddies" to come back to their suppers. That was always the time I saw best, though it was close upon the moment when the veil seemed to fall and the clear radiance became less living, and all the sounds died out of the street, and Aunt Mary said in her soft voice, "Honey! will you ring for the lamp?" She said honey as people say darling: and I think it is a prettier word.

Then finally, while I sat one evening with my book in my hand, looking straight across the street, not distracted by anything, I saw a little movement within. It was not any one visible — but everybody

must know what it is to see the stir in the air, the little disturbance
— you cannot tell what it is, but that it indicates someone here, even
though you can see even though you can see no one. Perhaps it is
a shadow making just one flicker in the still place. You may look at
a empty room and the furniture in it for hours, and then suddenly
there will be the flicker, and you know that something has come into
it. It might only be a dog or a cat; it might be, if that were possible,
a bird flying across; but it is someone, something living, which
is so different, so completely different, in a moment from the things
that are not living. It seemed to strike quite through me, and I gave
a little cry. Then Aunt Mary stirred a little, and put down the huge
newspaper that almost covered her from sight, and said, "What is it,
honey?" I cried "Nothing," with a little gasp, quickly, for I did not
want to be disturbed just at this moment when somebody was coming!
But I suppose she was not satisfied, for she got up and stood behind
me to see what it was, putting her hand on my shoulder. It was the
softest touch in the world, but I could have flung it off angrily: for
that moment everything was still again, and the place grew grey and
I saw no more.

"Nothing," I repeated, but I was so vexed I could have cried. "I
told you it was nothing, Aunt Mary. Don't you believe me, that you
come to look — and spoil it all!"

I did not mean of course to say these last words; they were forced
out of me. I was so much annoyed to see it all melt away like a dream:
for it was no dream, but as real as — as real as — myself or anything
I ever saw.

She gave my shoulder a little pat with her hand. "Honey," she
said, "were you looking at something? Is't that it is't that?" "Is it what?"
I wanted to say, shaking off her hand, but something in me stopped
me: for I said nothing at all, and she went quietly back to her place.
I suppose she must have rung the bell herself, for immediately I felt
the soft flood of light behind me, and the evening outside dimmed
down, as it did every night, and I saw nothing more.

It was next day, I think, in the afternoon that I spoke. It was brought
on by something she said about her fine work. "I get a mist before
my eyes," she said; "you will have to learn my old lace stitches, honey
— for I soon will not see to draw the threads."

"Oh, I hope you will keep your sight," I cried, without thinking
what I was saying. I was then young and very matter-of-fact. I had not
found out that one may mean something, yet not half or a hundredth

part of what one seems to mean: and even then probably hoping to be contradicted if it is against one's self.

"My sight!" she said, looking up at me with a look that was almost angry; "there is no question of losing my sight — on the contrary, my eyes are very strong. I may not see to draw fine threads, but I see at a distance as well as ever I did — as well as you do."

"I did not mean any harm, Aunt Mary," I said. "I thought you said — But how can your sight be as good as ever when you are in doubt about that window? I can see into the room as clear as —" My voice wavered, for I had just looked up and across the street, and I could have sworn that there was no window at all, but only a false image of one painted on the wall.

"Ah!" she said, with a little tone of keenness and of surprise: and she half rose up, throwing down her work hastily, as if she meant to come to me: then, perhaps seeing the bewildered look on my face, she paused and hesitated — "Ay, honey!" she said, "have you got so far ben as that?"

What did she mean? Of course I knew all the old Scotch phrases as well as I knew myself; but it is a comfort to take refuge in a little ignorance, and I know I pretended not to understand whenever I was put out. "I don't know what you mean by 'ar ben'," I cried out, very impatient. I don't know what might have followed, but someone just then came to call, and she could only give me a look before she went forward, utting out her hand to her visitor. It was a very soft look, but anxious, and as if she did not know what to do: and she shook her head a very little, and I thought, though there was a smile on her face, there was something wet about her eyes. I retired into my recess, and nothing more was said.

But it was very tantalising that it should fluctuate so; for sometimes I saw that room quite plain and clear — quite as clear as I could see papa's library, for example, when I shut my eyes. I compared it naturally to my father's study, because of the shape of the writing-table, which, as I tell you, was the same as his. At times I saw the papers on the table quite plain, just I had seen his papers many a day. And the little pile of books on the floor at the foot — not ranged regularly in order, but put down one above the other, with all their angles going different ways, and a speck of the old gilding shining here and there. And then again at other times I saw nothing, absolutely nothing, and was no better than the old ladies who had peered over my head, drawing their eyelids together, and arguing that the window had been shut up because of the old long-abolished window tax, or else that it had never been a window at all. It annoyed me very much at those dull moments to feel that I too puckered up my eyelids and saw no better than they.

Aunt Mary's old ladies came and went day after day while June went on. I was to go back in July, and I felt that I should be very unwilling indeed to leave until I had quite cleared up — as I was indeed in the way of doing — the mystery of that window which changed so strangely and appeared quite a different thing, not only to different people, but to the same eyes at different times. Of course I said to myself it must simply be an effect of the light. And yet I did not quite like that explanation either, but would have been better pleased to make out to myself that it was some superiority in me which I made it so clear to me, if it were only the great superiority of young eyes over old — though that was not quite enough to satisfy me, seeing it was a superiority which I ared with every little lass and lad in the street. I rather wanted, I believe, to think that there was some particular insight in me which gave clearness to my sight — which was a most impertinent assumption, but really did not mean half the harm it seems to mean when it is put down here in black and white. I had several times again, however, seen the room quite plain, and made out that it was a large room, with a great picture in a dim gilded frame hanging on the farther wall, and many other pieces of solid furniture making a blackness here and there, besides the great escritoire against the wall, which had evidently been placed near the window for the sake of the light. One thing became visible to me after another, till I almost thought I should end by being able to read the old lettering on one of the big volumes which projected from the others and caught the light; but this was all preliminary to the great event which happened about Midsummer Day — the day of St John, which was once so much thought of as a festival, but now means nothing at all in Scotland any more than any other of the saints' days: which I will always think a great pity and loss to Scotland, whatever Aunt Mary may say.

III

It was about midsummer, I cannot say exactly to a day when, but near that time, when the great event happened. I had grown very well acquainted by this time with that large dim room. Not only the escritoire, which was very plain to me now, with the papers upon it, and the books at its foot, but the great picture that hung against the farther wall, and various other shadowy pieces of furniture, especially a chair which one evening I saw had been moved into the space before the escritoire, — a little change which made my heart beat, for it spoke so distinctly of someone who must have been there, the someone who had already made me start, two or three times before, by some vague shadow of him or thrill of him which made a sort of movement in the silent space: a movement which made me sure that next minute I must see something or hear something which would explain the whole — if it were not that something always happened outside to stop it, at the very moment of its accomplishment. I had no warning this time of movement or shadow. I had been looking into the room very attentively a little while before, and had made out everything almost clearer than ever; and then had bent my attention again on my book, and read a chapter or two at a most exciting period of the story: and consequently had quite left St Rule's, and the High Street, and the College Library, and was really in a South American forest, almost throttled by the flowery creepers, and treading softly lest I should put my foot on a scorpion or a dangerous snake. At this moment something suddenly calling my attention to the outside, I looked across, and then, with a start, sprang up, for I could not contain myself. I don't know what I said, but enough to startle the people in the room, one of whom was old Mr Pitmilly. They all looked round upon me to ask what was the matter. And when I gave my usual answer of "Nothing", sitting down again shamefaced but very much excited, Mr Pitmilly got up and came forward, and looked out, apparently to see what was the cause. He saw nothing, for he went back again, and I could hear him telling Aunt Mary not to be alarmed, for Missy had fallen into a doze with the heat, and had startled herself waking up, at which they all laughed: another time I could have killed him for his impertinence, but my mind was too much taken up now to pay any attention. My head was throbbing and my heart beating. I was in such high excitement, however, that to restrain myself completely, to be perfectly silent, was more easy to me then than at any other time of my life. I waited until the old gentleman had taken his seat again, and then I looked back. Yes, there he was! I had not been deceived. I knew then, when I looked across, that this was what I had been looking for all the time — that I had known he was there, and had been waiting for him, every time there was that flicker of movement in the room — him and no one else. And there at last, just as I expected, he was. I don't know that in reality I ever had expected him, or anyone: but this was what I felt when, suddenly looking into that curious dim room, I saw him there.

He was sitting in the chair, which he must have placed for himself, or which someone else in the dead of night when nobody was looking must have set for him, in front of the escritoire — with the back of his head towards me, writing. The light fell upon him from the left hand, and therefore upon his shoulders and the side of his head, which, however, was too much turned away to show anything of his face. Oh, how strange that there should be someone staring at him as I was doing, and he never to turn his head, to make a movement! If anyone stood and looked at me, were I in the soundest of sleep that ever was, I would wake, I would jump up, I would feel it through everything. But there he sat and never moved. You are not to suppose, though I said the light fell upon him from the left hand, that there was very much light. There never is in a room you are looking into like that across the street; but there was enough to see him by — the outline of his figure dark and solid, seated in the chair, and the fairness of his head visible faintly, a clear spot against the dimness. I saw this outline against the dim gilding of the frame of the large picture which hung on the farther wall.

I sat all the time the visitors were there, in a sort of rapture, gazing at this figure. I knew no reason why I should be so much moved. In an ordinary way, to see a student at an opposite window quietly doing his work might have interested me a little, but certainly it would not have moved me in any such way. It is always interesting to have a glimpse like this of an unknown life — to see so much and yet know so little, and to wonder, perhaps, what the man is doing, and why he never turns his head. One would go to the window — but not too close, lest he should see you and think you were spying upon him — and one would ask, is he still there? is he writing, writing always? I wonder what he is writing! And it would be a great amusement: but no more. This was not my feeling at all in the present case. It was a sort of breathless watch, an absorption. I did not feel that I had eyes for anything else, or any room in my mind for another thought. I no longer heard, as I generally did, the stories and the wise remarks (or foolish) of Aunt Mary's old ladies or Mr Pitmilly. I heard only a murmur behind me, the interchange of voices, one softer, one sharper, but it was not as

in the time when I was reading and heard every word, till the story
in my book, and the stories they were telling (what they said almost
always shaped into stories), were all mingled into each other, and the
hero in the novel became somehow the hero (or more likely heroine)
of them all. But I took no notice of what they were saying now. And
it was not that there was anything very interesting to look at, except
the fact that he was there. He did nothing to keep up the absorption
of my thoughts. He moved just so much as a man will do when he is
very busily writing, thinking of nothing else. There was a faint turn
of his head as he went from one side to another of the page he was
writing; but it appeared to be a long long page which never wanted
turning. Just a little inclination when he was at the end of the line,
outward, and then a little inclination inward when he began the next.
That was little enough to keep one gazing. But I suppose it was the
gradual course of events leading up to this, the finding of one thing
after another as the eyes got accustomed to the vague light: first the
room itself, and then the writing-table, and then the other furniture,
and last of all the human inhabitant who gave it all meaning. This was
all so interesting that it was like a country which one had discovered.
And then the extraordinary blindness of the other people who disputed
among themselves whether it was a window at all! I did not, I am sure,
wish to be disrespectful, and I was very fond of my Aunt Mary, and
I liked Mr Pitmilly well enough, and I was afraid of Lady Carnbee.
But yet to think of the — I know I ought not to say stupidity — the
blindness of them, the foolishness, the insensibility! discussing it as
if a thing that your eyes could see was a thing to discuss! It would
have been unkind to think it was because they were old and their
faculties dimmed. It is so sad to think that the faculties grow dim, that
such a woman as my Aunt Mary should fail in seeing, or hearing, or
feeling, that I would not have dwelt on it for a moment, it would have
seemed so cruel! And then such a clever old lady as Lady Carnbee,
who could see through a millstone, people said — and Mr Pitmilly,
such an old man of the world. It did indeed bring tears to my eyes to
think that all those clever people, solely by reason of being no longer
young as I was, should have the simplest things shut out from them;
and for all their wisdom and their knowledge be unable to see what
a girl like me could see so easily. I was too much grieved for them
to dwell upon that thought, and half ashamed, though perhaps half
proud too, to be so much better off than they.

All those thoughts flitted through my mind as I sat and gazed across the street. And I felt there was so much going on in that room across the street! He was so absorbed in his writing, never looked up, never paused for a word, never turned round in his chair, or got up and walked about the room as my father did. Papa is a great writer, everybody says: but he would have come to the window and looked out, he would have drummed his fingers on the pane, he would have watched a fly and helped it over a difficulty, and played with the fringe of the curtain, and done a dozen other nice, pleasant, foolish things, till the next sentence took shape. "My dear, I am waiting for a word," he would say to my mother when she looked at him, with a question why he was so idle, in her eyes; and then he would laugh, and go back again to his writing-table. But He over there never stopped at all. It was like a fascination. I could not take my eyes from him and that little scarcely perceptible movement he made, turning his head. I trembled with impatience to see him turn the page, or perhaps throw down his finished sheet on the floor, as somebody looking into a window like me once saw Sir Walter do, sheet after sheet. I should have cried out if this Unknown had done that. I should not have been able to help myself, whoever had been present; and gradually I got into such a state of suspense waiting for it to be done that my head grew hot and my hands cold. And then, just when there was a little movement of his elbow, as if he were about to do this, to be called away by Aunt Mary to see Lady Carnbee to the door! I believe I did not hear her till she had called me three times, and then I stumbled up, all flushed and hot, and nearly crying. When I came out from the recess to give the old lady my arm (Mr Pitmilly had gone away some time before), she put up her hand and stroked my cheek. "What ails the bairn?" she said; "she's fevered. You must not let her sit her lane in the window, Mary Balcarres. You and me know what comes of that." Her old fingers had a strange touch, cold like something not living, and I felt that dreadful diamond sting me on the cheek.

I do not say that this was not just part of my excitement and suspense; and I know it is enough to make anyone laugh when the excitement was all about an unknown man writing in a room on the other side of the way, and my impatience because he never came to an end of the page. If you think I was not quite as well aware of this as anyone could be! but the worst was that this dreadful old lady felt my heart beating against her arm that was within mine. "You are just in a dream," she said to me, with her old voice close at my ear as we went downstairs. "I don't know who it is about, but it's bound to be some man that is not worth it. If you were wise you would think of him no more."

"I am thinking of no man!" I said, half crying. "It is very unkind and dreadful of you to say so, Lady Carnbee. I never thought of — any man, in all my life!" I cried in a passion of indignation. The old lady clung tighter to my arm, and pressed it to her, not unkindly.

"Poor little bird," she said, "how it's strugglin' and flutterin'! I'm not saying but what it's more dangerous when it's all for a dream."

She was not at all unkind but I was very angry and excited, and would scarcely shake that old pale hand which she put out to me from her carriage window when I helped her in. I was angry with her, and I was afraid of the diamond, which looked up from under her finger as if it saw through and through me; and whether you believe me or not, I am certain that it stung me again — a sharp malignant prick, oh full of meaning! She never wore gloves, but only black lace mittens, through which that horrible diamond gleamed.

I ran upstairs — she had been the last to go — and Aunt Mary too had gone to get ready for dinner, for it was late. I hurried to my place, and looked across, with my heart beating more than ever. I made quite sure I should see the finished sheet lying white upon the floor. But what I gazed at was only the dim blank of that window which they said was no window. The light had changed in some wonderful way during that five minutes I had been gone, and there was nothing, nothing, not a reflection, not a glimmer. It looked exactly as they all said, the blank form of a window painted on the wall. It was too much: I sat down in my excitement and cried as if my heart would break. I felt that they had done something to it, that it was not natural, that I could not bear their unkindness — even Aunt Mary. They thought it is not good for me! not good for me! and they had done something — even Aunt Mary herself — and that wicked diamond that hid itself in Lady Carnbee's hand. Of course I knew all this was ridiculous as well as you could tell me; but I was exasperated by the disappointment and the sudden stop to all my excited feelings, and I could not bear it. It was more strong than I.

I was late for dinner, and naturally there were some traces in my eyes that I had been crying when I came into the full light in the dining-room, where Aunt Mary could look at me at her pleasure, and I could not run away. She said, "Honey, you have been shedding tears. I'm loth, loth that a bairn of your mother's should be made to shed tears in my house."

"I have not been made to shed tears," I cried; and then, to save myself another fit of crying, I burst out laughing and said, "I am afraid of that dreadful diamond on old Lady Carnbee's hand. It bites — I am sure it bites! Aunt Mary, look here."

"You foolish lassie," Aunt Mary said; but she looked at my cheek under the light of the lamp, and then she gave it a little pat with her soft hand. "Go away with you, you silly bairn. There is no bite; but a flushed cheek, my honey, and a wet eye. You must just read out my paper to me after dinner when the post is in: and we'll have no more thinking and no more dreaming for tonight."

"Yes, Aunt Mary," said I. But I knew what would happen; for when she opens up her *Times*, all full of the news of the world, and the speeches and things which she takes an interest in, though I cannot tell why — she forgets. And as I kept very quiet and made not a sound, she forgot tonight what she had said, and the curtain hung a little more over me than usual, and I sat down in my recess as if I had been a hundred miles away. And my heart gave a great jump, as if it would have come out of my breast; for he was there. But not as he had been in the morning — I suppose the light, perhaps, was not good enough to go on with his work without a lamp or candles — for he had turned away from the table and was fronting the window, sitting leaning back in his chair, and turning his head to me. Not to me — he knew nothing about me. I thought he was not looking at anything; but with his face turned my way. My heart was in my mouth: it was so unexpected, so strange! though why it should have seemed strange I know not, for there was no communication between him and me that it should have moved me; and what could be more natural than that a man, wearied of his work, and feeling the want perhaps of more light, and yet that it was not dark enough to light a lamp, should turn round in his own chair, and rest a little, and think — perhaps of nothing at all? Papa always says he is thinking of nothing at all. He says things blow through his mind as if the doors were open, and he has no responsibility. What sort of things were blowing through this man's mind? or was he thinking, still thinking, of what he had been writing and going on with it still? The thing that troubled me most was that I could not make out his face. It is very difficult to do so when you see a person only through two windows, your own and his. I wanted very much to recognise him afterwards if I should chance to meet him in the street. If he had only stood up and moved about the room, I should have made out the rest of his figure, and then I should have known him again; or if he had only come to the window (as papa always did), then I should have seen his face clearly enough to have recognised him. But, to be sure, he did not see any need to do anything in order that I might recognise him, for he did not know I existed; and probably if he had known I was watching him, he would have been annoyed and gone away.

But he was as immovable there facing the window as he had been seated at the desk. Sometimes he made a little faint stir with a hand or a foot, and I held my breath, hoping he was about to rise from his chair — but he never did it. And with all the efforts I made I could not be sure of his face. I puckered my eyelids together as old Miss Jeanie did who was shortsighted, and I put my hands on each side of my face to concentrate the light on him: but it was all in vain. Either the face changed as I sat staring, or else it was the light that was not good enough, or I don't know what it was. His hair seemed to me light — certainly there was no dark line about his head, as there would have been had it been very dark — and I saw, where it came across the old gilt frame on the wall behind, that it must be fair: and I am almost sure he had no beard. Indeed I am sure that he had no beard, for the outline of his face was distinct enough; and the daylight was still quite clear out of doors, so that I recognised perfectly a baker's boy who was on the pavement opposite, and whom I should have known again whenever I had met him: as if it was of the least importance to recognise a baker's boy! There was one thing, however, rather curious about this boy. He had been throwing stones at something or somebody. In St Rule's they have a great way of throwing stones at each other, and I suppose there had been a battle. I suppose also that he had one stone in his hand left over from the battle, and his roving eye took in all the incidents of the street to judge where he could throw it with most effect and mischief. But apparently he found nothing worthy of it in the street, for he suddenly turned round with a flick under his leg to show his cleverness, and aimed it straight at the window. I remarked without remarking that it struck with a hard sound and without any breaking of glass, and fell straight down on the pavement. But I took no notice of this even in my mind, so intently was I was watching the figure within, which moved not nor took the slightest notice, and stinct than it had been.

Then I jumped up, feeling Aunt Mary's hand upon my shoulder. "Honey," she said, "I asked you twice to ring the bell; but you did not hear me."

"Oh Aunt Mary!" I cried in great penitence, but turning again to the window in spite of myself.

"You must come away from there: you must come away from there," she said, almost as if she were angry: and then her soft voice grew softer, and she gave me a kiss: "never mind about the lamp, honey; I have rung myself, and it is coming; but, silly bairn, you must not aye be dreaming — your little head will turn."

All the answer I made, for I could scarcely speak, was to give a little wave with my hand to the window on the other side of the street.

She stood there patting me softly on the shoulder for a whole minute or more, murmuring something that sounded like, "She must go away, she must go away." Then she said, always with her hand soft on my shoulder, "Like a dream when one awaketh." And when I looked again, I saw the blank of an opaque surface and nothing more.

Aunt Mary asked me no more questions. She made me come into the room and sit in the light and read something to her. But I did not know what I was reading, for there suddenly came into my mind and took possession of it, the thud of the stone upon the window, and its descent straight down, as if from some hard substance that threw it off: though I had myself seen it strike upon the glass of the panes across the way.

IV

I am afraid I continued in a state of great exaltation and commotion of mind for some time. I used to hurry through the day till the evening came, when I could watch my neighbour through the window opposite. I did not talk much to anyone, and I never said a word about my own questions and wonderings. I wondered who he was, what he was doing, and why he never came till the evening (or very rarely); and I also wondered much to what house the room belonged in which he sat. It seemed to form a portion of the old College Library, as I have often said. The window was one of the line of windows which I understood lighted the large hall; but whether this room belonged to the library itself, or how its occupant gained access to it, I could not tell. I made up my mind that it must open out of the hall, and that the gentleman must be the Librarian or one of his assistants, perhaps kept busy all the day in his official duties, and only be able to get to his desk and do his own private work in the evening. One has heard of so many things like that — a man who had to take up some other kind of work for his living, and then when his leisure-time came, gave it all up to something he really loved — some study or some book he was writing. My father himself at one time had been like that. He had been in the Treasury all day, and then in the evening wrote his books, which made him famous. His daughter, however little she might know of other things, could not but know that! But it discouraged me very much when somebody pointed out to me one day in the street an old gentleman who wore a wig and took a great deal of snuff, and said, That's the Librarian of the old College. It gave me a great shock for a moment; but then I remembered that an old gentleman has generally assistants, and that it must be one of them.

Gradually I became quite sure of this. There was another small window above, which twinkled very much when the sun shone, and looked a very kindly bright little window, above that dullness of the other which hid so much. I made up my mind this was the window of his other room, and that these two chambers at the end of the beautiful hall were really beautiful for him to live in, so near all the books, and so retired and quiet, that nobody knew of them. What a fine thing for him! and you could see what use he made of his good fortune as he sat there, so constant at his writing for hours together. Was it a book he was writing, or could it be perhaps Poems? This was a thought which made my heart beat; but I concluded with much regret that it could not be Poems, because no one could possibly write Poems like that, straight off, without pausing for a word or a rhyme. Had they been Poems he must have risen up, he must have paced about the room or come to the window as papa did — not that papa wrote Poems: he always said, "I am not worthy even to speak of such prevailing mysteries," shaking his head — which gave me a wonderful admiration and almost awe of a Poet, who was thus much greater even than papa. But I could not believe that a poet could have kept still for hours and hours like that. What could it be then? perhaps it was history; that is a great thing to work at, but you would not perhaps need to move nor to stride up and down, or look out upon the sky and the wonderful light.

He did move now and then, however, though he never came to the window. Sometimes, as I have said, he would turn round in his chair and turn his face towards it, and sit there for a long time musing when the light had begun to fail, and the world was full of that strange day which was night, that light without colour, in which everything was so clearly visible, and there were no shadows. "It was between the night and the day, when the fairy folk have power." This was the after-light of the wonderful long, long summer evening, the light without shadows. It had a spell in it, and sometimes it made me afraid: and all manner of strange thoughts seemed to come in, and I always felt that if only we had a little more vision in our eyes we might see beautiful folk walking about in it, who were not of our world. I thought most likely he saw them, from the way he sat there looking out: and this made my heart expand with the most curious sensation, as if of pride that, though I could not see, he did, and did not even require to come to the window, as I did, sitting close in the depth of the recess, with my eyes upon him, and almost seeing things through his eyes.

I was so much absorbed in these thoughts and in watching him every evening — for now he never missed an evening, but was always there — that people began to remark that I was looking pale and that I could not be well, for I paid no attention when they talked to me, and did not care to go out, nor to join the other girls for their tennis, not to do anything that others did; and some said to Aunt Mary that I was quickly losing all the ground I had gained, and that she could never send me back to my mother with a white face like that. Aunt Mary had begun to look at me anxiously for some time before that, and, I am sure, held secret consultations over me, sometimes with the doctor, and sometimes with her old ladies, who thought they knew more about young girls than even the doctors. And I could hear them saying to her that I wanted diversion, that I must be diverted, and that she must take me out more, and give a party, and that when the summer visitors began to come there would perhaps be a ball or two, or Lady Carnbee would get up a picnic. "And there's my young lord coming home," said the old lady whom they called Miss Jeanie, "and I never knew the young lassie yet that would not cock up her bonnet at the sight of a young lord."

But Aunt Mary shook her head. "I would not lippen much to the young lord," she said. "His mother is sore set upon siller for him; and my poor bit honey has no fortune to speak of. No, we must not fly so high as the young lord; but I will gladly take her about the country to see the old castles and towers. It will perhaps rouse her up a little."

"And if that does not answer we must think of something else," the old lady said.

I heard them perhaps that day because they were talking of me, which is always so effective a way of making you hear — for latterly I had not been paying any attention to what they were saying; and I thought to myself how little they knew, and how little I cared about even the old castles and curious houses, having something else in my mind. But just about that time Mr Pitmilly came in, who was always a friend to me, and, when he heard them talking, he managed to stop them and turn the conversation into another channel. And after a while, when the ladies were gone away, he came up to my recess, and gave a glance right over my head. And then asked my Aunt Mary if ever she had settled her question about the window opposite, "that you thought was a window sometimes, and then not a window, and many curious things," the old gentleman said.

My Aunt Mary gave me another very wistful look; and then she said, "Indeed, Mr Pitmilly, we are just where we were, and I am quite as unsettled as ever; and I think my niece she has taken up my views, for I see her many a time looking across and wondering, and I am not clear now what her opinion is."

"My opinion!" I said, "Aunt Mary." I could not help being a little scornful, as one is when one is very young. "I have no opinion. There is not only a window but there is a room, and I could show you ——" I was going to say, "show you the gentleman who sits and writes in it," but I stopped, not knowing what they might say, and looked from one to another. "I could tell you — all the furniture that is in it," I said. And then I felt something like a flame that went over my face, and that all at once my cheeks were burning. I thought they gave a little glance at each other, but that may have been folly. "There is a great picture, in a big dim frame," I said, feeling a little breathless, "on the wall opposite the window ——"

"Is there so?" said Mr Pitmilly, with a little laugh. And he said, "Now I will tell you what we'll do. You know that there is a conversation party, or whatever they call it, in the big room tonight, and it will be all open and lighted up. And it is a handsome room, and two-three things well worth looking at. I will just step along after we have all got our dinner, and take you over to the pairty, madam — Missy and you ——"

"Dear me!" said Aunt Mary. "I have not gone to a pairty for more years than I would like to say — and never once to the Library Hall." Then she gave a little shiver, and said quite low, "I could not go there."

"Then you will just begin again to-night, madam," said Mr Pitmilly, taking no notice of this, "and a proud man will I be leading in Mistress Balcarres that was once the pride of the ball!"

"Ah, once!" said Aunt Mary, with a low little laugh and then a sigh. "And we'll not say how long ago;" and after that she made a pause, looking always at me: and then she said, "I accept your offer, and we'll put on our braws; and I hope you will have no occasion to think shame of us. But why not take your dinner here?"

That was how it was settled, and the old gentleman went away to dress, looking quite pleased. But I came to Aunt Mary as soon as he was gone, and besought her not to make go. "I like the long bonnie night and the light that lasts so long. And I cannot bear to dress up and go out, wasting it all in a stupid party. I hate parties, Aunt Mary!" I cried, "and I would far rather stay here."

"My honey," she said, taking both my hands, "I know it will maybe be a blow to you, — but it's better so."

"How could it be a blow to me?" I cried; "but I would far rather not go."

"You'll go with me, honey, just this once: it is not often I go out. You will go with me this one night, just this one night, my honey sweet."

I am sure there were tears in Aunt Mary's eyes, and she kissed me between the words. There was nothing more that I could say; but how I grudged the evening! A mere party, a conversazione (when all the College was away, too, and nobody to make conversation!), instead of my enchanted hour at my window and the soft strange light, and the dim face looking out, which kept me wondering and wondering what he was thinking of, what was he looking for, who was he? all one wonder and mystery and question, through the long, long, slowly fading night!

It occurred to me, however, when I was dressing – though I was so sure that he would prefer his solitude to everything — that he might perhaps, it was just possible, be there. And when I thought of that, I took out my white frock — though Janet had laid out my blue one — and my little pearl necklace which I had thought was too good to wear. They were not very large pearls, but they were real pearls, and very even and lustrous though they were small; and though I did not think much of my appearance then, there must have been something about me — pale as I was but apt to colour in a moment, with my dress so white, and my pearls so white, and my hair all shadowy — perhaps, that was pleasant to look at: for even old Mr Pitmilly had a strange look in his eyes, as if he was not only pleased but sorry too, perhaps thinking me a creature that would have troubles in this life, though I was so young and knew them not. And when Aunt Mary looked at me, there was a little quiver about her mouth. She herself had on her pretty lace and her white hair very nicely done, and looking her best. As for Mr Pitmilly, he had a beautiful fine French cambric frill to his shirt, plaited in the most minute plaits, and with a diamond pin in it which sparkled as much as Lady Carnbee's ring; but this was a fine frank kindly stone, that looked you straight in the face and sparkled, with the light dancing in it as if it were pleased to see you, and to be shining on that old gentleman's honest and faithful breast: for he had been one of Aunt Mary's lovers in their early days, and still thought there was nobody like her in the world.

I had got into quite a happy commotion of mind by the time we set out across the street in the soft light of the evening to the Library Hall.

Perhaps, after all, I should see him, and see the room which I was so well acquainted with, and find out why he sat there so constantly and never was seen abroad. I thought I might even hear what he was working at, which would be such a pleasant thing to tell papa when I went home. A friend of mine at St Rule's — oh, far, far more busy than you ever were, papa! — and then my father would laugh as he always did, and say he was but an idler and never busy at all.

The room was all light and bright, flowers wherever flowers could be, and the long lines of the books that went along the walls on each side, lighting up wherever there was a line of gilding or an ornament, with a little response. I dazzled me at first all that light: but I was very eager, though I kept very quiet, looking round to see if perhaps in any corner, in the middle of any group, he would be there. I did not expect to see him among the ladies. He would not be with them, — he was too studious, too silent: but perhaps among that circle of grey heads at the upper end of the room — perhaps ——

No: I am not sure that it was not half a pleasure to me to make quite sure that there was not one whom I could take for him, who was at all like my vague image of him. No: it was absurd to think that he would be here, amid all that sound of voices, under the glare of that light. I felt a little proud to think that he was in his room as usual, doing his work, or thinking so deeply over it, as when he turned round in his chair with his face to the light.

I was thus getting a little composed and quiet in my mind, for now that the expectation of seeing him was over, though it was a disappointment, it was a satisfaction too — when Mr Pitmilly came up to me, holding out his arm. "Now," he said, "I am going to take you to see the curiosities." I thought to myself that after I had seen them and spoken to everybody I knew, Aunt Mary would let me go home, so I went very willingly, though I did not care for the curiosities. Something, however, struck me strangely as we walked up the room. It was the air, rather fresh and strong, from an open window at the east end of the hall. How should there be a window there? I hardly saw what it meant for the first moment, but it blew in my face as if there was some meaning in it, and I felt very uneasy without seeing why.

Then there was another thing that startled me. On that side of the wall which was to the street there seemed no windows at all. A long line of bookcases filled it from end to end. I could not see what that meant either, but it confused me. I was altogether confused. I felt as if I was in a strange country, not knowing where I was going, not knowing what I might find out next. If there were no windows on the wall to the street, where was my window? My heart, which had been jumping up and calming down again all this time, gave a great leap at this, as if it would have come out of me — but I did not know what it could mean.

Then we stopped before a glass case, and Mr Pitmilly showed me some things in it. I could not pay much attention to them. My head was going round and round. I heard his voice going on, and then myself speaking with a queer sound that was hollow in my ears; but I did not know what I was saying or what he was saying. Then he took me to the very end of room, the east end, saying something that I caught — that I was pale, that the air would do me good. The air was blowing full on me, lifting the lace of my dress, lifting my hair, almost chilly. The window opened into the pale daylight, into the little lane that ran by the end of the building. Mr Pitmilly went on talking, but I could not make out a word he said. Then I heard my own voice, speaking through it, though I did not seem to be aware that I was speaking. "Where is my window? — where, then, is my window?" I seemed to be saying, and I turned right round, dragging him with me, still holding his arm. As I did this my eye fell upon something at last which I knew. It was a large picture in a broad frame, hanging against the farther wall.

What did it mean? Oh, what did it mean? I turned round again to the open window at the east end, and to the daylight, the strange light without any shadow, that was all round about this lighted hall, holding it like a bubble that would burst, like something that was not real. The real place was the room I knew, in which that picture was hanging, where the writing-table was, and where he sat with his face to the light. But where was the light and the window through which it came? I think my senses must have left me. I went up to the picture which I knew, and then I walked straight across the room, always dragging Mr Pitmilly, whose face was pale, but who did not struggle but allowed me to lead him, straight across to where the window was — where the window was not; — where there was no sign of it. "Where is my window? — where is my window? I said. And all the time I was sure that I was in a dream, and these lights were all some theatrical illusion, and the people talking; and nothing real but the pale, pale, watching, lingering day standing by to wait until that foolish bubble should burst.

"My dear," said Mr Pitmilly, "my dear! Mind that you are in public. Mind where you are. You must not make an outcry and frighten your Aunt Mary. Come away with me. Come away, my dear young lady! and you'll take a seat for a minute or two and compose yourself; and I'll get you an ice or a little wine." He kept patting my hand, which was on his arm, and looking at me very anxiously. "Bless me! bless me! I never thought it would have this effect," he said.

But I would not allow him to take me away in that direction. I went to the picture again and looked at it without seeing it: and then I went across the room again, with some kind of wild thought that if I insisted I should find it. "My window — my window!" I said.

There was one of the professors standing there, and he heard me. "The window!" said he. "Ah, you've been taken in with what appears outside. It was put there to be in uniformity with the window on the stair. But it never was a real window. It is just behind that bookcase. Many people are taken in by it," he said.

His voice seemed to sound from somewhere far away, and as if it would go on for ever; and the hall swam in a dazzle of shining and of noises round me; and the daylight through the open window grew greyer, waiting till it should be over, and the bubble burst.

IV

It was Mr Pitmilly who took me home; or rather it was I who took him, pushing him on a little in front of me, holding fast by his arm, not waiting for Aunt Mary or anyone. We came out into the daylight again outside, I, without even a cloak or a shawl, with my bare arms, and uncovered head, and the pearls round my neck. There was a rush of the people about, and a baker's boy, that baker's boy, stood right in my way and cried, "Here's a braw ane!" shouting to the others: the words struck me somehow, as his stone had struck the window, without any reason. But I did not mind the people staring, and hurried across the street, with Mr Pitmilly half a step in advance. The door was open, and Janet standing at it, looking out to see what she could see of the ladies in their grand dresses. She gave a shriek when she saw me hurrying across the street; but I brushed past her, and pushed Mr Pitmilly up the stairs, and took him breathless to the recess, where I threw myself down on the seat, feeling as if I could not have gone a another step farther, and waved my hand across to the window. "There! there!" I cried. Ah! there it was — not that senseless mob — not the theatre and the gas, and the people all in a murmur and clang of talking. Never in all these days had I seen that room so clearly. There was a faint tone of light behind, as if it might have been a reflection from some of those vulgar lights in the hall, and he sat against it, calm, wrapped in his thoughts, with his face turned to the window. Nobody but must have seen him. Janet could have seen him had I called her upstairs. It was like a picture, all the things I knew, and the same attitude, and atmosphere, full of quietness, not disturbed by anything. I pulled Mr Pitmilly's arm before I let him go, — "You see, you see!" I cried. He gave me the most bewildered look, as if he would have liked to cry. He saw nothing! I was sure of that from his eyes. He was an old man, and there was no vision in him. If I had called up Janet, she would have seen it all. "My dear!" he said. "My dear!" waving his hands in a helpless way.

"He has been there all these nights," I cried, "and I thought you could tell me who he was and what he was doing; and that he might have taken me in to that room, and showed me, that I might tell papa. Papa would understand, he would like to hear. Oh, can't you tell me what work he is doing, Mr Pitmilly? He never lifts his head as long as the light throws a shadow, and then when it is like this he turns round and thinks, and takes a rest!"

Mr Pitmilly was trembling, whether it was with cold or I know not what. He said, with a shake in his voice, "My dear young lady — my dear ——" and then stopped and looked at me as if he were going to cry. "It's peetiful, it's peetiful," he said; and then in another voice, "I am going across there again to bring your Aunt Mary home; do you understand, my poor little thing, my —— I am going to bring her home — you will be better when she is here." I was glad when he went away, as he could not see anything: and I sat alone in the dark which was not dark, but quite clear light – a light like nothing I ever saw. How clear it was in that room! not glaring like the gas and the voices, but so quiet, everything so visible, as if it were in another world. I heard a little rustle behind me, and there was Janet, standing staring at me with two big eyes wide open. She was only a little older than I was. I called to her, "Janet, come here, come here, and you will see him, — come here and see him!" impatient that she should be shy and keep behind. "Oh, my bonnie young leddy!" she said, and burst out crying. I stamped my foot at her, in my indignation that she would not come, and she fled before me with a rustle and swing of haste, as if she were afraid. None of them, none of them! not even a girl like myself, with the sight in her eyes, would understand. I turned back again, and held out my hands to him sitting there, who was the only one that knew. "Oh," I said, "say something to me! I don't know who you are, or what you are: but you're lonely and so am I; and I only — feel for you. Say something to me!" I neither hoped that he would hear, not expected any answer. How could he hear, with the street between us, and his window shut, and all the murmuring of the voices and the people standing about? But for one moment it seemed to me that there was only him and me in the whole world.

But I gasped with my breath, that had almost gone from me, when I saw him move in his chair! He had heard me, though I knew not how. He rose up, and I rose too, speechless, incapable of anything but this mechanical movement. He seemed to draw me as if I were a puppet moved by his will. He came forward to the window, and stood looking across at me. I was sure that he looked at me. At last he had seen me: at last he had found out that somebody, though only a girl, was watching him, looking for him, believing in him. I was in such trouble and commotion of mind and trembling, that I could not keep on my feet, but dropped kneeling on the window-seat, supporting myself against the window, feeling as if my heart were being drawn out of me. I cannot describe his face. It was all dim, yet there was light on it: I think it must have been a smile; and as closely as I looked at him he looked at me. His hair was fair, and there was a little quiver about his lips. Then he put his hands upon the window, to open it. It was stiff and hard to move; but at last he forced it open with a sound that echoed all along the street. I saw that the people heard it, and several looked up. As for me, I put my hands together, leaning with my face against the glass, drawn to him as if I could have gone out of myself, my heart out of my bosom, my eyes out of my head. He opened the window with a noise that was heard from the West Port to the Abbey. Could anyone doubt that?

And then he leaned forward out of the window, looking out. There was not one in the street but must have seen him. He looked at me first, with a little wave of his hand, as if it were a salutation — yet not exactly that either, for I thought he waved me away; and then he looked up and down in the dim shining of the ending day, first to the east, to the old Abbey towers, and then to the west, along the broad line of the street where so many people were coming and going, but so little noise, all like enchanted folk in an enchanted place. I watched him with such a melting heart, with such a deep satisfaction as worlds could not say; for nobody could tell me now that he was not there, — nobody could say I was dreaming any more. I watched him as if I could not breathe — my heart in my throat, my eyes upon him. He looked up and down, and then he looked back me. I was the first, and I was the last, though it was not for long: he did know, he did see, who it was that had recognised him and sympathised with him all the time. I was in a kind of rapture, yet stupor too; my look went with his look, following it as if I were his shadow; and then suddenly he was gone, and I saw him no more.

I dropped back again upon my seat, seeking something to support me, something to lean upon. He had lifted his hand and waved it once again to me. How he went I cannot tell, nor where he went I cannot tell; but in a moment he was away, and the window standing open, and the room fading into stillness and dimness, yet so clear, with all its space, and the great picture in its gilded frame upon the wall. It gave me no pain to see him go away. My heart was so content, and I was so worn out and satisfied — for what doubt or question could there be about him now? As I was lying back as weak as water, Aunt Mary came in behind me, and flew to me with a little rustle as if she had come on wings, and put her arms round me, and drew my head on to her breast. I had begun to cry a little, with sobs like a child. "You saw him, you saw him!" I said. To lean upon her, and feel her so soft, so kind, gave me a pleasure I cannot describe, and her arms round me, and her voice saying "Honey, my honey!" — as if she were nearly crying too. Lying there I came back to myself, quite sweetly, glad of everything. But I wanted some assurance from them that they seen him too. I waved my hand to the window that was still standing open, and the room that was stealing away into the faint dark. "This time you saw it all?" I said, getting more eager. "My honey!" said Aunt Mary, giving me a kiss: and Mr Pitmilly began to walk about the room with short little steps behind, as if he were out of patience. I sat straight up and put away Aunt Mary's arms. "You cannot be so blind, so blind!" I cried. "Oh, not to-night, at least not to-night!" But neither the one nor the other made any reply. I shook myself quite free, and raised myself up. And there, in the middle of the street, stood the baker's boy like a statue, staring up at the open window, with his mouth open and his face full of wonder — breathless, as if he could not believe what he saw. I darted forward, calling to him, and beckoned him to come to me. "Oh, bring him up! bring him, bring him to me!" I cried.

Mr Pitmilly went out directly, and got the boy by the shoulder. He did not want to come. It was strange to see the little old gentleman, with his beautiful frill and his diamond pin, standing out in the street, with his hand upon the boy's shoulder, and the other boys round, all in a little crowd. And presently they came towards the house, the others all following, gaping and wondering. He came in unwilling, almost resisting, looking as if we meant him some harm. "Come away, my laddie, come and speak to the young lady," Mr Pitmilly was saying. And Aunt Mary took my hands to keep me back. But I would not be kept back.

"Boy," I cried, "you saw it too: you saw it: tell them you saw it! It is that I want, and no more."

He looked at me as they all did, as if he thought I was mad. "What's she wantin' wi' me?" he said; and then, "I did nae harm, even if I did throw a bit stane at it — and it's nae sin to throw a stane."

"You rascal!" said Mr Pitmilly, giving him a shake; "have you been throwing stones? You'll kill somebody some of these days with your stones." The old gentleman was confused and troubled, for he did not understand what I wanted, nor anything that had happened. And then Aunt Mary, holding my hands and drawing me close to her, spoke. "Laddie," she said, "answer the young lady, like a good lad. There's no intention of finding fault with you. Answer her, my man, and then Janet will give ye your supper before you go."

"Oh speak, speak!" I cried; "answer them and tell them! you saw that window opened, and the gentleman look out and wave his hand?"

"I saw nae gentleman," he said, with his head down, "except this wee gentleman here."

"Listen, laddie," said Aunt Mary. "I saw ye standing in the middle of the street staring. What were ye looking at?"

"It was naething to make a wark about. It was just yon windy yonder in the library that is nae windy. And it was open —as sure's death. You may laugh if you like. Is that a' she's wantin' wi me?"

"You are telling a pack of lies, laddie," Mr Pitmilly said.

"I'm tellin' nae lees — it was standin' open just like ony ither windy. It's as sure's death. I couldna believe it mysel': but it's true."

"And there it is," I cried, turning round and pointing it out to them with great triumph in my heart. But the light was all grey, it had faded, it had changed. The window was just as it had always been, a sombre break upon the wall.

I was treated like an invalid all that evening, and taken up-stairs to bed, and Aunt Mary sat up in my room the whole night through. Whenever I opened my eyes she was always sitting there close to me, watching. And there never was in all my life so strange a night. When I would talk in my excitement, she kissed me and hushed me like a child. "Oh, honey, you are not the only one!" she said. "Oh, whisht, whisht, bairn! I should never have let you be there!"

"Aunt Mary, Aunt Mary, you have seen him too?"

"Oh whisht, whisht, honey!" Aunt Mary said: her eyes were shining — there were tears in them. "Oh whisht, whisht! Put it out of your mind, and try to sleep. I will not speak another word," she cried.

But I had my arms around her, and my mouth at her ear. "Who is he there? – tell me that and I will ask no more ——"

"Oh honey, rest, and try to sleep! It is just – how can I tell you? – a dream, a dream! Did you not hear what Lady Carnbee said? — the women of our blood ——"

"What? What? Aunt Mary, oh Aunt Mary——"

"I canna tell you," she cried in her agitation, "I canna tell you! How can I tell you, when I know just what you know and no more? It is a longing all your life after — it is a looking — for what never comes."

"He will come," I cried. "I shall see him to-morrow — that I know, I know!"

She kissed me and cried over me, her cheek hot and wet like mine. "My honey, try if you can sleep — try if you can sleep: and we'll wait to see what to-morrow brings."

"I have no fear," said I; and then I suppose, though it is strange to think of, I must have fallen asleep — I was so worn-out, and young, and not used to lying in my bed awake. From time to time I opened my eyes, and sometimes jumped remembering everything: but Aunt Mary was always there to soothe me, and I lay down again in her shelter like a bird in its nest.

But I would not let them keep me in bed next day. I was in a kind of fever, not knowing what I did. The window was quite opaque, without the least glimmer in it, flat and blank like a piece of wood. Never from the first day had I seen it so little like a window. "It cannot be wondered at," I said to myself, "that seeing it like that, and with eyes that are old, not so clear as mine, they should think what they do." And then I smiled to myself to think of the evening and the long night, and whether he would look out again or only give me a signal with his hand. I decided I would like that best: not that he should take the trouble to come forward and open it again, but just a turn of his head and a wave of his hand. It would be more friendly and show more confidence, — not as if I wanted that kind of demonstration every night.

I did not come down in the afternoon, but kept at my own window up-stairs alone, till the tea-party should be over. I could hear them making a great talk; and I was sure they were all in the recess staring at the window, and laughing at the silly lassie. Let them laugh! I felt above all that now. At dinner I was very restless, hurrying to get it over; and I think Aunt Mary was restless too. I doubt whether she read her *Times* when it came; she opened it up so as to shield her, and watched from a corner. And I settled myself in the recess, with my heart full of expectation. I wanted nothing more than to see him writing at his table, and to turn his head and give me a little wave of his hand, just to show that he knew I was there. I sat from half-past seven o'clock to ten o'clock: and the daylight grew softer and softer, till at last it was as if it was shining through a pearl, and not a shadow to be seen. But the window all the time was as black as night, and there was nothing, nothing there.

Well: other nights it had been like that; he would not be there every night only to please me. There are other things in a man's life, a great learned man like that. I said to myself I was not disappointed. Why should I be disappointed? There had been other nights when he was not there. Aunt Mary watched me, every movement I made, her eyes shining, often wet, with a pity in them that almost made me cry: but I felt as if I were more sorry for her than for myself. And then I flung myself upon her, and asked her, again and again, what it was, and who it was, imploring her to tell me if she knew? and when she had seen him, and what had happened? and what it meant about the women of our blood? She told me that how it was she could not tell, nor when: it was just at the time it had to be; and that we all saw him in our time — "that is," she said, "the ones that are like you and me." What was it that made her and me different from the rest? but she only shook her head and would not tell me. "They say," she said, and then stopped short. "Oh, honey, try and forget all about it — if I had but known you were of that kind! They say — that once there was one that was a Scholar, and liked his books more than any lady's love. Honey, do not look at me like that. To think I should have brought all this on you!"

"He was a Scholar?" I cried.

"And one of us, that must have been a light woman, not like you and me —— But may be it was just in innocence; for who can tell? She waved to him and waved to him to come over: and yon ring was the token: but he would not come. But still she sat at her window and waved and waved — till at last her brothers heard of it, that were stirring men; and then — oh, my honey, let us speak of it no more!"

"They killed him!" I cried, carried away. And then I grasped her with my hands, and gave her a shake, and flung away from her. "You tell me that to throw dust in my eyes — when I saw him only last night: and he as living as I am, and as young!"

"My honey, my honey!" Aunt Mary said.

After that I would not speak to her for a long time; but she kept close to me, never leaving me when she could help it, and always with that pity in her eyes. For the next night it was the same; and the third night. That third night I thought I could not bear it any longer. I would have to do something — if only I knew what to do! If it would ever get dark, quite dark, there might be something to be done. I had wild dreams of stealing out of the house and getting a ladder, and mounting up to try if I could not open that window, in the middle of the night — if perhaps I could get the baker's boy to help me; and then my mind got into a whirl, and it was as if I had done it; and I could almost see the boy put the ladder to the window, and hear him cry out that there was nothing there. Oh, how slow it was, the night! and how light it was, and everything so clear — no darkness to cover you, no shadow, whether on one side of the street or on the other side! I could not sleep, though I was forced to go to bed. And in the deep midnight, when it is dark dark in every other place, I slipped very softly down-stairs, though there was one board on the landing-place that creaked — and opened   the door and stepped out. There was not a soul to be seen up or down, from the Abbey to the West Port: and the trees stood like ghosts, and the silence was terrible, and everything as clear as day. You don't know what silence is till you find it in the light like that, not morning but night, no sunrising, no shadow, but everything as clear as the day.

It did not take make any difference as the slow minutes went on: one o'clock, two o'clock. How strange it was to hear the clocks striking in that dead light when there was nobody to hear them! But it made no difference. The window was quite blank; even the marking of the panes seemed to have melted away. I stole up again after a long time, through the silent house, in the clear light, cold and trembling, with despair in my heart.

I am sure Aunt Mary must have watched and seen me coming back, for after a while I heard faint sounds in the house; and very early, when there had come a little sunshine into the air, she came to my bedside with a cup of tea in her hand; and she, too, was looking like a ghost. "Are you warm, honey — are you comfortable?" she said. "It doesn't matter," said I. I did not feel as if anything mattered; unless if one could get into the dark somewhere — the soft, deep dark that would cover you over and hide you — but I could not tell from what. The dreadful thing was that there was nothing, nothing to look for, nothing to hide from — only the silence and the light.

That day my mother came and took me home. I had not heard she was coming; she arrived quite unexpectedly, and said she had no time to stay, but must start the same evening so as to be in London next day, papa having settled to go abroad. At first I had a wild thought I would not go. But how can a girl say I will not, when her mother has come for her, and there is no reason, no reason in the world, to resist, and no right! I had to go, whatever I might wish or anyone might say. Aunt Mary's dear eyes were wet; she went about the house drying them quietly with her handkerchief, but she always said, "It's the best thing for you, honey — the best thing for you!" Oh, how I hated to hear it said that it was the best thing, as if anything mattered, one more than another! The old ladies were all there in the afternoon, Lady Carnbee looking at me from under her black lace, and the diamond lurking, sending out darts from under her finger. She patted me on the shoulder, and told me to be a good bairn. "And never lippen to what you see from the window," she said. "The eye is deceitful as well as the heart." She kept patting me on the shoulder, and I felt again as if that sharp wicked stone stung me. Was that what Aunt Mary meant when she said yon ring was the token? I thought afterwards I saw the mark on my shoulder. You will say why? How can I tell why? If I had known, I should have been contented, and it would not have mattered any more.

I never went back to St Rule's, and for years of my life I never again looked out of a window when any other window was in sight. You ask me did I ever see him again? I cannot tell: the imagination is a great deceiver, as Lady Carnbee said: and if he stayed there so long, only to punish the race that had wronged him, why should I ever have seen him again? for I had received my share. But who can tell what happens in a heart that often, often, and so long as that, comes back to do its errand? It is was he whom I have seen again, the anger is gone from him, and he mean good and no longer harm to the house of the woman that loved him. I have seen his face looking at me from a crowd. There was one time when I came home a widow from India, very sad, with my little children: I am certain I saw him there among all the people coming to welcome their friends. There was nobody to welcome me, — for I was not expected: and very sad was I, without a face I knew: when all at once I saw him, and he waved his hand to me. My heart leaped up again: I had forgotten who he was, but only that it was a face I knew, and I landed almost cheerfully, thinking here was someone who would help me. But he had disappeared, as he did from the window, with that one wave of his hand.

And again I was reminded of it all when old Lady Carnbee died —an old, old woman —and it was found in her will that she had left me that diamond ring. I am afraid of it still. It is locked up in an old sandal-wood box in the lumber-room in the little old country-house which belongs to me, but where I never live. If anyone would steal it, it would be a relief to my mind. Yet I never knew what Aunt Mary meant when she said, "Yon ring was the token," nor what it could have to do with that strange window in the old College Library of St Rule's.

SARAH TYTLER

A Harmonious Little Arrangement
(from *St Mungo's City*)

The three Miss Mackinnons have taken great exception to the will of their kinsman Fenton of Strathdivie, who has left £20 to each of the older sisters and £230 to the youngest.

To begin with, something closed the Miss Mackinnons' lips on this point, and not a word was said among them of the defrauding of Miss Mackinnon and Miss Janet to enrich Miss Bethia, sitting with downcast eyes, wringing the hands hidden in her lap.

At last Miss Janet said, not so much bitterly as with forced gaiety:

'You are up in the buckle [exalted], Betheye — an heiress; you'll no be speaking to me and Meye.'

'Oh, Janet!' burst out Miss Bethia, breaking down and sobbing with mingled 'pain and shame. 'Do you think I would touch the money? I'll gie it back, every penny, to you and Meye, the moment I've got it into my fingers.'

'But there's twa and whiles three at a bargain-making,' said Miss Janet, with wounded pride in her voice. 'Do you think we would tak' from anither — though she happened to be our sister — what was ours, but had been wulled awa' from us?'

'But that would be cruel!' protested Miss Bethia, in still greater distress. 'How could I help it? An ill-kinded man! Gude guide us!' pausing in horror; 'to think that I should speak ill of him, and him hardly in the mools. But I never set een on him, never.'

'You gowk, what does that signify?' Miss Janet was provoked into treating the heiress with little courtesy.

'What ails her?' cried Miss Mackinnon wrathfully. 'Is she pretendin' to greet for the man, now that he has left her the maist of his money? I cannot stand such hypocrisy.'

Miss Bethia wept on, regardless of the good fortune, which was misfortune to her, and equally unrestrained by the manner in which her sorrow was misunderstood.

'What can I do?' she lamented. 'I never wanted your shares; I never thocht money would come between me and you and Meye.'

Miss Janet was a little softened.

'You can do nothing — as long as the paper stands, the money's yours. But we're no blaming you, save for being silly — and we'll tak' the will for the deed.'

'Oh, thank you! thank you, Janet!' said Miss Bethia gratefully. 'If only Meye and you will not tak' me for a traitor and hypocrite — and me never to have seen the man! — I'll no mind so muckle. But is there no way to gie back the money, and share and share alike as we should have done? Why can I not do as I like with my ain, as he did?'

'You're fast enough with your ain,' said Miss Janet, in fresh displeasure. 'It has not been yours mair than an hour. I'll tell you what, Betheye,' the speaker relapsed into a sardonic mood, 'it's a' very weel to say what you'll do or not do the noo; but it's as likely as not that the word o' the sillar will bring some fair-spoken blackguard of a man after you. You'll marry him fast; then Meye and me will be left in the lurch, and he'll help you to spend the money that should have been ours.'

'Never!' declared Miss Bethia; and she failed to simper as of old, but a dull-red rose in her lined face and spread over it. She had, as she would have said, given up all thought of a man for many a day; but mercenary as were the notions attributed to this man, the sudden revival of the vision brought a shy, guilty sense of gratification, which the next moment covered poor Miss Bethia with confusion and remorse. Would she sacrifice her sisters even for the best man that ever breathed? 'I wonder at you, Janet!' she said, so vehemently that there was a suspicion of weakness and fear in the vehemence; 'an auld maid like me.'

'There's nae fules like old anes,' said Miss Janet jauntily 'and you'll cease to be an auld maid when the scamp has made you a young wife. Ye ken you'll be young among the mawtrons, though you're auld among the maidens.'

'It's cruel,' repeated Miss Bethia, with an ominous intensity of distress in the kindling fire of temptation. 'Oh! I wish I had the horrible money to fling into the fire, or cast it into Clyde.'

'What good would that do?' demanded the matter-of-fact Miss Janet, 'unless you wanted him to loup in and fish it out.'

Miss Bethia groaned.

'Stop her greetin',' broke in Miss Mackinnon, in greater disgust than before. 'I canna bide sic false pretences, Betheye; it's like haudin' an ingan [onion] to your een. Hoo can ye try sic a trick upon Janet and me?'

'I wull greet,' Miss Bethia suddenly turned upon her sisters: 'I have cause to greet. I thoucht my ain sisters liked and trusted me, and I was prood to slave wi' them and for them; but I find I was mista'en when they're ready to misdoubt me, for nae faut o' mine, and to tant me because of the wrongdoing of another.'

Miss Janet was taken aback by this new attitude of Miss Bethia, and the feelings reflected on her face were quickly caught up by her elder sister. They both paused, irresolute what to say next.

'We dinna misdoubt you, Betheye,' said Miss Janet, in a more subdued tone. 'But you maun grant this has been a shock as well as a hardship to us — the younger to be served out of the elders' proportions — the elder to be dependent on the younger's generosity, or whatever you like to ca't.'

'Oh, it is maist abominable!' admitted Miss Bethia, with all her heart. 'But it is no generosity — it's justice which ocht to be done; and surely I'll be helped to do't, though I've to get the Queen to back me.'

'It's an expensive road to the Queen, though her Majesty is very gude and kind,' said Miss Janet, not affording any encouragement to the scheme, but refraining from the strong derision she had been practising. The next moment she added: 'I think there may be an easier plan — it has just flashed upon me — if you're in earnest, Betheye, as I do not question.'

'Try me,' said Miss Bethia, with trembling eagerness.

'Weel, I apprehend there's just this parchment binding you doon — I said, as long as the paper stands we've but to submit. But what is to hinder us from making awa' wi't? The wull concerns nane but oorsel's and the servants — that dour, sly jaud of a housekeeper and her man. We are perfectly agreed, and we can easily settle wi' servants; we'll pay them every bawbee of their legacy, though it's twice as muckle as it need have been — and that is all they'll care for. What need is there to keep the paper and fash our heads with it? We'll tear it up, and think nae mair o't, while we divide Jean Mackinnon's money fair among oorsel's.'

'The very thing,' said Miss Bethia, with a great sigh of relief and of lurking regret that the legacy had not been ten thousand or ten hundred. In that case, even the third fraction of it might have constituted her an heiress, with all an heiress's privileges and trials. She might have been courted, she might have needed to stand firm, to decline to be wooed, to give her suitors a dignified yet amiable dismissal. There was glamour in the prospect, but it was not for Miss Bethia. 'To destroy the wull,' she hammered on at Miss Janet's project, 'which deals just with the servants, to whom we can make their legacy gude, while we are fully agreed on a fresh division of Jean Mackinnon's money, is so easy and natural. I wonder it did not occur to us at aince. Let us do it this minute, Janet, before Mr Mair or ony of the gentlemen come back.' Miss Bethia was opposed to the least delay. 'Shall I tak' out the paper and tear it?' she cried.

'On second thochts, it had better be burnt, and then there will be no trouble with the fragments,' said Miss Janet, gratified with having been the originator of a good idea, and full of importance in putting it into execution. 'I believe I have heard,' continued Miss Janet dogmatically, 'that, when a wull is burnt in this way, the parties interested stand round a can'le, and each holds a corner of the dockiment over the lowe, so as to mak' sure they're all consenting to the destruction; then if any wyte [blame] is incurred, it will fa' on all alike.'

'But is there ony fear o' wyte?' asked Miss Bethia startled. 'Maybe, after a', we had better wait and ask Mr Mair.'

'Maybe, after a', we had better let the wull stand,' said Miss Janet scornfully, for the resource hit upon had by this time recommended itself thoroughly to her. It would restore her own and Miss Mackinnon's birthright, by the curl of a flame, if not by the stroke of a pen, and thus immediately wipe out the insult and loss inflicted upon them. And the act would prevent any danger of Miss Bethia's wavering in her design, or being overborne by the arguments of others.

Not only was the plan Miss Janet's and therefore right in her eyes; she was proud of it, and sought to keep it in her own possession, and carry it out independently for herself and her sisters. She enjoyed the notion of astonishing and discomfiting Mr Mair by her sharpness and promptitude. In fact, Miss Janet had got out her head, and was bent on 'running her own road'.

'You ken I did not mean to let the wull stand,' said Miss Bethia, hurt and reproachful. 'But you'll speak to Mr Mair after. You'll tell him what you've done with the wull he gave up to you.'

'I'll speak to Mair when he speaks to me,' said Miss Janet, full of refractoriness. 'What has he, ony mair than his clerk, to do with Fenton of Strathdivie's wull, that was made on our account? Mair drew it up, as ony ither writer micht have done; but it was not his wull, or yours either, Betheye, as ane micht think, to hear ye speak. You've sune learnt to tak' a great deal upon you. You seem to forget, because you've been preferred without reason, that we're your elders, and Meye's the head of the hoose.'

'I dinna forget,' said Miss Bethia, with a full heart.

Miss Janet went on harshly:

'If you're in earnest in makin' reparation by being willin' to join Meye and me, in what we've had cause to suppose you had fixed to do, ye'll say no more about it.'

Miss Bethia said no more.

When it was put to Miss Mackinnon whether she would support her sisters in their spirited measure, she replied with hoarse emphasis, 'Certainly!' and looked about for a matchbox.

There was a wax taper by the inkstand, and Miss Janet was in such a hurry that she would not wait to ring for a candle, though it seemed doubtful at the first glance whether the little light could effectually consume the two or three broad-margined, widely-written, crackling pages of which the will was composed.

'We'll tak' it leaf by leaf,' said Miss Janet methodically. 'There are only three o' us; but I'll haud two corners, while you and Meye can tak' the other twa, ane each.'

The process was a slow one. Miss Janet and Miss Mackinnon stood unflinchingly, braving the little wreaths of smoke which seemed to rise out of all proportion to the performance, even daring the yellow tongues of flame that darted across the paper, and threatened the bony fingers.

Miss Bethia shook fitfully, disturbing the balance of the arrangement, and shrank nervously from the burning, as if it had been Archie Fenton putting forth fiery fingers to execute vengeance upon her for her contemptuous treatment of his will.

The whole fantastic incident — witnessed under the solemn splendour of a moorland sunset, which shone in through a western window; the three big, gaunt, hard-featured old women, in more or less fixed theatrically tragic attitudes, the right hand extended, grasping the sheet of paper; Miss Janet's dauntless, impassive face; Miss Mackinnon's glittering, restless eyes, lit up by an imprisoned spirit; Miss Bethia's features working with anxiety and dread; the shrivelling, blackening paper; the jets of flame, the smoke — all bore a marvellous, grotesque resemblance to the witches' incantations of the Middle Ages. Fenton of Strathdivie's will might have been one of those bonds, written in letters of blood, that sold souls to the foul fiend, and could be no more burnt in fire, which was their natural element, than the devil could perish in his own hell.

Towards the close of the strange proceeding there was a slight creaking of the door and rustling of something behind it, which caused Miss Bethia to look round in fresh terror; but the trifling noise ceased almost instantly. The charred fragments of the will dropped on the floor, and were carefully collected by Miss Janet in the fire-shovel and deposited in the empty grate. Another match was lit and applied to them, and she was soon warranted in the triumphant announcement:

'There's naethin' left but white aiss [ashes], let Mair or wha like mak' what they can oot o't. We've snapped our fingers at Fenton o' Strathdivie, in what was his ain hoose, too.'

'Oh! wheesht, Janet, wheesht!' implored the appalled Miss Bethia.

But Miss Janet did not heed her younger sister.

'We're free to do what we like wi' our ain,' she proclaimed exultingly.

Indeed, the Miss Mackinnons were not disturbed in their harmonious little arrangement, either on that night or before their departure next morning.

MARY FINDLATER

Void of Understanding

I

From every chink in the old door of the shed, red light forced itself out, penetrating far into the darkness of a night that was clear, but without stars. The windows were squares of scarlet, and Berry, crouching in the long grass beside the wall, could hear the fiddles play over and over again the same reeling air. On this the night of his father's second marriage, Berry had not been wanted in the merry-making that followed the ceremony, so he had wandered off by himself till the dusk fell, when the shadows about the roads began to get frightful, and he longed to be safe at home beside the fire. But the door of the house was locked, and someone in the barn had the key; so he found a dry corner by the wall, huddled himself up there, and began to look at the great, cloudless, grey sky, against which the farm buildings rose in a long row. The trees could be counted one by one, and he could see the meadow below him hoary with the first autumnal frosts. All was breathlessly quiet in the transparent dusk; the barn, with its light and noise, seemed another little world shut tightly up, with its own life going on in its own way, surrounded on all sides by a great quiet. Berry had one thought in his head — how much he would like to get to bed now, for it was so cold.

He crept again to the door of the barn, and peeped through a crack. Thump, thump, thump — the steps of the dancers went round and round, and then bursts of laughter came roaring out into the night, and someone threw down one of the windows for more air, and the keen giggle of the fiddles sung on above it all.

Berry turned away. He would go back and sit by the wall again. Berry's step was shuffling and uncertain, and his big head nodded about as he walked — a clumsy, piteous figure. No wonder they did not want him in there!

Now he was back beside the wall, and the window had been shut. He had not many thoughts at any time, but a sensation of fear began to pluck at his heart, left here alone out in the clear, moonless night. Something might be coming on him; he looked behind and saw the bank of wood against the sky. On one side was the wall, on the other a tangle of brambles and hemlocks, growing tall among some loose stones. Something moved there; he watched it, and it moved and moved. He went a little nearer to see; it stretched, and all the leaves began to quiver. Berry's heart was beating so fast that he could no longer hear the tune they played inside the barn. He must get away from this thing. He tried to run, but his feet were like weights of lead. Then it rose and rose, and screeched, and flapped, and gobbled, so that in his agony of terror Berry tumbled himself forwards through the weeds and loose stones down into the ditch, where the slime, pouring over him, made him scream aloud, and scrambling, dragging himself desperately up, he dashed at the door of the barn, while the great turkey-cock, whose rest he had disturbed, standing on the heap of stones, bubbled after him his angry disdain.

To be the heroine of the occasion begins to pall after six hours' enjoyment of that distinction amidst heat and noise. There was a lull in the music. The dancers sank on to the 'forms' and wiped their faces, and the bride, in her blue merino gown, seated blushing and smiling at the head of the long room, began to wish the wedding guests would go, for her head ached with the noise and the thick air, heavy with fumes of whisky and tobacco.

Amidst the general good feeling that prevailed, everyone — except, perhaps, lame Christina, the bridegroom's aunt and housekeeper, who was deprived of her employment by this marriage; and Janet Macnee, whose brother Elsie had jilted for the better match — everyone considered that Cameron was a happy man to get such a wife. Indeed, she was very pretty, and capable, and clever, and come of good people too. There was a distinct compliment in the manner in which the 'best man' now rose to sing during this pause in the dancing. He fixed his eyes on the bride as he sang —

'Her brow is like the snawdrift;
Her neck is like the swan;
And her face it is the fairest
That e'er the sun shone on.'

He was just beginning,

'Like dew on the gowan lying,'

when there came a crash at the door, followed by a chorus of exclamation; a current of cold night air swept into the room as the door flew open, and Berry, uttering a shrill, fearful cry, his clothes dripping with ooze and slime, came stumbling in among the wedding guests. His stupid face was drawn with terror, and he kept grasping at some invisible thing in front of him until he sank back, dazzled all of a sudden by the bright lights and the crowd about him. He would have fallen if Janet Macnee had not caught him up. 'Losh, losh!' she muttered, and a dead silence fell through the room. Janet wore her best black silk gown that night, and now the mud was all over it, but she lifted the boy on to her lap. 'Stand back an' let the creater get breath — he's a'most awa',' she said, propping the big head upon her arms; then lifting him up like a baby, she moved nearer to the bride.

'It's yer step-son, Mistress Cameron,' she said in a low voice. (Elsie's conduct to her brother got its payment then.)

The people around nudged each other, looking expressively at the bride as she bent over the boy, holding her skirt almost unconsciously out of the way (blue merino soils so easily). Berry opened his eyes and looked at her. She saw the white, vacant face, the open mouth, the bloodshot eyes, the misshapen limbs hanging limply from Mrs Macnee's arm, and as he lifted one of his coarse, cold hands to touch hers — on which glittered the new wedding-ring — she snatched it away, turning to her husband with a shudder.

'O John,' she said piteously, 'the bairn's got a fricht — he'd better be pit til his bed.'

'I'll tak' him hame wi' me,' said Janet dryly. 'We've no far tae gang, an' Donald'll carry him fine. Ye'll no be wantin' him the nicht, Mistress Cameron?'

She wrapped the child in a shawl, and turned to the door. Berry seemed confused and frightened still, and though Janet questioned him several times on his way home, he gave no intelligible reply.

'He's never been richt i' the mind, but he's waur nor I thocht,' she said to Donald after she had put the child to bed. 'Maybe Elsie'll no be sae weel aff aifter a' — the evil eye was on her the nicht — lame Kirsty's no a body I'd like tae cross — she micht nae hae done sae ill tae tak' oor Peter aifter a' — she's got a braw son tae stairt wi, ony hoo.'

Berry wakened out of his first sleep with a start. It was nearly two o'clock in the morning, and the fiddlers were passing on their way home.

II

Here was a very pretty young woman, just married to one of the steadiest, most respected men in the country-side, wishing to do her best, and make him a good wife — but here also was Berry, poor Berry, who, when the house was as neat as could be, and Elsie sitting in state waiting for a neighbour to look in, would trail, all slush and dirt, across the spotless floor, to sit on the fender and gabble vacantly when he was spoken to. And as time went on, matters, as they generally do in a home trial, got worse. With Elsie's own brown, bright-eyed baby in the cradle, was it pleasant to have the stranger lady who called one day inquire compassionately, 'What is the matter with your eldest little boy?'

And grievances grow like Jack's beanstalk when they are planted in one's own garden. This one became bigger than ever when the second baby had arrived, and when, on the day of the baptism, just as the minister was deep in the prayer, with everyone in the room so solemn, the idiot, standing behind the door, suddenly pulled out the concertina to its fullest length!

Could Elsie like that? Could she, who was young still, and thought a man could love but one, like to see the photograph of the first wife — the one done in Glasgow, showing her sitting with Berry as a baby on her knee — hanging always on the wall in front of her, to remind her every day that she was only the second.

Berry had been sent to school on trial for a day or two; but the master soon told them it was no use; he could never learn; so that instead of being sent off in the morning like other children, and only returning at five o'clock — for the schoolhouse lay two miles off over the moor — he was always there, loitering about the door, muttering to himself, or sitting opposite to Elsie at mealtimes, when he would spill every second mouthful that he tried to get into his poor open mouth. Elsie soon put a stop to this, however.

'It makes me fair sick,' she said. 'I'll give him his food when we're through, John,' and she did always. He got plenty to eat and drink.

It was quite hopeless to try to keep him clean, for he would be for ever with the ducks, ploutering away at the 'spout'.

At the Sunday school, where Miss Mackenzie was very patient, he was allowed to stay; and Elsie had a gleam of hope that he might learn something after all when she heard him mumble,

> 'On then to glorry-run,
> Be a-crown-an'-kingdom-won';

but it was all he could ever repeat of that or any other lesson.

Elsie tried very hard to be kind to him at first. When she married she held in her mind some idea of what a step-mother ought to be; but practice, with the most of us, means the slow disintegration of the ideal, and Elsie's crumbled quickly. He did not mind being scolded, for unless your voice was very high and harsh, he did not understand, so she got into the habit of giving him a tap on the head, sometimes briskly, when he would keep standing beside her baking-board; or a slap — a light slap — now and then if he tumbled things over; and she would push him aside with impatience when he came trailing, trailing 'amongst her feet', asking some pointless question for the hundredth time. This was all trying enough; but it was really after her own children were born that it became unbearable, for strangers would ask why she did not send her eldest boy to school.

John came home one night when the second baby was a few weeks old, and found her sitting by the cradle crying. Then for the first time she told him what she felt.

'It's the shame of it,' she sobbed, 'that onybody should take the likes of him for my bairn, an' Johnny sae well grown an' sae quick at the uptak, an' the baby —' She looked down at the warm, waxen face of the infant in its healthy sleep. 'The sicht o' him fears me whiles. He'll stand glowerin' at the bairn, an' talkin' a' the while, an' ye'll no ken a wurd he's sayin'. The bairn's like tae scream whiles when he'll poke yon great heid intil the cradle, an' no wonder either.'

John puffed at his pipe, and moved impatiently. He had not known quite how badly matters stood between Berry and his step-mother. Involuntarily as she spoke his eyes wandered from the cradle, and rested on the faded photograph that hung on the wall beside the fireplace.

Elsie watched his glance, and she felt that her opportunity was at hand. Rising softly from her low chair, she put her hand on his shoulder, and, so sweet, so pretty, looked down into his face. His eyes grew soft as they met hers.

'I'd be easier like, John,' she said gently, letting her eyelashes droop as she spoke, 'if ye'd just pit away yon picture. It's aye lookin' at me wherever I gae, an' — an' — Berry's no sense, I'm sure, to ken who it is.'

'No more he has,' said her husband shortly, and moved his face away that she might not see his expression. 'Would ye grudge her the picter on yer wa', lassie?' he asked at length.

'No me. I'm no grudgin' her naething that's hers; but ye may think what ye like.' She sat down again by the cradle. 'I hae my ain bairns,' she said, and lifted her baby and rocked it to and fro.

She did not look again at her husband, only in the long silence that fell between them she drew two or three slow sighs. The clock ticked away; the cradle rocked softly; and the green twigs on the fire began to bubble and hiss as the flames came near them. The man sat silent till half an hour had passed. Then he rose, and, stretching out his long arm, he took down the little photograph. Elsie did not turn her head. He held it in his hand, looking at it. She glanced round for a moment, and then buried her face in the cradle, cooing to the child.

'Will that please ye?' he asked.

Elsie made no reply.

He went slowly across the room to the big chest of drawers that was filled with clothing, from amongst which he took a handkerchief, and wrapping it carefully about the little picture, he laid it back in the drawer. Then he looked round at Elsie. Her head was bent over the cradle. He opened the door and shambled into the yard. 'Ways o' women,' he muttered to himself.

As the door closed behind him, Elsie lifted up her face. *'Thae men,'* she said expressively.

III

Berry found himself, after the arrival of the second baby, a good deal occupied in taking care of Johnny, who at first of course had been considered too precious to be allowed out of Elsie's sight. Berry had always shown a curious fondness for the little boy, ever since he first began to creep about the floor, for when he was in the cradle,

Berry was never permitted to touch him; when the child began to move about on his hands and knees, Berry too would get down on the floor, and with foolish laughter and meaningless gestures, make his clumsy efforts to amuse. He let Johnny tumble over him, pull his hair, slap him, do anything he pleased with him, and the child soon discovered that Berry was a more bidable playfellow than the cat, and did not scratch. So when Elsie had her hands full with the new baby, she found it very convenient to make Berry look after Johnny, and he carried out this, the only duty that he had ever known, with strange fidelity. Nothing else would keep him from messing about in the mud and water by the spout; but if Elsie put Johnny's hand in his, telling him to 'mind the bairn', he would pass hours at a time, on the safe, dry ground before the door, playing muddled little games with stones, games in which John was always the teacher; allowing Johnny to 'play horses', Berry always the horse. He had no jealousy of the little boy, and though the one thing that he liked best in the world was to stand at night between his father's knees and watch the fire blazing, and get warmed through and through, he never seemed to mind when Johnny, as was often the case, occupied the coveted position and he was left to creep away into a corner next to the door, where only a faint degree of heat could penetrate. He was intensely susceptible to cold, perhaps because his thin blood ran torpidly, and he had not the wits to jump about and warm himself like other children. As the nights drew on to frost he used to shiver almost continuously, so that it made Elsie quite uncomfortable to look at him, and she would sigh to herself in the morning as he stood chittering in the doorway — a pitiful object, with his ungainly head and cold, swollen hands.

As Johnny grew older, he managed to make Berry understand more than other people did. It was Johnny, and not Miss Mackenzie, who taught him to reply *'Jesus'* to every question that they asked him at the Sunday school, an answer which did wonderfully well, and gained him admission along with the others to the treat at Christmas time.

The smaller boys at the treat were all seated on the benches to the front, and as Berry had come to take care of Johnny, he was seated there too. He sat with one hand in Johnny's, the other grasping his orange, gazing in a kind of trance at the beautiful pictures that passed and repassed across the darkness at the end of the room, where Miss Mackenzie was showing the slides of a magic lantern.

When a picture of Queen Victoria, very richly dressed in her coronation robes, was on view, the superintendent asked who it was, and Berry's voice, shrill above the others, made his invariable reply. The little ones besides him burst into uncontrollable laughter, and Miss Mackenzie, shocked by the profanity, sternly demanded who said it. An angry juvenile teacher, not clearly understanding who it was, and not seeing Berry's poor face in the darkness, lifted him forward and turned him out at the door, without his orange.

So he went home alone, sobbing and slobbering, quite unaware of his offence. Miss Mackenzie tried her best next day to explain about it to Elsie — how they could not let the other children begin to laugh at such a reply, and so on.

'Johnny', for all he's that wee, was fair affronted, mem,' Elsie answered. Long afterwards she perhaps remembered the hard words with which she received Berry when he came back by himself in disgrace, having, as she thought, forsaken his trust, and left Johnny to find his way home alone.

'I wadna leave him — I wadna leave him,' sobbed Berry. 'They pit me oot,' — that had only made matters worse.

IV

The village school was reopened early in January, and Elsie made up her mind to send Johnny there for the first time. She did not like to see him constantly playing about with Berry, and though he was young enough to go such a distance, he was so quick and keen at learning for his age that she felt he ought to be with other boys, not all day long with a half-witted creature like his step-brother.

The schoolhouse lay about two miles over the moor, and she could not take him herself because of leaving the baby, so she gave Berry very strict charge concerning him. He was to go the whole way, not to loiter or to stop. He was to wait till the school came out, and take Johnny home. 'Go wi' him, an' be sure ye bring him back. Ye can show him the way — *it's all ye're good for*,' she said, giving Johnny's coat a final pull before they started. Her mind was still vexed by Berry's last disgrace, and she was scarcely aware of how sharply she spoke; she was anxious too, for it was a long way for her little boy, and the sky looked dark and threatening. Berry looked at her blankly, as if he did not understand.

'Ye'll mind no tae come back yer lane this time,' she repeated. 'Bring him back — *it's all ye're good for*.'

Berry fixed his expressionless eyes on her for a moment, then he took Johnny's hand, and turned humbly away.

She watched them go slowly on together till the road dipped down to the moor, and they were hidden behind the ridge.

V

The hours that he spent outside the door in the little porch of the schoolhouse, where he could hear the buzz of voices inside and the occasional drumming of the master's hand upon the desk, were very long hours to Berry, but he did not dare to move away. It began to get terribly cold. He watched the low winter sun, pale as straw, sink and sink further down the sky. Strange flights of birds flew twittering above in the darkening atmosphere, and the noise of a little burn that ran beside the door grew more distinct, until at last it ran with an almost metallic tinkle under the freezing grass. Berry rubbed his cold hands, swung his leaden feet, got up and walked a little way, and then came back to his post. He was afraid to go far lest the school should come out in his absence.

So cold! but even to his dull wits the 'bitter sky' did not 'bite so nigh' as the confused pain that moved in his uncertain mind — something about being shut out alone when all the other boys were in school — about having in some way done wrong to Johnny by leaving him before. He would not leave Johnny alone; he would sit on there though it was so cold.

When the sun, now red like crimson, had dropped upon the heavy rim of cloud that lay to the west, and a few flakes of snow began idly to flutter down upon the hard ground, the school-door opened, and the children tumbled out, shouting, into the sharp, evening air. In the first rush of egress, no one noticed Berry sitting in the porch. Then Johnny saw him, and called out; and then some of the bigger boys, riotous with spirits and freedom, made a ring round him and danced in a circle, mocking at his efforts to escape. He got hopelessly confused, and just ran round and round, always foiled whenever he attempted to creep under the barrier of arms that encircled him. At last, when the master himself came out, and shouted to them crossly that they must go home at once for the snow was coming, they desisted from the fun, and let their victim escape. They scattered away in groups, leaving Berry and Johnny standing alone, for they were the only boys whose way lay over the moor, and the sound of the young voices soon died away.

In spite of the hour — four in the afternoon — an oppressive darkness had fallen over the land; too early for night, some sort of unwholesome fellow to the dark seemed spreading wings like a great bird over the sky. Johnny said it was cold, and proudly wrapped himself in his grand, red muffler; and Berry trudged along beside him anxiously. The snow was falling thickly now, and the moor looked very gloomy.

'Div ye think we'll be hame afore it's dark, Berry?' said the little boy at length.

'Aye,' said Berry. 'It's no far.'

They went as quickly as they could, but the snow came ever quicker. At first it blew slowly from the east, so that only one side of their coats got white; then it became finer in quality, and fell faster and faster, until it danced about them in a blinding, white spray.

'I'm feared — it's that dark,' said Johnny. They could now see hardly a foot before them. 'Are we near hame noo, Berry?' he asked again. He was beginning to be very tired; they seemed to have gone such a long way.

Berry suddenly stumbled on something, and looked up at him. 'Hoo's there a wa' here?' he asked.

Johnny took his arm, and pulled him round. 'Ye've gone the wrang road,' he cried. 'Yon's no' the way we came.' The little boy was the quicker of the two,

'Oo aye, so we hae,' said Berry, obeying the push, and turning round to gaze into the white obscurity.

They plunged forward again, and went on steadily for some time, though now the snow was so deep, and the wind blew it in such stifling clouds against their faces, that their progress became very slow.

'I'm wantin' hame; I'm feared, Berry.' Johnny had begun to cry.

'Whisht, whisht,' said Berry, putting his arm round him. 'It's hame, hame we're gaen.' He led the little boy stumblingly forwards.

Johnny began to choke with the bitter, white dust that filled his eyes and mouth. He could hear Berry mutter to himself the same words, 'It's hame, hame.' Then they both sank deep into a bog-hole. Berry was out first, and dragged Johnny after him, now shivering and crying. Before them the snow was drifted so deep that they could scarcely move. 'It's hame,' Berry began to mumble. Then the little boy pulled at his arm, calling into his ear: *It's no hame — it's the wrang road; an' ye're a fule — ye're no' wise.* I'm wantin' hame; I'm wantin' ma mither.' And he sank down into the snow by Berry's side, sobbing and choking and hid his face in Berry's sleeve.

'Ye're a fule — ye're no' wise' — the words penetrated slowly into Berry's mind.

He staggered again to his feet, and pulled Johnny along with him a few yards further, but it was of no use. He could not carry the little boy, and he was too exhausted to go any further without help. The snow was numbing and blinding Berry; but all his mind had now centred on the one idea – to take care of Johnny, and not again incur his step-mother's anger by leaving him behind. He struggled out of his coat and wrapped it round Johnny. The sting of redoubled cold on his own back and arms roused him for a moment.

'Ye manna cry, laddie,' he said, wrapping him as closely as he could. They had sunk down together against a large stone; it seemed to give some protection from the storm.

'A'm cold — cold — cold,' sobbed Johnny; then raising his head he said: 'Shout, Berry, shout, they'll maybe hear.'

Clouds and clouds of snow swept across the moor. Gazing out before them, they could see nothing but a vortex of whirling, white confusion. Overhead the black, tempestuous sky showed every here and there, when, for a moment, the snow-clouds were driven apart by the wind.

Berry sat up and shouted as loudly as he could; Johnny joined in with a shrill cry. The wind took the feeble voices, and carried them away into the wild, white cloud.

'Shout again, Berry,' said the little boy, and Berry shouted loudly. No one answered, only a sheep bleated a faint reply.

'I'm near dead,' said Johnny: 'ye've ta'en the wrong road.' He could scarcely speak for cold. Berry silently fumbled away at his shabby, little vest; he took it off and rolled it round Johnny's legs. Then a great blast of wind came roaring over the moor, and swept the snow higher and higher, till it broke over them in a suffocating, powdery wave.

'*Whisht, whisht, are ye no warm noo?*' said Berry.

***

About noon on the following day, the men who had gone out to seek for the boys came to a standstill as the dogs began to scrape and search for something in the deepest drift.

The storm had long since abated, and the winter sun shone in an unclouded sky, pouring its light over the immaculate slopes of snow which the violence of the storm had piled like billows above the gentle undulations of the moor. Across such a pavement, so white and glistering, some heavenly vision might have floated from the blue.

The men raised their hands involuntarily to shield their eyes from the blinding radiance as they looked. There was breathless silence for a few moments whilst the dogs hurried to and fro, scraping, with short gasps, every here and there. 'She's on the scent noo,' cried one man, and the collie began to yelp and shiver with excitement. There was a deep drift piled up against a great stone, and they began to shovel the snow away — worked hard for a moment or two, and then stopped suddenly, and stood around in silence.

'Lord! Lord!' said the father, dropping on his knees.

The two boys lay huddled up beside the stone, Johnny under a heap of soaked clothing that was rolled and piled above him. He stirred slightly, and drew a deep breath as they uncovered his face. But beside him lay the idiot boy, dead and naked — one rigid hand still holding the clothes that he had heaped over Johnny.

There was not a rag of clothing left to cover the poor, misshapen body, and the men who stood around looked for a moment at the unsightly limbs that death had not been kind to; then with one accord, as if ashamed, each man turned his face away.

But as their eyes fell again upon the bewildering whiteness of the snow-covered plain, they had perhaps some vision also of that awful, unalterable Love, whose face we may not see.

JANE HELEN FINDLATER

The Pictures

The shores of Olnig on a summer night were like the shores of Heaven as weary mortals think of these: the long white beaches were just kissed by the scarcely moving tide, and on the horizon floated dim purple outlines that might have been the Isles of the Blessed.

There was no stirring of the atmosphere on such a windless night as this, but sometimes a great freshness would breathe in gently from the ocean and as suddenly die away — it carried with it the scent of leagues of sea. Then the sun would go down in a spectacular manner, lighting up the sky to a blazing scarlet behind the purple islands, . . . it was all unbelievably exquisite. Yet "wee Katie" (as she was always called) when released from her toil in the byre would stand and gaze out at this wonder of beauty without a single exclamation of surprise or pleasure.

Katie was one of the humblest creatures God ever made; she seemed scarcely to have a life of her own at all, just to have appeared on this planet to work for other people, toiling on, day after day, at her obscure tasks, without joy and almost without remuneration. She was thirteen on the day that she first arrived at the Farm, fresh from the tender mercies of an unloved aunt who had brought her up somehow on a pittance wrung from a very reluctant father. Such pittances are always joyfully discontinued at the earliest opportunity permitted by the law, so when Katie became a financial burden she had to go out to work at once. Her figure was stumpy and ill-proportioned, and she had a lamentable habit of never managing to hook her frock rightly, which did not add to her charms. Though Katie's hair was supposed to be "up", it was much more often half "down" her back in a tumbled, untidy plait, and wisps of it fell across her eyes and had to be brushed or tossed back when she looked up to speak to anyone: a doleful figure wee Katie as ever stepped. Her day was no sinecure: cows are milked three times a day on well-regulated farms, and Katie had the milking of five to attend to. Between times, there were pails to wash and churns to scald, and shelves to scrub, and basins to cleanse — an endless, fatiguing, unchanging round of work. And here was all the child's diversion when the long day was done — to wander down to the white shore, and look out to sea: a poor amusement Katie found it. What to her were the long white beaches, the lisping waves, or even the scarlet banners of sunset? The heart of man is unsearchable, and one never gets to the end of the surprises that are to be found in character; to look at Katie one would have thought her almost too dull to have any aspirations or longings — but this was far from being the case; in her heart there burned a wild thirst for amusement. How this had been stifled all the long, long winter months at Olnig, Heaven alone could tell! If little Johnnie Ross, the farmer's son, extracted a few screeching notes from his concertina, Katie would execute a clumsy caper on the stone floor of the dairy, and down her hair would tumble about her ears, and Mrs Ross would reprove her sharply, telling her to "mind her work and niver heed Johnnie and the concertina". Then sometimes Ran Reid, the lately demobilised tinker, would appear with his pipes at the door of the Farm. And at the first sound of the thin, gay, skirling notes, Katie flung down whatever she was doing and rushed to the door to listen.

Ran was quite a personage in the countryside since his return from Mesopotamia; he still by virtue of his late adventures, wore a ragged khaki coat, and it was only the outward sign of the profound inward awakening that the man had gone through.

Ran had seen the world, and though he preferred like the sow that was washed to return to wallowing in the mire, he wallowed, so to speak, with his eyes open. As he stalked alongside of his donkey-cart, his pipes under his arm, Ran had quite the air of a man of the world. Ross, the farmer, often came to the door to speak to him on a winter afternoon when there was little doing out of doors, and Katie would always manage to edge herself behind the door to listen, for his sanguinary tales of Mesopotamia delighted her fancy, and she pondered them as she went about her work in the byre.

Olnig in winter was indeed no foretaste of Heaven. Katie was often so buffeted by the gale that she almost failed to make her way between the house and the byre. Wrapped in an old oilskin coat, her hands blue with cold, she had to face the flying sleet that drove in pitilessly from the Atlantic. There were no purple islands and lisping waves then, only a hoarse, roaring waste of billows, desolate and terrible beyond description. Katie's one preoccupation was to get under cover as quickly as might be; but she had always a moment of acute struggle with the bolt of the byre door which refused to open at once to the touch of her benumbed fingers; then, dripping, blown about, exasperated by this fight with the elements, she gained the shelter of the byre. There at least the cows were warm, and Katie would lean against their hot, rough sides with a sigh of relief as their kindly breath thawed her frozen cheek. . . .

Then the snowstorms came, smothering and white, with sometimes, to follow, an awful frost that seemed as if it would nip life at its very sources. Grand pictures were to be seen in these winter storms by anyone with seeing eyes: but Katie's eyes were holden. On nights of intense frost, the great indigo vault of the sky, strewn with myriads of stars, was a sight to awe and terrify the beholder, making him turn back, with longings for the homely earth, from these pathless wastes of space. But no distressing thoughts of the terrors of space or the insignificance of man's place in it visited Katie's brain when she looked out of the skylight window of her freezing little attic bedroom. Her shudders, poor child, were of a much less subtle kind as she drew the heavy homespun blankets round her, and wondered if she would ever feel warm again. But snowstorms did not last for ever, even at Olnig, and the long despairing Highland spring began, with ceaseless rain and tireless wind, soaking and battering the farm for weeks on end, till it seemed as if summer must be only a fable that could never come true; yet there were signs of life — calves in the byre, and lambs — shivering little lambs — on the hillside, and frogs arriving in the pools of the old peat cuttings. Katie was constantly in the byre feeding the calves now, with her head tied up in a little tartan shawl, and her person wrapped in every additional garment she possessed.

She was young enough to find it rather fun, and would sometimes laugh outright at the gambols the creatures gave as they ran towards her, to guzzle up the milk from the pail. It was at this spring season that her feud with Flora Reid, the eldest of Ran Reid's six olive-branches, first began. Flora was what the expressive phrase "a limb" indicates. With her mop of fiery red hair, and her slanting blue eyes she was an incarnation of lawlessness and mischief.

The most importunate beggar of all the begging tinker clan, Flora had, as it were, acquired fresh powers in her trade during the troubled years of the war. For though she, her three brothers, her sister and her mother lived in affluence they had never dreamt of before, they would have been the last to acknowledge this fact. Instead of doing so, Flora added a new, long and very effective clause to her usual begging whine:

"Will ye no' gie me a puckle tea, Mistress? for faither's awa' fechtin' the Germans, an' mither's four weans, an' mysel', an' maybe faither'll no' come hame . . . could ye no' gie's an auld coat or a bit shawl for it's gey cauld the day? . . . faither's awa' fechtin' the Germans an' mither's a' her lane an' maybe faither 'll no' come back . . . have ye ony auld castin' wad keep the baby frae the cauld the nicht? he's no verra weel, an' noo that faither's awa' fechtin' the Germans . . . etc., etc. . . ."

So her endless tale of requests had gone on during the two war winters when Ran was away; but now that her father was safely home again, Flora had to change her tune. The sympathies of the country-side had been almost drained, so she invented what she called Mesoptamy Fever to revive sympathy afresh:

"Will ye gie's a puckle tea, if *you* please faither's back from fechtin' the Germans and he's bad wi' Mesoptamy fever . . . if ye'd an auld blanket by ye, mistress, could ye no' gie it for faither? He's come back wi' Mesoptamy fever on him, ye ken, aye, it gaes an' comes awful" (this to account for Ran's appearance of rude health); "while's he'll be near deid wi't. . . . Gie's a drop broth, if *you* please, Mistress. . . ."

Mrs Ross was much too liberal to the tinkers, and Flora never asked in vain; but one spring evening it happened that Mrs Ross had gone with her husband in the cart to Achinbeg, leaving Katie in sole charge of the house. Katie was very busy and *affairée*, with everything to do. She had swept out the kitchen, put fresh peats on the fire, and laid the table for tea to be ready for Mrs Ross on her return. Then in marched Flora, just about her own age and incredibly importunate. First, she wanted tea, of course; Katie refused; then a scone from the pile on the table; a second refusal; then a "drop milk"; refusal number three; then an old skirt — but at this Katie became impatient and told her to go away in no bated language.

"Awa' wi' ye, or I'll send Rover at ye!" she threatened, pointing to the collie on the hearth.

"I'll no' gang — the Mistress aye gie's me a puckle tea."

"Gang aff, ye're a fair torment!" cried the exasperated Katie, brandishing a broom, and advancing across the kitchen at Flora. Rover jumped up with a growl to join in the fray, and at sight of his bared white teeth, Flora ran out through the open door without further delay. But from that hour, war was declared between the two children — a war in which the stupid Katie was always the loser.

One of Flora's tricks was to make her way into the dairy and torment Katie to fili her "tinny" with milk. When Katie refused to do this, the little beggar ran off to the farmhouse and wheedled Mrs Ross into saying that she might get what she wanted; then Katie had the humiliation of having to fill the "tinny", and Flora carried it away in triumph. It was extraordinary in how many ways she managed to annoy Katie — she seemed to be endowed with an uncanny knowledge of how to do it. Mrs Ross might leave her whole family-washing on the hillside to bleach, and none of it would be touched; but if Katie left any of her poor little garments out at night, some of them would be sure to have disappeared before morning. Katie used to sit on an old log of wood near the door in her few spare moments, knitting herself a pair of black worsted stockings; if Mrs Ross called to her from the kitchen, she would lay down her knitting on the log, and perhaps not return for ten minutes or so. Twice, however, she had returned to find her needles pulled out and half the stocking pulled down.

Katie began to think her work was bewitched, for it was impossible to see how the needles could have come out by themselves. Mrs Ross said it must have been the kitten: Katie did not believe her. . .

One day all the milk pans had been scoured and put out in the sun to dry. An hour afterwards, they were found face downwards in the mud, and had all to be scoured over again. . . . Another day the dairy floor, newly scrubbed out, was covered with filth — the hens had been driven in from the yard across it, while Katie was having her dinner. . . . Yet this guerilla warfare was carried out with such cleverness that it would have been impossible to lay the blame on Flora — no one had seen her anywhere near the farm; but Katie knew that her little enemy was the cause of every trouble.

Remote as Olnig Farm was, some modern ideas had penetrated to it; so Katie suddenly demanded an "afternoon out", with as great determination as any town young woman; she had read about "afternoons out" in the *Weekly Scotsman*, and decided to have one. Her demand was granted, and then question was, what to do with these long vacant afternoons?

It was all very well for Katie to put on her Sunday gown, and even to cram her empurpled hands into a pair of cotton gloves; but when this was done, the poor child had nothing more amusing to do than to walk in solitary (albeit gloved) splendour, along the wind-swept moor road to Achinbeg. If she persisted in her determination to reach the village, the four long miles had to be walked all over again on the way home. And the village — what did it afford in the way of amusement? There was little to see there. The Hotel, closed for nine months of the year; the Post Office, presided over by old Mrs McIvor; the Shop where it was possible to buy sandy chocolate and liquorice lozenges — this was all the village had to offer as entertainment for Katie's young mind, unless you include the Station, where two or three trains came crawling in almost at a foot pace!

Still Katie persisted in her weekly pilgrimage to Achinbeg. It is difficult for those who have always lived in towns to understand the craving for variety that young people in the country feel so deeply. But the fact is, that what the human being wants to make him or herself happy is often the opposite of what he or she already has. The country-dweller hungers for stir and amusement; the town-dweller for quiet and repose; it is hard to say which craving is the stronger. Poor "wee Katie" trailing along the desolate hill road to Achinbeg in search of amusement, had a sick longing for variety that was pitiful to behold. Oh, for something — *anything* to happen! But week followed week, and month followed month, yet no excitement came poor Katie's way. And here she was on this beautiful midsummer evening, as dull as ever.

Her starved fancy projected itself into the week ahead, striving to see any hope of change in the monotonous round of her days. No: she could see no possible source from which help could come.

Tomorrow morning she knew she would have to rise at six, as she had done every day that summer, to light the kitchen fire, and sweep the floor, and put on the big black kettle to boil. Then the cows had to be milked, and the pails and pans had to be scalded, and there was the dairy floor to scrub, and the churn to work, and then the cows to be milked again, and more pails to scald, and so on, and so on. . . .

Katie shook her head, and repeated aloud to herself in a dismal little rhyme, *"Aye, aye, there's aye the kye"* — the cows seemed to fill the whole foreground of her life, there was no getting away from them, and the milk pails, and the churn, and the butter. . . .

"I wonder, will James the herring-man be here the nicht?" she thought. James was one of the few links that connected Olnig Farm with the outer world — didn't he drive all the way from Mallaig, and sometimes had a paper on him that he would leave with Ross? Not that Katie took any interest in the larger happenings of the world; but sometimes there was a thrilling murder case reported in the paper, and she liked to read it by daylight, though after dark the memory of its thrills had an unpleasant way of coming back into her mind.

Tonight she longed for some such unpleasant excitement. "Yon one aboot the corp found in the cellar was awfae interestin'," she meditated. . . . Beside her at that moment the sheep were nibbling the short green sward that grew close to the shore, all embroidered with thyme; and the tide was coming in, running up the long white shore with a gentle sound like millions of kisses — and Katie sat deaf and blind to it all, longing for a rag of a newspaper that might tell her more about a corpse found in a cellar.

Then, as if in answer to her longing, Katie saw the herring-cart come in sight round the curve of the bay. Maggie, the starved old black pony that drew the cart, always quickened her slow pace as the Farm came in sight, because she was allowed to graze for a few minutes on the turf beside the door, while her master sold his herrings to Mrs Ross.

"Ech! I wonder will James hae a paper wi' him the nicht?" Katie said to herself, making all haste across the shore towards the farm.

Mrs Ross had come out to the door with a dish, and stood waiting while James piled the herrings on to it.

"There ye are, mistress, there's the dissen for ye, bonnie fish, an' real cheap," he said, and then, turning to Katie, he added:

"Here's for ye, m' lassie — ye'll no' verra offen get the chance o' the likes o' this." He took from his pocket a bright pink bill, printed in startling black type, and handed it to Katie as he spoke. Her heart almost stood still for a moment as she read the announcement:

FOR ONE NIGHT ONLY

EAST LYNNE: (The World's most famous novel, filmed for
the first time by Ford's Cinema at Achinbeg).
Tickets 2s., 1s., 6d., and standing room 1d.

Katie read on, scarcely taking time in the fulness of delight that it might mean to her if she could really see a Cinema at last! Often she had read of this delight, but she had never hoped to enjoy it. She looked up into Mrs Ross's face, and there was a world of pleading in her voice as she asked humbly:

"Will I get tae gang, mistress? I'd like *awfae* tae gang."

"What aboot the kye, lassie?" Mrs Ross replied; but there was a smile lurking round her mouth as she spoke. Katie fingered the pink bill and looked down, making no answer; the cows were a solid obstacle not to be lightly put aside, she knew. There were ten of them, and five of these were her charge. Mrs Ross could never milk the whole ten. As she stood there in silence a blind fury of indignation surged up in Katie's heart. Could it be possible that the cows were going to deprive her of this wonderful treat? She was far too unsophisticated to question the justice of the universe; but this choking feeling of resentment overcame her, she had not a word to say, could not even plead her cause, could not raise her eyes from the ground, in case she should read final refusal in the face of her mistress. She stood there trembling, awaiting her fate.

Mrs Ross and the herring-man exchanged a wink of great amusement, then Mrs Ross spoke again:

"I might maybe get auld Annie from the Croft to help wi' the kye," she said, thoughtfully. "Johnnie'll be wantin' tae get tae see it, Katie, an' he's sic a laddie for playin' himsel' on the road, ye'd need tae look after him." Katie drew a long, slow breath of delight, and looked up. Mrs Ross and the herring-man were both laughing, and he added to her bliss by suggesting that Johnnie and she might drive the four miles to Achinbeg in the herring-cart if they chose. Here was a delightful suggestion, indeed! Katie had never driven to an entertainment in her life, and the prospect of this herring-scented drive filled her with ecstasy — she could wear her new blue merino, and her white cotton gloves, even if the night was wet!

"Ye see, I'm aye on the road on Fridays," James reminded them. "An' the cairt can hold the twa o' them fine."

What would many *blasé* persons give to have wee Katie's keen appetite for enjoyment? All the that week that followed was to her a blissful dream of anticipation. She looked forward to every moment of the evening's programme, from the one when she would mount the cart in her blue merino, to that of her return at night. It seemed to her that she would be a new creature then — she would have seen a Cinema at last. Though Katie appeared to be plodding in and out of the byre on her broken shoes just as usual, she really trod on air all that week. She began to count the days off one by one — six, five, four, three, two — at last she was able to say "tomorrow" would be the great day, and tomorrow would soon be here. She stood by the door that evening, and looked up into the clear amber-coloured sky. Ross was winding up his fishing reel beside her, and examining his fly-book. Katie, who was rather in awe of her master, never addressed him in general; but tonight anxiety conquered her shyness.

"Will it be fine the morn?" she asked timidly. Ross wound away at his reel with a practised hand, and looked up into the sky for a moment.

"Aye, that it will — a grand day," he pronounced, little guessing the delight his words gave.

Katie went to bed even earlier than usual that night. She wished to prepare for the great evening by a wonderful effort of the toilet. She had seen one of the maids at the Lodge crimp her hair by means of plaiting it into a great many tiny plaits and damping them. Katie resolved to follow her example. With extraordinary patience she damped and plaited till her head was a mass of hard little knobs all over. Pride often feels a great deal of pain, in spite of the proverb which tells the opposite, and certainly Katie felt a good deal that night. She could not rest her head for any time on the pillow, without feeling one of the knobby plaitits drive into her skull, till she writhed with discomfort. Far be it from her, however, to undo the plaits — they must remain as they were at whatever cost to personal ease. So Katie tossed to and fro until the breaking of the day. She heard the lisping tide run up the sands, the cries of the sea birds, the bleating of the lambs and the answer of the sheep; she even got up and looked out of the little window, across the blue Skye hills rising through the morning mists — but she saw them with unseeing eyes — she was thinking of nothing but the Cinema. At last, tired out with her vigil of vanity, Katie fell sound asleep. She wakened, startled, to find Mrs Ross speaking loudly in her ear:

"Rise, Katie! Rise, an' come doon the stair as quick 's ye can — the bairn's got convulsions, an' the Master's awa' tae Achinbeg for the doctor!"

The poor woman was so distraught with anxiety that she never noticed Katie's most comical appearance, with the armour of plaits all over her head. She ran downstairs again to attend to the child, and Katie still half dazed with sleep, jumped out of bed, rubbing her eyes as she struggled into her clothes.

Everything was in disorder downstairs — the fireside still choked with the ashes of last night's fire, the cupboard doors standing open after a frantic search for medicines had been made there. Katie could see into the bedroom beyond, where Mrs Ross stooped over the cradle of the sick child.

"Pit on the fire, lassie," she called through to Katie, who was standing in the middle of the kitchen, bewildered by this sudden summons. "Pit on the fire, an' boil the kettle, tak' the bellows tae it, an' a' the dry sticks ye can find, an' dinna stand glowerin' there."

Katie knelt down and scrabbled out the cinders on to the hearth with her hands; she was an untidy, badly trained worker, and this method of going to work sent clouds of dust and wood ashes out into the room. Then she seized the big black kettle and ran out to fill it at the spout by the door. When full, it was far too heavy for her to lift easily, and she had to heave it on to the hook above the fire by a tremendous effort of all her strength. This done, she went into the bedroom to look at the baby with great curiosity. She had never seen a child in convulsions, and all was fish that came to Katie's net.

"Ech! he's twitchin' awfae!" she cried, almost enjoying the excitement if the truth be told. But she was not allowed to sate her curiosity for long. As Mrs Ross bent over the cradle, she issued a long string of commands to Katie which might have dismayed even a practised worker:

"Get on the parritch for the men's breakfast, an' pit oot the plates an' the bannocks on the table, an' get a bit butter from the dairy, an' rin oot bye an' bring in the wee tub that's under the spout — I'm wantin' it for a bath for the bairn — an' bring ben the kettle when it's come through the boil, an' when yer through wi' a' that, gang up tae the Croft an' ask auld Annie will she come doon an' help us wi' the kye, for I canna leave the bairn a meenit."

At this last command, Katie stood stock still in the midst of all her work, for a dreadful fear had flashed across her mind; what if the bairn wasn't better by the evening? Old Annie couldn't milk all the ten cows, and there was no other woman anywhere near who could be got to help her. Could Fortune be going to play this cruel trick upon her? But Katie might have been a student of New Thought to judge by the swiftness and vigour with which she "repelled" this unwelcome suggestion; she refused to admit it for a moment, and, as it were, banged the door in its face. Then that protective instinct which comes to the help of all of us in times of anxiety, taught Katie that work was the best antidote she could find. She went plunging about the disordered kitchen, attacking one task after another, never giving herself time to think quietly in case this dreadful fear should steal into her mind again. To and fro she went, opening and shutting drawers, banging down plates and cups upon the table in a sort of maze of misery. Then the sound of the cows lowing in the byre, sent her running up to the Croft to fetch old Annie and begin the milking.

As she gained the crest of the hill, Katie paused to take breath. Stretched far below her was the sea, blue and sparkling, and across the strait, clear against the cloudless heaven, the astonishing outline of the hills of Skye . . . it did not astonish Katie in the least; she was so entirely preoccupied with the thought of how she could get to the Pictures, that she might have been blind, for any effect the beauties of the outer world had upon her.

She panted on up the steep little path that led to the Croft, the only cottage within miles of the farm.

Old Annie came to the door in response to Katie's knock, and eyed the child sourly. She was a most unpleasing old woman to look at, as she stood in the doorway, her hands rolled in her apron, her deep set, hard old eyes peering out from a little wrinkled face as brown as leather.

"Weel?" she asked laconically.

"Mistress Ross says," panted Katie, "will ye kindly come doon an' gie a hand wi' the kye, for the bairn's taen the convulsions an' she daurna leave him?"

Annie pushed out her under lip in an ugly grimace, and uttered a grunt that sounded like "Oo."

"Will ye come?" Katie asked again.

"She'll be payin' me for't?" Annie queried.

"She didna say," Katie had to confess; but in her eagerness to secure Annie's help she decided to encourage the idea that remuneration would be on an ample scale: "She'll be that grateful, ye ken," she said. Annie had always meant to come, her hesitation had only been assumed for the sake of being disagreeable; so she flung her little "shawlie" over her head and set off down the hill with Katie. Here was Katie's opportunity; she grasped it.

"Hoo mony kye can ye mulk by yersel, Annie?" she asked.

"I've seen the day I could mulk eicht — I wouldna' care tae try mair nor five noo — I'm auld, ye ken, lassie," the old woman said. Katie was dismayed.

"Five! but there's ten o' them!" she cried. "Ech! could ye no' manage them a', Annie?"

The old woman shook her head.

"Na, na, I'm ower auld for that — but ye're a stoot lass yersel' ye can mulk the five o' them fine."

"I'll no' be here the nicht — I'm tae gang tae the Picters," Katie blurted out.

The old woman stood still in the roadway, and gazed at Katie. "In a' the warl what'll that be?" she asked. As "The Movies" had not yet passed across her mental horizon, she might well be bewildered.

Katie burst into a fervent description of what she supposed the Pictures to be like, and the old woman listened with attention to all that she said, then as Katie paused for a moment, she gave her opinion on the whole matter.

"Sic a daft-like thing I niver heard tell o' in a' my days. Bide at hame, lassie, an' dinna gang stravagin' tae the likes o' that."

"Ech! I *canna* bide at hame — I maun get tae see the Picters! Will ye no' mulk a' the kye for me, Annie, an' let me gang?" Katie cried.

But she had come up against a heart as hard as flint. Her cry for help did not move Annie one whit; the deep disapproval of one generation for the amusements of another was expressed in every tone of her voice as she refused to countenance Katie's longings after pleasure.

"The lasses are a' daft for pleesuring noo," she said severely. "It's no' wurk ava, jist pleesuring."

"It's no' muckle pleesuring I get!" Katie cried, "I'm wurkin a' the week through in the byre, exceptin' the aifternoon on Thursdays. I'm up at six in the mornin' an' I'm no' beddit till nine — is that no' wurk?"

But Annie would not admit that it was. Her ideas on work had been formed in the stern times when afternoons out were unknown, and four o'clock in the morning was thought none too early for a young woman to rise from bed and attack an eighteen hours' day of work.

She had just imparted these stern views to Katie when they reached the farm, and there was no more leisure for discussion.

******

The doctor's hard-worked little car — as hard-worked as the doctor — did not pant up to the farm till the afternoon. It was then announced that the baby's gums must be lanced, an exciting operation which, another time, would have interested Katie mightily — today she was too much preoccupied with her own affairs to pay much attention to the sufferings of the baby. Her rather inept hands were indeed full, for as Mrs Ross could not leave the child for a minute, all the work of the house devolved upon Katie.

She was deep in very unscientific preparations for dinner, when, through the open door of the kitchen, her sworn foe Flora Reid effected an entrance. Never had Flora been more importunate; but her begging this morning was for a very definite object, and did not degenerate into the usual whine for "a puckle tea" that was generally on her lips.

"Gie's twa bawbees, mistress, if *you* please," she whined, calling through to Mrs Ross, whom she had unhappily caught sight of for a moment. Then, as Mrs Ross paid no attention to her plea, Flora went into detail about why she required the two bawbees. Ran, it appeared, had had a worse than usual attack of Mesoptamy fever last night, and hadn't the doctor in the Army told him that sulphur was the only cure; and wasn't Flora herself on the way to Achinbeg to buy the sulphur? "Jist twa bawbees, if *you* please," she chanted again and again, till Mrs Ross, exasperated and over-easily persuaded, called to Katie to find the sum that was required. Katie sought in an old jug where pennies were kept, and produced two battered halfpennies because she thought these insignificant coins were less gratifying to Flora than the one more important one would be.

"There's for ye — there's yer twa bawbees, awa' wi' ye, I'm ower thrang the day to have ye standin' there," she told her. And Flora, grinning with the pride of success in her trade, grabbed the bawbees into her little skinny yellow hands (which were tanned to the colour of finnan haddocks by the smoke of the camp fires) and skipped out of the kitchen. Relieved of Flora's presence, Katie went on with her cooking. It is to be hoped that Ross the farmer was no epicure, for Katie's preparation of the meal left much to be desired. If you had looked into the farm kitchen that morning, you would only have seen a very untidy, plain-looking girl hard at work, and you would never have guessed at the turmoil of feeling that was raging in her heart as she gashed away at the potatoes and tore the heads of the herrings with hasty, unskilled fingers. So separated are our souls from each other, that it never occurred to Mrs Ross that Katie was unhappy — her own anxiety had swallowed up any sympathy she might have had with the poor child at another time. As Mrs Ross knelt beside the cradle or paced up and down with the baby in her arms, she would call out directions to Katie of one sort or another; but she had completely forgotten all about the Cinema.

Long afterwards this August day would be remembered by the
mother as the one on which her child had nearly died, while to Katie
it would always just be "The Picture Day", when she had suffered
such unbearable suspense.

For, as the hours dragged past, her suspense grew more and more
acute. She longed to end it, by asking Mrs Ross plainly whether she
might go to the Pictures in the evening or not; but whenever she tried
to ask the question, she found it impossible to speak. The jangling old
kitchen clock struck five, then it struck half-past five, and Katie knew
that her fate must be sealed speedily: the pictures began at half-past
six, and how were the cows to be milked, she asked herself, in time
to allow her to dress and drive the four long miles to Achinbeg?

At this moment little Johnnie Ross ran noiselessly in on his bare
feet, and came up to where Katie stood washing the teacups in a basin
of greasy water.

"Are ye no' gettin' ready, Katie?" he whispered, glancing through
the half-open door that led into the bedroom, with a child's dim
perception of something he didn't understand going on there.

"Weesht!" Katie warned him, "I'm no' through wi' the tea things
yet."

"James is comin' along in the cairt, d'ye no' mind he's tae tak' us?"
the boy whispered.

"I mind fine — but I'm no' ready yet. Ye maun pit on yer buits,
Johnnie, an' yer Sunday claes, a' the folk in Achinbeg 'll be at
the Picters the nicht." Katie admonished him. She was yearning to
begin her own toilet, especially to see the effect when these most
uncomfortable plaits should at last be undone and her hair might
be combed out. It struck her that Johnnie's Sunday clothes would
introduce the subject of the Pictures as well as anything. With this
design in her mind she went across to the bedroom door.

Mrs Ross, with that almost awful maternal patience that seems as
if it could never tire, was still pacing up and down, up and down, as
she had paced the livelong afternoon, and at each step she gave a
tender little touch, as regular as the beating of her own heart, to the
baby's suffering body — it seemed to keep him quiet. . . .

Katie advanced into the doorway.

"Johnnie's seekin' his Sunday claes an' his buits, please," she said.
"It's the Picters the nicht, ye mind . . ." she added. Her words died
away into silence and she stood there dumb, awaiting her fate.

"The Picters — eh, I didna' mind — weel, get oot the laddie's claes

for him, Katie, I canna lay doon the bairn for a meenit — ye'll find
them in the drawer there." Mrs Ross spoke abstractedly, and without
pausing for a moment in her slow pacing up and down the room.

Katie opened the drawer, gathered up the suit in her arms, and
walked to the door; there she faced round and got the fatal question
out at last.

"Will I get tae go, mistress?"

Mrs Ross stood still and looked at her. She took in, perhaps,
something of the yearning there was in Katie's face, but at that
moment the baby sent up a thin trembling cry, and gave a horrible
jerk in her arms.

"Ech! puir wee mannie!" she said, all her attention turned to the
baby and away from Katie.

"Ye see I canna stand still a meenit," she said, then a moment later
she added:

"Ye canna get tae the picters the nicht, lassie, there's the kye tae
mulk an' a' thing tae sort forbye — ye'll maybe get anither time."

"*There's no' anither time!*" poor Katie blurted out; but Mrs Ross
scarcely heeded the anguish there was in the cry. To her, fighting
for the life of her child, this petty disappointment of Katie's seemed
beneath contempt. She resumed her pacing again, and only repeated,
as she passed Katie:

"Ye canna go, lassie, there's ower muckle tae dae."

Blind and choking with disappointment, Katie turned away
without another word. As if to make things worse, she saw James the
herring-man draw up in his cart at the door, and heard his hearty voice
call out to know if they were ready? She went to tell him the bad news;
but the words stuck in her throat, and she stood there, a grotesque, sad
little figure. Even to the old man's uncritical eye, Katie's appearance
suggested that she was not quite ready to start for the evening's
entertainment. Her whole head was covered with a sort of helmet of
plaits, she wore an old faded frock, and had tied a dirty sack round
her instead of an apron. The shoes she wore were large, and broken
across the uppers, and had seen service in the byre all winter.

Surely, James thought, the lassie wasn't going to Achinbeg like that?
He put the question in a more polite form.

"Ye'll no' be quite ready yet maybe — but there's no great hurry —
I'm glad o' a rest mysel' and Maggie here's glad of a bite," he said,
indicating the old black pony who was already hard at work snatching
her usual mouthfuls with famished haste.

Many children of Katie's age would have begun to cry at such a
crisis of misery as this was to her. But though Katie's voice was tense
with the effort she had to make to keep back her sobs, she did not cry
as she explained to James that she could not come with him. James
was much more concerned about the baby's illness than about Katie's
disappointment; to his elderly mind there was simply no comparison
at all between the two distresses, and he stood there exclaiming, "Ech!
I'm real sorry aboot the bairn, jist real sorry," and never bestowed a
thought upon poor wee Katie's grief.

Then Johnnie, hastily stuffed into his Sunday clothes and a pair of
loudly creaking boots, rushed out of the house and jumped into the
cart, his little sunburnt face shining with soap and anticipation —
never a thought did he give either to Katie's desolation. James got
more slowly to his place in the cart and tugged up Maggie's reluctant
head from the grass: a moment later and off they all went along the
sunny road to Achinbeg.

Katie stood in the doorway and watched until the cart disappeared
round the bend of the road. She felt as if her heart would burst with
pent-up tears.

But there was no escape yet from the inexorable wheel of Duty
— her grief could not be indulged in at present. For the cows came
streeling down from the field in a long, slow procession on their way
to the byre for the evening milking. Donald, the herd boy, appeared
behind them, flourishing his stick, shouting to Rover, and trying to
urge the cows beyond their usual slow pace. Fatally, Katie suspected
the reason for his haste — he, even he — was going to the Pictures!
He would only have time to "clean himsel'" (as Katie phrased it) and
be off to join the jubilant crowd at Achinbeg.

She had guessed truly. As Donald drove the cows past the door,
he shouted to her in huge excitement:

"I'm awa' tae the Picters, Katie! Are ye no' comin'?"

But he was in too great haste to wait for her reply. Then, the last
cow driven in, Donald went off at a tremendous pace to clean up for
the entertainment, and once more Katie was left alone. Her bitter
cup was not drained to the dregs yet, however. With a rattle over the
stony road, the Reids' donkey cart drew near. Ran stalking beside
it, Flora seated in the cart. Katie felt in no mood to cope with her
enemy at that moment; but no tinker's cart ever was known to pass
the door of a farm without stopping at it, so there was little hope of
escape from Flora. Sure enough, Ran called to the cuddy to halt, in

a stentorian military voice acquired in Mesopotamia, and then, too fine (like all tinker men) to beg himself, he affected to arrange the harness while Flora slipped out of the cart and tried to dart into the kitchen as usual. But Katie barred the way.

"No' the nicht — ye'll no' get onything: the mistress has a bairn ill — awa' wi' ye" she said roughly.

Flora persisted, and even pushed at Katie in her effort to get in through the doorway. The struggle became almost a fight, and Ran stood by and laughed delightedly. Then what did poor Katie hear? Did her ears deceive her, or did Ran address his daughter in these words:

"*Bing Avree* (come away), Flora," he cried, in the ancient lingo of his race, and then, with a sudden descent into modernity, "*We'll no' be in time for the Picters, lassie!*"

It was too much for Katie altogether. "They'll no' let tinklers in," she cried, hot with indignation and none too polite in consequence; but Flora had the best of the situation in a moment.

"I'm a sojer's bairn, an' that's mair than ye'll ever be," she assured poor Katie. "My faither's been awa' fechtin' the Germans, sae I'll get in."

And then she began to caper about, executing a triumphant sort of jig upon the doorstone, both her skinny little hands held high above her head, while she chanted out these words:

"*Standin' room for twa bawbees, Standin' room for twa bawbees!*" and Katie saw that between the finger and thumb of each hand Flora was displaying the ha'pennies she had begged from Mrs Ross in the morning. Truly the wicked flourish like the green bay tree: Katie, who had toiled late and early, must now continue to toil with never a ray of amusement to brighten her days, and Flora, who habitually ate the bread of idleness, was off to the Pictures on the money she had begged on false pretences. Is it any wonder that Katie's fortitude broke down as she watched the up-to-date tinkers rattle off along the road to Achinbeg? She turned away from the house and rushed into the warm darkness of the byre. There, among the cows, she was alone at last; and might weep out her bitter tears.

******

Two hours later, when the cows had been milked, and old Annie had gone home, Katie still sat in the byre and refused to come in to the farm for supper. Her face was swollen with much weeping, and a sob would still, at long intervals, rise in her throat, though she had now dried her tears. Everything was quiet round the house; the hens gone to roost, Rover asleep on the doorstone. Then Katie heard Ross come out, and knew that he was probably looking for her.

"Katie! Are ye there, Katie!" he called. She made no reply. Again he called:

"Come out an' ye'll see something ye'll no' see the likes of twice in a lifetime."

Katie's curiosity was faintly roused.

"What is't?" she called back in a husky voice.

"Come you an' see," Ross persisted.

Reluctantly Katie emerged from the gloom of the byre and came out to where the farmer stood.

He pointed to the horizon. "Look West, Katie — as far's ye can see — d'ye ken that's the Island of Barra ye're seeing there — like a wee boat it's that far away? D'ye see it?"

Katie raised her swollen eyelids and gazed out towards the blazing West. The whole arch of the sky was scarlet, the sea ran in scarlet waves, and the mountains of Skye were purple against the glow. But as far as the eye could venture — so far that it seemed more like a delusion of the senses than a reality — away on the utmost horizon, another island had become visible.

"D'ye see it! Yon's Barra! I've no' seen it for years," the farmer repeated.

But Katie did not see anything to be excited about.

She turned away without a second glance at the land that was very far off.

"I'm no' carin'," was all she said.

VIOLET JACOB

Thievie

The side street of the Angus town was as grey a thing as could be seen on this grey dripping day. The houses, thick-walled, small-windowed, sturdily uniform and old-fashioned, contemplated the soaking cobble-stones and the 'causeys' which ran like rivers on either side; the complacent eyes of their dark panes, made yet darker by the potted geraniums whose smouldering red gave no liveliness to a reeking world, stared out, endlessly aloof, upon the discomfort of the occasional passer-by. Under their breath they seemed to be chorusing unanimously the words of St Paul and saying, "None of these things move me." The dried haddocks, which usually hung on their wooden 'hakes' nailed to the walls, had been brought in, as had the small children whose natural playground was the pavement; chalk-marks made by schoolboys in their various evening games had been obliterated from the flags. Newbiggin Street was a featureless place given over to the sulky elements.

All night it had rained steadily, for with evening the fitful drizzle of the day before had settled down to business. The woman who stood framed in the only open doorway of the street looked up and down, frowning. She was a thickset, bony woman, one of those who, unremarkable in feature, are yet remarkable in presence, and though in daily life she made no bid for attractiveness, it was because she did not happen to know where, or in what, attraction lay. Her eyes were steady, and full, at times, of a purposeful though not alluring light. Her hair was dark and thick, her skin sallow, and her head well carried. She was dressed tidily, in stout, ill-fitting clothes, in strong contrast to which she wore a cheap, new hat with a crude blue flower; this was a recognition of the occasion, for she had walked yesterday from her home, five miles away, with her bundle in her hand, to see an aunt whose voice could now be heard in conversation behind her. She was not paying the smallest attention to the old woman's talk; her return journey was before her and the prospect did not please her.

A lad came up the street with his hands in his pockets and his head ducked into his collar under the downpour.

"Bad weather," she observed, as he passed the doorstep.

"Bad weather!" he exclaimed, with a half-contemptuous laugh; "wumman, hae ye seen the river?"

Her face changed. She stood hesitating, staring; then, without a word to the unseen aunt within, she gathered up her bundle and stepped out.

Soon she was in the movement of the main street which declined in a steep hill to the lower levels; there were many others making in the same direction and as she went along she could hear, above the noise of wheels and footsteps, a steady roaring. Not a breath of wind was stirring to make the sound fluctuate, and the even relentlessness of it awed her a little. She crossed the way that lay at right angles to the bottom of the street and stood looking down over the iron-railed wall which held up the road at the riverside. The grey, moving mass that slipped by was almost up to the railings.

Beyond her and all along the row of houses, the people were gathered to watch the rising water. The doors of the one-storied dwellings were choked with furniture that was being lugged out and carried away. Chairs, tubs, tables, birds in cages appeared and disappeared up the hill; women screamed angrily to venturesome children whose curiosity had lured them from the maternal skirts, frightened infants cried, men pushed about laden with cooking-pots and bedding; boys shouted to each other, running about in the crowd, the thud of their bare feet lost in the changeless, covetous voice that rose from between the banks. A blind man was being led toward the rise of the hill; he too was playing his part, for he carried a 'wag-at-the-wa'' clock with a gaudily painted face clasped in his arms. She paused a few minutes to look up and down the torrent and then struck away from the crowd, making through the outlying streets for her straightest line home.

Janet Robb's life had been much concerned with the elements. The house for which she was making at her steady, uncompromising tramp was a waterside cottage just above the spot where the river wound into a lake-like estuary on its way to the North Sea. Here she was born, here she had lived out her thirty-four years, for her father had been ferryman until the building of a new bridge a short distance up-stream had shovelled his trade into the limbo of outworn necessities. She had kept house in it almost ever since she could remember; for her mother, who had been an invalid, died when her girl was thirteen, and the ferryman, in spite of the prophecies of his neighbours, did not marry again. Women had no attraction for him, and the need of a housekeeper, which, more than any other cause, drives middle-aged working men into matrimony, did not exist while he had a daughter like Janet, so well able and so well accustomed to grapple with domestic needs. She was a hardy woman now, close-fisted and shrewd. She had been an invaluable help, both in the house and out of it; the two had worked the ferry between them, for the river was not wide and the traffic was small. Carts and horses had to go round to a point about a mile westward, and only foot-passengers on their way to the town troubled that part of the shore; when her father was out she could leave her house-work to put them across to the farther bank without much interruption to it.

The ferryman was not an inspiring acquaintance. Though he belonged, in company with publicans, barbers, and blacksmiths, to a trade essentially social in its opportunities, he cared nothing for that part of it. He could put over a boatful of people without addressing a word to any of them and with scarcely an answer to any man enterprising enough to attack his silence. He was not popular, and, as those who give nothing of their mind to the world must perforce submit to have the gaps they create filled up according to the taste of their neighbours, a whole crop of tales sprang up at the water-side like so much duckweed. He was a secret drinker; he was worth ten thousand pounds; he had a woman in the town whom he ill-treated — had she not been seen with her head bandaged, crying ill names after him on the public road? — he starved his daughter; she starved him — all these whisperings surrounded his unconscious head. He was a spare man, smaller in build than Janet, lined and clean-shaven. Besides his recognised business he had a cart and an old horse by means of which he did a little carrying, going townwards three times a week, whilst she took charge of the boat; and though nobody outside the cottage knew anything about it, he received substantial help from a son who had left home early and was making a good income in Canada. While the neighbours went wide of the mark in most of the rumours they set afloat about him, one of these had a fragile foundation of truth. Davie Robb kept no woman and cared as little for drink as he did for company; there was only one thing that he cared about at all, and that lay in a box under his bed. The contents of this box did not amount to ten thousand pounds, but they went into several hundreds. They were his soul, his life. Waking, he thought of them; and sleeping, they were not far from his dreams. When he opened the lid to add to the hoard he counted and re-counted them, running up the figures on paper. It mattered not to him that he knew them by heart; he would roll them about in his brain as a child rolls a sweet about in its mouth.

Not even Janet knew the amount of these savings, though she made many guesses and was, perhaps, near enough the truth. The box was never spoken of between father and daughter. It was the ferryman's god, and in one sense it had the same place in their household as God has in most others: it was never mentioned, even when taken for granted. In another sense, its place was different: for it was continually in the mind of both.

Janet thrust along the road, leaving the country town quickly behind her, urged on by strong necessity. Her father was now permanently disabled, for some years almost crippled by rheumatism. He was an old man, shrunken and very helpless. The cottage was two-storied, and its upper floor was approached by an outside staircase running up at the gable end. There was a stair inside, too, which had been added later because of the occasional spates in the river, to allow the inmates to move to the upper room without opening the door when water surrounded the walls. Old Robb slept upstairs and was able to get down by himself, though he could never manage to get up again without assistance; and yesterday, leaving home, Janet had arranged with a boy who lived up-stream near the new bridge that he should come in the evening to convey the old man to his bedroom. The lad had consented reluctantly, for, to the young, there was something uncanny about 'Auld Thievie.' Scottish people are addicted, perhaps more than any others, to nicknames, and the ferryman's surname, combined with his late extortions as a carrier, had earned him the title by which he was known for some miles round. Nobody liked Thievie.

Not even Janet. It was scarcely affection that was hastening her. Perhaps it was duty, perhaps custom. Something was menaced for which she was responsible. That, with capable people, is generally all that is wanted in the way of a key to wind them up and set them going. The rain had stopped and she put down her dripping umbrella. The blue flower in her unsuitable hat had lost its backbone and flagged, a limp, large thing; there was a fine powdering of wet on her thick eyebrows and the harsh twist of hair at the back of her head. Mist was pouring in from the sea, the wind having sat in the south-east — the west quarter on the east coast — for three days; and though it had dropped like lead with last night's tide, the 'haar' was coming miles inland as though some huge, unseen engine out seaward were puffing its damp breath across the fields. The cultivated slopes of the Sidlaws, a mile on her right, diminishing in height as they neared the estuary, were hidden. The Grampians, ten miles away on her left, were hidden too; that quarter of the horizon where, on ordinary days, they raised their blue and purple wall, being a mere blank. The river whose infancy they cradled had burst from them angrily, like a disobedient child from its parents, and was tearing along, mad with lust of destruction, to the sea.

When she was some way out of the town a figure emerged from the vapour ahead, growing familiar as the two wayfarers approached each other. Her expression lightened a little as she recognised the advancing man. He was smiling too.

"Hey, Janet!" he cried, "I was wond'rin' what-like daft wife was oot on sic a day."

His face was red and moist with the mist.

"I've been at Newbiggin Street. I'm just awa' hame," said she.

He was a connection of the Robb family, so her words conveyed something to him.

"An' foo's auntie?" he inquired.

"Weel eneuch — but I maun awa' back. There's an awfae spate, ye ken."

"Tuts, bide you a minute. I haena seen ye this twa weeks syne."

She made no move to go on. Willie Black had a different place in her mind from anyone else. It was not easy to deflect Janet Robb from her way, but she would do more for this man, a little younger than herself and infinitely her inferior in will, than for any other person. He was the only male living being who approached her from the more easy and lighter standpoint from which such men as she knew approached girls, and their quasi-relationship had brought them into a familiarity which she enjoyed. He was one of those who looked upon women in a general way with a kind of jocose patronage, always implied and often expressed. He meant no harm by this manner; it was natural to him, and he was not nearly so bold a character as his attitude would suggest. Janet was so much unlike the other women he knew that he would have thought it right to assume superiority even had he, in her case, not felt it. She attracted him, not through his heart and certainly not through his senses, but as a curiosity to be explored in a mildly comic spirit. He knew, too, that Thievie was well off; for once, in a moment of confidence, Janet had hinted at her father's savings, and Black felt vaguely, but insistently, that in the fullness of time he would be wise in proposing to her. The day was distant yet, but meanwhile he sought opportunities of considering her and discovering how far she would be endurable as a wife.

Janet fidgeted from one foot to the other. By one half of herself she was urged to continue her way; the other half being impelled to stay by the invitation in his eyes. She did not know for how much this counted, so great was her ignorance of the amenities of men. Black was the only man who had ever come nearer to her life than the baker's cartman from whom she took the bread at her door or the cadger from whom she bought the fish. She had a great longing to be like other women, a factor in the male world. She was too busy to brood over the subject, and had inherited too much of her father's love of money-making to be deeply affected by any other idea. But when she was with Black she was conscious of all she lacked and was lured beyond measure by her perception of his attitude. It suggested that she took rank with the rest of her sex.

"I'll need awa'," she began, "feyther's himsel' i' the hoose. There's an awfae water comin' doon an' he canna win up the stair his ane. I maun hae tae gang on."

"I didna ken ye thocht sic a deal o' Thievie. Yeicht think o' me a bittie," he added, with knowing reproachfulness.

She looked away from him into the blankness of the mist.

"Heuch! — you!" she exclaimed.

"Haud yer tongue!" she cried, actuated purely by a sense of what was fitting.

"Weel, what's the advantage o' him sittin' yonder, an' a' that siller just nae use ava' till him — an' nae use tae ony ither body?"

She made no reply. There is something silencing in hearing another person voice an idea one believes to be one's private property.

"Ye'd be a real fine lass wi' yon at yer back," he continued; "it's a fair shame ye should be dancin' after the like o' yon auld deil when ye micht be daein' sae muckle better."

She withdrew her gaze from the mist and met his eyes.

"What would I be daein' better!" she inquired, rather fiercely.

He gave a sort of crowing laugh.

"What wad ye be daein'? Gie's a kiss, Janet, an' maybe I'll ye."

Before she had time to think he had flung his arm about her and the roughness of his dripping moustache was on her lips.

She thrust him from her with all her very considerable strength. He laughed again.

It was the first time that a man had ever attempted such a thing and her heart almost stopped. She was torn between wrath and a thrilling, overmastering sense of something achieved. She stood panting, her bundle fallen into the mud. Then she snatched it and dashed into the greyness. It took but a moment to swallow up her figure, but he stayed where he was, staring, his coarse shoulders shaking with laughter. She could hear his jesting voice calling after her as she went. When she had gone a little distance she paused, listening to discover whether he was following; but there was no sound of footsteps.

She hurried on though she had ceased to think of her goal. Her thoughts drove her, rushing and tumbling like birds with beating wings, crowding and jostling and crying in her ears. Black's words had let them loose, stirring her as much as his action. Yes, it was quite true. She was tied, as she had been all her life, to her father and his box. She drudged for him, year in, year out, and got nothing by it, while he clung like an old dog in the manger, to the thing he would neither use nor share. She would be a wife worth having for any man with the contents of that box to start housekeeping on! Willie Black would realise that. She remembered her years at the ferry in fair weather and foul, the picking and scraping she had done and suffered in the house, that the hoarding might go on that was no good to anyone. There had never been any love lost between herself and Thievie, and though he was her father she had long known that she hated him. Yes, she hated him. She had no fear of work and had taken it as a normal condition, but it had come between her and all that was worth having; the toil that had been a man's toil, not a woman's, had built a barrier round her to cut her off from a woman's life. All this had lurked, unrecognised, in her mind, but now it had leaped up, aroused by a man's careless, familiar horseplay.

Her breath came quick as she thought of her own meagre stake in the world. She knew herself for some kind of a power, and that was awaking the dormant realisation of her slavery, all the more bitter for its long sleep. She pushed back her hat and the drops came tumbling to her shoulder and from the draggled blue flower, now a flower in name only, a sodden streak of blackened colour. She found herself shaking all over and she longed to sit down, but the milestone, which had often served her for a seat on her walks to and from the town, was a good way on.

The roadside landmarks were growing a little clearer. It was almost noon, and the flash of false brightness which that hour will often bring hovered somewhere in the veiled sky. She heard the ring of a hammer coming muffled from the smithy ahead, and pushed on, thinking to sit a little in some corner behind the ploughs and harrows. She was unnerved by the tumult in her; anger and self-pity were undermining her self-control; she was a self-controlled woman, and the agony of the disorganised feeling was, in consequence, all the worse. It seemed that she had never been aware of the large injustices of life till now. Her difficulties had been small, physical ones and she had known how to scatter them with a high hand; but these new ones pressed round her like a troop of sturdy, truculent beggars, clamouring and menacing. Another woman might have wept but she only suffered.

She reached the smithy door and looked in. The smith was at his anvil, holding a red-hot horseshoe with the tongs. The blowing had ceased and in the dimness of the shed a pair of huge, patient Clydesdales were in process of being shod. A young 'horseman' was standing by, his hands in his pockets, watching the sputter of flaming sparks that rose with each blow andd fell here and there. The hot scent of horses and leather and scorching hoof seemed one with the rich browns and warm shadows that hang about smithy fires. Behind the mysterious limbs of the bellows the elf-like face of the smith's 'prentice-lad peered at Janet, though both the men's interest in the matter in hand made them unaware of the woman who slipped noiselessly in.

She laid her bundle down behind a cart that stood jacked up with a wheel off, amid a medley of implements, and sat down, concealed by the litter, in a cobwebby corner of the long building. The hammering stopped and one of the cart-horses shifted its feet and blew a shattering sigh into the rafters; the horseman gave one of those sudden expostulatory cries that his profesion addresses to its charges, and all was still again. The smith threw down his manner and left the shoe to cool a little.

"They'll be haein' a bad time doon at the hooses yonder," said he, nodding his head backwards in the direction of the low ground.

"Aye, coorse," said the horseman.

"I wad believe that," continued the smith, whose noisy trade gave him less opportunity of hearing his own voice than he liked. "I mind weel eneuch when we got a terrible-like spate — saxteen year syne, come Martinmas. I was doon aboot Pairthshire way then, an' I wasna lang merrit, an' the wife was that ta'en up aboot it. She was frae the toon, ye understan', an' she didna like tae the swine an' the sheep jist rowin' past i' the water. Ah weel, ye see, we'll jist hae tae dae oor best."

"Aye," said the horseman.

"Na," said the horseman.

"An' I doot auld Thievie doon at the ferry'll be swampit. Aye, ye see, ye canna tell when yer time's tae come."

"The auld scabbit craw," said the horseman.

The smith took up his tools, and approaching one of the horses, laid hold of an enormous hind foot and began, strenuously, to pare the hoof. The beast looked round with an all-embracing toleration. The horseman spat.

Janet sat still, trying to quell the storm within her and to think connectedly. There had been no need for the blacksmith's words to bring her father's plight before her. In all likelihood the riverside cottage was already surrounded, and the fact that the few neighbours were well aware that none knew better than she how to handle oars might easily make them slow to bestir themselves on Thievie's behalf. The old ferry-boat, still seaworthy, lay in its shed some way up the bank, ready for the occasional use to which it was put; and no one but the little boy who had been in to help the old man on the preceding night knew that Janet was absent; and the boy was probably at school.

Even now her freedom might be coming to her on the rising spate! She shivered, chilled after her excitement and her transit from hot heart-burning to the cold horror upon which, with the inward eye, she looked. Thievie could not get up the ladder-like stair — not even with the gurgling water behind him — without a helping hand. It was years since he had even been willing to try. Perhaps she had only to stay where she was and to take what gift this day might bring! Her hands were shaking, though she had clasped them tightly on her lap, and she set her teeth, almost fearing that their chattering would betray her to the smith and his taciturn companion. Of what use was that old withing life by the riverside to itself or to any other living thing! It was as dead, already, as the dead money in the box below the bed. But the money would be dead no longer. Willie Black would not think it dead. She would wait where she was; the smith might go to his dinner when the shoeing was done, but the smithy door stood always open and she would sit, unmolested, till such time as she judged. . .

Her thoughts stopped there and she closed her eyes, leaning her head against the wall.

She could not hang about the road in such weather, waiting. She had not the courage to do that, for fear of drawing attention and making her neighbours ask inconvenient questions . . . afterwards. Though she assured herself that no one would guess, or be sufficiently interested to try to guess, what was causing her to loiter, her nerves would not allow her to face so much as an innocent stranger. She wished the lad behind the bellows had not peered at her in that way. Suppose he should tell the smith — but anything was better than the public road! She tried to force herself into composure.

All at once a loud voice sounded at the door. She opened her eyes and recognised a local carrier through her screen of lumber. He took off the sack which enveloped him and shook it till the drops flew.

"No muckle daein' the day," he began. "Dod aye, the water that's oot" Whiles I couldna get forrit."

The smith looked up from the hairy foot gripped between his knees.

"Queer times, queer times," he said. "Weel, we canna change it, ye see."

"How's a' wi' you, Ake?" said the carrier, turning to the horseman.

"Whoa. S-ss-ss!" cried the latter, for the horse, feeling the smith's movement, tried to release its foot.

"I was thinkin' Thievie wad be drooned," continued the carrier, grinning from ear to ear and remembering the days when they had been rivals on the road.

"And is he no?" inquired the horseman, roused to interest at last.

"No him. I'm tae a word wi' some o' they folk by the brig. I saw the river-watcher's boat gaein' oot nae lang aifter itwas licht, an' I cried on him, whaur was he gaein'? Dod, when he tell't me he was awa tae seek Thievie, I was fairt angert. 'Let him be,' I says, 'wad ye cast awa' the Lord's maircies yon way?' But there's the auld thrawn stock safe an' soond, and folk lossin' their guid cocks an' hens. Fie!"

The horseman gave a loud shout of laughter and relapsed immediately into gravity.

"Aye, the ways o' Providence," observed the smith.

"Weel, I maun be movin'," said the carrier. "Thievie'll be on the pairiah yet. There's mair water tae come doon frae the hills afore it's finished. There'll be naething left o' the sma' hoosies on the bank. A'thing 'll just gang traivellin' tae the sea. There was naebody believed it wad be sae bad the morn, airly, when I was doon by the auld ferry, but lord! they tellt me an hour syne that there's no been onything like it this aichty year past. An' the tide's comin' in, ye ken."

He called the last sentence over his shoulder as he turned from the door.

Janet had all but cried out aloud during the carrier's speech. Her father was gone — sitting safe now under some sheltering roof above the reach of the insurgent river!

But it was not thought of this which overwhelmed her. She knew from long experience that there was hardly anything he would not do to prevent anyone, even herself, from seeing his precious box, and she could sear that he would never consent to expose it to a strange human eye while there was the smallest possibility of keeping it hidden. At that hour, soon after daybreak, when the carrier had seen the goat go for him, the torrential rain which was to follow had not yet turned the ordinary spate into something unknown for a half a century. That being so, it was plain to her that, sooner than disclose the box to his rescuer, Thievie would leave it in what had been, at other spate-times, the perfect security of the upper story. So completely was she convinced of this that she would have staked everything she had on it. But she had nothing; and all that she had a prospect of having was surely lying in the rickety upper room waiting for the abnormal torrent to wreck the little house and carry its precious contents to the fathomless recesses of the sea.

She sprang up, the frantic idea banishing all else; and she had dashed boldly out of the smithy under the astonished gaze of the two men before it struck her with measureless relief that she had now nothing to fear from the most suspicious eye. Her father was safe; her secret design thwarted by the river-watcher; the reason for anything she did was of interest to no one. She saw now how futile her fears had been; the outcome of disorganised nerves. Conscience had almost made her believe that she carried her thoughts outside her body like her clothes.

At last, breathless, the perspiration on her face mingled with the wet, she reached the diverging road that led to the river, and as she turned into it the mist began to lift. It grew brighter behind the cloud-wrappings that veiled the world. She stopped, listening for the river's voice. The noonday gleam had strengthened and she came out suddenly from a belt of vapour into comparative clearness and saw the submerged levels lying some little way before her. The broken water above them was all that told her where the banks were, and here and there she could recognise certain tall clumps of alder above the swirl. She redoubled her pace till, at the place in the road from which Thievie's cottage could be seen, she noted with rising hope that the flood had not yet reached the tops of the ground-floor windows. The outside stair was still practicable.

At the water's edge, at the nearest spot to the little house, she stood still. She had hung her bundle and her umbrella on a stout thorn-tree growing on a knoll by the wayside. She would need both hands for what she was going to do. She drew up her skirts and walked into the chilly water.

She felt its steady push against her legs, and her riverside knowledge told her that the tide at the eastuary's mouth had turned and was coming in. It was thrusting the overflow out from the banks on either side and the area of dry fields was diminishing. She looked up apprehensively, for the gleam of brightness had paled in the last few minutes and she dreaded lest the mist should close in again before her task was done.

At last she reached the shed. The oars were afloat inside, kept from sailing away by the pressure of the incoming tide on the flood-water. She waded through the doorway and mounted, hampered by the weight of her soaking boots, on a projecting wooden ledge; then as she clung to an iron hook in the wall, she stretched out her foot and drawing the old craft towards her, stepped in. When she had secured the oars, she loosed the painter from its ring and guided herself out between the narrow walls.

It was easy work rowing, in spite of the slight current against her. The boat was not a heavy one, and only built to carry a few people at a time across fifty yards of water. She rowed as fast as she could, for the damp vapour was drifting in again, and the sun's face, which had looked like a new shilling above her, had now withdrawn itself, leaving a blurred, nebulous spot in its place. Pulling across the shallows on the skirts of the spate, she refused to picture what might happen should she find, on emerging from the cottage with the box, that all landmarks were lost in the mist. Her only guide would then be the sound of that menacing rush from which it would take all the strength of her arms to keep clear.

When the boat's nose bumped against the outside stair she made the painter fast to the railings and stood up, wringing the water from her petticoats. As she clambered out and ascended to the stairhead, small steams trickled down the stone steps from her boots. The door of the upper room was locked inside, but she was not much perturbed by this, having expected it, and moreover she knew the old crazy wood could not stand much ill-usage. Its thin boards were gaping inside and had been pasted up with brown paper by her own hands. She drew back to the outer edge of the stairhead and flung her whole weight against them. The door cracked loudly, and though the lock held, she saw that another couple of blows would split it at one of its many weak places. Again and again she barged into it, and at last the wood parted in a long, vertical break. She was down the steps in a moment and dragging one of the short stout oars from the boat. She stood on the stairhead, looking round. She could still see the boathouse, a dark blur, no more, but from the south-east there came a splash or rain. She struck the door with the butt end of the oar, once, twice. It gave suddenly, almost precipitating her into the room. She recovered her balance, and then, with that boatman's prudence which never left her, carried her weapon down and threw it into its place.

In another minute she had thrust her way in and was face to face with her father.

Thievie was sitting crouched under the tiny widow with his box in his arms. His nostrils were dilated, his eyes looked as though he would strike, though his hand was still. He had sat listening to the bumping of the boat below and to the blows that burst in the rotten door; humanity seemed to have gone from him, leaving in its place the fierce, agonised watchfulness of some helpless, murderous thing, some broken-backed viper. His eyes fixed Janet, unrecognising. Nor a word came from his lips.

"What are ye daein' there!" cried Janet hoarsely.

Her knees were shaking, but not from her exertions at the door.

His tongue passed over his lips. He looked as though he would bite. She sickened, she knew not why, but revulsion passed shuddering through her.

"Foo is't ye're no awa'!" she exclaimed, mastering herself.

"I wasna gang."

He smiled as he said this and held the box tighter. As she looked at it in his grasp, some inherited instinct rose in her, and though it had been mainly valuable to her for what it would bring, should it pass from his drowned hands into her living ones, it became, at that moment, a thing desired and desirable for itself. She did not know what sum was in it, but the rage for possession of it came to her.

He laughed quietly, his toothless mouth drawn into a long line. She pounced on him, shaking his arm.

"Weel, awa' ye come noo — the boat's waitin' on ye!"

He shook his head.

She had never laid rough hands on him before, but she gripped him now. She was strong and he was helpless; and he knew, in his helplessness, that she had come for the box. He had feared the river-watcher, and he now feared her. He did not know know what she meant to do to him; his mind was obsessed by the box and the fear of its loss, and unhinged by the flood. He would like to resist her, but he could not, should he dare try. His concentrated hate shot at her like a serpent's tongue.

"I ken what's wrang wi' ye!" she shouted. "Ye're feared for yer box! Ye're feared yon man gets a sicht o' it! Aye, but he'll be here syne —he's aifter ye." I saw his boat i' the noo, an' him in it — ye'd best come."

His face changed. On the dusty window-pane the drops beat smartly.

"Ach, ye auld fule!" she cried savagely "wad ye loss it a'? Dive ye no see the rain? Div ye no ken the water's creepin' up? Muckle guid yer box'll dae ye when the pate's owre yer heid an' you tapsalterie amang the gear the water's washin' doon! Haste ye noo. We'll need awa' frae this."

She dragged him to his feet and he leaned on her, clutching his burden and unable to resist her violence.

They struggled across the floor and through the broken-down door. It was raining pitilessly. Thievie took no notice of it. He, who had known the river in every phase of drought or flood, should have had small doubt of the danger in which they stood. The roaring of its voice was increasing and there were fewer stone steps to be seen than when Janet made her entrance. It was pouring in the hills and the tide had yet a few hours to rise before it turned. Thievie looked this way and that. What he feared most was to see the river-watcher slide out of the mist in his boat; for the elements, the world and all the men and women in it were, to his disordered imagination, intent on one thing — the box. He would never sleep peacefully again should a strange eye see it. He would be robbed. He had long since been the slave of this one thought, and now it overwhelmed his dim, senile mind, even as the resistless water was overwhelming the land about them.

It took all her force and resolution to get him into the boat; he was so crippled and his arms so much hampered by the burden he carried. Though he cursed her as they went down the stair, his thoughts were of the river-watcher. In the middle of their decent he laughed his mirthless laugh.

"God-aye, but he'll be comin'!" he said, "but it'll no be there – he'll no get a sicht o't!"

At last she got him safely afloat, and having loosed the boat, rowed away from the stairs. The surrounding floods were peppered by the onslaught of heavy drops from the low sky, and then, as though a sluice-gate had been pulled up in the firmament, a very deluge was upon them. The little they could see was washed out and they were isolated from everything in a universe without form and a void, at the inmost heart of the hissing downpour. The river's noise was lost in it and all sense of direction left Janet. She pulled blindly, believing that she was heading for the boathouse. Soon they bumped and scraped against some projection and the stern swung round. She felt the boat move under her, as though drawn by a rope. She tried to straighten it, but the blinding descent of the rain bewildered her; a branch of an alder suddenly looped out of it, the lower twigs sweeping her face. Thievie cried out and crouched, clinging with frenzy to his box, and she guessed they had drifted above the deep, wide drain whose mouth was in the river. Her blood ran cold, for its swollen waters must inevitably carry them into the very midst of the tumult.

The drain was running hard under the flood-water and she despaired of being able to struggle against it. They were broadside on; besides which she dreaded to be swept out of her seat by another branch, for there were several alder trees by the edge of the channel. The rain began to slacken.

As its fall abated, the river grew louder and the sky lifted a little and she could see the large alders, gaunt and threatening as spectres, blurred and towering over them. With that strange observance of detail, often so sharp in moments of desperate peril, she noticed a turnip, washed out of the ground and carried by the torrent, sticking in a cleft between two straggling branches just below water-level. She made a tremendous effort and slewed the boat straight; and working with might and main at her oars, got it out of the under-tow that urged it riverwards.

All at once the river-watcher's voice rang out from the direction of the boathouse, calling the old man's name. She answered with all the breath she had left.

"Yon's him! Yon's the river-watcher!" shrieked Thievie, from where he still crouched in the bottom of the boat.

She ignored him, tugging at her oars and pulling with renewed strength towards the sound.

He raised himself, clinging to one of them, tried to drag it from her. She wasted no breath but set her teeth, thrusting out at him with her foot. He clung with all his weight, the very helplessnes of his legs adding to it. She dared not to let go an oar to strike at him. She could not have believed him able to hamper her so — but then, neither had she believed he could get himself up the inside stair of the cottage unaided; and yet he had done it. It was as though the senseless god of his worship, lying in the box, gave him the unhallowed tenacity by which he was delivering them over to the roaring enemy they could not see, but could hear, plain and yet plainer.

She was growing weary and Thievie's weight seemed to increase. Could she spare a hand to stun him she would have done so for dear life. She had heard of the many-armed octopus of the southern seas, and she remembered it now in this struggle that was no active struggle because one would not, and one dared not, lose grip.

The boat, with one oar rendered useless, swung round anew into the channel between the trees. Again the river-watcher was heard calling and again Janet tried to answer, but her breath was gone and her strength spent. The current had got them.

Thievie relaxed his grip as he felt the distance increase between himself and the voice. A branch stayed their progress for a moment, whipping the sodden hat from Janet's head; her clothes were clinging to her limbs, her hair had fallen from its ungainly twist and hung about her neck. They went faster as they neared the racing river. Then the swirl caught them and they spun its grip and were carried headlong through the mist. Janet shut her eyes and waited for the end.

Time seemed to be lost in the noise, like everything else. They sped on. At last they were not far from the estuary and the river had widened. Once they were all but turned over by a couple of sheaves, the spoil of the late harvest, which came driving alongside; once they pased within a foot of a tree which rode the torrent, plunging, its roots sticking up like gaunt arms supplicating mercy from the shrouded sky.

Finally they found themselves drifting in the comparative quiet of the broad sheet of tidal water, among the bits of seaweed carried inland above the deeps of the river-bed. The terrors of death had blinded Janet as they were swept along, and she now awoke as from a nightmare. An oar had been reft from her grasp in the stress of their anguished journey. Thievie was staring at her like an animal; his sufferings, as they were battered between one death and another on the boiling river, were nothing compared to hers. His god had upheld him. He had crawled back to his seat in the stern.

"Aye, he micht cry on us," he said. "We're no far awa' frae him noo —he'll no ken what I've got here!"

He began to rock about, laughing as he thought of the river-watcher's fruitless attempt to find him.

"Haud still," said Janet sternly. "God, hae ye no done eneuch mischieve the day? Gon yon mist doesna lift an' let them see us frae the shore we'll be oot tae sea when the tide gangs back."

"Naebody'll see us, naebody'll see us!" he exclaimed, hugging the box and rocking himself again.

Janet rose to her feet, fury in her eyes; she could no longer keep her hands off him.

As he saw her movement, he snatched the box from where it lay at his feet.

"Stand still, or I'll tak' it frae ye!" she cried loudly, making towards him.

He gave one cry of horror and, with the box in his arms, hurled himself sideways into the waters that closed over him and his god.

The tide was on the turn and the rain had ceased. A wind had sprung up in the west, driving the 'haar' before it back to the sea when it came. Some men from the fishing village near the lighthouse were rowing smartly out into the tideway where a boat drifted carrying a solitary human being, a woman who sat dazed and frozen and who had no so much as turned her head as they hailed her.

As they brought her ashore one of them took of his coat and wrapped it round her. She seemed oblivious of his action.

"Hae," said he, with clumsy kindness, "pit it on lass. What'll yer lad say gin ye stairve?"

Janet thrust the coat from her.

LORNA MOON

Wantin' a Hand

The moisture from the tub curled her hair into babyish ringlets that hung about her flushed face. Despite her form made broad with the daily travail of washing clothes, and her face pouchy with drink, suggestions of beauty still lingered about her as perfume might cling to a garment after it was soiled and torn.

There was no hint of age or decay in the square tower of her body, no thought of handicap in her actions as she squeezed and rubbed the clothes upon the board with her one powerful hand. The small stump of her missing arm jerked vigorously from the shoulder in time to the hand upon the board. She would stop at times to pin the empty sleeve more snugly to her side and then resume the crawling, gripping motion of her one hand in the tub. It was a great-jointed hand, corded along the back, and broad, and when it had squeezed the water from a garment she could defy any woman with *two* hands to wring one drop more from it. The clothes washed by Jean Sclessor were truly washed, and clear and fragrant when she took them from the line.

And so, although she tried them sorely by her frequent drinking spells, the good wives of Drumorty would rather wait for Jean than have some feckless two-handed woman wash in her stead. And the greatest church-goers among them would ignore the smell of whisky on her breath and would even comment sympathetically upon her bunions when her steps began to waver.

But Jean was long past caring what Drumorty thought about her drinking, long past the time when she turned her head away so that they wouldn't catch her breath. She cared only for evening to come, and she worked through the day with a driving force which became a frenzy of haste as night-fall drew near, for she was going home to

the kist under the stairs, home to dreams, home to love and revenge
and despair, home to forgetfulness, home to the flat-sided bottle of
whisky wrapped in a grey petticoat.

And when at evening she groped her way toward the kist in the
musty hole beneath the stairs filled with the odour of sprouting
potatoes, she was already tearful with welling memories, melting
with the vision of the lass that was once Jean Sclessor and the lad
that had been Sandy Morrison. They came to her as always, bright
with the sunlight of a harvest day and fragrant with the breath of
reaping time. *He* stood by the reaper bareheaded in the high noon
sun. Lesser lads had sought the shade panting and weary, but he,
foreman of them all and master of them all by height and strength,
stood stretching in the glare. And *she* came laden with the scones
fresh from the griddle and the mulled ale cool in its great earthen
bottle. There was a power in him that brought her eyes to his, and
whether she would or no' she looked at him, and he looked back at
her.

And then at milking time he came. She knew it was his shadow
in the door as she sat milking there. But never a move made she,
and never a turn of her head, although her heart was singing louder
than the milk that struck the pail. And never a word she said about
the singing of her heart, and never a word said he. But every night
he came and watched, and every night he waited while she strained
the milk.

Lightsome days they were, and work was easy in the doing. And she
would sing and scrub the yard for Mary Tate, the second lass, and
often she would do the work for both when Mary's cough confined
her to her bed. Nor did she care about the extra tasks, but rather
she welcomed them, knowing that Sandy loved her all the more
that she was strong. And though at times he looked on Mary with
admiring eyes, seeing her hair that lay like silken wheat against her
head, Jean did not care; she knew the kindling of his heart was but
for her, and the strength that lay in her round arms. And nearing
thrashing time he said:

"Come Martinmas, I'll go a-cotterin'."

And Jean replied with hurrying heart, tossing her head to give the
words a careless lilt:

"'Deed? An' wha will cotter wi' ye?"

"Yersel', I'm thinkin'," he made answer. And lingering by the
stooked grain that stood like little tents beneath the moon, he told

her of the fine bay mare he had his mind upon; and of the farm, come time, they'd rent together; and of the butter she would make for marketing, and of the long, long hours that they would work, he, with his back that had the strength of two, and she, with arms that had the strength of any man's. And by and by they'd own a farm, and *she* would go to kirk in taffetas, and *he* would wear a tall gray hat on market days.

Down on her knees she fumbled for the bottle, pulling it with avid hand from its wrapper in the kist. Seizing the cork with yellowed teeth, she spat it out, and drank, gulping dryly in her haste. She settled back upon the piled potatoes in the fusty murk, her heavy throat racked with bitter sobbing. The thrashing machine sounded in her ears again. She stood in its sucking wind, feeding the yellow sheaves to its hungry mouth. Sandy swung by calling her above the roar, love glimmering in his face. She stopped to wave at him — to watch his glinting head go by — the crunching mouth reached for her fingers — drew them onwards with the wheat — seized them, pulled them in, — the hand, the arm, up, up, the arm:— Oh, God, stop it! — stop —

She jerked from side to side with the pain of sharp remembering, thumping the potatoes with the splashing bottle. And then she licked the whisky from her hand, and drank, whimpering as the glow stole round her heart.

Sandy came to the hospital, silent and down-looking, and every time he came his stay was shorter. The smell of medicine made him fit to spew, or the second man was away gallivanting with a lass, and he must hurry back to do his work. And then he got to bringing Mary Tate along, and she would sit and look at him and giggle when he looked at her as if they had a joke between the two of them. And Jean could never speak to him alone or ask a word about the cottering.

Long after thrashing she came back from hospital, and Martinmas was drawing near. Lads were speaking of feeing time and whether they would stay, or seek a better place. But Sandy never spoke a word, but had some business in the byre, or other work to do when she would question him. And Mary Tate would make his brose with extra butter, and mealy-mouth about him in the evening, and make as if she knew what she would never tell. When Jean could bear no more of that she asked:

"Is Sandy biding here or goin' cotterin'?"

And Mary laughed and said:

"If he's yer man ye've little need to ask."

And Jean could barely keep from riving her. "What mean ye by that taunt?" she cried.

But Mary laughed, smirked and simpered while she stepped about as if the kitchen were a dancing hall, and all the lads had come to look at her.

So she cornered Sandy in the stubble field at loosing-time. He bore the harness on his arms and round his neck, for he would sooner break his back than tire a horse for no good end. He saw her, and he tried to pass, making as if the horses needed him, but Jean put out her hand.

"A word wi' ye. What's come o' a' yer talk o' cotterin'?"

"Oh, nathin'," he replied. And cried, "Whoa, Bess, whoa!" as if the horses were astray.

"Nathin'?"

"No." And looked ahead, straining as if to see the horses reach the watering trough.

"Look at me, Sandy Morrison: why will ye no' go cotterin'?" she cried, shaking his harness-laden arm with her one hand.

"I'll cotter come time, nae doot," he said, with more ease in his voice than in his face.

"Wi' me?" Her voice was shrill and cut him like a lash. The red rose up his throat. "Wi' me? Will ye go cotterin' wi' me? Answer me *that*, Sandy Morrison."

He could not look at her, and tried to turn away.

"Answer me!" she screamed and beat his breast, and as she struck her dangling stump jerked to the motion of the beating. Sandy's eyes were on it.

"I canna, Jean," he said. "I've nae use for a wife wantin' a hand."

And so he married Mary Tate and took her cottering, her that could never wet her feet, her with arms like matches, and legs like clay-pipe stems. He took her cottering for a year, and then the baby came, and Mary couldn't leave her bed for many a month, and when she *did* they said she'd creep about more like a ghost than anything that drew the breath of life.

Sandy left the cottering and hired out again. Soon there was another wean to feed and tend; and every year or two another wean, another mouth for Sandy Morrison to feed, and Mary always lying in the bed. And he that had so proud a head left the farming to do what work he could about the town by nights, and tend the weans and make their porridge by day. He that spoke of fine bay mares, and cottering, and rented farms, and tall gray hats, was doing work that none would do — emptying garbage in the night. She lived again that first night of his shame, when he crept up the lane at dawn, his head hung low, hoping none would see. But *she* was there and screamed her scorn, as many a dawn since then she'd screamed her scorn:

"Nae use for a wife wantin' a hand, eh? Fine for ye emptying garbage, fine for ye." He never looked toward her, crying in the window there, nor raised his head. And all the years he never looked nor spoke, but moved about as if her jeering fell on ears that could not hear.

Why did he not cry back at her or lift his head? Oh, to make him give a sign, to get her hand upon his shrunken flesh and rive it with her nails. To tear him open that her eyes could see him bleeding. To make him scream his pain as *she* must scream — to make him cry her name — to *know* that he was suffering. She rocked, tortured, on the shifting pile of potatoes, breaking their white sprouts as her hand grabbed, anguished, for the bottle.

Oh, what was he to her? He was a dour, down-looking chiel, thin he was, thin and withered, withered like a turnip at the winter's end. And his hair, his bonnie hair that shone like a Michaelmas penny, was grizzled and sparse and dry like dusty moss. And the shoulders of him that had filled the door from side to side as he stood watching her at the milking, were shrunk and bent, and bent and shrunken was his neck that had been straight and pink and moist with the sweat of the fields. And the eyes of him were bleared and wavering, and his gait was like a weary dog's.

Oh, what cared she? Why wait to shame a bleary dog — a bleary dog — a weary dog? Why sit and rock and wait, and cry at dawn? She'd stop her rocking and her crying. She'd stop her drinking and her wailing. She'd buy a dolman trimmed with bugle beads and go to kirk on Sunday. She'd cry in by to her that lay a-coughing in the bed, and him that pottered about wiping noses. She'd stop a while and sweep the floor, and wash the faces of the glowering weans. And all the time that image in bed would hate her for her strength. And Sandy would be shamed and he would see what he had cast aside. She'd stop and bake and throw her dolman on the chair so that its beads would shine. She'd feed the weans and tend the image in the bed, and it would choke with rage and cough, and cough, and cough.

She'd stop her drinking, this would be the last. She'd be looked up to and respected; she'd go to kirk, she'd make red petticoats for naked heathens, she'd stop her drinking. The higher she was held the more would be his shame. She'd stop her drinking, break the bottle — break it on the wall — but first she'd drink — No use to waste good whisky — this would be the last — the very last — the last.

She started to sway pendulum-wise, settling deeper in the pile, rolling her head as if in time to some well-remembered chant. Her vacant eyes were bleared with tears that fell on this shoulder, and on that, with the rolling of her head. Her purple lips forming the silent words twisted in a half-forgotten pain, and then her voice meaningless as a wind in a hollow place took up the dirge: "Nae use for a wife wantin' a hand, wantin' a hand. . . ."

WINIFRED DUKE

Captain Pert

I

She lived with her mother, who was a widow, in the one cottage. He lived in the other with his mother, who was not a widow, but whose husband stayed away so much at sea that she might equally well have been for all the use that he was to her. Mrs Paton, being a widow, enjoyed a small pension through the bounty of her late husband's employers. Mrs Pert, not being a widow, subsisted on her own irregular earnings as a charwoman and an occasional postal order from her man at sea, when he deigned to remember the existence of his wife and child.

The coast road which linked the villages from Finhaven to Aberdeen trailed its white and dusty miles between many-coloured fields that ran up to the skyline on the one hand and tilted down towards the sea upon the other. It was a bit of country that tugs at the heartstrings. Dark woods, the plainness of ploughland, rough stone dykes sunken at the edge of the lanes that severed the fields on their way to isolated farm or cottage, rejoiced the eye with their angles and outlines softened and effaced by the pervading sea mist which stole up to cloak the landscape. Midway between Bush and Berbie, seen from the highroad as if flung down haphazard by some giant's hand, lay the scattered roofs and dwellings of Sandhaven, the fishing village where Mrs Pert and Mrs Paton lived.

A dark lane, rough to the tread, moist and sodden for weeks after any spell of rain, turned off from the highroad, and went down in a steady descent to the village and the quay. At the bottom, where half the houses seemed to have turned their backs upon the only means of approaching them, as if in contempt or defiance, the lane split into several directions. One ran on through the village, ending parallel with the railway line cutting the fields above it; another dived sharply towards the quay; a third slanted up directly to the little station, a collection of windy sheds and a strip of pebbled platform, sunk in green banks and gay with flower beds. In the middle of this triangle of ways, seemingly uncertain which one to take, and deciding after all to remain where it was, there stood against the side of the road, the blunt end turned towards it, a house. Looking at it more closely, it was really two cottages, built together. Each had its warped, green-painted door set in the solid stone, with a window on either side and one above. These stared out upon a rough little garden, where hens perambulated and picked up a scanty living.

The cottage dwellers had all things in common. They shared the moss-smeared, leaking rain barrel, the garden, as exercise and feeding-ground for mutual fowls. The same gate, creaking, ill-hung, set in a high wall, admitted themselves, or any who came to see either woman. The gate always creaked. In a high wind it swung and squealed. On winter nights, calm nights, wet nights, it could be heard, whining a faint, insistent protest against its own impotence.

Mrs Paton, who lived in the first cottage with her daughter Elizabeth, was rosy, bustling, and popular. Elizabeth was not like her, being lean and dark, with a bitter mouth, a mean eye, and an unfriendly disposition. Mrs Paton's husband had been head gardener at Benholm, a neighbouring estate. Consequently she enjoyed basking in the twilight of his reputation as a sober and esteemed servant, a hard worker, a non-smoker, and a good Presbyterian. She lived in her cottage rent-free. Mrs Pert had to pay rent for hers.

Mrs Pert was thin and querulous. She found it hard to make ends meet, and to hold up her head in Sandhaven circles as triumphantly as Mrs Paton did. There were no stories afloat about Mrs Paton's husband. There were plenty current concerning Mrs Pert's. Some people declared that he had never existed, and that the "Mrs" in her case was purely a courtesy title. Others insisted that they remembered a big, bearded, truculent man who had arrived unexpectedly one night, roaring drunk, slept off his potations in the little front garden, and vanished next morning before his identity could be established or the story substantiated. Mrs Pert's hourly nightmare was a repetition of this episode. Her bitterest moments were when she watched her neighbour, habited in her weeds, carrying a bunch of flowers, and accompanied by her creditable daughter, making a pious pilgrimage to the little cemetery that lay halfway up the lane. The laird, whose father the late Paton had worked for, had not merely provided the widow with an annuity and a cottage. He had put up an expensive tombstone, recording the name, age, and virtues of the deceased gardener. Mrs Pert's thin bosom swelled as she contemplated the gross unfairness of things in this unsatisfactory world.

Her son John added to her trials. He was the same age as Elizabeth Paton, a sullen, unruly lout, for ever hanging about the harbour. The sea, ships, boats, sailors, were his secret passion. Mrs Pert had been a farmer's daughter, and yearned for her son to display some of the qualities and ideals of his yeoman forebears. Instead, he was growing alarmingly like his seafaring father in appearance, disposition, and inclinations. Elizabeth, of course, was destined for good service, preferably in the laird's family. Mrs Paton's ambitions for her daughter were bounded by the genteel dependence of lady's maid to the laird's daughters.

With all these puzzles, differences, inequalities, disadvantages, and propinquity, it may easily be seen that the two women were not congenial. The poor can never get far away from one another. Neither could go out at her own door without being seen by her neighbour. Sounds could be overheard, even conversation, if voices became incautiously raised. They met perpetually, each feeding her hens, looking for her child returning home, shaking a mat in the fresh air. They spoke. They nodded. They commented, dryly, briefly, on weather or local events. Even their religion divided them. Mrs Pert went to the ugly kirk along the village street, when she went anywhere. Mrs Paton, from years of good service, borrowed her form of worship from her employers. She called herself an Episcopalian, was occasionally — O bitter pill to Mrs Pert — driven in to church at Finhaven by the laird's wife, and talked glibly of Elizabeth's approaching confirmation. She and Cecilia Carnegie, the laird's youngest daughter, were to be "done" together.

Despite all this, there is just a bare possibility that the two women might have existed more or less tolerantly side by side, had it not been for the drying-green. The drying-green represented the last straw to Mrs Pert. To Mrs Paton it was the final aggravation in the long list of minor aggravations that had piled up steadily since she had been neighbour to John's mother.

The cottage garden in the front was a wilderness devoted to poultry. The ground behind was a rough rise of bare earth, cut by a high wall. It was useless for growing things, drying things, or burying things. From its ineligibility as a suitable spot for hanging out the weekly wash, a substitute had to be sought. Beyond the cottage that was Mrs Pert's dwelling there sloped a small field of rough grass. It "went with" the bargain when both women took their houses — Mrs Paton at the laird's expense, Mrs Pert at her own. The field became a perpetual bone of contention. Mrs Pert insisted that, as it was at the side of *her* cottage, she should enjoy the sole use of it. Mrs Paton, in her effective role of the lone widow, evoked the aid of the laird and landlord. They shook their heads over a clause in the agreement, appointing the occupants of both cottages joint use of the field as a drying-green. Each refused to give up her poultry, and utilize the front garden instead. They continued to share their hatred and a long clothes-line. It hung saggingly across the wind-bitten grass, as if conscious of the unpleasantness which it caused. Mrs Pert had from the pole to the hook in the side of Mrs Pert's house. Every Monday they met on the field of battle, the mouth of each bursting with venom and bristling with clothes-pegs. They tried washing on separate days, with dismal results. Mrs Paton declared that Mrs Pert's Johnny, by leaning out of his mother's kitchen window, had cut Mrs Paton's end of the clothes-line, causing the damp garments extending from it to fall on the muddy grass. Mrs Pert vowed that the boy had been out all day, and that Mrs Paton's Elizabeth was seen running in the field with the laird's dogs, who had jumped up, tearing and dirtying Mrs Pert's spotless wash. Each woman accused the other of encroaching on her portion of the line. Each woman could have cut off her share of it, and strangled her neighbour with the same. The children carried on the feud. Elizabeth threw clothes-pegs at John. John dressed up in Mrs Paton's nicely drying print and apron to frighten Elizabeth. Monday became Black Monday, a day of dread. In windy spring mornings, blazing summer ones, veiled autumn ones, bitter winter ones, both women, with bared arms and burning hearts, hung out their wash. On Mondays — washing-day — they never addressed one another. Each would fulfil her task, and go back into her house, voiceless, hating the other. The children learned to keep out of the way, or to stay very quiet, on washing-days.

The years went on. In the little front garden rank weeds grew and flourished. In the two cottages flanked by the little garden, hate, a ranker weed, throve riotously, luxuriously, fed by envy, impotent and undying.

II

The outstanding happenings in Mrs Pert's barren life during its last years were the death of her husband and the departure of her son John. These events did not coincide. Several months divided them. The first was much the pleasanter, although it could not be denied that the second brought a certain measure of relief. The first removed a nightmare, and meant actually a small increase in money. The second deprived her of her son's companionship, but he had begun to get into bad ways, and Mrs Pert heard the village comments without being able to contradict them.

She always suspected that it was Elizabeth Paton who drove him away.

Mrs Paton had continued to prosper. Elizabeth had done her credit at school, whereas only the intervention of the minister, pitying Mrs Pert, had saved John from expulsion and scandal. The two mothers, each at her door, used to watch the boy and girl coming up the slope at the end of the long street on their way home from their mutual studies. They were a great contrast — Elizabeth, slim and graceful, "a real lady", her mother reflected proudly; John, hulking and awkward, swinging his books, talking in the harsh East Coast accent which sounded so oddly beside Elizabeth's mincing refinement. She was endeavouring to speak like the Misses Carnegie, and nourished a secret and undying grievance against her mother for having sent her to the village school, instead of to some superior establishment in Finhaven. Mrs Paton pleaded her poverty. Elizabeth's thin mouth curled. The laird could quite well have managed it, would have, if taken the right way. Why had not her mother cried, and regretted that her husband's death should deprive his only bairn of so much advantage in the shape of a good education? Her mother did not make half enough use of rich folk like the Carnegies. Elizabeth would play her cards better, once she was safely an inmate of their house. She glanced at John with aversion and dislike. It was not by any choice of hers that he had taken to walking home with her every afternoon, although their ways lay together. She had her choice of schoolboy escorts. In her soul there lurked a secret germ of fear. After the last house ended there was a dark, rough bit of laneway to be groped before reaching the gate that led to safety and home. In winter it was eerie, with only the station lights far up the fields, and the one blurred lamp set in its iron frame in the wall running past the two cottages. The other night. . . . She bit her lip. There had not even been the lamp. A storm had broken the glass, and the high wind blew out the flame. As she fumbled along the wall in the blackness, the sea in her ears, John had come up from behind, seized her, and kissed her. She had thrust him off, fury lending her a nervous force alien to her slight body. A medley of feelings surged up in her heart, amongst which disgust, alarm, and rage predominated. He was sullenly conscious of her soft cheek shrinking from his rough lips, her girlish weakness beating down his brute strength. A sudden skurry of wind raving up from the quay flung their bodies against each other. She clutched at her hat, and found his arms round her. . . .

"Foo dare ye?" she stammered furiously. In moments of wrath her surface gentility of speech and manner dropped from her. She relapsed into becoming what she was, primitive, countrybred, common.

"Elizabeth!" He muttered her name, his head hanging, his arms still girdling her soft body.

"Let me gang!" Fear was fast swamping anger.

"No for a minute." Strength was giving way to abject pleading. "Elizabeth, listen," he begged. Dinna gang ben. I — I love ye."

She released herself, throwing back her head. Her laughter, shrill, mocking, was cruel as the sea lipping the stony beach not many yards away. Her contempt chilled him like an east wind.

"You love me? A lout the like o' you!" She rocked to and fro, maddening in her warm nearness, her scornful mirth.

"What way no?" Suddenly he stood over her, masterful, terrifying. "Elizabeth, gin ye'll wait, gin ye'd care — some day, A'll dae wonders." He drew a long, struggling breath.

"I believe ye." Her laugh was wavering, and faintly curious.

"A tell ye A wull." He squared his shoulders. "A'll mak' money — a lot o' money. Div ye suppose A'll stay here a' my life?" His boastful tones changed to pleading. "Elizabeth, wull ye no' wait? It'd be something tae work for, gin A thocht ye liket me."

The lane was black and unlighted, noisy with great wind. Her hand, searching desperately along the wall, unexpectedly encountered the latch of the gate. She thrust it open, and stumbled into its protecting shelter. Away from his looming presence, its menace and vague terror, with the lights and solidity of home just at her back, she felt reckless and emboldened. "A wonder foo many lasses ye've tellt that till," she jeered.

"Elizabeth!" He made a clumsy rush, but she had slammed the gate.

"Wait for you!" Her voice, silvery and mocking, had sloughed the Doric. "I hope to do better for myself, thank you. I'm to be trained at Benholm, under Mistress Carnegie's own maid, and I'll have plenty of chances there. Do you suppose I'd wait, and grow old and ugly, on the chance of you making a fortune?"

This was all that passed between them. They had gone in together, parting wordlessly at their respective doors. Schooldays ended. She vanished into the mysterious, semi-sacred precincts of Benholm. He idled for a time, hung about the harbour, finally disappearing on a boat that halted at Sandhaven for some trivial repairs on its way to Sunderland with a cargo of wood. Mrs Pert talked vaguely of her son's seafaring instincts, his love of the life. At intervals he sent her money, but, beyond a curt statement that he was "all right", he neither wrote nor returned.

III

In a life drab of episode, barren of events, save her marriage and her son's birth, Mrs Pert, like a dying fire flaming up before its final extinction, experienced a few glorious, glowing weeks of undiluted, unmitigated triumph. For years she had lived beside a woman who made her feel her inferiority at every turn. For years that washing-green sundered and divided them. Mrs Paton's successful, ladylike creditable daughter was held up as model and rival to Mrs Pert as the mother of an unsatisfactory and roving son. At the end, however, it was Mrs Pert, the despised, the downtrodden, the under-dog, who rose up, the triumphant mother, the satisfied, the superior. She was old and widowed and worn-out when her son came home.

John, the slouching lad, the unsteady and sullen, this upright, keen-eyed, prosperous man! She could not believe it. He was first mate on the *Bella*, with good prospects of becoming captain. *Captain Pert*, she crooned the name over to herself. . . . John had money, as well as success. He crackled Treasury notes before her astonished gaze. What would she like? he demanded. He was going off on a longer voyage this time, and wanted to leave her comfortable before he went. Her dim eyes lit up. She had wild visions of staying with him at a Finhaven hotel, only to strangle these sternly. She must not prejudice his chances. Already he had hinted that his captain's daughter was interested in him. She trembled, then faltered out her dreams. Would

John buy the cottage for her — and yon field? She'd like fine to die in her own house, and to have her drying-green to herself first.

John laughed and promised. For his week's stay she tasted bliss, pure and unadulterated. It was balm to reintroduce "my laddie" to the gaping village mothers who had prophesied, one and all, that "Mrs Pert's Johnny" would end on the gallows. They had tea at the manse, John more than holding his own in conversation, his mother wearing a black satin from one of the best Aberdeen shops. Even the laird was interested and sympathetic. Mrs Pert hoarded her golden moments, her hope approaching its realization, until the blow fell.

The cottage was not for sale. The owner was in an asylum, and it could not be disposed of until after his death. The utmost that John was able to secure for his mother was a lease of it for fifteen years, with a half-share of the drying-green. Mrs Paton still reigned secure in her possession of the other half. John paid her a visit before he left, partly at the entreaty of his mother, desirous of showing off to her rival this creditable son, partly on his own account, to glean news of Elizabeth. She was abroad, he learned, as lady's maid to the youngest Miss Carnegie, now Mrs Fullarton.

John did not mind. She had slipped from memory, the slim girl whom he had kissed in the windy darkness of an October night. He had kissed so many other girls since that her image was nebulous and dimmed. Mrs Paton, that tremendous, overwhelming shadow in his mother's life, had shrunken and dwindled to a deaf and complaining old woman. On his return from seeing her John made a jesting request to his mother. She'd have to promise him to see Mrs Paton out. Then, maybe, he'd be able to buy both cottages, knock 'em into one, and she'd enjoy her drying-green to herself. The gleam in her sunken eyes amazed him.

"Aye, that'd be fine, laddie. But" — her brow clouded —"it's no' likely. A've had a hard life, an' her a saft ane. She'll live tae bury me."

"No' her!" He laughed.

"Aye" She was stubborn in her dreary conviction. "But gin A'm deid, laddie, an' she, buy yon hoosies a' the same. When A'm in my grave, A'd like weel tae think that baith an' yon green was *oors.*"

IV

Twenty years later John Pert came home for the second time.

News of his mother's death had reached him in Shanghai. It was several months before he could arrange his affairs satisfactorily and return to his native spot. At long intervals he had heard from his mother, every letter bringing the same tidings. The lunatic owner of the cottages and Mrs Paton both lived, bidding fair to become centenarians. Mrs Pert had died, beholding her dream unfulfilled a great way off. She would never live in a cottage which belonged to her, or have her drying-green to herself. A much lesser spot than either sufficed her now.

The place, save for its ludicrous smallness to eyes that had seen great cities and wide spaces, was oddly unchanged. John motored from Finhaven, and leaving his car at the top of the lane, went, a wealthy prodigal, first to the little cemetery, where with difficulty he found his mother's grave. He vowed, standing beside it, that she should have the biggest tombstone that money could buy, and her son at least should become owner of her coveted field and cottage. It was all that he could do for her now. Her last years had been comfortable, although she resolutely refused to leave the draughty, old-fashioned place which occasioned her such heartburnings. He walked down to it, smiling a little over her clinging to the same so tenaciously.

He saw a slender spiral of smoke wavering up from the near chimney. So old Mrs Paton — she must be over seventy now — still lived there? He hated her for her power to peer behind the blinds whilst his mother's coffin was manoeuvred out at the narrow door. He pushed the gate open, and, with its familiar whine in his ears, walked up to the first cottage.

No one answered his knock. After a few seconds he repeated it, impatiently, noisily. The sunshine — it was a bright day — fell upon his powerful figure as he stood there, a man of fifty, well-clad, prosperous, one who had fought for his own hand, and won. The place was very still. He heard the slow cluck and little noises of hens, a whistle from the railway, children screaming at their play in the village street. A queer sensation stole over him. It was as if his mother's spirit stood beside him, whispering in his ear, urging him not to desert her, to laugh aside her unsatisfied cravings and desire. His eyes went past a tall and ragged hollyhock, over the wall, beyond the slanting housetops, to the sea. It glittered, blue and beckoning. He remembered the little boy who had lain awake on windy nights listening to its voice. He had heard that voice through his dreams in foreign lands. Well, he was back again, he, Johnny Pert, the village wastrel, now Captain Pert, the well-off, the independent. If money could buy them, these two cottages should become his. He thought that it was reverence for his mother's memory, this craving to carry out her last, her only wish. In reality, something of her insane, obsessing desire had passed into himself.

The door opened unexpectedly. It swung back, the narrow aperture framing a woman. He stared into her face, not recognizing her. A spare body, a withered, spectacled countenance, with thin hair brushed primly from a prematurely lined brow. "Is Mrs Paton in?" he asked sheepishly. No doubt this was some neighbour who looked after the old woman. Her own daughter — she must be the same age as himself — was probably married long since.

"Mother's dead." Where had he heard that mincing, refined voice, that aping of gentility? Good heavens!

"Elizabeth!" he stammered.

She drew back. "I am Miss Paton I'm afraid I don't remember —"

He broke in. "Div ye no' mind Johnny Pert?"

Her face did not change, save to harden the merest trifle. "Oh! Your mother's dead too, I suppose you know?"

They stood looking at one another. The sunshine was very cruel to her fifty years.

"Can I come ben?" He spoke awkwardly.

She led the way without a word. He remembered the Patons' cottage even in his childhood as twice as comfortable as his mother's. Now he was struck by its modest luxury — yes, that was the only word — its taste, its elegancies. Had Elizabeth inherited money? Her mother's slender pension — if continued to her — would hardly account for these amenities. She was not married, nor a widow. She had called herself "Miss Paton".

She motioned him to a chair. "I'm sorry I can't offer you anything to drink. I don't keep spirits in the house."

"Oh, that's all right." He remained standing, feeling awkward and enormous in the low-ceilinged room. "A'm — A'm sorry aboot your mither. Foo lang?"

"Three months." She looked down at her black dress.

"An' you stay here?"

"Yes."

"Are ye no lonely?"

She shook her head.

His rough voice took a gentler tone. "Ye're no merrit, Elizabeth?"

Again that slow movement of the lean neck and small head, with its primly braided hair.

"No. I'm not married."

He stared at her helplessly. "A'd hae thocht ye was merrit lang syne, or still wi' yon Carnegies."

"Oh, not since my accident." She held up her left hand, encased in a black silk glove. "Miss Cecilia — Mrs Fullarton, I should say — upset a lamp in one of the Italian hotels, and I got pretty badly burned putting out the fire." She smiled faintly. "The laird says I saved her life, and the family can't do enough for me." Her smile deepened to a smirk. "I've been with mother this good while. She'd a long illness, and now I'm to have her pension, and another from Mr Fullarton, and I'm always to and from the place — Benholm — when the family's there. Did you hear that the laird's bought this house for me?"

John could hardly believe his ears. "But it was no for sale?" he gasped.

"Oh, hasn't anyone told you about Mr Gascoigne?" Her thin smile was pitying. "He died six weeks ago, so the cottages were to be sold. Colonel Carnegie bought both, and made them over to me. I'm going to have them turned into one as soon as this builders' strike is over and we can get the workmen."

He looked at her, this lean, middle-aged woman, who had so effectually killed both his cherished dreams. Where was the soft-cheeked Elizabeth whom he had kissed in the dark thirty-four years ago? Where was his chance of buying field and cottages to appease his mother's memory? Lost by six weeks!

"The laird micht hae waited." He found himself stammering in his fury.

"He'd no idea where you were, and when your mother was dead you couldn't want them." Her voice sounded sharp and acid. "You can't live in them, and, as he said himself, it was only right that I should have a place of my own, after losing the use of my hand saving his daughter. What was more natural than that it should be my old home, my mother's house?" Her tones grew shrill.

John smiled grimly. The Carnegies would find out their mistake, establishing this cadging virago not far from their own gates. She was not the sort to let them forget the obligations which they owed her. And she loomed between him and the fulfilment of a desire now fast becoming an obsession.

The veins stood out on his flushed forehead. "A'll buy the place frae ye, Elizabeth."

"My name's Miss Paton, an' the cottage is no for sale." Un-consciously she dropped into the vernacular.

"A'll gie ye yer ain price. A'm no a poor man."

"It's not of any interest to me what your means are." She clutched the cloak of her gentility round her again. "I tell you, the place is not for sale."

The place! From her manner she might be referring to Benholm. "What did the laird pay for it?" He was dogged and determined.

Her eyelids dropped. "Eight hundred pounds, I believe, and he's giving me three more for the alterations and putting in electric light."

John choked. "A'll mak' it twelve hundred."

She shrugged her thin shoulders. "I don't want to have to tell you again that I am not selling my house."

He stood looking at her. The window, framed in spotless muslin, was open. Through it came the drone of the sea. She was as obstinate, as immovable as the sharp-toothed rocks against which the sea beat, untiringly, uselessly. . . .

In his rage he said a brutal thing to her. "Ye juist want it because ye think ye'll get a lad, auld as ye are. Some chap tae hang up his hat —"

Her smile widened, showing her false teeth. "I'm quite happy by myself, thank you. Oh, you needn't think I haven't had offers. The head gardener at Benholm, and Mr Fullarton's gentleman." She laughed. "You were sweet on me yourself once. You had the impudence to kiss me, a rough village boy like you!"

He writhed. She had defiled his golden moment, defaced his last memory of the Elizabeth who was gone. "A'll see the laird!" he threatened vaguely.

"Do." Her voice was silken.

He went out, without ceremony or farewell. The garden, no longer hen-haunted, sloped neat and gay. The poultry had been removed to the disputed drying-green, where their houses shone white and cared-for in the sunshine. Across the hard blue of the sky a thin, dark thing stretched. It was the ancient clothes-line, cause of continual heartburnings.

V

It was fifteen years before John Pert saw Sandhaven again.

In the interval he had further prospered, married, begotten children,

157

and well-nigh ceased to remember the disputed cottage and Elizabeth
Paton. He did his best at the time. The laird, the lawyer, the trustees
of mad Mr Gascoigne's property were all in turns interviewed,
blustered at, brow-beaten, threatened, and abused. The last-named
would have been glad to accept his offer of the higher price. The
laird, secretly afraid of Elizabeth Paton, waveringly left the decision
in her hands. She remained adamant. The cottage was now her own,
and she intended to keep it. She declined to see Captain Pert again,
and any offer in writing would be put in the fire. He left Sandhaven,
wondering which was the greater — his hatred of her, or his desire
to dispossess her?

On a September night, fifteen years later, his ship put in at Finhaven
Harbour. Her stay was brief, but her crew for their few hours' liberty
scattered gladly about the little town. Captain Pert, a trifle stouter,
otherwise unchanged, strolled up from the harbour, and looked around
him with amused eyes. In his boyhood a day in Finhaven, with its
quiet streets and simple shops, its quay and ships, so much finer than
anything at Sandhaven, had been a foretaste of Paradise. Now all was
dwindled, lessened, provincial, slow. He turned into the Salutation
Inn for a drink. The east wind, haar-laden, coming up from the Basin,
had chilled him, reminding him of incipient rheumatism. He was not
getting any younger. He had a bonny wife, a pretty daughter, fine boys,
and ample means on which to retire. The last time he was home his
wife had hinted strongly that she wanted her man beside her. The
children were growing up, requiring a father's hand and authority. Yes,
he would forsake the sea, and enjoy his leisure and ease. At sixty-five
a man needed a home for himself, and peace and relaxation.

A name, passing between two farmers who were exchanging drinks
and gossip, caught his attention. Sandhaven! He looked up sharply.
The mention of the old place had stirred his pulses. "Talking of
Sandhaven?" he asked them. "I'm a Sandhaven man myself." The
Doric had slipped from him in the years of wandering. "How's things
there?"

"Oh, nae sae bad. A've a fairm mysel' 'atween Bush and
Sandhaven." The speaker looked with careless interest at the grizzled
sea captain. "Aye, it's a great place for seafarin' folk. Mistress
Carnegie's deid. Ye'll mebbe mind her, the laird's leddy at Benholm?"

He remembered Benholm. It awed him in the old days. Mrs

Carnegie, driving past, had been his ideal of a royal queen. Another name stirred in the burned-down ashes of old memories. "I mind folks called Paton," he said slowly. "Any living still?"

The two farmers exchanged winks and laughs. "There's ane — she's eneuch. Auld Elizabeth — likes tae be ca'ed Miss Paton. She'd like fine tae be Mistress Carnegie, an' dod! A'd no be surprised gin she managed it yet. The laird's owre eighty."

In the low-ceilinged, smoke-grimed room, foggy with tobacco rings, fuggy from ale, Captain Pert heard the whole story. Elizabeth Paton had grown insatiable in her demands upon the Carnegies. She visited them, no longer as a former valued dependant, but as an equal. She took money, privileges, repairs to her house from them as freely as she accepted their garden produce and coal. They bowed meekly to her blood-sucking. It was whispered in the neighbourhood that she levied a species of ladylike blackmail. The story of the overturned lamp and her gallant rescue of Cecilia Fullarton were skilled fictions. Mr Fullarton, extremely drunk, had made amorous advances to his wife's maid, in the virginal repelling of which they upset the lamp between them. Elizabeth valued her damaged hand, and the Carnegies valued Mr Fullarton's damaged reputation. She had been the secret terror of their lives. Her sinister nearness, her unabashed requests, had driven Mrs Carnegie into her grave, and it was freely rumoured that Elizabeth was set upon becoming her successor. Captain Pert chuckled, nodded, swallowed his ale, and after standing drinks all round, departed in a general atmosphere of beery benediction.

In spirit he had dropped the last fifteen years. He was once more the man of fifty, impotent in the knowledge that his money could not buy him the one thing which he coveted. That infernal woman! He ground his teeth at the thought of her. How she had prospered, fastening herself, leech-like, upon this unfortunate family, who had been her mother's benefactors. He recalled her, smug and sallow, the black glove upon her damaged hand symbol of her black heart. A desire suddenly seized him to see her again.

He knew that they would not sail until the morning. It was barely seven o'clock now. In the High Street, cobbled, unchanged, he squeezed his bulk into the last seat in a crowded, mud-splashed motor bus, and was soon jolting through familiar landscape. There was the old tollhouse at the crossroads, and further along, the woods and wide fields and distant glimpses of the sea. They drove across the great bridge spanning the Esk, the shore, a misty curve, below and beyond. The road ran up and tilted down. They dropped passengers at solitary farms and cottages, or took up others. The sky was deep and brooding, and the country darkening for the night. A wind blew across the fields, rough and empty after the ingathering of a late harvest. Ahead he saw the steeple and tall outline of Kirkside Church.

The bus dropped him at the top of the lane running down to Sandhaven. It was eight o'clock, and nearly dark. He glanced at the locked gates of the cemetery as he passed, and strode on. At the junction of the ways he halted, peering up at the cottage-end silhouetted against the sky. There was a tiny window set high in it, and he saw with satisfaction that a stone had evidently been aimed, shattering the glass. No doubt the laird would have the privilege of putting in a new pane.

Captain Pert watched the house for a long time. Then he turned, very leisurely, and retraced his steps. He would walk back to Kirkside, get a snack at the inn, and if he found that he had missed the last bus returning to Finhaven, would hire a taxi. . . .

He walked slowly, not because he was tired, but because something seemed to drag him back at every yard. Hate — monstrous, malignant, obsessing — obliterated all other feeling. He told himself impatiently that it was absurd to wish to injure a woman whom he had not seen for fifteen years, and scarcely thought of during their passing. What urged him to return, to have sight of her, to speak with her face to face? The motionless fields fell behind him as he tramped on doggedly. He was no longer Captain Pert of the *Merry Maid*, the husband of a pleasant, well-dowered wife, the father of three children, the idol of his crew. He was Johnny Pert again, the lout whom Elizabeth Paton had mocked in the dark lane, the man whom she had baulked of his desire for four walls and a plot of land. She was there alone, defenceless, too unpopular in the village, he shrewdly surmised, for any to come to her aid were a cry heard from her cottage. Its surrounding darkness had struck him, and he suddenly remembered noticing that the lamp, against the wall, was gone. Long afterwards he learned that she had complained about it as unnecessary and unsightly, insisting upon its being removed. It was nothing to her if half the villagers broke their legs groping towards the houses and the quay.

He saw the lights of Kirkside pricking the darkness ahead as he plodded up a long rise. He supposed irritably that he should find the inn shut. Ten o'clock had chimed from the high steeple when he was a quarter of a mile from the village. He'd have to tramp the length to Finhaven, if he did not want to miss his ship, unless a passing motorist overtook him and gave him a lift. It was too late for a train, or any tradesmen's carts calling at the intervening villages.

He came through Kirkside, with its forge, its solitary shop, its modest post office. He passed the inn, like these others inhospitably curtained and shut. Further along, a line of stuffy little cottages bordered the road. He saw a light glimmering behind a sun-bleached blind in the last window. It was a tiny general store, and his hand, incredulous of the chance of finding it open so late, lifted the old-fashioned latch.

The place was dark and confused, crowded with packing-cases, dusty, half-empty boxes, derelict tins. A smell of sawdust and cheese hung in the air. An old woman came forward from some mysterious inner premises, peering and blinking. He bought a packet of biscuits, and, whilst she wrapped them up, took out his tobacco pouch and refilled his pipe.

"A braw nicht." She handed him the little bag.

"Aye. No bus to Finhaven, I suppose?"

"No till the morn's morn. The last gangs by aboot six." She scrutinized him, idly curious. "Ye're no frae hereaboots?" she asked.

He was suddenly cautious. "No." He handed her a coin. "Got change? Sorry, I've nothing smaller."

The old woman examined it critically. "The licht's no verra guid, nor my eyes. Is yon a florin noo, or a hauf-croon?"

He was anxious to be gone. "A florin. I think you said the biscuits'd be sixpence."

She dropped the coin into a tin box, from whence she extracted a battered shilling and six worn pennies. He thanked her and went out, unceremoniously cutting short her interminable tale of how it was early closing, but the Kirkside policeman winked at her keeping open on Thursdays. It brought a little custom, especially in the tourist season, when people looked in to buy chocolates and picture postcards. All the villages up the coast had Thursday for their half-holiday, but it was Wednesday in Finhaven. He muttered "Yes, yes" impatiently, and went.

Outside, it was quite dark, with a wind blowing in from the sea.

He walked irresolutely to the top of the road, stood about, turned. Steadily, unfalteringly, unweariedly, he took the miles that he had already trodden. An unlighted house was before him, a house shorn of its protecting, revealing lamp, and in the house there slept a woman

161

whom he hated. It was nearly midnight when he stood once again beside his Naboth's vineyard.

The gate in the wall yielded to his touch. It whined as if in protest as he swung it back. He remembered every inch of the place, and groped his way unhesitatingly round to the far side of the house. The drying-green was a drying-green no longer, but his hand encountered a sodden knot of fibre twined about the same rusty hook in the wall. With his stout jack-knife he hacked off the dangling, rain-saturated length of rope remaining.

Miss Paton had no fear of midnight marauders apparently, for he found it ludicrously easy to push up the low, unlatched window, and effect an entrance. He stood listening. The house — once two cottages — was naturally less familiar than the garden, and he wondered suddenly where she slept, or if she had servant or neighbour for company. As he pondered, feeding his hate on half-submerged memories, awakened by the sight of these, his boyhood's surroundings, he heard a door open.

The gaunt and scraggy figure in the nightdress had not time even for cry or prayer before he flung himself upon her, bearing her to the ground.

VI

The Sandhaven murder passed into the category of unsolved crimes. In Sandhaven itself it was the chief topic of interest for months, and the house in which Elizabeth Paton had lived many years, and had been found strangled with a piece of rope from her own drying-green, was displayed delightedly to inquiring visitors. No clue could be discovered as go to her murderer. A few grains of strong tobacco, dropped from pipe or pocket during the brief struggle, pointed to a man, possibly a seafaring man, but that was all. She was not popular in the village, yet no one was known to have had such an active grudge against her as to go to the length of taking her life. Robbery was not the motive for the deed. Nothing in the cottage had been touched or disturbed, and she had plenty worth a thief's appropriating. There were indications in the rough ground behind the cottage that the murderer had endeavoured to dig a shallow grave amongst the rubble and stones in which to hide his night's work, but by the time that the police arrived the place had been explored and trampled over by half the village, whose boots obliterated the original footmarks, had any remained. Elizabeth Paton had not been seen talking to any stranger. She was in the village, buying stamps at the post office, on the evening of her death, and had appeared well and cheerful. Her daily servant had left her at six o'clock, aware of her intention of going into Finhaven next day for some shopping. She had made out a list of the articles she intended to purchase, which was afterwards found in her bureau, but the only things that she subsequently required — a shroud and a coffin — were not amongst these. She was buried beside her father and mother, and would no doubt have appreciated the large concourse assembled to watch her murdered body lowered to its last home.

Six months later Captain Pert, now retired and living at Weymouth, chanced to be paying a visit to his wife's people, who lived in Aberdeen. Wrapped round some fish, he noticed a copy of the *Finhaven Review*. He rescued the sodden sheet and read it, out of curiosity. There was nothing in it to interest him until he came to the advertisements, and saw — "Desirable Freehold Cottage for Sale at Sandhaven."

The Dwelling-house, known as Benholm Cottage, Sandhaven, to be sold by public roup on Friday first, April 12th, consisting of two Public, three Bedrooms, Bathroom (h. and c.), Kitchen, Scullery, etc. Good Garden and Drying-Green. Immediate entry. Property in excellent repair. Low Feu-duty. For further particulars apply to Burness and Christison, Solicitors, Bridge Street, Finhaven."

Captain Pert pondered. No doubt the place had a sinister reputation since a certain happening within its walls on a dark September night. His heavy-jowled face set itself into lines of sudden resolve. He would go to Sandhaven, buy the cottage, and once it was his, pull it down, stone by stone. His old dream was bidding fair to be fulfilled. He was to become the owner of the disputed drying-green at last.

A week later the express from Aberdeen ran smoothly parallel with the long platform of Finhaven station. It was a day of high winds, with sudden squalls of rain, out of a sky alternately brilliantly blue and sombrely grey. Captain Pert alighted, gave up his ticket (afterwards a predominant feeling in his mind was annoyance at having flung away for nothing the price of the return half), and crossed over to the siding where the dingy little local train waited. It was more crowded than usual. Curiosity, morbid interest, the desire to be present at the epilogue to the tragedy, evidently were taking people, who had no intention of buying it, to see the house sold. He recognized no faces that he knew, and settled down in his corner behind a newspaper.

The April fields were green and windy. The railway line ran along the cliff top, with the shore curving far below, and the sea dancing beyond the rocks. The roofs and outlines of the solitary farms that the train passed, dotted about the countryside, were sharp and clear-cut in the keen, salty air. Everywhere ploughing was in progress. The smell of the turned earth, and a lark's lessening singing, came in at the carriage window. The stations slid past — Northesk Bridge, Kirkside, Bush, Berbie, Sandhaven. He stepped out on to the little platform, with its smell of salt and tar from the harbour, and the first daffodils, pale and brave, just beginning to show in the black mounds that broke the green banks framing the twin gleaming rails. He made his way slowly, a unit in a grimly excited crowd, down the road, muddy and rutty, to where the chimneys of the cottage stood stark against the sky.

The furniture and effects had been removed and disposed of privately. An empty shell, the house itself kept its grim secret to itself. He wandered over it, re-living, though his dour, tanned face betrayed no signs of it, that night. Here was the doorway which had framed her, her scraggy neck and withered face in ludicrous, pitiable contrast to the nainsook and embroidery of the girlish nightdress. Here was the very spot where the lean body had lain. He went out, expecting somehow to meet her. Dully he began to wonder what had brought him back here, to this house of grisly remembrance, of ugly ghosts that refused to be laid. Who said that murderers were always, in the end, forced to return to the scene of their crime, unwilling, unrepentant, goaded? He laughed in his trim beard to think how impossible was the chance of discovery and identification in his case. No one had seen him, coming or going. He had walked back the black miles without meeting a solitary soul, and sailed with his ship next morning. The only thing that worried him was the loss of his tobacco pouch. He had missed it suddenly during that dark return tramp to Finhaven, and memory refused obstinately to aid him to think where he could have left it. Was it in the Salutation Inn? No, for he recalled refilling his pipe from it on the bus. Was it in the little shop when he was buying the biscuits? He could not tell. Was it — O agonizing thought — in the room where the body lay? Had he dropped it there, or in the garden, or on the drying-green? It bore his name in roughly inked letters under the flap, but, if found, there must be other John Perts. He had not dared to advertize for it. As weeks went by he came to the conclusion that he must have lost it on the road, and whoever picked it up considered it too valueless to hand to the police. It was as well that they had not done so, after the discovery of the scattered grains of tobacco near the body. . . .

He stood idly about the neglected little garden. Sightseeers had tried their best to trample it down, but a few springing things, rank and straggling, were pushing their heads above the dark earth. In the drying-green, empty of poultry, the grass was long and tangled. He noticed, still fastened by a sodden lump round the hook in the wall, the remains of the rope that he had hacked the end from that night. A solitary star had watched him as he sawed doggedly through the fraying strands. . . .

He saw that the loitering crowd of curiosity-mongers were massing before the windows. He joined them, and shrugging his broad shoulders at the keen, sunless wind, stood listening idly to the auctioneer's persuasive patter. In spite of his insistence upon the attractions and superiority of the house, the answering bids were reluctant, few, and low. A man beside Captain Pert turned to him.

"Are ye for buyin'?" he asked.

"Maybe." The other shrugged his shoulders again.

"Ye'll get a bargain, as far as yon hoosie gangs." The speaker lowered his voice. "But gin ye're a stranger, it's no fair no tae tell ye that there's a story aboot yon." He nodded towards the cottage.

Captain Pert had an odd illusion that the place was watching him, waiting to pounce upon him. The chimneys were like an animal's ears. He could fancy them flattened, laid back, as the creature gathered for a spring. . . .

"Aye?" he queried, with vague civility.

"The woman —a spinster body — wha stayed here, she was murdered last September." None knew this better than Captain Pert, but he merely nodded. "Found strangled with a bit of rope frae her ain drying-green." He jerked his head to indicate.

"And who did it?" Captain Pert stared at the blank windows, which stared stolidly back.

"Naebody kens. She wasna juist verra well liket hereaboots, but she'd nae enemies. Naething was tuk', an' they found nae footprints. Ye wouldna think a wee, quiet place the like o' yon would hae a murder in it, would ye?"

Bids had gone up slowly to five hundred and twenty pounds. There was a pause. Captain Pert, breaking from his garrulous acquaintance, stepped forward and offered six hundred. He had forgotten everything but that the laird had paid eight hundred for the place, and repairs and alterations had swallowed up another three. Could his mother and his enemy butbe alive to witness this belated triumph! There was a little further chaffering, ending in capitulation and congratulations. He wrote a cheque then and there, the sharp wind fluttering the leaves of the cheque book as his fountain pen travelled across the page. The auctioneer scrutinized it. "Pert? Yon's a Sandhaven name," he remarked.

Captain Pert was anxious to be gone. He made his way quickly through the still lingering groups of people. All the faces were strange to him, and his equally, it seemed, to them. A few words of sly chaff about his "guid bargain", and inquiries as to whether he intended to live in the house himself, he answered by a curt nod or head-shake. He had a driving feeling that he must leave the sinister place behind, or it would run after him, overtake him. . . .

Heads oscillated in eager conference after his departure. What was the name of the man who had bought the property? Captain Pert. Aye, weel, a Mrs. Pert and her son Johnny used to stay in the end cottage, years past, when it was two houses. He'd done grandly at sea, and tried to buy the cottages after Elizabeth Paton got them from the laird. He was fair mad when she refused to sell. Auld sweethearts? No them! Hated him, and used to say so.

Captain Pert, on his way to the inn to inquire about a conveyance to take him to Findhaven, found a small boy pattering after him. He turned and waited. The boy panted —"The auctioneer says wull ye please come back? Something aboot an address."

He went, oddly reluctant to face the garden and the crowd again. As he swung back the gate, the familiar creak and whine reminded him of its attenuated, long-drawn scream that had followed him up the hill that night (for he had not dared to risk returning and closing it properly) an old woman detached herself from a group of others, and made towards him.

"Eh, but I'm glad tae see ye," she exclaimed. She detained him by a skinny hand on his thick sleeve. "Div ye no mind leavin' yer tobacco pouch in my shop six months past? It was the verra nicht the puir body here was murdered." She nodded towards the cottage. "Ah've got it lockit up safe —————"

In his relief, his confusion, he stammered out a fatal admission. "Yes, I missed it, but I thought I'd dropped it here. It's all right as you have it. Keep it. I don't want it. It's of no value."

He finished his business —a trivial, overlooked detail — with the auctioneer, and went. People stared after him. He fancied that they fell away from him. The old woman had not rejoined her companions. She was talking eagerly to a tall man, the village police constable off duty. Presently he detached himself from her and came quickly up the hill after Captain Pert.

WILLA MUIR

Clock-a-doodle-doo

They were all wag-at-the-wa' clocks, but of every conceivable size and
shape, and they covered three walls of the room, which had a fourth
wall of clear glass as if it were an enormous show-case. Every day a
Woman opened a little side-door and came in to wind up any weights
that had run down. She always came in just when the sunlight,
having fingered its way round half the room, touching clock after
clock, had withdrawn for a siesta on the floor-boards before creeping
back to finger the clocks on the other half of the walls. She handled
the weights lovingly as if she liked feeling them, and the clocks were
excited and glad to see her, so that they all whirred and chimed in
unison no less than twelve strokes, the maximum effort of which they
were capable. A great deal of their tick-talking and clack-clacking was
concerned with her and her doings, yet she never showed the least
interest in their mechanism, except for the weights, and the clocks,
who were proud of the cog-wheels inside their heads, especially when
daylight failed and they could not see each other, were puzzled by her
indifference. In the dark they lived only in their cog-wheels and so
the shadow that hid each clock from its neighbour was also a shadow
of fear, for if a wheel were to fail in the night or a spindle break the
damaged clock could not even show a face to the world but was as if
annihilated. In the dark, therefore, they were resentful of the Woman's
indifference, but they did not discuss her except to accuse her of
stupidity, for they were eager to forget their fear by speculating on
the nature of cog-wheels and propounding theories for their repair.
Every night the discussion waxed in liveliness until the defiance of
the clocks culminated in striking midnight, after which they relapsed
more contendedly into the hum-drum routine of the small hours where
little effort was needed.

On moonlight nights, however, the liveliness continued as long as

discussion waxed in liveliness until the defiance of the clocks culminated in striking midnight, after which they relapsed more contendedly
into the hum-drum routine of the small hours where little effort was
needed.

On moonlight nights, however, the liveliness continued as long as
the moonshine lasted. And on these occasions they speculated about
the moon, arguing that it must be a super-clock, permanently lit-up and
delivered from the fear of darkness, not to speak of its power to move
freely, if erratically, across the wall of the sky. One very grandfatherly
clock, reputed to be the oldest inhabitant, sought in vain to discourage
what he called the heresy of revering the moon; the other clocks were
tired of hearing his admonitions to honour the punctual sun, which
was, he said, the Author of their Being "He is like ourselves, only
greater. He too vanishes from sight in the darkness. He too is regular
in his movements — does he not visit us daily, each in turn, to watch
over our welfare and to remind us that we belong to the great cosmic
rhythm of Time? Your moon is no clock-face, your moon spins round
until only its edge is visible, your moon is merely the sun's pendulum."

"Bah!" said the young, impatient clocks, and they said it loudly ten
times so that the wheezing, grandfatherly clock was quite inaudible.
"Of course the moon is a clock-face. Can we not see the signs upon
it although they are difficult to read?"

"Use your cog-wheels, old fool, use your cog-wheels," added a very
Clever Clock, who claimed to have twice as many cog-wheels as any
of the others. "It's face-values you're trying to foist on us, face-values
wrapped up in pious sentimentality. If the sun takes the trouble
to visit us it's because he thinks it worth his while. And as for you,"
he addressed the young clocks, "it's face-values you're serving too,
the whole clacking of you, when you say that you admire the moon
although you can't read its face! Admire it rather *because* it is illegible,
because its meaning lies hidden in its private cog-wheels, because it is
an intricate and baffling piece of mechanism, unlike your hum-drum,
bourgeois sun."

The moon shone straight in upon the Clever Clock. "Ah! I am lit-up
too!" he cried. "Now I shall tell you the truth. The numbers on your
faces are only a device to keep us marking time, to prevent us from
inquiring into the nature of reality ———"

He had to break off to strike Eleven, and this made him furious;
besides, in spite of his multifarious cog-wheels, his voice was not the
loudest in the room. A much simpler-looking clock on his right had

a fuller, more resonant chime, and the Clever Clock, aware of his superior intricacy, kicked his pendulum petulantly as far as it could go.

"I appeal to my friends on the left," he exclaimed, as soon as the echoes had died away. "What is this so-called Time to which we are bound in slavery? Can anyone define it? Is it anything but an ideological figment?"

These words impressed the young clocks. And when the Clever Clock went on to point out that the Truth of things lay inside their own heads, and was to be discovered only by the study of their own cog-wheels, they were interested. But when the Clever Clock said that a knowledge of the springs of their own conduct would enable each of them to detach himself from routine and become an independent moon, they were elated.

"Let us make a beginning — any beginning!" they cried.

"Good," said the Clever Clock. "Watch me."

He shrugged and twisted himself until he had dislocated the numbers on his face, so that they were all in the wrong places.

"That is the first step towards illegibility," he announced, "the first step on the road to freedom. *A nous la liberté!*" And he struck Twelve on a high, tinny note of exultation, with both his hands pointing to the number One. "Now I shall withdraw into myself and meditate on my cog-wheels," he said. "I have already made several important discoveries ———"

"Do tell us," buzzed the clocks. But at that moment the moon fled behind a cloud-bank and the clocks began to be a little fearful at the return of darkness. The Clever Clock felt their fear creeping into him, and muttered "Fools!" so savagely that the clocks did not dare to address him again that night.

Now the Clever Clock had really discovered something. By listening very intently to himself he had discovered that his cog-wheels were interlocking and moved each other. But which of them was the *primum mobile*? He groaned in private over the difficulty of his task. "If I could only be quit of this nonsense of striking the hours!" he reflected. "What I want is Pure Horological Thought. . . ." He fell into a kind of trance, murmuring to himself: "I am. I. I am my cog-wheels." This so refreshed his self-conceit that on the morning after, when the other clocks looked uneasily at his face, wondering what the Woman would say, he tick-tocked and clack-clacked more arrogantly than ever. "She won't dare to say anything. She is a mere servant of the cog-wheels.

Does she not handle our weights simply and solely to minister to the cog-wheels?" he declared, and was proved right, too, for the Woman did not look at his face at all. He was a clock who could run for months at a time without her, and she disregarded him. "In any case," said the Clever Clock, after she had gone, "she is stupid. And so are most of you — all of you. Marking time is all you're fit for. Not one of you is capable of becoming a free agent, except myself. However, when I am a moon I shall be lit-up for ever, and I shall be famous when you are all on the scrap-heap."

"No, no!" cried several young clocks, so young that they were almost watches. "We want to be lit-up too!"

"How can you take him seriously?" growled the grandfatherly clock.

The Clever Clock interrupted him. "We must free our terminology from the materialism of content, if we are to discover the laws of Pure Horological Thought," he said, rapidly, impressing his audience once more.

At that moment the finger of the sun touched him, giving him a warm, tickling sensation which was so pleasant that, even while reminding himself how much he despised sensation, he forgot momentarily to continue talking. As the sun slid over him the carved detailed on his case stood out clearly, and one could see what a very fine clock he had been meant to be. Twelve little wooden figures stood in niches around the clock-case, and an angel with a little trumpet was perched on the very top. There could be no doubt that his intricate machinery had been planned to set these figures in motion, but something must have gone wrong, for they were gathering dust, and looked a little forlorn. And the Clever Clock, pondering his cog-wheels, had never even suspected that what they really needed was the adjustment of a minute pinion to set the little figures dancing. There was a tiny screw loose in the Clever Clock, but he was too busy boasting and studying Pure Horological Thought to observe anything of the kind.

He felt restless again when the finger of the sun left him. The Daily Dope! he muttered to himself, sneering at the travelling beam of light. And he shrugged to himself so hard that his numbers fell into confusion; one of them even came off and tinkled on the floor. That delighted the Clever Clock.

"Now I am well on the way to become unintelligible," he said. "I am among unique among clocks!"

"But you are still marking Time," retorted the grandfatherly clock, for at that moment the Clever Clock had to strike Two along with all the others. This so exasperated him that with a violent kick he dislodged the balancing weight from his pendulum.

"Now I am Really Unique," he gasped, somewhat out of breath, since his pendulum was clacking wildly. "Now I can swing from one extreme to the other as much as I like! There is no other clock like me in the whole universe. Clack-clack! Clack-clack! Clack CLACK! Not one of you can do this! Clack-clack-clack-clack!!"

"Oo-oo-oh!" cried the young clocks, feeling excited. "What marvellous high-kicking!"

And that night, when he was lit-up, the Clever Clock set all the other to shrugging and kicking in imitation of him, crying at top-speed:

"This is — clackety-clack — this is the Horological Renaissance!"

When the Woman came in the next day her foot struck against a little pile of discarded numbers and a pendulum balance. Also, she reached up and took him from the wall and blew dust off the little wooden figures.

"Watch me!" said the Clever Clock to the admiring young clocks. "Now I move from the wall as I promised you. This Woman is the servant of my will."

And he went out in her arms and the door shut behind him.

CATHERINE CARSWELL

The Zoo: The Dream

I had to do something. For more than a week out of sorts, possessed by melancholy, afflicted by strange pains and by that lassitude which is in itself a pain, I could neither rest nor concentrate. Though equable by nature and, for the most part, able to nourish cheerfulness from a dozen familiar sources should the day's routine fail in providing any, I have all my life been subject to such attacks. Their onslaught has in it something of the violence of an epileptic seizure. At least, as with the victims of epilepsy, the malady has a way of following with precipitance upon a state of equally unaccountable wellbeing. After a day in which all one's fountains have played to the sky; a day in which the common ills of life, and even one's own particular sorrows, are shown by irrefutable clairvoyance to be needful dissonances only waiting their time to be resolved in a universal music; a day in which love, truth and worth, no matter how ill-bestowed or unrecompensed, stand beyond question as eternal verities; after such a day, all in a moment, the solid-seeming structure melts into mud leaving the spirit homeless. Then the mildest sunshine, the blossoming trees of spring itself afford no relief. The foundations of life and the incentives for maintaining it are gone. But why attempt to describe an affliction so well known even in better times than those we now endure?

The only comfort in this condition is to have near one a familiar, loving human being in whose smiling 'there, there!' one can take refuge till the cloud goes. I have had this best of all possessions. I have it no longer. So I thought I would walk in the sunshine, following the vast, unending, drab crowd of my fellows who were bound for the Zoo.

I had not been to the Zoo for over thirty years, though it lies not far from where I live now. When I last went it was on a Fellows' day to meet in the then Galsworthian fashion a lover and friend and teacher who is now dead. I was young and had made my toilette with care. On the farther side of the Gardens lay the region of pictorial art into which I had deliriously dipped upon first coming to London. On the nearer side lay marriage, a long history of work, motherhood, success of a sort, friends, tragic and sudden deaths, a penniless condition, the war. The air had used to sparkle with magic. Yesterday, though the sun shone and the air was mild there was nothing of sparkle and less of magic. I drifted as part of the dingy procession zoo-wards and was possessed by sick loathing and melancholy.

Inside the grounds there was hardly moving room. I had glimpses of imprisoned animals and wondered at the beauty of their coats — especially the red dingoes and bright brown wolves. Then by some chance of shifting I found myself in front of a giggling, inquisitive crowd and close to the bars before an outdoor prison of small monkeys. THESE ANIMALS ARE DANGEROUS. I read the printed sign. I held out my finger. The little ape held it and we looked into one another's eyes. 'No trees,' he seemed to say, and he let my finger go. I looked at the horrible contraption of blackened sticks — mockery of a tree — in his cage, which, with the bars was all our provision for two agile geniuses. 'No trees,' said his melancolic eyes, 'but at least *you* can remember them. I have not so much as the memory of trees. I do not even know that that distant greenness in the park outside is made by trees.'

'There there!' I murmured as I turned away. I dragged myself home determined never again to visit the Zoo.

As a child I adored all animals and greatly longed to have a monkey, but my wish was not realised. My father, as a boy in the Fife manse, had a monkey about which I was never tired of hearing. It had escaped, he told us, from a travelling circus in the company of a dwarf. Both had arrived at Collessie manse by night, and for years afterwards they had formed part of the household. The monkey grew uppish. He used to steal a tumbler and tooth-brush, run up a tree with them, and brush his teeth conceitedly. The dwarf, quite an old man, had, like so many dwarfs, a sour temper. But the children loved him, and they were sad when their parents decided that the little man must go. What his and was I never heard.

In our local Pet Stores in Camden Town I was once tempted to buy a chimpanzee. Almost as tall as I, but 'tame end gentle,' I was assured, 'well behaved, he will give no trouble.' 'Buy me!' his eyes pleaded. But the price was £50, and would he not eat me outof house and home during war-time? Besides I have no trees. Guiltily I shook my head. The chimpanzee followed me to the door as far as his chain would allow. More practicable, I thought, would be this goose in a cage on the pavement — an unusual bird; she had three legs. I might tour the country with her, charging a penny admittance, and I could live on the eggs she laid. Fortunately for me, next day both chimpanzee and goose were gone.

Returning more dejected than when I had set out I repented of my visit. But next day I was glad I went, because the dream I had in the night afterwards, though it might have been of the sort which carries its peculiar sense of pleasure far into the subsequent hours of daylight, and might so have restored something of the magic my daylight hours lacked, could hardly have been of the same substance and circumstance.

Unhopeful of conveying its ecstatic quality I shall yet try to set it down now.

I walked, in my dream, along a narrow path which skirted a steep hillside. Sloping up on our right through patches of woodland to the summit, and down on our left to a stream which meandered through clumps of bushes and reeds, the place put me in mind of a short-cut at Mount Quharrie, known in the district as the Fairy Path, and used by us to avoid a stretch of hard road when going on foot to or from the village.

I say 'our', because several of us walked there, both young and old, I being one of the children of the company. I did not identify any of the others till I found myself clinging to the front of an upright piano which threatened to fall forward upon me as I stood on its closed keyboard holding by the candlebrackets. Then I saw my father. He was reclining fully dressed on a bed on the other side of the path from me and the toppling piano. Unperturbed by my peril he leaned on his elbow and smiled across at me. "Help me!" I cried." The piano is falling on me!" "Jump!" he said, still smiling, and he moved a little back to make room for me on the counterpane, patting it to encourage my obedience. I jumped and landed in safety. The piano and the bed disappeared. We all went on along the path. Then, looking down to the left, I saw a pool partly reed-covered, and my attention was held by an agitation within the water. Some hidden life below was covering the surface with gleaming rings. As I watched the head of a red-haired animal emerged, soon followed by its bulky red body, as the creature rose into the sunlight and scrambled on to the bank. There, while it shook a rainbow shower from its pelt, it was joined from the pool by a second, far smaller animal of the same species and ruddy colour, clearly a kid, which also shook itself in the bright, warm sun.

I regarded them with careful, extreme delight. The mother — as an unusually large and clumsy udder showed her to be — was something between a deer, a goat and a large dog in shape and size, but she exactly resembled no beast I ever saw in reality or in picture. Her curiously formed forehead was without horns, her neck was short and thick, her legs awkward. The most beautiful thing about her was her pelt of long and silky hair, like that of a red setter, but falling in irregular swathes about her, reaching in places almost to the grass. Even her udder trailed these long red wisps of hair. Though this was unbeautiful, and though her proportions were somehow wrong and her movements clumsy, so that she struck me as no better adapted for walking on land than for living under water, I felt inexplicable joy and emotion in her aspect.

Followed by her kid, neither of them uttering any sound, she lumbered through a group of birch trees in young leaf bordering the stream and made her way to where there was a stretch of level sward. There, having turned her blunt head as if to summon her young to emulation, she suddenly curved her whole body like a stretched bow, and, in relaxing it, sprang into the air. All was now revealed. Rapture flooded me. I saw her rise higher and higher in her proper element, threshing with her four thrusting legs and her flexing spine in powerful unison, wingless, yet able to spurn and mount in the air by her own motion. How describe her aerial progress, which was totally unlike that of bird or aeroplane, having a manner, an energy and a satisfaction that were all her own? She rowed her great bulk easily, strongly upwards on a steep line towards the brow of the hill behind, gaining impetus and height together.

What particularly ravished me was the way her swathes of hair, now made alive by the air of her motion, streamed and rippled back all around her, so that they became part of her motion, while at the same time, both transparent to and illumined by the bright sun, they formed an aureole round her. And within the aureole the outline of her body was revealed in its magnificent adaptability to her true element. I cannot express the extreme delight begotten in me by this heavenward canter of the red beast.

Soon she would disappear high over the hill behind. My one intent became to see her kid spring up and follow her. But he showed no sign of taking to the air. He nibbled at the reeds, looked about him, and presently decided to go farther down hill, where I now saw that there were some cottages and even little grass-grown shops far below the level of the stream on the far side. I feared, as he was very pretty, that he would be taken into one of the houses as a pet, and might then never be able to fly and rejoin his mother.

"Come along, child," said my father who had seen nothing of all this. "You know we have a train to catch. If you loiter like this we shall miss it." Here my dream ended and I woke. But all that day, going about, I saw at intervals the flight of the strange mother beast and her emergence from the quivering pool. And though I still felt out of sorts and useless, some of the magic had returned. Each dog and horse I saw in the street had the air of being about to leave the road and to fly over the housetops. It made no difference that I knew they would do no such thing. They none the less reasserted the marvel of their creation. Let it be admitted that without something of this magic and marvel I cannot happily move, breathe, exist. I am neither proud of this nor ashamed, glad nor sorry — though there have been moments of gladness and of sorrow for which it is responsible. It is merely something I have never been able to avoid or discard.

Yes, I know that there is a Freudian interpretation of my dream of the flying red beast; moreover, I think I know how it would run. And the clinical reading may be correct. I have no objection to this. But it does not greatly help me. I have faithfully narrated the dream by way of a pictorial record of what brought with it an access of serenity and joy. It was a dream essentially delightful which had the power to carry delight forward, as have all those of my dreams which involve landscape, sky, colour and strangeness. May I have many such.

NAOMI MITCHISON

The Teeth

He turned on the walkie-talkie and listened. In the old days they had
shouted across from boat to boat. But it was the same words they
were at still. 'Anything doing?' 'Not yet.' 'A wee spot below the
Pluck.' '*Silver Queen* calling: anything doing, boys?' 'No, nothing
at all.' 'Johnnie had a ring, not more than five baskets.' 'Aye, big
herring if they could be got!' 'Anything doing, boys, anything doing?'

There'd be old Jelly-Piece fishing with his lights off as like as not,
dirty old bugger! But he — aye, by God, if he saw herring now
and them to be got without the rest of fleet knowing, it would be
without lights he'd be fishing them! There was a way for a fisherman
to be. Hellish, aye, hellish altogether. You'd get so you'd not trust
your neighbour. There'd been a bunch of leads stowed in at the foot
of his bunk. And now they were gone! Who ever heard of thieving
a puckle leads? When you needed to keep the leads locked up you
might as well stop being a fisherman.

He was steering north again, up the coast, nosing along past the
marks he knew so well, a glance back now and again at the echo
sounder. Nothing doing there. Not the wee black tick of a spot of
herring. He'd make a ring for that, God he would not wait for a
right showing! Davie at the stern had the wire out as well. Any kind
of an appearance of herring and there'd be the ring out. He looked
at his watch. Ten o'clock. He had said he would speak to Jean at
ten. She would be waiting with the thing, turned on to the trawler
band. Maybe there'd be a two-three of the women folk in by at the
fire for a cup and a bit ceilidh. And each one with her own reason
to listen. To listen and hope and not to be able to do one thing to help.

He began to speak into the thing. Wonderful what the head ones
would be doing, inventing away at this gear! 'This is the *Honest
Lassie* calling. Are you there, Jean, are you hearing me? The *Honest*

Lassie . Nothing doing yet, but a good enough night by the look of it. We're up and down. If there's a herring in it I'm thinking it will be got. There was a Dunure pair got twenty baskets. But none of our own boats, no' yet. But the night's young and we're in good heart. Good-night then, good-night.'

In good heart — was he? By God, with the bills in his pocket eating away at his heart! There, he was back at them again. He'd need to pay the insurance at least. He'd let it stretch to the last day. And the repair bills, he could not bear to look at them even. And he'd need to. Bad enough for the share fishermen, one black week after another. But worse for the skipper and him needing to take everything, every kind of knock.

Jean would have switched off now, she'd wash the cups and go to her bed. Aye, it was hard on the women folk, too. Good heart? Aye, you'd need to say that. He had kept the worst of the bills away from her. How would she take it if she knew? Maybe she did half know. The way she'd been looking at him when he was home.

He altered his course a few points. It was cold getting. There must be herring somewhere! The night wore on. Here and there he could see the bright working lights where some pair had a ring, and the rest would come hurrying. But nobody got more than a lift. And the crews tired and cold and out of heart. No boat's echo sounder showed the good, definite dark mark of a shoal, no wire felt the pattering of fish. The gannets were somewhere else.

In the cold of the small hours the *Honest Lassie* had a ring. It had seemed like small feel of herring on the wire. But they got nothing, and the wet, heavy net to lay again, a thing that was easy enough with a hold full of herring but sad work on an empty boat. He was worried a bit over his engine, too; there was a kind of blurred feel about the gears, especially the reverse. He tried to put the gear lever in as canny as he could. Now with the dawn coming the shore seemed to get darker, the hills some way threatening. They swung round, making back. He steered on the harbour lights, the same as the rest. It made no sense. For here he was with good gear and the best of boats, and he had been working the hardest he knew for night after night, and so had his crew been working. He had nothing against the boys, nothing at all, no fault there. And no fault with the Board and the prices if once there was to be herring in it. But in spite of it all there was no money in his hand, but instead these rustling papers of debt, these paper teeth biting him.

Some way the money thing was not real. Not like his boat and his net were real. And yet if you hadn't it, everything was wrong. There was the jag-jag of money at you all the time like a stomach pain, and things not going right between himself and Jean, for they were both afraid. Aye, there it was, a terrible great fear standing beside him in the wheel-house.

Now the night all round them was turning grey, easing into a chilly dawn. They were almost in the harbour. He slowed down, his neighbour boat close across they grey, oily water, the crew's pale, dirty, tired faces showing up now in the first light. Above the harbour the houses were still asleep. He glanced round, turned the wheel and put her into reverse so as to come in gently. In reverse? The gear was not engaging. He shoved hard, no good, shouted to Davie and Jock to stand by with the fenders and spun the wheel again, felt the glancing bump on the neighbour boat, but not praise be, the splintering of wood.

'What in God's name are you at?' shouted his neighbour. 'You've sheared two of my fenders, you crazy wee sod, you!' He shouted back: 'It's my reverse, she's not engaging. If it hadna been me being so quick it's more nor your fenders'd ha' been sheared!' He was panting and frightened — aye, by God, frightened to the heart!

They made the pier, edging in gey slow and throwing out a rope. After they'd made fast he and Davie went down the hatch to look at the engine. They tried again to engage, but there was nothing doing. The others had turned into their bunks. They could be little help over this. Gradually he and Davie began to strip her down, rising sometimes to stretch and rub their tired eyes. Oil from the engine crawled down necks and wrists, smudged hair and stubbly cheeks.

He watched while Davie went up to the wheel-house to move the gear lever about. What was it had happened? God be about us, he thought, we'll need to get one of the engineers from the yard. He began to think of his bill there. They were beginning to look at him when he came their way so that he felt ashamed.

And now this. If only it could have been an insurance job! If he could have found a thing broken and no fault of his own. Surely there must be something broken, some flaw in the casting. He knew suddenly that this was what he had been hoping for and looking for. But the gear teeth were sound. Only worn a bit. Ay, the whole thing was worn when you came to look at it. Five years. Five years hard work and everything worn, himself and his gear. And nothing to show for it but a pocket full of bills! Davie had said just that: 'Wear and tear on the reverse gear.' Davie would know what he was thinking and hoping. You cannot live so close as a crew must live and not have a good enough idea of the other's thoughts. A new reverse drum. He could not do it. No. No. The money was not in it at all. And they would never give him this on credit.

He stared down at the gear. Then he called up through the deck to Davie to leave it be. They would go and have a lie down, the two of them. When it was right day he would take the thing up to the yard.

They went down into the hot, sleepy, snoring fo'c'sle. There dreams gripped him almost before he had his boots off. As he lay down he saw the gear with a tooth broken, saw it as plain as a thing you'd touch, the jaggy, bluish metal. As the dream deepened he seemed to be in the hold of a bigger boat, a black hold full of teeth; he was working between them looking for a way out, something broken that he could slip by. He knew there was what he could not face coming after him. By the end he was that frightened he woke with a start, sweating.

The others were all sleeping. Davie? Aye, like the rest. He put down stocking feet and so up the fo'c'sle hatch and along the deck and down in the engine-room. He got a cold chisel and a hammer. He was going to do a terrible thing, to cut himself off from the company of the decent and honest. It was like a voice almost. Jean crying on him not to be doing this. Jean. She did not know, her. She did not know the stress he was under. A stress that would break metal.

He thought hard now. There would not need to be suspicions over this. At last he struck, cannily. A flaw in the metal could have shown up this way. He stuck it on lightly with grease. Then he tiptoed back to the fo'c'sle and for a short time slept undreaming.

They breakfasted meagrely on tea and bread with a scraping of marge and jam. A hold full of herring and they would have had eggs or mince. Nobody spoke much. Davie and Jock at least knew that anything extra on the expenses might mean that their skipper just could not carry on, that he would need to lay the boat up, sell her at a loss if he could find a buyer, go into bankruptcy maybe, with all the misery and shame that would be for a decent namely family. And themselves? None of the boats were doing anything but badly, and few enough other jobs to be had at Port Fada. You cannot go on for ever on the unemployment money, not if you are a married man with a home to keep up. They would need to leave the place, leave the Highlands altogether maybe. Go down to Corby and the steel mills. Take to some other job. And they so skilled at their own.

Once or twice they looked at him, but he said nothing. Had he any kind of a plan for meeting this trouble? He got up abruptly and went along to the engine-room hatch, Davie following. They began to strip out the reverse. Suddenly there was a tinkle on the planking. 'By God!' said Davie. 'There's a tooth broken on her right enough!' He stooped and picked it up. 'And me not to see it before.'

The skipper came near. 'Is that so?' he said with a kind of waver in his voice. 'Man, Davie, are ye sure?'

'Aye,' said Davie, 'ye're lucky. That makes it an insurance job.' He looked hard at his skipper under the naked bulb in the engine-room. The skipper looked back at him and swallowed. And then all at once Davie found himself not saying as he had intended to say, that it was queer altogether he had seen no sign of this when they were working on the engine earlier. Instead he gave his skipper a friendly kind of thump on the back and stooped again over the engine.

Between them they got it into a barrow and took it up to the yard. Aye, it was an insurance job right enough. The boss there knew how things were with the fishermen and did what he could to help them. But beyond a certain point he could not go. He mentioned the account again. 'You could surely let me have something towards it,' he said. And then: 'I don't want to be hard on you, but — maybe I could give you a lend of a reverse gear. I'd not want to see you stuck. Twenty pounds towards the account, say.'

Twenty pounds. Twenty pounds, by God! No use asking the bank for any more. And them ladling it out to the ones that had it! He told Davie what the boss had said; the crew had a right to know. If they got the lend of a new reverse gear they could go out again at once. And the luck might turn. Must turn one night.

He went back to the boat, to another meal of tea and bread. He could not find it in himself to go begging for the twenty pounds. He could not move off the bench he was sitting on to do that. It was too far to go home, a shilling on the bus and Jean to be questioning him, or just to sit on the far side of the table with a wee scared look in her eyes. No twenty pounds there. Nothing that was worth selling.

Poor Jean. A bonny, cheery lassie she'd been, aye, poor Jean right enough. He half slept thinking on her.

In the early afternoon Davie came in. He had fifteen pounds in dirty notes crumpled in his fist. He plunked them down on the table. 'Tak this doun tae the yard and see what the has the boss to say. It's the best I can dae for ye.'

The skipper could smell the drink on his breath, a heartening kind of smell, and hear a sharp edge on his voice. 'Where got you it, Davie, man?' he asked.

'Ach,' said Davie, 'that would be tellings. And I'll need to pay it back. But — och, we're bound to strike a bit luck one o' these nichts!'

'But,' said the skipper, yammering away, 'but — och, Davie, I'm mostly sure we'd get the lend o' gear on this — but — was it honest got?'

'You'd need to take a bit risk once in a way,' said Davie, and he spoke gey soberly now, 'when things are that bad. Go you on, man, and get us the reverse gear.'

He took the notes in a tight grip and went over to the yard. After a little humming and hawing the boss said, well, yes, he could have the lend of the reverse gear, seeing he was a decent man and times so bad. He went along to his stores, leaving the skipper stand there, shamed from his hair to his boots, wondering how long folk could go on saying that of him. A decent man. He had been.

They fitted the new reverse gear and tried it out. It seemed to be right enough and the crew pleased to get it, yet the skipper some way had little confidence. Neither in the new gear nor in any other thing. It seemed by now he could look none of the crew in the face right, least of all Davie. He spoke angrily. He had the terrible thought of himself and the hammer and chisel and the gear teeth for ever in front of him. Yet when dusk fell and the rest of the fleet all came alive and the diesels started up and there was movement and shouting and hope again, the *Honest Lassie* went out with the rest.

He was on the wheel-house, the same as he always was, and when the time came he set the echo sounder ticking across, lining the clammy paper with its jags and curves. But the uncertainty and misery had him gripped. He would have missed the black speck on the paper if Davie had not come in out of the cold to the warmer wheel-house and looked at the echo sounder. He did not know if it was himself shouting or Davie, but the winkie was overboard and he had rounded her up. It seemed to be the boat and the crew doing everything on their own and he a kind of machine, not thinking, only going through the movements of a skipper correctly, only listening to his own shouting voice, and in time hearing himself crying hoarsely to the others on the net to haul away for dear life, for look, there was a fine mashing, ay, thet were into the herring right enough!

Even when the brailer was swung out and he saw them tumbling, tinselly beautiful, flapping with strong life and goodness, down into the hold, h was hardly himself. Then Davie said quietly, as his elbow: 'You'll get cash down on this, will you no'? I — I'd like fine to pay back yon fifteen pound. Before the polis —' And then he he shut his mouth. And the skipper nodded, understanding well.

NANCY BRYSSON MORRISON

No Letters, Please

He sat in his consulting-room, hearing without listening to it the hurried ticking of the small clock on the mantelpiece behind him eating up the silence. With all the inhibited reserve of the man who is never interrupted, only now, when the servants were in bed, did he feel that he had the house to himself, free to go through the letters lying on top of his desk.

There were shoals of them. He let them run through his fingers like a pack of cards, only he never played cards. That was something for which he had never had time. He knew that his thoughts were only playing with him, while they staved off the moment he would have to open these squares and oblongs, every one of them.

His reluctance was only natural to read the letters of condolences on his wife's death. This day last week he had not known she was going to die, and as a specialist such prognosis was surely his stock-in-trade. Nobody had known; she herself had received no warning — he had ascertained from Dr. Bolton she had not consulted him for years. His thoughts were numbed solid, as if frozen: the act of thinking cut into them like a snowplough, but they still remained blocks of ice.

If he had known he was going to be faced by this problem, swamped by a sea of condolences, he would certainly have inserted in the intimation. "No letters, please." That was what some people did, wasn't it? Only "No letters, please," was usually accompanied by the clause "No flowers," and she had always loved flowers. He could not have refused them on her behalf.

He simply had not thought about the letters. If he had, he was bound to know he would receive some. But not this avalanche: that was what startled him. He looked down at the varied handwritings: all these people had known her intimately enough to feel they wanted to write to him.

Only one envelope had a black border. He remembered when his

186

father died the scattering of letters his mother had received from far out connections had all been heavily framed in black. Times had changed since then, he thought as he picked up the solitary mourning envelope. No, he contradicted himself, catching sight of his name incorrectly sprawled across it in an illiterate hand, perhaps this class still sent out black-edged notepaper as a token of their respect. He had associated so long with his wife's class that he was inclined to forget he, not the times, had changed in certain things.

He picked up the ivory paper knife lying on his desk and slit it through the envelope in his hand. He must begin some time. From a person called Susan: she had written pages in her clumsy writing that told him her fingers were unaccustomed to a pen. This was more an outpouring than a letter, all about his wife's goodness to the writer not only when she was her mistress but since she married. Never a Christmas or birthday passed but she remembered Susan, some one called Alec, and, of course, the children.

Susan . . . he must have known her, she had lived in this house. His mind tried to work back in an effort to retrieve her from the past, but for the life of him her could not remember her.

And he felt it was vital for him to remember her, as though something, he knew not what except that it was something tremendous, depended on that memory. She wrote how good her mistress had been to her when her mother died — every sentence of the letter, if Susan had gone in for sentences, contained the words "I'll never forget." Susan would never forget; and he could not remember one detail about her.

She had called her eldest daughter after his wife. They had no children of their own to be called after her or him, and she had always wanted children. How long ago it was since he had remembered that.

He put Susan's letter to one side. He would have to answer it himself. He could not possibly send to her one of the acknowledgment cards on order. Nor could he allow to pass out of his life the only child to bear her name. He would have to begin and remember Susan from now on, since he could not find her in the past.

It was as though her letter had broken the ice. He did not hesitate opening the next: his name, correct with all his degrees on its envelope, was written with the long "f's" of foreign script. He noted the signature first — even to him, untutored in such matters, the name rang a bell. Music, like cards, had been another of these things for which he had never had time.

187

His well known correspondent remembered that the specialist's wife had been his most brilliant pupil; between the lines of his letter it was not difficult to read the frustration of one artist for another whose career had never come to fruition.

He had forgotten all about his wife's piano playing. That must be, he thought, because she never played now, and hadn't for years, although her grand piano still stood, always open, in the drawing room upstairs. Perhaps she had thought piano playing not quite suitable for a specialist's house, when for certain hours each day he used it for consultations. Unless she played it while he was out.

God, he knew nothing about her. This music man, and Susan, knew more about her daily life than he did who had lived with her for well nigh quarter of a century.

He put the letter on top of Susan's — another he would have to answer himself. His hands, with their long, strong, spare fingers, fumbled as he picked up the next envelope, and he peered at the postmark as though his sight were not eagle-clear, as it always was, until he deciphered the name Yetts sealing the stamp.

Yetts! The small country place where he had been born. He saw it again in his mind's eye, the squat grey cottage bordering the patch of village green, and the doctor's house, embosomed in trees, at the other end.

Dr. Elliot had always been good to him: when he, the lad of pairts, came through the university, he knew the doctor had been prepared to have him as a partner; and his practice, in that residential district, was one of the finest in the shire. But everything the lad of pairts did he did with distinction: he had won every honour and prize there was to win. Instead of partnering Dr. Elliot he had married his daughter and specialised. He even looked distinguished now, as though he had been born with a silver not a horn spoon in his mouth.

Whoever could be writing to him from Yetts! He would have thought the last link had been cut years ago. He held the inconspicuous, good envelope in his hand, as though weighing it. But before he opened it, he knew whom it would be from, the only person who would be writing to his from there these days — Kincaid. How long ago it was since he had given him a thought.

Yet how this man had once filled his mind, like an obsession, because both loved the same girl. He could remember the black hatred he had felt for a rival who had everything that he hadn't, everything the world could give him without working or fighting for it. Yet despite that, the girl had chosen not Kincaid but him, the unknown quantity.

How she must have loved him to do that. Now she was no longer there he tried to burrow back into her love for him; to stretch it like a covering over the span that separated now from then. He could read Kincaid's letter with impunity, clothed in the knowledge that he, the reader, was the man who had won, the writer the one who had lost.

Yet no such thoughts filled his mind by the time he had read to the end. It had a curiously humbling effect upon him. Here was one person who knew what he, her husband, must be feeling. The knowledge that Kincaid knew because he had been, perhaps still was in love with her now served to unite him to this man, as though there were kinship between them.

He wrote that he had met her recently when he had been into town. She had not mentioned this visit to her husband, but he thought nothing of that. The musician had said in his letter that he had seen her the last time he was playing with the Scottish Orchestra, and she had not mentioned that to her husband either.

He realised now, when he would never hear her voice again, how little she had mentioned to him. He was, he supposed, a particularly silent man: perhaps that was why she had attracted him so strongly, because she was everything he wasn't, with a quality of gaiety about her. But looking back now, he realised that for years past she must have conformed to his pattern.

He was absorbed by his work nothing else mattered to him, or had the smallest significance. His reputation was now international. One did not reach where he had reached without a concentration that annihilated, relinquished everything that did not bear on one's subject.

But while he was climbing to the top of his profession, what about her? Had his preoccupation, his silence, had a calcifying effect upon her love for him? He looked down at the sea of letters on his desk. Had she turned to others for the simplest of contacts that he, isolated by himself, had denied her?

You could look at a woman, sit at the same table with her, every day of your life, and not see her. That was what he had done. He had taken her as much for granted in his life as he took a piece of furniture in a room he used every day.

But she would understand: she had always understood. Understood what? That he loved her, although he had taken her for granted, that she was the background to his life, as necessary to him as the air he breathed. Because she knew him as no one else knew him, she must have known what he felt for her, what he would feel if she were taken from him. If only he could be sure that she knew that —

He must speak of her to some one, some one who had known her. Only thus could he feel in touch with her as he had been once upon a time. Kincaid — he was the one person he could contact. In some unexplained way he felt Kincaid came into this, because he could remember her, himself, the other fellow when they had all been young.

As he waited while the call was put through he realised how the intervening years had evened things out between him and the man he was now telephoning. No longer did he smart under a sense of inferiority. He and his one-time rival were equals now. Indeed, he was more than equal to him, he was his better — because she had chosen to be his wife.

Kincaid did not sound surprised to hear who was ringing him at that hour, but if had been he would not have revealed it. There were some things he would never need to learn, because they were part and parcel of him. The specialist heard his own voice stumble, he who was customarily incisive and to the point.

"Your letter . . . it was good of you to write as you did . . . I telephoned to say to you what I could not write." The sigh that escaped him reached the other prolonged and exaggerated. "I cannot tell you what I feel about what happened, but I know you understand. Despite his faltering, he found he could speak to this disembodied voice as he could never have spoken to him in person. He began to feel disembodied himself. "It all happened within a matter of hours, you see."

"Always those you love are young to die."

He understood, this man at the other end, understood as no one else could

"I did not know you had seen her so recently."

So anxious was he to reach what he was leading up to that he was unaware of the infinitesimal pause before the other replied.

"No? She did not mention it to you then?"

"No, but of course she wouldn't. I've always been so busy that I'm afraid I got out of the way of listening to the come and go of daily life. But you do think that she knew what I felt for her, don't you? That although perhaps I gave no sign it didn't mean that I didn't love her? If only I could be sure of that, what a difference it would make to me. This last time you saw her, for instance, did she — what I mean is

— well, did she let fall anything which made you know whether she were happy or unhapppy?"

Eternity yawned for him in chasm of a pause as the other remembered back.

"As a matter of fact, her last words to me were ——"

He had the feeling that Kincaid had the strongest reluctance to tell him.

"Yes?" he asked desperately. "What did she say to you?"

"There is only one man in my life. There will always only be one man."

His relief was such that only then did he realise how much had hung on this man's reply.

"She said that of me?" His grip tightened on the receiver as he waited for the joy of hearing it repeated.

But Kincaid's voice sounded remote, almost formal, as he replied, "These were her very words."

No wonder he had been reluctant to tell him what the woman he loved had said of him, her husband. Naturally he could not guess what her words meant to the man at the other end — only he knew that, because only he could feel as he felt now.

When he had rung off he returned to his desk. Although his unfrozen feelings hurt him with their pain, pain was better than that deadening numbness. You had to be alive to feel.

He sat far into the night reading the letters on his desk, piling each one he read on top of Susan's. As he must answer hers by hand so would he have to answer every single one. They were no longer letters of condolences. They were life-lines to his love.

MURIEL SPARK

The Black Madonna

When the Black Madonna was installed in the Church of the Sacred Heart the Bishop himself came to consecrate it. His long purple train was upheld by the two curliest of the choir. The day was favoured suddenly with thin October sunlight as he crossed the courtyard from the presbytery to the church, as the procession followed him chanting the Litany of the Saints: five priests in vestments of white heavy silk interwoven with glinting threads, four lay officials with straight red robes, then the confraternities and the tangled columns of the Mothers' Union.

The new town of Whitney Clay had a large proportion of Roman Catholics, especially among the nurses at the new hospital; and at the paper mills, too, there were many Catholics, drawn inland from Liverpool by the new housing estate; likewise, with the canning factories.

The Black Madonna had been given to the church by a recent convert. It was carved out of bog oak.

'They found the wood in the bog. Had been there hundreds of years. They sent for the sculptor right away by phone. He went over to Ireland and carved it there and then. You see, he had to do it while it was still wet.'

'Looks a bit like contemporary art.'

'Nah, that's not contemporary art, it's old-fashioned. If you'd ever seen contemporary work you'd *know* it was old-fashioned.'

'Looks like contemp —'

'It's old-*fashioned*. Else how'd it get sanctioned to be put up?'

'It's not so nice as the Immaculate Conception at Lourdes. That lifts you up.'

Everyone got used, eventually, to the Black Madonna with her square hands and straight carved draperies. There was a movement to dress it up in vestments, or at least a lace veil.

'She looks a bit gloomy, Father, don't you think?'

'No,' said the priest, 'I think it looks fine. If you start dressing it up in cloth you'll spoil the line.'

Sometimes people came from London especially to see the Black Madonna, and these were not Catholics; they were, said the priest, probably no religion at all, poor souls, though gifted with faculties. They came, as if to a museum, to see the line of the Black Madonna which must not be spoiled by vestments.

The new town of Whitney Clay had swallowed up the old village. One or two cottages with double dormer windows, an inn called The Tyger, a Methodist chapel and three small shops represented the village; the three shops were already threatened by the Council; the Methodists were fighting to keep their chapel. Only the double dormer cottages and the inn were protected by the Nation and so had to be suffered by the Town Planning Committee.

The town was laid out like geometry in squares, arcs (to allow for the by-pass) and isosceles triangles, breaking off, at one point, to skirt the old village which, from the aerial view, looked like a merry doodle on the page.

Manders Road was one side of a parallelogram of green-bordered streets. It was named after one of the founders of the canning concern, Manders' Figs in Syrup, and it comprised a row of shops and a long high block of flats named Cripps House after the late Sir Stafford Cripps who had laid the foundation stone. In flat twenty-two on the fifth floor of Cripps House lived Raymond and Lou Parker. Raymond Parker was a foreman at the motor works, and was on the management committee. He had been married for fifteen years to Lou, who was thirty-seven at the time that the miraculous powers of the Black Madonna came to be talked of.

Of the twenty-five couples who lived in Cripps House five were Catholics. All, except Raymond and Lou Parker, had children. A sixth family had recently been moved by the Council into one of the six-roomed houses because of the seven children besides the grandfather.

Raymond and Lou were counted lucky to have obtained their three-roomed flat although they had no children. People with children had priority; but their name had been on the waiting list for years, and some said Raymond had a pull with one of the Councillors who was a director of the motor works.

The Parkers were among the few tenants of Cripps House who owned a motor-car. They did not, like most of their neighbours, have a television receiver, from being childless they had been able to afford to expand themselves in the way of taste, so that their habits differed slightly and their amusements considerably, from those of their neighbours. The Parkers went to the pictures only when the *Observer* had praised the film; they considered television not their sort of thing; they adhered to their religion; they voted Labour; they believed that the twentieth century was the best so far; they assented to the doctrine of original sin; they frequently applied the word 'Victorian' to ideas and people they did not like — for instance, when a local Town Councillor resigned his office Raymond said, 'He had to go. He's Victorian. And far too young for the job'; and Lou said Jane Austen's books were too Victorian; and anyone who opposed the abolition of capital punishment was Victorian. Raymond took the *Reader's Digest,* a magazine called *Motoring* and the *Catholic Herald.* Lou took the *Queen, Woman's Own* and *Life.* Their daily paper was the *News Chronicle.* They read two books apiece each week. Raymond preferred travel books; Lou liked novels.

For the first five years of their married life they had been worried about not having children. Both had submitted themselves to medical tests as a result of which Lou had a course of injections. These were unsuccessful. It had been a disappointment since both came from large sprawling Catholic families. None of their married brothers and sisters had less than three children. One of Lou's sisters, now widowed, had eight; they sent her a pound a week.

Their flat in Cripps House had three rooms and a kitchen. All round them their neighbours were saving up to buy houses. A council flat, once obtained, was a mere platform in space to further the progress of the rocket. This ambition was not shared by Raymond and Lou; they were not only content, they were delighted, with these civic chambers, and indeed took something of an aristocratic view of them, not without a self-conscious feeling of being free, in this particular, from the prejudices of that middle class to which they as good as belonged. 'One day,' said Lou, 'it will be the thing to live in a council flat.'

They were eclectic as to their friends. Here, it is true, they differed slightly from each other. Raymond was for inviting the Ackleys to meet the Farrells. Mr Ackley was an accountant at the Electricity Board. Mr and Mrs Farrell were respectively a sorter at Manders' Figs in Syrup and an usherette at the Odeon.

'After all,' argued Raymond, 'they're all Catholics.'

'Ah well,' said Lou, 'but now, their interests are different. The Farrells wouldn't know what the Ackleys were talking about. The Ackleys like politics. The Farrells like to tell jokes. I'm not a snob, only sensible.'

'Oh, please yourself.' For no one could call Lou a snob, and everyone knew she was sensible.

Their choice of acquaintance was wide by reason of their active church membership: that is to say, they were members of various guilds and confraternities. Raymond was a sidesman, and he also organized the weekly football lottery in aid of the Church Decoration Fund. Lou felt rather out of things when the Mothers' Union met and had special Masses, for the Mothers' Union was the only group she did not qualify for. Having been a nurse before her marriage she was, however, a member of the Nurses' Guild.

Thus, most of their Catholic friends came from different departments of life. Others, connected with the motor works where Raymond was a foreman, were of different social grades to which Lou was more alive than Raymond. He let her have her way, as a rule, when it came to a question of which would mix with which.

A dozen Jamaicans were taken on at the motor works. Two came into Raymond's department. He invited them to the flat one evening to have coffee. They were unmarried, very polite and black. The quiet one was called Henry Pierce and the talkative one, Oxford St John. Lou, to Raymond's surprise and pleasure, decided that all their acquaintances, from top to bottom, must meet Henry and Oxford. All along he had known she was not a snob, only sensible, but he had rather feared she would consider the mixing of their new black and their old white friends not sensible.

'I'm glad you like Henry and Oxford,' he said. 'I'm glad we're able to introduce them to so many people.' For the dark pair had, within a month, spent nine evenings at Cripps House; they had met accountants, teachers, packers and sorters. Only Tina Farrell, the usherette, had not seemed to understand the quality of these occasions: 'Quite nice chaps, them darkies, when you get to know them.'

'You mean Jamaicans,' said Lou. 'Why shouldn't they be nice? They're no different from anyone else.'

'Yes, yes, that's what I mean,' said Tina.

'We're all equal,' stated Lou. 'Don't forget there are black Bishops.'

'Jesus, I never said we were the equal of a Bishop,' Tina said, very bewildered.

'Well, don't call them darkies.'

Sometimes, on summer Sunday afternoons Raymond and Lou took their friends for a run in their car, ending up at a riverside road-house. The first time they turned up with Oxford and Henry they felt defiant; but there were no objections, there was no trouble at all. Soon the dark pair ceased to be a novelty. Oxford St John took up with a pretty red-haired book-keeper, and Henry Pierce, missing his companion, spent more of his time at the Parkers' flat. Lou and Raymond had planned to spend their two weeks' summer holiday in London. 'Poor Henry,' said Lou. 'He'll miss us.'

Once you brought him out he was not so quiet as you thought at first. Henry was twenty-four, desirous of knowledge in all fields, shining very much in eyes, skin, teeth, which made him seem all the more eager. He called out the maternal in Lou, and to some extent the avuncular in Raymond. Lou used to love him when he read out lines from his favourite poems which he had copied into an exercise book.

> *Haste thee, nymph, and bring with thee*
> *Jest and youthful jollity,*
> *Sport that . . .*

Lou would interrupt: 'You should say jest, jollity — not yest, yollity.'

'Jest,' he said carefully. 'And laughter holding both his sides,' he continued. *'Laughter* — hear that, Lou? — *laughter.* That's what the human race was made for. Those folks that go round gloomy, Lou, they . . .'

Lou loved this talk. Raymond puffed his pipe benignly. After Henry had gone Raymond would say what a pity it was such an intelligent young fellow had lapsed. For Henry had been brought up in a Roman Catholic mission. He had, however, abandoned religion. He was fond of saying, 'The superstition of today is the science of yesterday.'

'I can't allow,' Raymond would say, 'that the Catholic Faith is superstition. I can't allow that.'

'He'll return to the Church one day' — this was Lou's contribution, whether Henry was present or not. If she said it in front of Henry he would give her an angry look. These were the only occasions when Henry lost his cheerfulness and grew quiet again.

Raymond and Lou prayed for Henry, that he might regain his faith. Lou said her rosary three times a week before the Black Madonna.

'He'll miss us when we go on our holidays.'

Raymond telephoned to the hotel in London. 'Have you a single room for a young gentleman accompanying Mr and Mrs Parker?' He added, 'a coloured gentleman.' To his pleasure a room was available, and to his relief there was no objection to Henry's colour.

They enjoyed their London holiday, but it was somewhat marred by a visit to that widowed sister of Lou's to whom she allowed a pound a week towards the rearing of her eight children. Lou had not seen her sister Elizabeth for nine years.

They went to her one day towards the end of their holiday. Henry sat at the back of the car beside a large suitcase stuffed with old clothes for Elizabeth. Raymond at the wheel kept saying, 'Poor Elizabeth — eight kids,' which irritated Lou, though she kept her peace.

Outside the Underground station at Victoria Park, where they stopped to ask the way, Lou felt a strange sense of panic. Elizabeth lived in a very downward quarter of Bethnal Green, and in the past nine years since she had seen her Lou's memory of the shabby ground-floor rooms with their peeling walls and bare boards, had made a kinder nest for itself. Sending off the postal order to her sister each week she had gradually come to picture the habitation at Bethnal Green in an almost monastic light, it would be bare but well-scrubbed, spotless, and shining with Brasso and holy poverty. The floor boards gleamed. Elizabeth was grey-haired, lined, but neat. The children were well behaved, sitting down betimes to their broth in two rows along an almost refectory table. It was not till they had reached Victoria Park that Lou felt the full force of the fact that everything would be different from what she had imagined. 'It may have gone down since I was last there,' she said to Raymond who had never visited Elizabeth before.

'What's gone down?'

'Poor Elizabeth's place.'

Lou had not taken much notice of Elizabeth's dull little monthly letters, almost illiterate, for Elizabeth, as she herself always said, was not much of a scholar.

James is at another job I hope thats the finish of the bother I had my blood pressure there was a Health Visitor very nice. Also the assistance they sent my Dinner all the time and for the kids at home they call it meals on Wheels. I pray to the Almighty that James is well out of his bother he never lets on at sixteen their all the same never open his mouth but Gods eyes are not shut. Thanks for P.O. you will be rewarded your affect sister Elizabeth.

Lou tried to piece together in her mind the gist of nine years' such letters. James was the eldest; she supposed he had been in trouble.

'I ought to have asked Elizabeth about young James,' said Lou. 'She wrote to me last year that he was in a bother, there was talk of him being sent away, but I didn't take it in at the time, I was busy.'

'You can't take everything on your shoulders,' said Raymond. 'You do very well by Elizabeth.' They had pulled up outside the house where Elizabeth lived on the ground floor. Lou looked at the chipped paint, the dirty windows and torn grey-white curtains and was reminded with startling clarity of her hopeless childhood in Liverpool from which, miraculously, hope had lifted her, and had come true, for the nuns had got her that job; and she had trained as a nurse among white-painted beds, and white shining walls, and tiles, hot water everywhere, and Dettol without stint. When she had first married she had wanted all white-painted furniture that you could wash and liberate from germs; but Raymond had been for oak, he did not understand the pleasure of hygiene and new enamel paint, for his upbringing had been orderly, he had been accustomed to a lounge suite and autumn tints in the front room all his life. And now Lou stood and looked at the outside of Elizabeth's place and felt she had gone right back.

On the way back to the hotel Lou chattered with relief that it was over. 'Poor Elizabeth, she hasn't had much of a chance. I liked little Francis, what did you think of little Francis, Ray?

Raymond did not like being called Ray, but he made no objection for he knew that Lou had been under a strain. Elizabeth had not been very pleasant. She had expressed admiration for Lou's hat, bag, gloves and shoes which were all navy blue, but she had used an accusing tone. The house had been smelly and dirty. 'I'll show you round,' Elizabeth had said in a tone of mock refinement, and they were forced to push through a dark narrow passage behind her skinny form till they came to the big room where the children slept. A row of old iron beds each with a tumble of dark blanket rugs, no sheets. Raymond was indignant at the sight and hoped that Lou was not feeling upset. He knew very well Elizabeth had a decent living income from a number of public sources, and was simply a slut, one of those who would not help themselves.

'Ever thought of taking a job, Elizabeth?' he had said, and immediately realized his stupidity. But Elizabeth took her advantage. What d'you mean? *I'm* not going to leave my kids in no nursery. *I'm* not going to send them to no home. What kids need these days is a good home-life and that's what they get.' And she added, 'God's eyes are not shut,' in a tone which was meant for him, Raymond, to get at him for doing well in life.

Raymond distributed half-crowns to the younger children and deposited on the table half-crowns for those who were out playing in the street.

'Goin' already?' said Elizabeth in her tone of reproach. But she kept eyeing Henry with interest, and the reproachful tone was more or less a routine affair.

'You from the States?' Elizabeth said to Henry.

Henry sat on the edge of his sticky chair and answered, no, from Jamaica, while Raymond winked at him to cheer him.

'During the war there was a lot of boys like you from the States,' Elizabeth said, giving him a sideways look.

Henry held out his hand to the second youngest child, a girl of seven, and said, 'Come talk to me.'

The child said nothing, only dipped into the box of sweets which Lou had brought.

'Come talk,' said Henry.

Elizabeth laughed. 'If she does talk you'll be sorry you ever asked. She's got a tongue in her head, that one. You should hear her cheeking up to the teachers.' Elizabeth's bones jerked with laughter among her loose clothes. There was a lopsided double bed in the corner, and beside it a table cluttered with mugs, tins, a comb and brush, a number of hair curlers, a framed photograph of the Sacred Heart, and also Raymond noticed what he thought erroneously to be a box of contraceptives. He decided to say nothing to Lou about this; he was quite sure she must have observed other things which he had not; possibly things of a more distressing nature.

Lou's chatter on the way back to the hotel had a touch of hysteria. 'Raymond, dear,' she said in her most chirpy West End voice, 'I simply *had* to give the poor dear *all* my next week's housekeeping money. We shall have to starve, darling, when we get home. That's *simply* what we shall have to do.'

'O.K.,' said Raymond

'I ask you,' Lou shrieked, 'what else could I do, what *could* I do?'

'Nothing at all,' said Raymond, 'but what you've done.'

'My own *sister*, my dear,' said Lou; 'and did you see the way she had her hair bleached? — All streaky, and she used to have a lovely head of hair.'

'I wonder if she tries to raise herself?' said Raymond. 'With all those children she could surely get better accommodation if only she —'

'That sort,' said Henry, leaning forward from the back of the car, 'never moves. It's the slum mentality, man. Take some folks I've seen back home —'

'There's no comparison,' Lou snapped suddenly, 'this is quite a different case.'

Raymond glanced at her in surprise; Henry sat back, offended. Lou was thinking wildly, what a cheek *him* talking like a snob. At least Elizabeth's white.

Their prayers for the return of faith to Henry Pierce were so far answered in that he took a tubercular fit which was followed by a religious one. He was sent off to a sanatorium in Wales with a promise from Lou and Raymond to visit him before Christmas. Meantime, they applied themselves to Our Lady for the restoration of Henry's health.

Oxford St John, whose love affair with the red-haired girl had come to grief, now frequented their flat, but he could never quite replace Henry in their affections. Oxford was older and less refined than Henry. He would stand in front of the glass in their kitchen and tell himself, 'Man, you just a big black bugger.' He kept referring to himself as black, which of course he was, Lou thought, but it was not the thing to say. He stood in the doorway with his arms and smile thrown wide: 'I am black but comely, O ye daughters of Jerusalem.' And once, when Raymond was out, Oxford brought the conversation round to that question of being black *all over*, which made Lou very uncomfortable and she kept looking at the clock and dropped stitches in her knitting.

Three times a week when she went to the black Our Lady with her rosary to ask for the health of Henry Pierce, she asked also that Oxford St John would get another job in another town, for she did not like to make objections, telling her feelings to Raymond; there were no objections to make that you could put your finger on. She could not very well complain that Oxford was common; Raymond despised snobbery, and so did she, it was a very delicate question. She was amazed when, within three weeks, Oxford announced that he was thinking of looking for a job in Manchester.

Lou said to Raymond, 'Do you know, there's something *in* what they say about the bog-oak statue in the church.'

'There may be,' said Raymond. 'People say so.'

Lou could not tell him how she had petitioned the removal of Oxford St John. But when she got a letter from Henry Pierce to say he was improving, she told Raymond, 'You see, we asked for Henry to get back the Faith, and so he did. Now we ask for his recovery and he's improving.'

'He's having good treatment at the sanatorium,' Raymond said. But he added, 'Of course we'll have to keep up the prayers.' He himself, thought not a rosary man, knelt before the Black Madonna every Saturday evening after Benediction to pray for Henry Pierce.

Whenever they saw Oxford he was talking of leaving Whitney Clay. Raymond said, 'He's making a big mistake going to Manchester. A big place can be very lonely. I hope he'll change his mind.'

'He won't,' said Lou, so impressed was she now by the powers of the Black Madonna. She was good and tired of Oxford St John with his feet up on her cushions, and calling himself a nigger.

'We'll miss him,' said Raymond, 'he's such a cheery big soul.'

'We will,' said Lou. She was reading the parish magazine, which she seldom did, although she was one of the voluntary workers who sent them out, addressing hundreds of wrappers every month. She had vaguely noticed, in previous numbers, various references to the Black Madonna, how she had granted this or that favour. Lou had heard that people sometimes came from neighbouring parishes to pray at the Church of the Sacred Heart because of the statue. Some said they came from all over England, but whether this was to admire the art-work or to pray, Lou was not sure. She gave her attention to the article in the parish magazine:

While not wishing to make excessive claims... many prayers answered and requests granted to the Faithful in an exceptional way... two remarkable cures effected, but medical evidence is, of course, still in reserve, a certain lapse of time being necessary to ascertain permanency of cure. The first of these cases was a child of twelve suffering from leukaemia... The second... While not desiring to create a *cultus* where none is due, we must remember it is always our duty to honour Our Blessed Lady, the dispenser of all graces, to whom we owe . . .

Another aspect of the information received by the Father Rector concerning our 'Black Madonna' is one pertaining to childless couples of which three cases have come to his notice. In each case the couple claim to have offered constant devotion to the 'Black Madonna,' and in two of the cases specific requests were made for the favour of a child. In *all* cases the prayers were answered. The proud parents . . . It should be the loving duty of every parishioner to make a special thanksgiving. . . . The Rather Rector will be grateful for any further information. . . .

'Look, Raymond,' said Lou. 'Read this.'

They decided to put in for a baby to the Black Madonna.

The following Saturday, when they drove to the church for Benediction, Lou jangled her rosary. Raymond pulled up outside the church. 'Look here, Lou,' he said, 'do you want a baby in any case?' — for he partly thought she was only putting the Black Madonna to the test — 'Do you want a child, after all these years?'

This was a new thought to Lou. She considered her neat flat and tidy routine, the entertaining with her good coffee cups, the weekly papers and the library books, the tastes which they would not have been able to cultivate had they had a family of children. She thought of her nice young looks which everyone envied, and her freedom of movement.

'Perhaps we should try,' she said. 'God won't give us a child if we aren't meant to have one.'

'We have to make some decisions for ourselves,' he said. 'And to tell you the truth if *you* don't want a child, *I* don't.'

'There's no harm in praying for one,' she said.

'You have to be careful what you pray for,' he said. 'You mustn't tempt Providence.'

She thought of her relatives, and Raymond's, all married with children. She thought of her sister Elizabeth with her eight, and remembered that one who cheeked up to the teachers, so pretty and sulky and shabby, and she remembered the fat baby Francis sucking his dummy and clutching Elizabeth's bony neck.

'I don't see why I shouldn't have a baby,' said Lou.

Oxford St John departed at the end of the month. He promised to write, but they were not surprised when weeks passed and they had no word. 'I don't suppose we shall ever hear from him again,' said

Lou. Raymond thought he detected satisfaction in her voice, and would have thought she was getting snobbish as women do as they get older, losing sight of their ideals, had she not gone on to speak of Henry Pierce. Henry had written to say he was nearly cured, but had been advised to return to the West Indies.

'We must go and see him,' said Lou. 'We promised. What about Sunday after next?'

'O.K.,' said Raymond.

It was the Saturday before that Sunday when Lou had her first sick turn. She struggled out of bed to attend Benediction, but had to leave suddenly during the service and was sick behind the church in the presbytery yard. Raymond took her home, though she protested against cutting out her rosary to the Black Madonna.

'After only six weeks!' she said, and she could hardly tell whether her sickness was due to excitement or nature. 'Only six weeks ago,' she said — and her voice had a touch of its old Liverpool —'did we go to that Black Madonna and the prayer's been answered, see.'

Raymond looked at her in awe as he held the bowl for her sickness. 'Are you sure?' he said.

She was well enough next day to go to visit Henry in the sanatorium. He was fatter and, she thought, a little coarser: and tough in his manner, as if once having been nearly disembodied he was not going to let it happen again. He was leaving the country very soon. He promised to come and see them before he left. Lou barely skimmed through his next letter before handing it over to Raymond.

Their visitors, now, were ordinary white ones. 'Not so colourful,' Raymond said, 'as Henry and Oxford were.' Then he looked embarrassed lest he should seem to be making a joke about the word coloured.

'Do you miss the niggers?' said Tina Farrell, and Lou forgot to correct her.

Lou gave up most of her church work in order to sew and knit for the baby. Raymond gave up the *Reader's Digest*. He applied for promotion and got it; he became a departmental manager. The flat was now a waiting-room for next summer, after the baby was born, when they would put down the money for a house. They hoped for one of the new houses on a building site on the outskirts of the town.

'We shall need a garden,' Lou explained to her friends. 'I'll join the Mothers' Union,' she thought. Meantime the spare bedroom was turned into a nursery. Raymond made a cot, regardless that some of the neighbours complained of the hammering. Lou prepared a cradle, trimmed it with frills. She wrote to her relatives; she wrote to Elizabeth, sent her five pounds, and gave notice that there would be no further weekly payments, seeing that they would now need every penny.

'She doesn't require it, any way,' said Raymond. 'The Welfare State looks after people like Elizabeth.' And he told Lou about the contraceptives he thought he had seen on the table by the double bed. Lou became very excited about this. 'How did you know they were contraceptives? What did they look like? Why didn't you tell me before? What a cheek, calling herself a Catholic, do you think she has a man, then?'

Raymond was sorry he had mentioned the subject.

'Don't worry, dear, don't upset yourself, dear.'

'And she told me she goes to Mass every Sunday, and all the kids go excepting James. No wonder he's got into trouble with an example like that. I might have known, with her peroxide hair. A pound a week I've been sending up to now, that's fifty-two pounds a year. I would never have done it, calling herself a Catholic with birth control by her bedside.'

'Don't upset yourself, dear.'

Lou prayed to the Black Madonna three times a week for a safe delivery and a healthy child. She gave her story to the Father Rector who announced it in the next parish magazine. 'Another case has come to light of the kindly favour of our "Black Madonna" towards a childless couple. . . .' Lou recited her rosary before the statue until it was difficult for her to kneel, and, when she stood, could not see her feet. The Mother of God with her black bog-oaken drapery, her high black cheekbones and square hands looked more virginal than ever to Lou as she stood counting her beads in front of her stomach.

She said to Raymond, 'If it's a girl we must have Mary as one of the names. But not the first name, it's too ordinary.'

'Please yourself, dear,' said Raymond. The doctor had told him it might be a difficult birth.

'Thomas, if it's a boy,' she said, 'after my uncle. But if it's a girl I'd like something fancy for a first name.'

He thought, Lou's slipping, she didn't used to say that word, fancy.

'What about Dawn?' she said. 'I like the sound of Dawn. Then Mary for a second name. Dawn Mary Parker, it sounds sweet.'

'Dawn! That's not a Christian name,' he said. Then he told her, 'Just as you please, dear.'

'Or Thomas Parker,' she said.

She had decided to go into the maternity wing of the hospital like everyone else. But near the time she let Raymond change her mind, since he kept saying, 'At your age, dear, it might be more difficult than for the younger women. Better book a private ward, we'll manage the expense.'

In fact, it was a very easy birth, a girl. Raymond was allowed in to see Lou in the late afternoon. She was half asleep. 'The nurse will take you to see the baby in the nursery ward,' she told him. 'She's lovely, but terribly red.'

'They're always red at birth,' said Raymond.

He met the nurse in the corridor. 'Any chance of seeing the baby? My wife said . . .'

She looked flustered. 'I'll get the Sister,' she said.

'Oh, I don't want to give any trouble, only my wife said —'

'That's all right. Wait here, Mr Parker.'

The Sister appeared, a tall grave woman. Raymond thought her to be short-sighted for she seemed to look at him fairly closely before she bade him follow her.

The baby was round and very red, with dark curly hair.

'Fancy her having hair. I thought they were born bald,' said Raymond.

'They sometimes have hair at birth,' said the Sister.

'She's very red in colour.' Raymond began comparing his child with those in the other cots. 'Far more so than the others.'

'Oh, that will wear off.'

Next day he found Lou in a half-stupor. She had been given a strong sedative following an attack of screaming hysteria. He sat by her bed, bewildered. Presently a nurse beckoned him from the door. 'Will you have a word with Matron?'

'Your wife is upset about her baby,' said the matron. 'You see, the colour. She's a beautiful baby, perfect. It's a question of the colour.'

'I noticed the baby was red,' said Raymond, 'but the nurse said —'

'Oh, the red will go. It changes, you know. But the baby will certainly be brown, if not indeed black, as indeed we think she will be. A beautiful healthy child.'

'Black?' said Raymond.

'Yes, indeed we think so, indeed I must say, certainly so,' said the matron. 'We did not expect your wife to take it so badly when we told her. We've had plenty of dark babies here, but most of the mothers expect it.'

'There must be a mix-up. You must have mixed up the babies,' said Raymond.

'There's no question of mix-up,' said the matron sharply. 'We'll soon settle that. We've had some of *that* before.'

'But neither of us are dark,' said Raymond. 'You've seen my wife. You see me —'

'That's something you must work out for yourselves. I'd have a word with the doctor if I were you. But whatever conclusion you come to, please don't upset your wife at this stage. She has already refused to feed the child, says it isn't hers, which is ridiculous.'

'Was it Oxford St John?' said Raymond.

'Raymond, the doctor told you not to come here upsetting me. I'm feeling terrible.'

'Was it Oxford St John?'

'Clear out of here, you swine, saying things like that.'

He demanded to be taken to see the baby, as he had done every day for a week. The nurses were gathered round it, neglecting the squalling whites in the other cots for the sight of their darling black. She was indeed quite black, with a woolly crop and tiny negroid nostrils. She had been baptized that morning, though not in her parents' presence. One of the nurses had stood as god-mother.

The nurses dispersed in a flurry as Raymond approached. He looked hard at the baby. It looked back with its black button eyes. He saw the name-tab round its neck, 'Dawn Mary Parker.'

He got hold of a nurse in the corridor. 'Look here, you just take that name Parker off that child's neck. The name's not Parker, it isn't my child.'

The nurse said, 'Get away, we're busy.

'There's just a *chance*,' said the doctor to Raymond, 'that if there's been black blood in your family or your wife's, it's coming out now. It's a very long chance. I've never known it happen in my experience, but I've heard of cases, I could read them up.'

'There's nothing like that in my family,' said Raymond. He thought of Lou, the obscure Liverpool antecedents. The parents had died before he had met Lou.

'It could be several generations back,' said the doctor.

Raymond went home, avoiding the neighbours who would stop him to inquire after Lou. He rather regretted smashing up the cot in his first fury. That was something low coming out in him. But again, when he thought of the tiny black hands of the baby with their pink fingernails he did not regret smashing the cot.

He was successful in tracing the whereabouts of Oxford St John. Even before he heard the result of Oxford's blood test he said to Lou, 'Write and ask your relations if there's been any black blood in the family.'

'Write and ask *yours*,' she said.

She refused to look at the black baby. The nurses fussed round it all day, and came to report its progress to Lou.

'Pull yourself together, Mrs Parker, she's a lovely child.'

'You must care for your infant,' said the priest.

'You don't know what I'm suffering,' Lou said.

'In the name of God,' said the priest, 'if you're a Catholic Christian you've got to expect to suffer.'

'I can't go against my nature,' said Lou. 'I can't be expected to —'

Raymond said to her one day in the following week, 'The blood tests are all right, the doctor says.'

What do you mean, all right?'

'Oxford's blood and the baby's don't tally, and —'

'Oh, shut up,' she said. 'The baby's black and your blood tests can't make it white.'

'No,' he said. He had fallen out with his mother, through his inquiries whether there had been coloured blood in his family. 'The doctor says,' he said, 'that these black mixtures sometimes occur in seaport towns. It might have been generations back.'

'One thing,' said Lou. 'I'm not going to take that child back to the flat.'

'You'll have to,' he said.

Elizabeth wrote her a letter which Raymond intercepted:

'Dear Lou Raymond is asking if we have any blacks in the family well thats funny you have a coloured God is not asleep. There was that Flinn cousin Tommy of Liverpool he was very dark they put down to the past a nigro off a ship that would be before our late Mothers Time God rest her soul she would turn in her grave you should have kept up your bit to me whats a pound a Week to you. It was on our fathers side the colour and Mary Flinn you remember at the dairy was dark remember her hare was like nigro hare it must be back in the olden days the nigro some ancestor but it is only nature. I thank the almighty it has missed my kids and your hubby must think it was that nigro you was showing off when you came to my place. I wish you all best as a widow with kids you should send my money as per usual your affect sister Elizabeth.'

'I gather from Elizabeth,' said Raymond to Lou, 'that there *was* some element of colour in your family. Of course, you couldn't be expected to know about it. I do think, though, that some kind of record should be kept.'

'Oh, shut *up*,' said Lou. 'The baby's black and nothing can make it white.'

Two days before Lou left the hospital she had a visitor, although she had given instructions that no one except Raymond should be let in to see her. This lapse she attributed to the nasty curiosity of the nurses, for it was Henry Pierce come to say good-bye before embarkation. He stayed less than five minutes.

'Why, Mrs Parker, your visitor didn't stay long,' said the nurse.

'No, I soon got rid of him. I thought I made it clear to you that I didn't want to see anyone. You shouldn't have let him in.'

'Oh, sorry Mrs Parker, but the young gentleman looked so upset when we told him so. He said he was going abroad and it was his last chance, he might never see you again. He said, "How's the baby?", and we said, "Tip top."'

'I know what's in your mind,' said Lou. 'But it isn't true. I've got blood tests.'

'Oh, Mrs Parker, Oh wouldn't suggest for a minute . . .'

'She must have went with one of they niggers that used to come.'

Lou could never be sure if that was what she heard from the doorways and landings as she climbed the stairs of Cripps House, the neighbours hushing their conversation as she approached.

'I can't take to the child. Try as I do, I simply can't even like it.'

'Nor me,' said Raymond. 'Mind you, if it was anyone else's child I would think it was all right. It's just the thought of it being mine, and people thinking it isn't.'

'That's just it,' she said.

One of Raymond's colleagues had asked him that day how his friends Oxford and Henry were getting on. Raymond had to look twice before he decided that the question was innocent. But one never knew. . . . Already Lou and Raymond had approached the adoption society. It was now only a matter of waiting for word.

'If that child was mine,' said Tina Farrell, 'I'd never part with her. I wish we could afford to adopt another. She's the loveliest little darkie in the world.'

'You wouldn't think so,' said Lou, 'if she really was yours. Imagine it for yourself, waking to find you've had a black baby that everyone thinks has a nigger for its father.'

'It *would* be a shock,' Tina said, and tittered.

'We've got blood tests,' said Lou quickly.

Raymond got a transfer to London. They got word about the adoption very soon.

'We've done the right thing,' said Lou. 'Even the priest had to agree with that, considering how strongly we felt against keeping the child.'

'Oh, he said it was a good thing?'

'No, not a *good* thing. In fact he said it would have been a good thing if we could have kept the baby. But failing that, we did the *right* thing. Apparently, there's a difference.'

JOAN LINGARD

An Edinburgh Lady
(from *The Prevailing Wind*)

Agnes Robertson comes to vist her daughter Janet, who has returned to Edinburgh with a small child but no husband.

Emptied trunks and a broken tea-chest stood in a pile against the wall, dwarfing the low room; clothes, books and toys lay strewn across the floor. Janet pushed a hank of hair out of her eyes and looked up to see her mother's feet come along behind the railings and stop at the gate.

Agnes Robertson descended the steps slowly, not trusting the smooth worn edges, trying each one tentatively with the sole of her soft suede shoe. A heather tweed skirt with two swinging pleats came into view, then a jacket with three purple buttons and a pale lilac jumper showing at the neck straddled by two rows of neat, unostentatious pearls. The face appeared at the window, and Janet realized with a shock that her mother was getting old.

Agnes Robertson picked her way through the various objects and seated herself on the edge of a springless chair. She accepted a cup of tea which she held on her lap with both hands. There was a dirty thumb mark on the side of the cup; after a few minutes she laid it aside without touching the tea. The place smelt. Her nostrils twitched, trying to discover what it was that was so offensive. She came to the conclusion that it was a collection of smells: fried food, stale tobacco smoke, dampness, cat. She made a mental note to bring a bottle of air-freshener the next time she came. She wiped her hands on her handkerchief and watched Sally with an air of wistfulness that made Janet want to scream. She had brought a plastic doll in a pink frilly dress but after a cursory glance the child had tossed it onto the bed in the recess, preferring the things on the floor.

'I thought you might have come to see me?'

'I meant to.' Janet poured herself another cup of half-cold tea. 'I've been working. I've not had time.' It was a lie: she could have gone when she was out on her canvassing rounds. Once she had walked along the road, hesitated with her hand on the gate, and turned away.

'This is a terrible place.' Agnes Robertson stared at the stove with its spewed porridge enamel and cracked mica windows. 'Surely you don't mean to live here?'.

Janet swallowed the remains of her tea. Of course she meant to live here. What else was she doing here? She meant to distemper the walls, put up new curtains, hang some pictures. . . . A bird was chirping on the railings and she thought she could smell burning leaves. Sally began to transfer the coal, lump by lump, from the bucket to the window sill. Agnes Robertson looked at the child and then at Janet.

'It doesn't matter,' Janet said. 'She's playing at shops.'

Agnes Robertson sighed. No, perhaps it didn't matter. The room was filthy anyway. This daughter of hers had never had much idea of cleanliness though she had been brought up in the same way as the others. Even as a child she had differed from the rest: she had fought with her father, roamed the streets after dark, came home with dirty hands, cut knees and an unsuitable vocabulary. In her teens she had been wayward and uncontrollable, she had refused to go to church, to tell them where she spent her time and most of the time she was at home she had locked herself in her room. What had gone wrong? What had made Janet so different? She had spent many sleepless nights pondering the question. Fergus blamed an eccentric old aunt on her side. Aunt Emily had been housekeeper to a retired civil servant from Rangoon but it was said she had done more than keep his house. Fergus said that Aunt Emily's wickedness had come out in Janet.

'It can't be healthy down here. I smelt the damp as I came into the hall. Why can't you live in a decent place?' She knew a woman, a member of her church, who had recently been left a widow and wanted to let part of her bungalow. She had declared herself willing to discuss terms with Janet. 'She remembers you, dear, when you were in the Guides. You cut her grass during Bob-a-Job week.'

'I'm no longer a Girl Guide.'

'Consider it, please, Janet. It's a nice house and there's a big garden for Sally to play in.'

Janet considered the idea and rejected it at once. Her mother tried to reason with her but, as she said to Fiona afterwards, it was impossible to make Janet see reason once she had made up her mind about something. At the end of it all she said that Janet was stubborn and did not deserve sympathy, then she wept. Janet, although she had anticipated the tears from the moment she saw her mother's legs come down the steps, was surprised and uncomfortable.

Agnes Robertson soon had herself under control again. She dabbed her eyes and smiled bravely at her daughter. In the silence that followed Janet raked desperately round in her mind for something to talk about. The subject scarcely mattered: it was only to mask the blankness. She started to talk about a book she had read, talking quickly and animatedly. Her mother stared past her with glassy eyes.

'You should read it, mother. It's very evocative. You went to Bruges for your honeymoon, didn't you? I could write down the title for you.'

'Do you remember Betty Parker?'

Janet started. 'Betty Parker?'

'She married Bob Morrison. I met her the other day. She has two lovely children and a house on the Braids. Bob's got a good job, straight in line to be managing director.'

'I'll write down the name of this book . . .'

'I've had to sack my daily woman. She would bring her two-year-old child with her. He had dirty habits. It was disgusting — stains on the carpet and pools on the linoleum. I warned her several times but it was no good. She had to go.'

Janet began to tear an empty cigarette packet into strips.

'It's so difficult to get help these days, and they ask three and sixpence an hour plus bus fares. I can remember when you and Fiona were babies . . .'

Janet tore the strips into small pieces like confetti.

'Of course they can get big money in the factories now. People like me can't hope to compete. It's perfectly true that it's our class that's been hit the hardest. Before the war . . .'

There was a clatter of feet on the steps outside. Janet swivelled round to see Khalil's brown face pressed against the window.

He came in and shook hands politely with Agnes Robertson before settling himself on the settee.

'I see you have a typewriter,' he said, prodding it with his foot. 'I have a friend who wishes to borrow one. I will bring him to meet you.'

of Khalil's friends wished to borrow something. Janet protested that she needed it herself. Khalil said that nevertheless he would bring his friend and they could discuss the matter. Agnes Robertson preserved a prim-lipped silence interspersed with quick vacant smiles; Sally sang over her black knobbly patterns; Khalil told them of a typewriter he had once owned — this Janet did not believe — which would only work in a downhill position. On fine summer days he would take it into the Queen's Park, lay it on a soft green slope high above the smoky tenement roofs and gently tap out love poems. 'Love poems to your city, madam,' he added with a little bow towards the skewered felt hat under which flickered another of those anxious smiles. 'Ah yes, on the few days of summer it is beautiful: sun on grey stones, the smell of grass, flowers . . . But in winter' — he shivered — 'the blood runs cold in my veins, the wind cuts me like a thin wire, I waken in the morning with icicles on my lashes and my breath freezes against the sheet. Soon it will be winter again. I feel it in my hands.' He stretched out his thin fingers, then linked them together behind his head. 'And yet I stay. Do you love your city, madam?'

A faint blush stained Agnes Robertson's powered cheeks and she looked away from the dark inquiring eyes as though she had been asked something vaguely obscene. The word 'love' was a difficult one for her. Janet had never heard her say she loved anyone or anything. She had often said: 'You know I'm very fond of you dear,' when she had meant something more.

'There are worse places to live,' she said, rearranging the pleats of her skirt.

'Yes indeed. I have lived in them all. Places where nothing ever freezes, where the sun beats hot all day on dry earth, where flowers push through the stones only to die, where are no sheets for the breath to freeze against. And places the sun never finds, where all is cold and green and grey.'

Agnes Robertson coughed and stole a glance at the wrist watch under her tweed cuff. 'Yes, we are fortunate here. We have no extremes. I must go, Janet, or I'll be late for your father's tea. It's been nice meeting you, Mr — er —'

'Khalil. Just Khalil.'

Janet walked up the steps with her mother.

'Who on earth is that? What rubbish he was talking! I know you've got to lead your own life and all that but I don't think it's good to have someone like him hanging round you. People start talking. I mean you've got to think of Sally too, haven't you? Poor wee mite. I'm sure he hasn't had a bath for a month: his neck looked filthy to me though of course it's hard to tell when his skin's that colour anyway. I don't know what your father would say. I wouldn't trust him if I were you. There's something shifty about those dark eyes.'

They embraced, skiffing one another's cheeks with their lips, caught for one moment into a feeling of pure tenderness where all judgments were suspended. Then they drew apart and the wind swirled between them. Agnes Robertson looked back from the corner to wave. Janet moved forward a step. She wanted to run after her and tell her that she would be all right, that Sally would be all right, that she need not carry her worry home with her in the bus; but she went back down the steps into the room where Sally and Khalil were playing with a red and yellow beach ball, where Muffin purred in the folds of a faded rug, where all the objects of her life lay on the floor like exhibits for all to see and pick over.

'You think I made a hit with your mother?' Khalil asked. 'No?' He flicked his tongue. 'At the top of the steps she said to you: "Beware, this man is dangerous"!' They laughed and Sally joined in. 'She is a nice lady even though she thinks I am not nice. A nice Edinburgh lady who is never late for her husband's tea.'

An Edinburgh lady who is loyal to her husband, who loves her children and worries over them during long sleepness nights, who goes faithfully to church, delivers its magazines along suburban roads, stands behind cake stalls with hands sticky from soft sweet icing and shiny red cherries, who works diligently sweeping the dirt from the corners of her house, whose tear-washed eyes betray a self-induced martyrdom of sadness; a wife and mother who has known what it is to be peacefully content with a fire at her feet and children sleeping in upstairs rooms but who has never known what it is to be wildly, deliriously happy and want to shout it out of every window up to the stars in the sky. An Edinburgh lady, standing now at a bus stop, feeling the chill of a September afternoon round her legs, waiting for the dark red bus to come and carry her back to her close-carpeted villa where she can take the long pin out of her hat and sit down beside a tidy hearth to drink tea from a thin cup that bears no mark of a dirty thumb. Standing on the pavement thinking. Thinking of her children. Ian: he is all right, he is in Canada, he has a good job, a nice home, a big car, he has two children whose eyes laugh out of their photographs making her sad. Fiona: she is all right, she has a good husband, a nice little house, fitted carpets, a wrought-iron gate, a car, she will soon have a child. Isobel: so far she is all right, she stays out late sometimes but not too late, she is not as openly defiant as Janet was, she is not as sensible as Fiona but not as irresponsible as Janet. There is hope yet for Isobel. Robert: he is not clever but he seems to be all right, he has some nice friends who will help him. But Janet: she has a child who has no father and whose face is black with coal dust, she has a dark dank basement where paper clings to the walls like burst blisters and chairs erupt their entrails onto stained coconut matting that hides the rottenness of the floor, where strange men lie on the sofa and say strange things. No, Janet is not all right, she has made a mess of her life . . .

'You look sad, Janet,' Khalil said. 'Are you?'

'Sad! Why should I be sad? Come on, help me clear up this mess. It looks like one of mother's jumble sales.'

JOAN URE

It's My Day for Leaving Home

"It isn't possible for me to leave home." The woman sat on her suitcase by the bus stop. She talked all the time.

"That's my trouble. It's not that they don't understand me. They don't but that doesn't matter. My trouble is I am the only one there is to understand *them*.

How it begins is that I am afraid. I am whimpering. I go about almost whimpering and I realise the time. I lead, as they say, a double life. And, because I lead a double life. I am ashamed of both halves of it. Not really.

I am not grumbling. Grumbling is irrelevant to my predicament.

Yet if had the money I could pay someone to look in and cook their good meals! I could say, All right. I have deprived them of my precious company but I do know that Mrs So-and-So is looking in and cooking their good meals, and being paid for it. But who is there to see that they eat their good meals in an atmosphere of sweetness and light? Who can be paid for that? Who is there to cheer them both up, to see that they do not quarrel in the middle of the soup thus depressing the salivatory releases and hastening the adrenalin response before the potatoes and the stew and vegetable have cooled enough to taste? Thus are they preparing their linings for the ulcers to follow in their riper years. I shall survive them both, I say to myself, as my grandmother did before me; and she did too.

Even if I had money to pay for a good cook for the main mid-day meal, or dinner as we call it, there would still be the chance of their cocking a snoot at — I know my own boys — Who should know them better than I do? Who but I nursed them, one to each breast, encouraging — incidentally — an upper arm muscular development in myself that an old-time steel worker

216

would have been proud of. They were heavy babies. Twins. And as unlike as their father and I were, put together.

Twin sons. Not that I ever lifted a hand to either of them. I think that there being two of them was their real safeguard. No wonder their father cracked under the strain but he had taken them through a good schooling and up to the University before he had realised his time had come. He had been replaced. Twice over. It was more than he could bear. For us it was fortunate that we'd had him so long, I said at the graveside. Everyone said I was wonderful. I was. I am still.

Our daughter, Janet, left us in the previous Spring. For me it was no loss. She borrowed my sheer tights. But my husband missed her. He wore the old-fashioned socks and suspenders. I tell her when I can bring myself to hold a pen that this is so. Janet, I say, your going killed your father. You might as well stay where you are, wherever that is. I have enough on my plate with your two strapping young brothers to love and cherish and good riddance. I send this *poste restante* with little hope that you have mended your ways, Janet. Not that it matters now since you have killed your father already and one crime is enough on your conscience at a time since you are not intent on any large-scale enterprise if I know you at all.

I have no doubt this is ture. She did not have a classical education. Neither had I but my eyeshadow wasn't good enough for her. Always made me feel older than my years. Her brothers on the other hand keep me young. We have a little giggle from time to time and there are two of them. Janet used to resent the educational advantages her brothers were given by right of their sexual advantages, although I admit they are too light-hearted when they are not quarrelling at meal times to be really intelligent. She was a clever girl and she brought a teacher home to explain this to her father who had not noticed it and therefore did not hold it against her. But she'll be getting married, I said — the teacher was wearing a very unfortunate spreadeagled tie. And what good will her cleverness do her? I added. It is what my own father said to me and I never quite forgave Janet's father for not saying the same to her so that I could make something out of it. What if she does marry? he said. It isn't a full-time job, is it? I felt I had been kicked in the teeth — Do you know the feeling? — Little *did he* know, I told Janet's father. There is no limit to

888888888888888888

the unspoken demands. There are unspoken demands made of a man too, he retorted. And not always unspoken either.

All he wanted was central heating! It was practically a necessity in the quadrant where we had moved by that time. We already had a fridge, which without the addition of central heating would have constituted a waste in the winters we suffer here, from time to time.

The father worked late that final year but I had always the boys to wind my wool for me. The central heating was paid for by the time the father was taken. I rent the front room upstairs to a very quiet couple who eat out and look too old to have children so I can't grumble. I don't believe in grumbling when I can get something done about it with a smile. In the advert I said all meals to be taken out. This, of course, cuts out small children without my having to lose sympathy with the man in the newsagent's by expressing what I mean in clearer terms. All meals out. And no washing.

When the boys are educated is time enough for girls. I tell them. Haven't they got each other? Isn't that incest? they say. And buggery forbye. No sodomy. They are very amusing, with their meaningless babble. They crosstalk like Morecambe and Wise. But some of the things they say make me glad that Janet has gone to the devil already and won't be corrupted by her brothers if they meet in an afterlife. I myself am too old to need corrupting but I read my Bible still to keep my mind open.

When the boys leave. They are always threatening me. What'll we do with our dear old cosy mother? Have her put away for her savings? They are only joking. What savings could *I* have? I playfully retort with a wink. It keeps them interested.

When they go. I'll take to a chair. I'll call Janet home. She can't have gone far. There's no guile in her. And she hasn't got the education. Haven't I given my life to her brothers?, I'll say. And lost a good husband towards their betterment.

Of course she'll come home as soon as I tell her I've taken to my chair. She'll not want to miss that. I know how I was at her age. How could *she* be any different? — No, — Meantime it is my day for leaving home. I've set everything over a low gas, of course. Simmering. What I do on my days for leaving home I am not prepared to divulge even to a stranger at this point. Leading a double life is something I have good reason to be ashamed of but I would not be without it. I should miss such a very great deal.

The bus came. The conductor helped the woman and I handed her case up to her. There was room for one only — with a case that size. I had to wait another twenty minutes. It was a Sunday service.

JESSIE KESSON

The Gowk

You'd felt pity for the Gowk, when yourself was young. And he was a boy — debarred. Clutching the school gates. Engrossed in the rough and tumble of the playground.

In manhood, this on-looking compulsion was still with him. But you had outgrown pity. Revulsion, tinged with apprehension, had taken its place. Until you thought about it, and realised that maybe, maybe the half-witted dribbling boy was now imprisoned grotesquely in the flesh of manhood.

But you didn't often think about that. And certainly the boys on the inside of the school playground never thought about it at all. Ettling always to get out, and within taunting distance of the Gowk.

> We saw Gowkit Jockie
> We saw him run awa
> We saw Gowkit Jockie
> And his nakit Bum and a'!

'Come *inside*, Rob! *And* you, Peter!' Jean Aitken shouted from her kitchen window.

'And stop tormenting the life out of that poor bloody Gowk!' Her father admonished, over her shoulder.

'That "Poor Gowk", as you call him,' Jean Aitken shrugged, 'should have been lockit up and away a long time ago. Terrifying the life out of the bairns.'

'Jockie's harmless enough,' the old man defended. 'He wouldna mind *them*. If they didna keep tormenting *him*!'

'You try telling Kate Riddrie that, Father, She's had her bellyful of the Gowk!'

'That's true enough,' her Father agreed. 'But not until the Gowk's father put the wedding ring on her hand!'

'And she's living to regret *that*!' Jean Aitken pointed out. 'Forbye, the Gowk was but a bairn, then. He's a man. Full-grown, now.'

'. . . and the older he grows, the worse he grows,' Kate Riddrie was complaining. 'He's started to abuse himself again. In broad daylight now! You'd think he hadn't got the wit for *that* even!'

'Maybe it's the instinct he's gotten,' Hugh Riddrie said. 'Even the brute beasts have gotten *that*.'

He had long since found that words failed to justify to himself the existence of his idiot son. And was beginning to discover that they failed even to protect him.

'I could *cope*,' his wife claimed. 'I could *cope* when he was young. But he's getting beyond me now.'

'You could never cope, Kate.' Hugh Riddrie reached above the dresser for his bonnet. 'You could only pretend he wasna there at all.'

'*Better*!' Kate Riddrie flared. 'Than pretending he wasn't an idiot *born*! But then, of course, he's *your* son.'

'So you aye keep reminding me, Kate.'

'And you *need* reminding! Do you know something?'

Hugh Riddrie shook his head. 'No. But I know you're just about to *tell* me something.'

'High time somebody did! You puzzle me,' Kate Riddrie admitted. 'Where other folk would try to keep a Gowk out of sight, *you* seem to like flaunting him in the face of the world.'

'Letting everybody share the *shame*, like, Kate?'

'I don't know what you'd call it!' Kate Riddrie snapped. 'But Nell Crombie was saying that she gets a red face, every time she puts her foot across this door!'

'She would,' Hugh Riddrie agreed. 'A very modest woman, Nell. Forever bragging that her man has never seen her nakit. In his life. Come to think of it,' he reflected, 'neither have you! What the hell is it makes you all so feared to *look*!'

'Decency!' Kate Riddrie said. 'Just plain *decency*!'

'Is *that* the name they've gotten for't? Ah well. I'm aye learning.'

'Not fast enough!' Kate Riddrie shouted, as he made for the door. '*Something's* got to be done. About the Gowk!'

'*Jockie*! *You mean.* Don't you Kate?' Hugh Riddrie spun round on his heel. '*Jockie!*'

'I meant *Jockie*. She flustered. 'It was just . . . it was just that everybody else calls him. . .'

'*THE GOWK*!' Hugh Riddrie finished the sentence for her. His quiet anger rising loud. Out of control. 'What do you suggest I do with him, Kate? *Lib* the poor bugger! The way I'd lib a young calf! Or would you have rather I had thrappled him at *birth*! With my bare hands! . . . . I've killed a calf for less. For just being shargered. . . .'

He could hear the school bairns taunting in the distance. Forcing his forefingers between his teeth, the shrillness of his whistle brought the taunting to a halt. And evoked the memories of the workers on their way home from the farm.

Old Riddrie. Whistling his Gowk again. Poor bugger. Other men had dogs to whistle for. Still. The man himself could be more sociable. Oh, but they minded on Riddrie, young. Another man then. Another man, altogether. That, of course, was before the Gowk was born. They themselves found little enough wrong with the Gowk! A pat on the head. A word in his ear, in the passing. A chew of tobacco slippit into his hand. And God! The Gowk was as happy as if he was in his right mind!

The shrill whistle halted their wives on their way back from the baker's van. Myth and memory blending in a confusion of truth.

The *minute* the Gowk was born. The *instant* the doctor set eyes on him . . .'Poultice Jimmy', as he was known. For he believed that a bread poultice could cure anything from a blind boil on your bottom to a broken heart. Though a poultice was of little use to the Gowk. But at least the doctor knew *something* was far wrong.

It was the midwife, of course, that had let the cat out of the bag. In *confidence*, mind you! Though she should never have done the like. Not in a job like hers. According to her, the doctor cursed and swore like a tinker when he set eyes on the Gowk. Roaring away at the midwife. To pay heed to the *mother* . . . The midwife swore to the day she died, that Poultice Jimmy *knew*. That he hopit, if they paid no attention to the bairn, it might just dwine away. But the Gowk had survived. Never a day's illness in his life. To the great regret of Mistress Riddrie the Second.

Still. There was nothing on the *women's* consciences. The Gowk, young, had never been debarred from *their* games as girls. Always willing to be 'poor Gracie' lying dead and in her grave. While they circled mournfully around him . . .

> We planted an Apple-tree
> Over his head
> Over his head
> We planted an Apple-tree . . .

. . .'Did you not hear me the *first* time? I'll comb your hair for you!' Jean Aitken threatened. 'If you don't come inside. And stop crying after that Gowk!'

'The Gowk was following our Liz.' Young Rob dodged his mother's upraised hand. 'Liz didn't see him. That's why Peter and me was shouting. They were going down Sue Tatt's road.'

'Sue Tatt's road!' The information halted Jean Aitken's enraged intention.

'There you are, then!' Dod Aitken laughed. '*There's* something for you to pick your teeth on! We know Sue's not all that particular. But even Sue Tatt would draw the line at the Gowk!'

'Are you *sure*, Rob?' his mother demanded.

'Positive!'

'*Certain*!' Peter added. Enjoying the effect the information had produced. 'We was trying to warn Liz. That's why we was shouting.'

'Our Liz,' Jean Aitken remembered. 'Should have been home by *this* time! The school bus gets in at the back of five. What on earth would Liz be seeking down Sue Tatt's road?'

Liz Aitken, herself, knew what she was seeking. But was not sure whether it was to be found.

'Sue Tatt will know what to do,' Chris Forbes had informed Liz. 'They say she's had more men than we've had suppers.'

That had sounded reassuring enough, last night. But then night had always brought reassurance to Liz. Expecting its very privacy to produce the dark, quiet miracle. And herself waking up. To confirm it, in the morning.

'I've *often* been late,' Chris had said. Sounding it like some special privilege rather than a comfort. 'Sometimes a whole *week* late.'

But then Chris Forbes had never been enticed up into the woods. How glad Liz had always been that she was herself. And not Chris Forbes. Never Chris Forbes. Now, she could have torn Chris right out of her skin. And gone inside it. To be safe. Like Chris was safe.

The rumours surrounding Sue Tatt were such that her house, itself, should have imparted an aura. Secret. Erotic. Its ordinariness disappointed Liz. But then the ordinariness of familiar things had begun to confuse her.

They should *know*. They should look *different*. The thing that had happened to herself should lie distorted, reflected in everything she set her eyes on. The skeleton of Rob's bike, stripped of essentials, lying out in the shed. The handles of her father's old plough, curving high above the nettles.

But it was her landscape that was the ultimate traitor. Lochnagar couldn't *stand* there. The Dee it should flood . . .

> The sky it should fall
> Since I am with bairn
> Unwedded and all . . . .

'This *friend* . . . this friend of yours, Liz' Sue Tatt asked. 'About how old would she be, then?'

'Sixteen-and-a-half. Nearly seventeen!' Liz extended her age, thinking somehow that it might advance her cause. 'Chris Forbes said you could help!'

'Oh, she *did*, did she? It could be nothing, Liz,' Sue Tatt concluded, transforming her irritation with Chris Forbes into an attempt to reassure Liz Aitken. 'That whiles happens to young lassies. Till they become regular, like.'

'But I *am* regular!' Liz protested. 'I've always been regular. Till *now*.'

'Oh Liz! Liz Aitken, Not *you*!'

The roof at home would have fallen in, under such an admission. It was the echo of its fall that sounded in Sue Tatt's voice.

'But you could *help*!' Liz urged. 'Everybody says . . .'

'Everything except their prayers, Liz. The thing is,' Sue stood pondering the paradox. 'Everybody knows the cure. Till the ailment happens. Syne, they know nothing. For *myself,*' Sue recollected, 'I just fell back on the old Penny Royal. Quinine. And the skin of my legs peeling off in a pail of hot water and mustard. Knowing they were all useless. But always just . .

hoping. Nothing ever budged mine an inch! Not until they were good and ready to be born. But cheer *up*, Liz! It *could* be a "wrong spy"! And I've had my share of them! You might just waken up the morn's morning to find that everything's just fine, again. And oh, whatten a fine feeling *that* is, Liz, stroking yourself under the sheet. As if your hands loved your body again. And the sweat pouring out of you. What relief, just. And thanking God. Even though you're not a Christian. Because you cannot think of anybody else to thank. And promising never to do it again. Not as long as you live . . . But of course you'll do it again, Liz!' Sue Tatt bent towards her, laughing. Pressing her hands on Liz's shoulders, as if they might leap up, and dance together, to a bright reel of Sue's composing. 'Again. And again, Liz! And it will be *right* then. And fine. For some lad will have *wedded* you! There's no chance of *this* lad wedding you?' Sue asked, as if the music itself had ended, and the bright bubble of hope drifted high up. Out of mind's reach.

'*None*!' That was a certainty. And Liz merely confirmed it. 'He's sitting his Highers,' she explained, 'and I'm trying for a Bursary. I'm going to the University. My mother's *set* on that. And my father will kill me. You'll not tell!' she urged. For, although hope had gone, secrecy still seemed essential. 'You'll never tell.'

'I'll not tell,' Sue Tatt promised. 'But you should, Liz. Tell your mother. And tell quick! Before other folk get in there first. That's what "gets" mothers. Not having the time to get their faces ready. To look on the world again.'

'It's my *father*!' Liz rose to go. 'He'll kill me. When he finds out.'

'I doubt that, Liz, I very much doubt that!'

'You don't know my father.'

Liz Aitken could well be right, Sue Tatt thought, as she watched Liz turn the bend of the road. But still Sue doubted. It was with the *mothers* of the parish that she had a mere 'nodding acquaintance'.

'A fine night, again, Jockie!' Sue Tatt cried out to the Gowk, as he shambled past her gate. Poor silly creature, he wouldn't understand a word she was saying. But he might just know that somebody was speaking to him. 'Another fine night again, Jockie!'

The brambles down in the King's Howe were always the first to ripen. Liz Aitken stood amongst the bushes, caught up once more in a deceptive sense of security. The taste of childhood on her tongue. The colour of it staining her mouth. Savouring a fallacy.

The reeshling in the bushes behind her didn't disturb her peace of mind. It was the unseen hands that gripped her shoulders, that sent her cry rising across the Howe.

Such cries breaking the silence of the quiet Howe were common enough. Easily enough analysed by listeners in the passing. A screaming rabbit cornered at last by the watchful weasel. A bleating ewe worried by a stray dog. The black sweep of the Hoodie Crow. And the rising protest of its victim. Distress traced easily enough to its unseen source. It was the source, itself, that could always momentarily stop the listening heart.

The Gowk, was no solitary. Hugh Riddrie nearly always knew where to find him. The smiddy, the general shop, the bus stop. For Jockie liked to be amongst folk. A pity, that. For folk either ignored his presence. Or acknowledged it, the way they acknowledged old Moss, the shepherd's dog. With a pat on the head.

In all the years, Hugh Riddrie had never got rid of the ache that caught at him at the sight of his son, standing with, but not of, normal men. It was rare. But easier, at times like now, when they came upon each other alone. In the nakedness of their relationship. When communication, though primitive, was natural. When tone of voice transcended interpretation. And monologue, comprehended by the listener, gave release to the speaker.

'*There* you are, Mannie! I've been whistling on you all night.
What have you been up to, Jockie?
Riving head first amongst the bushes!
Steady! Steady now! Till I get you wipit down.
Let's see your mouth now! You've been dribbling again!
The moustache of you's all slavers!

Steady now! Steady *on*!

Your flies are wide open again! Will you *never* learn to button yourself up!

You know fine that drives her clean mad.

She's gotten such a spite to flies.

Especially open flies.

STILL!

You're *fine* now!

In you go, then, Jockie.

Up the stairs. As nippit as you can!

Hold it! Hold it, Jockie. Till I get the boots off you.

That's *it*! *That's* it!

She'll not hear you, now.

We'll better her, this time!

In you go, then! You're fine, now.

All present and correct!

NO! Jockie, *NO*!

Let my hand *go*!

I'm *coming* in! Right *behind* you.

Let my hand go!

Do you not *see*, Jockie?

You've got go in *first*!

As if you'd been a *good* mannie!

And come all the way home. By *yourself*!

It's easier, that way, Jockie.

In you go then. We'll be all right!

'It's all *wrong*! All wrong, I tell you!' Jean Aitken insisted. 'That Gowk should never be allowed to roam the countryside. Just look at the state Liz has come home in. Are you all *right*, Liz? What did that mad bugger of a Gowk *do* to you?'

'We tried to warn Liz,' Young Rob remember. '*And* me!' Peter confirmed. 'We was shouting after the Gowk.'

'Off up to your beds! The pair of you!' Jean Aitken commanded. 'Are you *sure* you're all right, Liz? Are you *sure*!'

'Liz will be all right.' Rob Aitken said. 'She got a fleg just.'

'She's gotten more than a fleg! She's looking *terrible*.'

'He grabbed me,' Liz explained. 'And I didn't see him. *That's* what it was. I didn't *see* him. I ran all the way from the King's Howe. But I thought I'd never get out of the spot.'

'What took you down to the King's Howe, like?' her father asked. 'That's a bit out of your road, isn't it?'

'My homework. I forgot to take it down. I went over to get it from Chris Forbes.'

'I wouldn't bother about homework the hight,' Jean Aitken advised. 'You should hold straight on up to your bed. You've had a gey shake-up.'

'I'll be all right. I couldn't sleep if I went to my bed.'

'Liz is right!' her Father agreed. 'Stop fussing her, woman!'

'Well then!' Jean Aitken turned in attack on both of them. 'If she's all right, and can't go up to her bed, and can't sleep, she's *not* going to sit molloching here all night! She can just take herself through to the sink. And make a start to the washing-up!'

She would 'tell them on Saturday'. The decision taken, Liz leant against the sink, comforted by the postponement of time that lately she had begun to allow herself, when days could seem almost normal.

'I could have sworn I put preserving ginger down on the grocer's list.' Her mother's voice drifted through to the scullery. 'I'm sure I noticed some at the back of the press, the other day . . .'

There *couldn't* be anything wrong with Liz! Her mother would *know*. She could never be worrying about preserving ginger, if there *was* something wrong . . .

'But I think it's *last* year's preserving ginger that's in the press. The strength will have gone out of it . . .'

If there *was* something wrong, her mother would stop going on about preserving ginger forever . . .

'I could be speaking to *myself*!' her mother was complaining to her father. 'I *told* you she would be better off in her bed! Standing through there in a dwam. She's had a bigger upset than she'll admit. And if it's the last thing I do, I'll make Hugh Riddrie's ears, blister! Him and that Gowk of his.'

The Gowk, himself, was beginning to take on a subtle new dimension in the eyes of the Howe. A curious kind of normality. An ability to share in the venial sins of ordinary men. It was Liz Aitken who began to lose dimension to its inhabitants.

You could have 'knocked them all down with a feather', they

swore. Liz Aitken of *all* people. And her set to sit for the bursary.
She was just about the *last*! Not that anybody was perfect, of
course. But Liz Aitken was . . .

'As liable as the *next* one!' Teen Rait had snapped, in an
attempt to keep her own image of perfection intact. God help
whoever was the father, they agreed. It was bound to be somebody.
That was for certain. Though it had happened *once*. Just once.
But that was two thousand years ago. And, though they were
regular kirk-goers, and believed in every word the psalms uttered,
they'd just never quite managed to 'swallow *that* one'. It was
for papers. Although Cis Coutts, the simple creature, had tried
it on when *she* was pregnant. And syne forgot. And admitted to
the doctor that she 'had pink knickers on at the time'. Still,
and seriously, though, God help whoever was the father when
Rob Aitken got his hands on him. He couldn't get a word out
of Liz herself. She wouldn't say a cheap. There was a rumour.
Only a rumour, mind you! But then, there always was. They
would have died without one. A 'speak'. Oh! A *whisper* just.
That it was — *the Gowk.*

'You haven't got Liz to admit it, yet, then?' Kate Riddrie asked.

'No.' Jean Aitken shook her head. 'But she will. The state
Liz came home in, that night. Her jumper torn, legs scratit. And
herself, nearly hysterical . . .'

I can believe *that*! Your Liz would never have had the strength
against a brute-beast like the Gowk!'

'Never a one for the lads, Liz. Her head aye buried in some
book, just . . .'

'I was just saying Liz would never have had the strength!
Something will have to be done about the Gowk, *now*! And you've
gotten witnesses!'

'Aye some book, just . . .'

'You've gotten witnesses!' Kate Riddrie urged.

'Young Rob. And Peter. They were trying to warn Liz.'

'WELL! THEN! That's *it*!

'She never crossed the door at night. Except whiles. Down
to Chris Forbes for her homework.'

'You've gotten *witnesses*! All it needs now, is to testify before
the board!'

'But Liz. Liz is so unwilling. So unwilling to do that! Do you think? Do you think, maybe . . . ?' Jean Aitken hesitated, unable to put her own apprehension into words. 'Maybe, it's because he is a *Gowk?*'

'That's where you've *got* him!' Kate Riddrie got to her feet, in triumph. 'That's what I'm trying to *tell* you. It's Liz's word against a Gowk's word. And he's got none. At least none that anybody could make any sense out of. Forbye! The whole Howe can testify that the Gowk's forever shambling all over the place. *Exposing* himself!'

'You'll be satisfied *now* then Kate. You've gotten your will. You've gotten rid of Jockie, at last . . .'

'*My* first job. The first fine day. Will be to get that stinking mattress of his outside. And set fire to it.'

'*That* was what you always wanted, Kate . . . .'

'It stank the house to high heaven.'

'Wasn't it, Kate?'

'At least we'll get a bit of fresh air into the house, at last . . . '

'Speak! you *bitch*! Or have you lost your tongue! A damned pity you didn't lose it in front of the board!'

'It wasn't *me* that got rid of the . . . *Jockie.*'

'NO! But you said damn all to prevent it!'

'What could *I* say to prevent it? The board could see for themselves. Liz Aitken's belly was getting big enough!'

'*Jockie* didn't make it so.'

'You've got no *proof* of that.'

'Nor of the *t'other*!' Hugh Riddrie concluded, making for the door. 'All that Jockie ever wanted was for somebody to *speak* to him.'

'*Speak* to him!' Kate Riddrie snorted. 'What on earth can anybody say to a GOWK!'

'I'll tell you what they can say to a Gowk, Kate! I'll *tell* you.'

Hugh Riddrie turned to face her. Searching dumbly for words, that could be put into words. *Knowing* them. Thousands of them. Words that often weren't words at all, but instincts. Transmitted by tone and touch. A language acquired and mastered in a confusion of pain and frustration.

'You can *anything* to a Gowk, Kate!' The realisation took him by surprise. 'Anything at all. That's the best thing about Gowks. They never tell. And that's the worst thing about them.

They cannot tell. But I'll find somebody, Kate. I'll find somebody who *can* tell!'

... Liz Aitken O Liz Aitken ...

'Come on, Liz! Come on, lass,' her mother persuaded. 'Moping around the house like this is doing you no good. No good at all. And it such a fine night. Why don't you take yourself off for a bit walk?'

'Because she's feart!' Young Rob blurted out. Unable to contain his knowledge.

'*FEART?*'

'That's right!' Peter confirmed. '*Feart!*'

... Liz Aitken O Liz Aitken ...

'Feart of what, Liz!' It was her own fear that Jean Aitken probed. Convinced that such a fear had not touched her daughter. Oh, but the young were lucky. One danger at a time. Clear and cut. Over and done with. With little hindsight — and not very much foresight. If only the father had been a normal lad. And not a Gowk. 'Fear of *what*, Liz?'

'Nothing. Nothing, just.'

... Liz Aitken O Liz Aitken ...

'Well then!' Jean Aitken urged. 'Off into the fresh air with you. Young Rob and Peter will go with you for company.'

'Never *ME!*'

'*ME neither!*' Peter echoed his brother's determination. 'The other bairns will cry after us!' "Gowk's bairn! Gowk's bairn!" *That's* what they'll cry.'

'Is that right, Liz?' her Father asked. 'Is that what they cry?'

'Sometimes. It's only the bairns, though.'

... Liz Aitken O Liz Aitken ...

'I wouldn't let that worry you, Liz. Folk have always needed somebody to cry after. And they've got no Gowk, now.'

'If only it had been some other lad ...' Regret slipped out of Jean Aitken's control. And sounded itself in her voice.

'Some *other* lad!'

Her father's astonishment confirmed Liz's own certainty.

'If it had been some *other* lad, Liz would have been out of here. *Bag* and *Baggage*! What happened was no fault of her own. It took half a dozen of us grown men, to hold the Gowk down, till they got him off to the asylum.'

'Come on, Liz. Up you get. Her mother piloted her towards the door. 'Just you take a turn round the steading. I used to like fine a walk when darkness was coming down,' her mother confided, as they stood on the doorstep. 'I suppose I felt ashamed in daylight. *Not* because I was carrying a bairn, Liz. But just because I felt so ungainly. And ugly in myself. Still!' her arm found her daughter's shoulder. 'Every creature's *bonnie* when it's little, Liz.'

A daft thing to say, Jean Aitken thought, as she watched Liz from the door. The wrong words sometimes came out. When you couldn't find the right ones to say.

'Just the length of the steading, Liz!' she called out reminding her daughter . . .

But the Gowk's father roamed freely enough. On the prowl. Night after night. They said. Neither Gowk to whistle on, nor dog for company. His croft running to wreck and ruin. His oats rotting in the stack. And the threshing mill had gone long since past his road end. His turnips neither howked nor stored for his cattle-beasts. And winter nearly on top of the man. Bad enough when his first wife died, and the Gowk was born. Worse than ever *now* since they'd carted the Gowk off to the asylum.

Come to think of it, they themselves missed the Gowk. You would never believe *that*! But they'd just got used to him, like. Popping up here and there. And everywhere around the Howe. Still. It was an ill wind. And it had fair suited *Katie Riddrie*!

'I'm not sure that it did!' Meg Tait informed them. 'I'm not so sure at all! Kate Riddrie *herself* was telling me only the other day . . .'

'There's no living with him. No living with him at all. On the prowl all night. And sitting amongst my feet all day. Never taking his eyes off me. And never opening his mouth to me. Just mumbling away yonder to himself. He aye maintained that his first wife was at fault for the bairn being born a Gowk. But

I'm beginning to have my doubts. The way he sits mumbling to himself. He'd aye gotten such an *obsession* with that Gowk.'

. . . Liz Aitken O Liz Aitken . . .

LIZ!

So it hadn't been merely in her imagination. Or, maybe it had been created out of her imagination.

LIZ AITKEN!

Strange how prepared she was . . .'I'm in a hurry, Mr Riddrie.'
'Aye, Liz. You've been in a great hurry this past few weeks!
What is it that you're running from like?
Hold on, Liz! Just hold *on,* there!
You're no *feart* are you, Liz?
No! Of course you're not feart!
You know fine that the *Gowk* canna jump out on you the night.
No. He canna do that. He's far enough away, the night.
You made sure of that!
You *all* made sure of it! The whole bloody jing bang of you!
No! No! Liz! Hold on!
It wasn't Jockie? Was it, now?'

'I told the board . . .'

'I know damned fine what you told the *board*!
You try telling *ME*!
Struck suddenly dumb are you, Liz!
It's some late in the day for that.
It was never Jockie, Liz. *Never* Jockie.
You see Liz, he wouldn't even have kent *where* to *PUT* the bloody thing.
But *I* ken, Liz.

I ken *for* him.'

DOROTHY K. HAYNES

Dorothy Dean

When Mrs Dean called at the Remand Home, shamefacedly and on foot, she was surprised to find it both respectable and anonymous. It was the kind of house where you might expect to find a brass plate, a doctor or dentist's or architect's; but only the brass bell glinted, and worn gilt on the fanlight scrawled the signature "Tintagel":

The door was unlocked to admit her, and locked behind her again, and the superintendent looked a cross between a hospital matron and a gaoler as she led the way to her room. Mrs Dean sat in the warm study, her white gloves screwed to grubbiness, her jersey suit smudged with train dust. Already, she was on the verge of breaking down. Only her indignation kept her going, a resentment against everyone concerned with placing Dolly in this halfway house between court or prison, or perhaps, if one dared to hope, a second chance in life.

"I can't understand it," she said peevishly, forgetting that she had come to plead for help rather than to excuse. "She's always been a good girl. She's highly strung; but what she did to Mrs Stanley, and then carrying on like that afterwards — well, I mean, it's just not *like* Dolly. . . ."

"That's what we want to investigate," said Miss Gallacher gently. "We want to find out *why* she did it." She felt that, at short notice, it was too much to expect her to unravel her charges' kinks for the benefit of persons who should have seen trouble coming a long time ago. The girls were here for such a short time. Some you were glad to see the last of, some you liked on sight; but you learned to distrust the lot of them, Veronica, with her bronzed hair turning to mouse, Barbara, who stole, Jean, who lost her head whenever a man looked at her, and Dolly Dean, who wouldn't talk, and who rejected all offers to help her.

"We're having her checked up, of course," she said. "There's this nervous tic that she's got —"

"She can stop it if she wants to," said her mother sharply. "You don't need a doctor for that. It's not the first time I've smacked her out of a bad habit. . . ."

. . . .she had always had some mannerism or other, like jerking her head or flicking her hair back. "My hair gets in my eyes," she complained, and so her mother clipped back her fringe and put the long mane into a pony tail. Next there was blinking, screwing her eyes to squeeze the blackness till it ached ecstatically, but by this time she was at school, and they sent her to the eye clinic and made her wear glasses.

The blinking stopped, but it gave way to yet another habit, an uncomfortable twitch to keep the glasses from sliding down her nose. She indulged in it when she was reading, and her mother would watch in exasperation, breaking in on her with complaints. "You read far too much. Wasting your eyesight, that's what you're doing. No wonder you have to wear glasses."

She sat reading all day in a dark corner, newspapers, comics, or catalogues, whatever she could lay her hands on. She spent long hours with Mrs Beeton; but her mother's library was limited. There was a more fascinating selection at Mrs Stanley's, and Mrs Stanley's house was itself an attraction. She lived across the landing, on the sunny side of the building, and her kitchen was bright with geraniums and green linoleum. Dolly went across sometimes to see the budgie. "Wee Joey, Kiss wee Joey!" it chattered, and Mrs Stanley chattered back; and when they were both chattering away, Dolly would slip away from them and go into the parlour with the dark chenille curtains and the glass bookcase. There were old annuals there, *Chatterbox*, and musty bound volumes of *Atlanta*, and the *Home Doctor*, banded with gold, and too heavy to hold.

Dolly went through them all. The first time she opened the Home Doctor she was fascinated. There were men with stumps and moustaches, enduring terrible things; and then a folded diagram opened to show networks of nerves and arteries in a man stripped of skin. . . .

She shut the book and locked the glass door, and for a long

while she would not go back. Her mother could not understand it, nor could Mrs Stanley "I don't know," she said. "She just walked out without a word, as white as a sheet. Did she say anything to you?"

"No. Just that she didn't want to go back."

But she went back, eventually, because she had to have another look; and when the first horror of the Home Doctor had spent itself, she discovered the book about martyrs, and this time she did not run from it, though it frightened her even more. The saints suffered willingly, too willingly, but they did not hide their pain. Wide mouths yelled, eyes rolled to Heaven. The pictures were red with fire and blood, but the saints did not die. They stayed screaming; and reading about it was worse than looking, because it told *everything*, the pincers and the burning, and how they dragged themselves about. She gnawed at her nails, trying to get the thought of it out of her mind.

"Don't bite your nails," her mother said to her, *"and don't suck your thumb!* Honestly, Dolly, if it's not one thing with you, it's another!" She went to Mrs Stanley's to escape, and there, in the bookcase, was a scissor man, lean, leaping, and a child screaming in a shower of blood, or sprouting flames from every finger. "Struwwelpeter," said the sprawling letters, and she dreamed about it at night, but she did not tell her mother why she wakened and screamed. Her mother would have blamed it on her reading, and forbidden her to go to Mrs Stanley's again.

It was about this time that Mrs Stanley had what she liked to call, with a certain amount of pride, "her accident." A car battery that her husband, who was a garage attendant, had put, for some reason, on the top shelf of the cupboard, overturned and showered her with acid. She was alone at the time, but she managed to get to the door and shout for Mrs Dean. There was a great crying and running to and fro between the two houses, and for a while the doctor came every day; and then Mrs Stanley appeared again, as cheerful as ever, and looking almost the same. She had a tendency, however, to dwell on the accident, and Dolly saw her draw her blouse down and show the red weals on her breast before she covered them up tenderly again. She noticed the wry pull on her mouth as she touched the scars; and there was a blouse, a white blouse, eaten into holes, that was shown off sometimes to the gloating neighbours.

Dolly could not get the accident out of her head. Her mother and the other neighbours had taken turns at nursing her when she was in bed, and their whispers rolled down the echoing stairs ". . . couldn't bear the blankets over her . . . . marked for life. If you'd seen what I seen, Mrs . . ., Oh, I never knew a woman to suffer like that!"

Somehow, because of this, Dolly could not feel the same towards Mrs Stanley. She was always afraid that she would draw her blouse down and show her scarred bosom; and yet she wanted to see . . . .

She was always drawn to forbidden things. From the landing window, three stories high, she could see into the next backyard, uneven with stones, and with great coarse dockens sprouting in the corners. Her mother called it "the dirty yard" and warned her not to go near it; but one day she stared and stared till she couldn't resist it any longer, and at last she climbed over the crumbling wall and into the forbidden yard.

Her own window was high, high above her, her own yard looked strange and unfamiliar. Here she could see into doors which from above were only shapes to her, wash houses with dripping taps and broken tubs, and a dirty lobby stretching into darkness. A sour, soupy smell came from the lobby, and suddenly there was a man at her side, a thin, high shouldered man in a dirty pink jersey.

She knew who he was. She had seen him from a distance standing in the yard, with his high shoulders and dingy grey head. He was deaf and dumb, and nobody cared what happened to him. "It's a shame," her mother said. "Three women next door, and not one of them sees that he gets a decent meal. He'd be better off in a home somewhere."

For all that, she warned the child not to speak to him, never to speak to anyone from the dirty yard; and here he was now, his hand on her arm, grunting and making queer noises. His eyes were cold blue stones in a tiny skull. She screamed, and a fat woman in a rubber apron came and pulled him away. He shuffled over to a stone stair in the corner, and the woman shook her fist at him. Before Dolly could make up her mind to run, the woman had gone into her house and came back with a chunk of bread and rhubarb jam. "Here, love," she said coaxingly, and Dolly was afraid not to take it. She carried it back to her own yard, and then she dropped it in the dustbin.

She wanted to tell her mother about it, but she knew she would get into trouble for going, so she kept quiet, though she could not get the thought of the man out of her head. The house up the stone stairs had dirty windows, and she knew just wwat it would be lie inside. She would like in bed, seeing it, and where did the images come from, a furnace room with a black boiler taking up nearly all the space, and the floor all ashes? In the middle of the ashes the man would lie on an iron bed, blinking at the grey dark.

She did not know how she knew this. She did not like knowing. Then one day the bed was outside, poised on top of the stairs, and the man still in it. Rain fell on him, wind plucked at the covers, but he didn't move. With a sick horror on her, Dolly ran crying to her mother, and told her to make the man go away. Her mother took one quick, astounded glance, and shook the child till she was stupid. "There's no bed there, do you hear? There's nothing. Telling lies like that — you try that nonsense again, my girl, and I'll have something to say to you. The very idea!"

It was never mentioned again. Her mother did not believe in encouraging nonsense, and Dolly was afraid of her mother. She loved her, she ached with love of her, but somehow she could not talk to her. There was never time. He mother had been rushed off her feet ever since she had been left a widow, and Dolly came back from school now to an empty house. The house was growing more and more neglected, dust on the dresser, spiders' webs in the corners, cold grease in the frying pan. The mirrors were dim, and Mrs Dean never swept up the crumbs until Dolly was in bed; and Dolly was always glad to go.

Hunched up, eyes screwed, she would lie tense with a terrible pleasure, imagining things, the things she was afraid of, Mrs Stanley sizzling away in acid, the high-shouldered man doing horrible things, the saints with their eyes turned up and their mouths yelling. The pictures would come to her small, miles away, but so clear that they *rocked* with intensity; then they would rush together and explode in a black star, and she would feel herself trembling and somehow ashamed.

"Why don't you go out and play?" her mother said irritably. "Mix with the other girls. Haven't you any friends at school?" She could not explain that at school the other girls laughed at her. Where authority saw her as a quiet child, sweet faced and docile, her classmates saw only lank hair, glasses, and a tendency to fidget. Even the teachers could not ignore her fidgetting."For goodness' sake, Dolly, sit still. You'd think you had St Vitus' Dance!" Who was St Vitus? A long, deranged monk, continually on the twitch? Sometimes, as she walked home alone, he jerked and hobbled beside her; and when she got in she would sit quiet, so still that her mother noticed it; and dull as it was, she would wish that things could always be like that, because it pleased her mother.

She had a great and touching urge to be good. Sometimes she was happy, in a peculiar sort of way, as if she was living each day with a touching devotion to everyone she loved. Surely, then, things had been happier, the times long ago, when she was small, and her mother took her on her knee and sang to her,

"Oh, Dorothy, Dorothy Dean,
Oh, Dorothy, where have you been?
She's suddenly flown
To regions unknown,
Along with a man in a flying machine!"

Funny how it came back to her now, the old-fashioned song, through the racket of records the girls played in the Common Room, the heartsick crying of the Top Twenty and the pop charts. Funny how it frightened her, the Regions Unknown, sadder than anything wailed out by the boys with guitars.

"I just can't understand it," said Mrs Dean querulously. "She's had every chance. Of course, she's been left on her own a bit, but who hasn't? You've just got to trust them. You can't be around all the time."

"Do you have to go out to work, Mrs Dean?"

"How else do you think we'd manage? It could be done, I suppose, but it would only be a bare living. I wanted to give her nice things, things I could never afford myself. And they *need* so much nowadays, record players, school trips — you just can't keep up with them. Not that Dolly ever asked for anything. She was quite happy, just reading and imagining things. I know some have said she'd too much imagination, but I saw to it that she kept it under control. I soon knocked the imagination out of her."

"What did Dolly do when you were out, Mrs Dean?"

"Oh, she went over a lot to Mrs Stanley's. That's why I can't understand it. Ever since she could walk she's been in and out as if it were her own house. And Mrs Stanley wasn't the one to stand for a lot of nonsense either. There's no imagination about *her*. That's why I always felt she was so good for our Dolly . . ."

It was Mrs Stanley who first put the idea into her head. Dolly had gone over quite happily — but she did not look happy. She had a new mannerism now, a habit of peering round and rubbing her chin on her shoulder. There was no pleasure in it for her, nothing but an uncomfortable desire to do it once and for all and be finally rid of the temptation; but the temptation grew with every indulgence, until her mother sometimes slapped her in frustration, and the teachers checked her at school. It was time, everyone agreed, that Dolly grew out of that sort of thing; and Dolly knew it better than anyone.

That morning, Mrs Stanley took it on herself to do something about it. She started as soon as the girl came in, before she could lift a magazine from under the cushions. "Do you know this, Dolly? People will think you've got something on your shoulder if you keep looking round like that. I knew a girl once that had a black imp on her shoulder. Nobody but her could see it, but she knew it was there, and she was always looking at it —"

"What happened to her?"

"The girl? Oh, I don't know. They took her away, I think. But she used to look round just like you —"

"I think I'll go back to my own house now," said Dolly, her mouth tight smiling, her heart nearly choking her.

She did not really believe there was an imp on her shoulder. She could not see it in the mirror. She stared in the smokey glass, and the room looked odd and fascinating, all the furniture back to front, and her face not at all as she imagined it. Her cheeks were red, guiltily red, her hair dark, and her tongue sly pointed at the edge. Suppose the imp *was* there? She jerked her head sideways, to surprise it, and thought she saw the flick of a black tail; but it was only her hair, flung round. There was nothing. Of course there wasn't. Then, sitting quiet at the fireside, reading her book, she felt it on her shoulder, the slight weight and warmth of it, and a sweat came out on her as she sat rigid, waiting for it to move.

"Will you set the plates for me, Dolly?"

"Mummy." She said it experimentally, her voice casual, but with screaming undertones. "Mummy, there's something on my —"

"What dear?" Her mother was at the sink, pouring the potatoes, her mind already on the next task, and Dolly knew that she would never be able to tell.

"Nothing," she said, and went carefully, steadily to the table.

In time, her mother noticed it. "What are you holding your shoulder like that for?" she asked, irritable at always having to criticise. "Your left shoulder's higher than your right. Have you got a stiff neck, or something?"

"No. No, it's all right." She relaxed carefully, so as not to disturb the resting fiend.

"If it's not one thing, it's another. Why you've got to get up to all these capers, I don't know . . ."

She walked at a slow, gliding pace, because she was afraid that a jerk might send the invisible thing flying. Or would it dig in its claws? She was afraid to put it to the test. It was like having an animal that could be vicious, but what kind of an animal she didn't know. Black, maybe, with sharp ears and a bat's wings and a tail like a devil's?

Her mother poked the fire, and flirted the brush from the companion set.

"Do you *feel* anything wrong with your shoulder?"

"It — it feels heavy. As if there was something on it."

"Well, there isn't. And the quicker you get those ideas out of your head, the better."

But her mother was wrong. The weight shifted, the clutch of small feet tightened, and sometimes there was a warmth of breath at her ear. Once or twice she put up a hand to feel, but there was nothing — unless it had edged away. It seemed able to move. At night, reluctantly, it let her undress, but in bed it sat, touching her, on the pillow. And all the time, she wanted to tell about it.

There was sun in Mrs Stanley's kitchen, and she blamed her mother because their house was at the dark side of the building.

"Oh, come in, Dolly. My, what's wrong with your shoulder?"

"It's nothing." She walked in, casual and cautious, but her voice went high with the effort of not tilting the fiend. "Any magazines, Mrs Stanley?"

"There might be one or two. Go and have a look." She handed her a biscuit from the tin, pink mallow and coconut. "You're a great girl for the books. How are you getting on at school?"

"Fine, thank you." She chewed the biscuit, but the crumbs went dry in her mouth. "Mrs Stanley, remember the girl with the black imp?"

"What girl, dearie?"

"The girl that used to look round like me." Her voice broke, and she swallowed. "And you said she'd an imp on her shoulder."

"Oh, that one? I don't know. Nobody knew for sure that there *was* an imp. It was just the way she kept looking round, and people said —"

"Mrs Stanley, I think there's one on my shoulder!" It was out now, in tears and wild panic. "I know I kept looking round, but it wasn't for that, honest it wasn't! I just did it because . . . I just did it! But now I feel one there. . . ."

Mrs Stanley smoothed her skirt, and swallowed two or three times. Her eyes, fearful suddenly, looked over the child. "Tell me where it is," she said nervously. "*I* can't see anything."

"No, but neither could the other girl. And neither can I. But I can *nearly* see it. Just here. . . ."

"Oh, get away with you!" Mrs Stanley was becoming more confident. "You've far too much imagination. I — I was just kidding about the other girl. I said it to get you to stop that habit you've got."

"I can't stop. I can't stop now it's there."

"But it isn't there! Did you tell your mother about it?"

"No. She'd have been angry. She shook me when I told her about the man in the bed —"

"What man?" said Mrs Stanley, sharply, almost eagerly.

"The man in the dirty yard. He used to lie in bed, on the stairs. I could see him . . . . there was a furnace in his room, and he used to get burnt squeezing past . . ." She could not stop herself, the horrors mounting, crowding out of her mouth to the woman who did not want to hear —

Mrs Stanley went white, and the sunlight in the room seemed to sicken. Jerkily, she went over to the window and craned out. There was the shabby yard, the stone stairs and the iron railing; but there was not a bed to be seen, and no room for one on the landing; and the deaf man had been taken to a home long ago.

"You're making it up," she said. "You imagined it."

"I know," said the child. "But it comes into my mind and frightens me, and it's *there*! And now there's the imp — you shouldn't have *told* me —"

"I know what'll happen to you." Mrs Stanley picked her duster nervously, and inched her way among the ornaments. "There's a place for people who let their imaginations run away with them. I remember one girl who was always making up stories. She got so she didn't know what was real and what wasn't; and one day they came for her in a black van —"

"NO!" Dolly screamed, seeing the van draw up, knowing that, if Mrs Stanley said so, it would be so. There was desolation and terror in knowing that now, at last, she had gone too far. She lifted a knife, a poker, a candlestick, she didn't know what it was, and screamed and screamed as she went for her; and somehow there was a queer pleasure in it, the twisted pleasure of the martyr book, and the cruelty of Struwwelpeter.

Nobody scolded, everyone was very kind as they took her, Dolly, back to her own house, and her mother, and the people who came for her in a closed van. And now all she felt was the desire to be safe and good. She was played out and weary, and chastened at the thought of what she had done. But it would be all right. She could behave if she wanted to. She sat quiet and conscious of her self restraint, and there was nothing on her shoulder. She looked around, she moved her shoulder, but the imp had gone. Surely that was a good sign? Surely, if she did what they told her, they would let her go home . . . . she thought of her mother, her face tired, her hands tired, and her mouth squared with the strain of not crying. All she had to do was to run into her arms, and never let go as her mother petted her.

"Oh, Dorothy, Dorothy Dean,
Oh, Dorothy, where have you been. . . ?"

Her mother was standing with Miss Gallacher, all dressed up for visiting, with her pearls on, her navy suit, and her gloves all grubby with train dust, and as soon as Dolly saw her she knew she was angry. "Well? I hope you've been behaving yourself. You'll have to pull yourself together, you know, if they let you out of here. . . ."

It went on like that all the time. She did not cry when the visit was over, and her mother gone, still indignant and hurt. Stiff, icy cold, she sat alone, and there was nothing behind her, nothing good or bad to remember, and nothing to look forward to or dread. And then, suddenly, there was a slight pressure on her shoulder, a warmth of hair or fur on her face. For a moment, she almost saw it; and then it settled down, invisible but familiar, the fiend, the friend; its weight no longer a burden, and its touch a caress.

MARGARET HAMILTON

Bung

In bright, blown-up raincoats they bobbed slowly along like bunches of balloons tied to a ragman's cart. Women and kids coming to watch the launching.

By the yard gate men stood waiting for them: workers in faded blue or brown overalls, fishing in pockets for a half-smoked cigarette. John Laurie, sulky-faced under the pushed-back welder's goggles, could see a bloated bit of green that was his wife, Katy, bending to jerk the child Ian's clothes to rights.

For a moment the two heads were together, insolently alike, with eyes like plumped-up raisins in the smooth warm faces. There was nothing of John in the boy, he sometimes half-wondered if. . . Ah, no good thinking like that two years after he'd married her because Ian was on the way. He glanced inside at the shed where Ginger Bain and the rest of the scrap-metal ring were standing in a corner, nervously flicking fag-ash behind them as they plotted their latest scheme for nicking brass from the yard in a big way. Ginger and Katy had once been pretty thick, but Ginger wasn't the marrying kind. The kid had ginger hair, but so had Katy — a crimpy auburn that sparkled and crackled if a man ran his work-horned fingers through it.

As she crossed the street, a gust hurled grit and dirty paper in Katy's face. John could sense her muttering through the plastic shield of her dentures: *Shut up, Ian. What a climate, we can't be away too soon.*

Above him, as he stepped out to meet her, a Union Jack and a red-and-gold house flag snapped and snorted at each other. He dived to pick up Ian, grasping him by the thickly-clad waist to swing him high and clear of his mother. At once her attack began. 'You could have stayed at your work another quart'ran hour, you're only flingin' away dough!'

A lorry, backing into the yard, was silenced by the din inside — but not Katy. Men waiting to take children off the hands of their wind-ravaged mothers, could still respond to the rough comedienne's voice, which gave her words a blatant fearlessness and would make strangers grin indulgently at what she said.

He muttered: 'You needny worry. When did you ever get less than your pound o' flesh?'

What in heaven's name did she do with it, the unopened pay-packet handed to her every week? He never was away from work, except once when he'd had to go and see about that bit of skin trouble, brought on by her rotten cooking, beans and chips instead of the good grilled steak his mother always gave him. Tenderly exploring his chin with a blackened finger, he wished Katy would let him grow a beard. She was dead against it, remembering that at one time he had experimented with facial ornaments — handle-bars, beards, exaggerated sideburns — to attract certain girls who were said to be sporting.

Katy herself had been one of them. . . working at the time in a department store, conning women into buying clothes that made them look like frowsy tarts, and herself borrowing the clothes to wear with dazzling effect in the evenings. Till she was found out and sacked.

As he tried to settle the child more comfortably on his shoulders, she narked on as if he had not spoken: '*And* I'll bet you forgot to post the form about goin' to Australia. Nothin' gets done unless I do it myself . . . *Don't, Ian*! She gave the kid's leg a stinging slap for trying to kick the wind bellied front of her coat.

His automatic howl was cut short by the appearance of Thomson, the yard foreman. Wearing a grey, well-pressed suit for the occasion, he shot out on to the pavement, as if catapulted from the ways where the ship, *National Progress*, clung ready for launching. Before you could hear him, you knew he was muttering, *Where the hell have they got to?*

'Hear anything?' he roared to Paddy McGuire, the gateman. Slowly the old man cupped his hand to his ear whose drum had been mangled by years of boiler-shop din.

Thomson fiddled violently with his watch-strap, then turned to look inside the yard again — as if the minute his back was turned that ship would probably ramstam into the river on her own. Then he was out again — glaring along the street — pushing back the natty tweed hat as if it had been his usual squashed homburg.

(It was not so many years since Thomson had discarded the black reinforced bowler, traditional foreman's protection against bolts and rivets dropped 'accidentally' from a height.)

Fathers of families, lingering by the gate, nipped out their cigarettes to become workmen again, hands forward, listening. Children were shushed. Against the yard noises, against the wind and the thunder of main road traffic fifty yards away, everybody listened. 'Is it too quiet for you, Mister, will I drop a pin?' said Katy, but softly listening too.

Her husband moved back against the wall. 'They're comin'!' Then to Ian, squirming above his head: 'Here's the band, son.'

Thomson waited only long enough to make sure the small group of pipers and drummers was heading for the yard. Maybe he'd hoped for some hitch like the lack of a band to give him an excuse to approach the directors again about postponement. They must have insisted on the launching — Thomson would know it was daft to let her go today, a big empty hulk with no sense in her to tack and manoeuvre with a gale.

Ah, she had to go now, for the band was here. They were not a stylish turn-out, but a scratch bunch of local men who had learned piping or drumming in boys' organisations or the Orange Lodge, and now hired themselves out for football matches and launchings. The wind sported among their thick kilts and even tried to snatch the mace which the pipe-major tossed bravely as he entered the yard. There was a cheer from some of the men as he grabbed and caught it, less bravely.

'Well held, son!'

'That's a rare job, I wonder what bung they've to pay *him*.'

'It's nothin' to what some folk'll do for love!' roared Paddy the gateman with a wink at John Laurie. Paddy was Katy's uncle, and she turned with a grin and a casual 'H'llo, auld yin!'

A grey-painted bow, with the name, *National Progress*, in gleaming white letters, dominated the yard. On either side the iron uprights, bare now of staging planks, swayed in the wind, while underneath her the shipwrights hammered away one by one the huge wooden supports, which they might almost have left for the wind to winkle out. Job No. 798 she had been, from the day the number was first pencilled on a blueprint by the foreman patternmaker till it was stamped on the last small prefabricated metal part imported into the yard. Two berths away lay No. 799, a few months off completion, with a prickle of staging planks on her stern. Between the two, No. 800, with only her keel laid, made a fine platform for watching 798 take the water.

Men glanced at the two unfinished shells, estimating how much work was in them for this or that trade. The speeches at the celebration luncheon were quoted in the afternoon papers, which had been given advance copies.

'D'ye see what the chairman's been sayin'?'

'Aye — "There may have to be sacrifices all round." All round about himsel', he means. Sacrifices in every home on Clydeside, but none for him and his pals!'

'Ach, they canny make work —'

'They canny make ships, you mean. We're the mugs that do that.'

Clouds hurtled over the sky, dropping a few fat samples of their load on waiting ship and people, then moving restlessly on. As restlessly as Katy, darting about with Ian by the hand, looking for a vantage point but choosing none.

'That's a nice boat you've got, son.' Paddy the gateman chatted kindly to his great-nephew, Ian. 'You should get the lady to launch it too.'

'Lady launch my boatie too!' the child cried excitedly, waving the toy sailboat he had insisted on bringing. 'Lady launch my boatie too!' he crowed, so that people standing near them laughed nearly as proudly as if he had been one of their own.

A man came up behind Katy, Ginger Bain putting his arm round her waist, his dirty hand crumpling the stiff P.V.C. coat with casual insolence. 'Hello, Katy, long time no' see. 'Ve you come to see the launchin'?'

(Did he think maybe she'd come to get down to it with a rivetting hammer.)

She answered with husky affability: 'Ach, Ian's daft about ships. Not that a tanker's much – just a big petrol can gettin' heaved into the water on its backside.'

'It makes a change for the kids.' Ginger was very civil now, treating her as a respectable matron only good for looking after another man's brats. Then deliberately he turned his back on her and sidled towards John, the ferret face full of imitation joviality.

'Is this your kid then, Johnny? Fine wee chap. Takes plenty dough to keep 'em goin' these days, eh, Johnny? . . . Now — me and the boys was just talkin'. We were hopin' you'd change your

mind about comin' in wi' us. If it's only a matter o' steppin' up
the bung, Johnny — just say what you want an' we'll see what we
can do . . .'

John looked at him distastefully. The ring was dead keen to get
him: a welder working for long spells near the keel of the ship where
all the dirt and refuse gathered — he could hide stuff among the
rubbish till they were ready to take it away. And his wife's uncle
was a gateman who might be persuaded, for family reasons, to turn
a blind eye on what was being carried out.

John had always steered clear of big theft, thinking you were
bound to cop it sooner or later. It must be big stuff they were after
this time — probably brass portholes by the dozen, since nothing
smaller would pay off enough. They'd give him his whack for a week
or two, but then his share would be cut, and if he tried to break
with them the pressure would go on. Only last year Bill Carey, one
of his mates, had got a prison sentence because he'd been made a
scapegoat for the ring.

John shook his head. 'It wouldn't be worth while for all the time
I'll be here — Katy wants to emigrate to AustraliaT. . .'

Suddenly they were everywhere, overalled men who knew they
had to stop work now if they were to see the launching. On the
ship herself riggers lined the deck-rails, and on the roofs of sheds
or underneath them other men stood close-packed as for a cup-tie
football match. Every now and then a single ironic cheer went up —
for the band, changing position, for someone in the official launching
party being photographed by a pressman. For Katy Laurie, diving
and swearing after Ian who, while John was talking to Ginger Bain,
had run dangerously near the prow of No. 8oo.

'Some folk's no' fit to be in charge o' a mongrel pup, let along
a kid!' Lugging and shaking Ian, she strutted away on steel club
heels that John had not seen before. Another new pair — she must
spend a fortune in shoe-shops. Or . . . there was that place in Copland
Road where they had shoes on display on a rack outside. Katy was
a compulsive picker up of ashtrays and glasses in pubs, toilet rolls
from lavatories. *Ach, they owe us a bit o' bung for the prices they charge!*
she would grin with those ugly false teeth. All the beauty had gone
out of her smile when she had to have her own quartz-pebble teeth
hauled out because they went rotten after Ian was born.

Catching sight of Ginger Bain still hovering near, she stopped in
her tracks and began shamelessly to make up to him. 'Just like old

times, i'n't it, Ginger? D'you mind what the old bitch said when she saw the van waitin' outside?'

As they went off together, John suddenly knew that her dismissal from the shop had not been on account of borrowing clothes to wear in the evenings. She and Ginger had been in cahoots, she slipping out bundles of garments to a waiting van and telling her boss they had been shoplifted...

'That one needs her backside warmed, and if her mother was livin' she'd get it.' Paddy McGuire, Katy's uncle, was looking at her and Ginger.

John shot him a look, but had an urge to confide in the old man. 'She wants to go to Australia,' he said.

'Ach!' Paddy spat, grinding his spittle with his boot. 'I remember a green frock she once wanted when she was just a lassie — nylon wi' a bunchy skirt. It was in a shop window in the Govan Road and she thought if only she could get wearin' it at the school dance she'd be queen o' the Clyde.'

'Likely she wasn't far wrong —'

'She never had half the looks o' her mother, nor the contented nature . . . Her brother Mike bought her the frock, but she never wore it because she discovered the other lassies were goin' to the dance in sweaters and jeans . . . . Now it's Australia. Her brother's in Melbourne, doin' well for himsel'. He spoiled her rotten when she was wee, so now she thinks everything would be hunky-dory if she was there too. As if every thousand miles she travelled was a bit o' bung she was payin' for life to give her the best o' everything. . . .'

Bung, the shipyard term for bribery or graft. You slipped the craneman a bit of bung, a packet of fags for lifting a hunk of prefabricated shell into position so that you needn't stand idle waiting for him. Or you gave the foreman a bottle of whisky or a few quid (if he was known to be the kind who'd take it) so he'd put you on jobs where there was most money to be made on piecework, or when times were bad — as they were now on Clydeside — he wouldn't list your name among the men to be sacked.

Bung. . . some folk thought there was nothing it couldn't do if you offered enough of the right kind.

'Johnny!' Suddenly Ginger Bain was back beside him, grinning like a mangy cat that had just swallowed a bird of paradise. 'Johnny, I've got her talked out of it for you — she says she's no carin' aboot goin' to Australia, providin' she gets a bit more dough to make ends

meet. So gettin' back to that wee bit business we were discussin',
Johnny —'

'*Ach-aw!*' A low growl went round the yard as men realised the
ship was 'coming alive' — trying to creep down the ways on her
own. Thomson, the foreman, was hopping about, muttering, 'For
Christ's sake, hold on to her!' — his talk profane because the
shipwrights' foreman would expect it, but subdued in deference to
the platform party. They were now reshuffling for the launching,
the official kicking of *National Progress* out of the yard with a broken
bottle at her head.

A shout from Thomson was the signal for it to begin, for the bottle
to be flung, the last stay to be knocked out, the *National Progress* to
start moving. Eyes and cameras took her to themselves in a series
of nose-to-tail impressions chasing each other with growing rapidity.
Everything moved to receive the ship, turbulent water, hovering tugs,
draggled sky . . . and wind.

Now she was cleaving the water. . . . and a scream cleaved the air.
The familiar outraged protest of Ian Laurie being prevented from
doing what he thought was right and just to himself.

Unnoticed by either parent, he had snaked to the very front of the
people on No. 800. He laid down his boat, the better to clap and
jump to the music of the band as the ship went down the ways. As
Paddy had prophesied, there was a second launching, for the wash
from the ship flooded the new keel and swept away his boat.

Ian tried to snatch it back, and was himself snatched by his
great-uncle Paddy who, unlike the child's parents, had seen what he
was up to. Struggling in mid-air, Ian screamed against the injustice
of a world where boats were launched and taken from you.

It was different with the *National Progress*. Before tugs could control
her the wind rushed in, forcing her sideways, slowly, back to the
land. With a splintering crack of staging-planks, her stern rammed
the stern of the partly-finished No. 799.

And John Laurie rammed his wife.

Triumphantly, even as the tugs got busy charging and leaping and
putting out smoke, he roared at her: 'Of all the bloody rotten
mothers — he could easy have been drowned — I suppose that would
suit you fine — save you the bother o' lookin' after him —'

'You might as well know it now, you're goin' to Australia, whether
you like it or not. I've made up my mind.'

'*You've* made up *your* mind.'

'And you're goin' nowhere near Melbourne, you're goin' to the outback where there's nothin' but sheep and you'll have to pay attention to the kid . . .' She'd have to be nice to her man too, there'd be no competition but kangaroos and Aborigines.

She laughed in his face and strutted away, still yapping at Ian. 'Shut up, you'll get another boat the very same. Oh, all right, you'll get one o' the big clockwork ones that go round and round the pond' — as if she were already confident of having extra money between her fingers. A few yards away Ginger and the rest of the ring stood grinning, confident too.

Other men, moving slowly back to work, looked at the damaged ship, already on her way down-river for fitting out. 'That'll be a bit o' overtime for somebody, goin' to Greenock to sort her plates.'

Paddy McGuire, staring at the wind-scoured empty berth, said: 'You miss a ship when she's awa'. She kept the draught oot o' the yard.'

'There's others comin' on.' John waved towards the growing No. 799 and the embyro No. 800.

'And after that?' Paddy as a young man had lived through the hungry thirties, when this and other yards had been a forest of rotting cranes and empty uprights.

There were hard times coming again. You couldn't lift a paper or switch on the telly without getting more bad news. Maybe he'd better take a chance with Ginger and the rest, John thought, for the sake of having a few quid behind him when the crash came.

As if he read the thought, Ginger moved in close to John. 'Look at Thomson messin' his pants for what he'll say to the directors about the bad launchin'.'

'What's he worryin' aboot?' Paddy McGuire, time-pitted hook by which the ring must hang or fall, looked John in the eye. Then he roared above the growing sounds of work re-starting: '*Even the directors ken the wind's like a guid gateman — it'll no' tak' bung frae anybody!*'

ELSPETH DAVIE

Pedestrian

A great patch of scoured and gravelly land at either end marked the approach to the motorway cafe . Beyond that were flat fields and a long horizon line broken here and there by distant clumps of trees. At no point on this line was there a sign of a building. A glass-sided, covered bridge joined the car park to the café, and people if they wished could stand in the middle and look down onto the road below. The four lanes of the motorway carried every sort of traffic. The long vehicles were the most spectacular and there was no limit to their loads — lorries carrying sugar and cement and tanks of petrol went past, carrying building cranes and wooden planks, barrels of beer, cylinders of gas, sheep and horses, bulls in boxes, hens, furniture and parts of aeroplanes. There were lorries carrying cars and lorries carrying lorries.

The café itself was filled day and night with a periodic inrush of people and changed its whole appearance from half-hour to half-hour throughout the twenty-four. It had its empty time and its time of chaos. Habitual tough travellers of the road mixed here with couples stopping for the first time for morning coffee. Here buses disgorged football fans and concert parties, and stuffed family cars laboriously unloaded parents, children, grandparents, for their evening meal. The cars far outnumbered other vehicles. And no pedestrian, as opposed to hitchhiker, was ever seen here, for it would be nearly impossible to arrive by foot. Any person unattached to a vehicle was as unlikely as a being dropped from the skies. There was no place for him on the motorway.

Nevertheless there were still pedestrians in everyday life. A married couple who were queueing at the counter of this café one evening found themselves standing beside a man who admitted to being one himself. The couple had been discussing car mileage with one another and they kindly brought him into it. 'And how about you?' asked the wife. 'How much have you done?' The other smiled but said nothing. He had obviously missed out on their discussion, and she didn't repeat the question. From his blank look she might have just as easily been asking how much time he had done in jail. Behind the counter a woman with a long-armed trowel was shovelling chips from a shelf, while her companion dredged up sausages from a trough of cooking fat. 'Sorry,' said the man suddenly. 'I didn't pick you up just now. No, I'm not in a car. I'm in the bus out there. Long distance to Liverpool.'

'Good idea,' said the woman's husband. 'Good idea to leave it at home once in a while. No fun on the roads these days. No fun at all!'

'No, I haven't got a car.'

'You don't run one?'

'No, never had one.'

'Then you're probably a lot luckier than the rest of us,' said the man after only the slightest pause, at the same time giving him a quick look up and down. He saw a well-set-up-fellow, well-dressed and about his own age. Not a young man. This look, however, cost him an   outsize scoopful of thick, unwanted gravy on his plate. He slid cautiously on towards a bucket of bright peas. His wife, who had kept her eye on her plate, now bent forward and asked politely. 'Have you ever thought about it?'

'Thought about . . . ?'

'Getting one.'

'No, I can't say I have.'

The woman nodded wisely, blending in a bit of compassion in case there was some good reason for it — a physical or even a mental defect. For a moment the hiss of descending orange and lemonade prevented further talk. The three moved across to a table which had just been vacated by the window. From this point they had a straight view of the bridge and a glimpse of the road beneath. Every now and then, in the momentary silences of noisy places, they could hear the regular swish of passing traffic. On the far side of the bridge glittering ranks of cars filled one end of the parking space with lorries at the other. Long red-and-green buses were waiting near an exit for their passengers.

'You don't mind if I go ahead?' said the man from the bus. 'There's only twenty minutes or so to eat.'

'No, go right on. Don't wait for us,' said the woman. The couple were occupied with some problem about the engine of their car and the unfamiliar sound it had been making for ten miles back. They discussed what kind of sound — tick or rattle or thump — and with almost musician-like exactitude queried the type of beat — regular or irregular? There was the question of whether to look into it themselves, have it looked into or go straight on. Even now they were careful to include the other in the talk in case he should feel left out. They let him into the endless difficulties of parking, of visiting friends in narrow streets, or of visiting friends in any street, wide or narrow, because of the meter. They told him how much for twenty minutes, how much for forty minutes, how much if you were to talk for an hour. They discussed the price of petrol and of garage repairs and the horrors of breakdown on the road.

'And the hard shoulder can be a very lonely place on the motorway,' said the woman. 'All those cars rushing past you. Have you ever had to pull over yourself?'

'No, I haven't,' said man said, with a hint of apology in his voice.

'Oh no, no — of course you haven't! I absolutely forgot for the moment that you haven't got . . . Excuse me. I am being so stupid.'

The man said no, there was nothing to excuse. It was easy to forget. He added that the hard shoulder did indeed sound a very unsympathetic place to rest on in the night.

The three of them had now finished their first course and had turned towards the door to watch the next group entering. Half a dozen families were coming in, and a carload of men carrying trumpets. Two policemen were moving slowly about among the tables. At the far end of the room a waitress was mopping up the floor where someone had let a plate slide from a tray. The policemen bent and spoke to a man at a table, then sat down, one on either side of him while he put ketchup on a last wedge of steak pie and ate it with seeming relish. The three of them left the café together. 'This is where you find them,' remarked the car owner to his wife and the passenger from the bus. They had now started on their squares of yellow sponge cake with a custard layer between. The custard too had been sliced into neat and solid squares, and their plates when they had finished were as dry and clean as when they had started. 'One job less for the staff, I suppose,' said the husband examining his dish with distrust.

The other man — seeing they had confided in him — began to tell them what it felt like to walk along the edge of an ordinary country road while the cars went by. The husband looked vaguely aside. It was not a believable thing for a grown man to do and he did not hear it beyond the first sentence. But the woman said: 'You mean hitch-hiking?'

'No, no — just getting about from one place to another, sometimes by bus and train, naturally, and sometimes walking.'

'As a pedestrian?'

'Yes, I suppose so. In cities naturally one walks a good deal.'

'Yes, I see —a pedestrian,' said the woman, looking at him with a vague interest.

Her husband had now brought coffee for the three of them and the man drank his quickly, for the time was up.

'I'm sorry to rush,' he said, 'but the bus leaves in eight minutes, and they don't wait long. Thanks for the coffee — and a very good journey!'

'And the same to you!' They watched him go, weaving between the tables, and a few minutes later saw him hurrying down the glass bridge and starting to run as he reached the far end.

'A pedestrian,' murmured the woman musingly.

'Well, a bus traveller.'

'But he tells me he walks a lot of the time, in country as well as city.'

After a while her husband looked at his watch. 'Shall we get on then?'

'Might as well. We can take our time.' They wandered slowly away from the windows, looking back to see one of the buses moving off. *'His* bus, I expect,' said the woman. 'Careful and don't slip on that chip,' she added as they passed the spot where the plate had fallen.

The glass bridge over the motorway was the only viewing point for miles. The man and woman paused in the middle and looked down onto the great streams below. Four or five chains of long vehicles happened to be coming up on one side with a second line going down the other. Great grey roofs slid beneath them in opposition like extra roads moving along on top of the others. At this time of day the cars too were coming one after the other with scarcely a second between them, and — seen from above —scarcely an inch.

'I can't say I've met many non-drivers in my time,' said the man broodingly, 'but there's usually a perfectly legitimate reason for it. Certainly not money in his case though.'

'Physical disablement, maybe,' said his wife. 'Remember Harry Ewing. *He* didn't drive. He had one short leg.'

'You'd never have known. Anyway, with all the dashboard gadgets these days, what's a short leg, or arm for that matter?'

'Some people have bad eyes,' suggested the woman.

'Funny thing, but I've seen cross-eyed people driving about and nobody stopped them yet. And as for one eye at the wheel — that's common enough, believe me!'

Watchers on the bridge, or any persons not in a hurry, invariably attracted others. Something about the static bridge, sealed in above the speed, made company acceptable. So, before long, the two who had been standing there found that another couple had joined them — a man in a blue summer jacket and his wife in a cream coat. For a while the four of them stood comfortably together, silently watching. Then the first man said, 'My wife and I were speaking about non-drivers — their reasons, I mean, for not having a car. Most disabilities can be overcome, you know.'

'Maybe it's nerves,' said the man in the blue jacket. 'Or more likely psychological.'

'You mean,' said his wife, 'like that woman who'd never let her boy touch a machine — not even a child's scooter. So he never had a car all his life, not even when she was dead. Well, I suppose he loved his mother.'

'Well, I've heard that story the other way,' said her husband. 'His mother *wants* him to own this super-car since ever he opened his eyes. Nagged him all his life. And he won't do it, not even when she's dead.'

'Sure,' said the other man, 'because he *doesn't* love his mother.'

They turned and sauntered slowly along the bridge together like old acquaintances, looking down at the motorway to the left and right of them as though it was still a long, long way off.

'That man in the café — maybe he just didn't want one,' said the first wife. Her husband looked aside again with his vague and un-believing smile. The four of them now seemed reluctant to reach the end of the bridge. They began to walk more and more slowly as they neared the opening. In front the great gravelled space was, if anything, more closely packed than ever — some cars edging out, others slowly burrowing in like beetles into hidden corners. The two couples paused and stared intently at this space, searching for their own. 'Well, nice to have met you,' they said to one another, 'very nice indeed to have the pleasure . . . ' For one more moment they hesitated on the sloping ramp of the bridge. an overpowering whiff of loneliness reached them from the fumy air beyond. Then they stepped down and out into the narrow lanes between the cars and the glittering maze of metal divid-ed them.

EONA MACNICOL

The Pigeon

ELLA was dressing in the bathroom, because you cannot use the sittingroom as a bedroom until everyone has gone to bed. She called out to him, "See if you can find my nylon blouse with the long sleeves, Jan." Jan hesitated before going to the bedroom. He looked through the crack of the door, and wondered if he and Ella would ever get it straight again: the possessions of son and daughter-in-law lay in piles all over it, on the chest of drawers, on the floor, on the bed even though they were trying to coax the two little ones to go to sleep.

He wondered why he and Ella had bothered to paper and paint it. But Ella said it was her family custom to get everything very nice for the New Year.

He wished he did not have to go in and ask for the blouse. But Ella's voice came again. "Jan! Are you bringing me the blouse?" So he put his lips to the crack, and said quietly, "Please, Robert! Please hand me your mother's nylon blouse with the long sleeves."

Robert said, "O.K.," and after a creaking of the wardrobe which woke the baby he lumbered across the piles of things and handed the blouse out.

The passage also was full of things, suitcases and the larger of the children's Christmas toys. Jan had to pick his way among them to the bathroom. But Ella said, "Oh ta, dear!" in her warm friendly voice, and he felt rewarded.

Ella went on singing in the bathroom. She was very happy, with Robert and Moira and the two little ones in the house. He was glad she was happy and singing, glad she had children of her own so that he need not feel he had disappointed her.

She came out of the bathroom in a cloud of scented steam, fully clothed even with make-up on. Very handsome she looked, big and

258

full-bosomed and bright-hued, like a mother goddess. He looked at her with love, and she smiled back at him.

Then she cried, "Hurry up, Jan! Get dressed. It's time. We're going out first-footing."

He shook his head.

She cried, "Why not? You came with me last year. And you enjoyed it. Don't you remember? You danced an eightsome with me, and Moira taught you to rock-and-roll."

"This year I will stay in."

"To baby-sit? Sweet of you. But you needn't. Moira's not going out. You know she's — in June."

"I am glad," he said politely. Then he managed to squeeze his bulk past her, and went into the kitchen and from there into the scullery.

The pigeon lay in a basket or soft rags which he had found in the duster bag. He had managed to get an old oilstove going, so it was not very cold. He thought at first that the pigeon looked better. Its eyes were open at any rate, round eyes like the centres of flowers. He examined the soapdish of milk and imagined it had taken some.

But he knew that, whatever he wanted to believe, the pigeon was now very sick. Worse than when he'd got it, for then it had fluttered a little, now it lay still. He had discovered it on the ledge above their bedroom window ten days ago. For three cold nights he saw it sheltering there. Then he realised it was injured and could not fly or find itself any food. So one night he had opened the window, letting the cold air in to Ella, and stretched himself painfully up till he reached it, got his hand round it, and drawn it in. It had not struggled, that was the odd thing. Maybe it was too weak to offer resistance: but he really felt it knew it belonged to him.

"A stray homer," Ella had said. "You'd best take it along to Jimmie Telfer's. It's likely to be one of his."

— "Are you hearing me, Jan?" she'd said. "Take it to Telfer's. He has a loft for them. Even if it's not one of his, he'll know how to see to it."

"It is not Telfer's," he'd said stubbornly. "It belongs to me. I am not taking it to any other person."

"Well, but you can't keep it in the house! — Och," she'd shrugged, "Have it your own way. But do me a favour, keep it in the scullery. For the mess."

She was a good-natured woman. When first he had gone to work

and brought a pay packet home he had tipped it all out on to her
lap, as he had done at home. Only her brothers laughed at him, so
he had stopped. But he still wanted to give her all of it. She was
like a mother to him.

Now like a rebellious child he decided to disobey. He would not
go. He did not want to go out among her large family, did not want all
the laughing and shouting they went in for at this time of New Year.
"Happy New Year, Mother!" "A good New Year, Tom!" "Archie —
Andrew — Joanne!" Robert would love it, home on leave. He and
his mother could go out together and enjoy themselves without him.

They were waiting for him at the front door. "Jan, what have
you been doing? You're not dressed yet! Fussing over that old bird
again?" Ella said, teasing. And she laughed when he retorted, "It's
a young bird."

"Well, whatever it is, if you ask me it's on its last legs. Come on
now, Jan. You'll have to help Robert carry the bottles. I've the cake
for mother to carry and I don't want to break the icing."

"No," he said, hanging his head. "No. I will not go."

Ella remained good-tempered even then. "Are you going to the
pub then? Well, mind and be up at mother's by half past eleven. To
take in the New Year."

"O.K.," he muttered. "O.K."

He waited till the gate clicked. In the cluttered passage he found
his overcoat fallen on the floor underneath Robert's khaki one and the
children's tiny anoraks. He put it on. All was quiet in the bedroom,
where Moira must have fallen asleep beside her babies. Then he
stole into the scullery again. He lifted the pigeon carefully out of its
basket and placed it inside his cardigan, under the lapels of his coat.

It wasn't queer to be taking the bird out, he said to himself.
Sometimes people called him queer, but this time he was perfectly
sensible. He had taken it out before. To the Library first, to ask the
assistant there if she had a book on the care of a sick bird. Very
sympathetic she had been, and had looked up a number of books
for him, explaining what he did not understand. But the bird was
still sick. Then he taken it to the pit, to the First Aid Centre, where
Alec MacColl worked. Alec had felt over the bird, whilst he, Jan,
stepped from one foot to the other in his anxiety. At last he had
given his opinion. "It's a goner, Jackie. You'd best put it in a pie,
boy." Last of all he had gone to the Clinic, though for some reason
he did not like the place: it was too white and cold, reminiscent

of something. The lady in the reception had opened her eyes wide when he explained who the patient was; in the end he had seen a doctor but had been sent away with a sedative for himself.

It was not queer, but it might be unwise to venture it out in the cold of a winter night. Yet what else could he do? He could not leave it in the house, lest one of the children should wake up and go into the scullery and worry it. He had to keep it safe with himself. And he had to go out, he had to be alone.

Curiosity drew him first to Main Street. Such a jolly rollicking din! He stood by the wall opposite the Thistle Tavern, his hand over the breast of his coat, and watched in wonder the people standing about it, slapping one another on the back, shouting, "Here's tae ye!" "And whit will the New Year be bringing you, Geordie man?"

"Hullo there, Sugar! You coming over?" Someone took him by the arm. And he jumped. He never could get used to sudden shouts and even yet he hated to be unexpectedly touched.

"No. No. Thank you but no." He got loose easily enough, the man's mind being on the Thistle Tavern. But others came round him. "Is it Jackie Sugar? Come along in, Jackie man. It's Hogmanay."

"No. No." He struggled out from among them, and went quickly up the street, his hand pressed all the time over his breast. Under one and another lamp post all the way up Main Street he could see groups of people gathered. It made his heart thing. Didn't they know? Didn't they realise it was forbidden? — It took an effort to recall that he was where people could congregate on New Year's Eve without arousing suspicion.

But if he walked on he would come to the other tavern. So he turned up Sixth Street. Many of the uncurtained windows displayed Christmas trees, and from most of the houses he could hear sounds of parties going on, gramophone records, high excited talking and drifts of laughter. One or two front doors stood open with people welcoming arriving guests. "Hullo there, Auntie Grace! Come away in. Jim! — And wee Marlene!" There was a tremendous lot of hugging and kissing. But no one saw him go by. He put his hand into the breast of his coat and touched the pigeon reassuringly.

Once he was seen and recognised. "There's Jackie Sugar. Are you out on your own,. Jackie? We'll no tell on you!"

"Care to come in, Sugar? Have a wee drink to celebrate."

"Thank you. No. No."

"Oh come on! Just a few friends. Folk you know."

"Thank you! Thank you!"

They let him go. He turned left and followed the course of a narrow vennel which threatened the tops of all the streets. He thought he would be safe here. But he ran full tilt into the midst of a band of chattering people. They recognised him, and cried, "Hello, Sugar! Where are you off to?" He had almost got past them when suddenly a girl left the group, ran up behind him, and before he could do anything put her arms round him and gave him a tight squeeze. She said something very kind, leaning forward to kiss him; he smelt the whisky on her breath. He struggled angrily from her. At which she screamed with laughter and ran away to the others.

His pigeon! What had she done to it? He cried out in Polish. Under the next lamp post he opened his coat. The pigeon was limp, its eyes closed. Yet as he whispered to it, it opened them slowly. Until the shutters of the lids came down.

He turned into the road that led to the hill above the village. No more houses, only the factory that stood empty with dead windows for the holiday. It was peaceful and quiet.

– Yet he was startled by a car which came nosing down towards him, and he shrank out of the headlights' glow. My God, a police car! He had not gone unnoticed either. The car slowed in passing him, then stopped. Something fluttered inside his coat: he did not know whether it was the pigeon or his heart. A voice shouted, "Hullo, Sugar! Is this where you're taking in your New Year?" And then came a hearty laugh. His beating pulses grew still. Of course, it was Britain, he was safe. The police were only Angus Bell, the big red-faced sergeant, and young Graham Anderson who was a cousin of Ella's.

Graham got out of their car and came up to him. "You all right, Sugar? Taking a wee walk to yourself, is that it? Working off your surplus fat, eh? Are you wanting a lift back to the village?"

"No," he said, backing away, pushing himself right into a holly hedge. "No. I thank you, I am enjoying the quiet."

"What's he say?" he heard the sergeant ask as the young man got into their car again. He heard the beginning of the answer. "Wants to be quiet." A laugh escaped before the window was wound up.

Now they were gone. He slipped his hand under his coat and stroked the smooth neck with one finger, and said to comfort both it and himself, "They've gone away."

He was near the top of the hill. There was no one now. The faint moonlight patterned the countryside with dark places and pale. His eyes sought the dark places, bushes and wind-warped trees. You could hide there, supposing anyone did come.

He stopped to get his breath and looked down on the village. It had lights all over it, like a Christmas tree fallen prone. He could still hear voices, only they were muted and made tolerable by distance: shouts and laughter and bagpipe music and the drumming of dancers' feet.

He sat in the lee of a bush, till there was silence, then the sound of the church clock striking twelve. One, two, three — he counted in Polish. At the twelfth stroke came a burst of cheering, and then the song which Ella had taught him, where all must take hands.

But the thought of Ella was blurred in his mind now. His eyes no longer saw the little town, nor the city lying beyond it about its lion-shaped hill, nor the sliver of sea, nor the long lines of lights twinkling that were towns on the opposite shore. The lights twinkled and danced before his eyes . . . the lights of another town, his own, the town where he and Hannah lived, where he went to work every day, where their baby Anyusha had been born, where she waited for him every evening ready to climb up into his arms. His own town, his own doomed and violated city, where they had come for him because his great grandfather had been Jewish, where they had come for Hannah and the child dancing in her arms.

He had to think. He had to remember. He had to let it come up into conscious thought.

— The day of his release, the loud vigorous soldiers who had come in and freed them. He had managed to get a lift and gone to Hannah's camp. The officer in charge had a camp list on the table before him. He had red hair and a reddish moustache that moved as he spoke. And he, Jan Szager, had stared at him, at the moustache that moved and the red hair, as he endeavoured to grasp what it was he said. "I'm very sorry. She is listed among those who died. On the 20th of September last. I'm afraid it's clear. — The child? Was there a child? There's no mention of any child of your name."

So had begun his frantic search for Anyusha. "Let me see the women who survived." They were scarcely human, some of them. It seemed indecent to question them who desired only to be left in peace. "Don't you remember a child? A small girl? Fair hair, soft smooth hair, blue eyes always laughing. You could not forget such a child."

"I saw no child with her."

"I never knew she had a child. She used to weep. But then who did not?"

He had searched for Anyusha for years. Until at last he found a girl who was crazed. "I was in the same truckload with her, arriving. She had a little girl in her arms."

"What became of her?"

A burst of hysterical laughter. "What do you think? They had no nursery for children!"

"You mean they killed her?"

"We envied those who died so quick."

A cousin of his, who had escaped before the war, heard of him and asked him to come in Britain. A miner, expert on ventilation, he had found work here, had made a new life for himself and married Ella. Only rarely now did the question spring up like a tiger within him: How was she killed? Did she know? What did she suffer first?

Sometimes in dreams he saw her as she might have been, grown into a woman, married maybe. With children. Like Moira. Sometimes she came and found him. She did not know much English, let alone Scots. He would see her approaching people in Main Street, "Excuse me, please! Is there by chance a Mr Jan Szager here living?"

But always in the mornings when he awoke, like a wind blowing away a sweet perfume, came the realisation. If Anyusha by any chance had survived, in what shape would she be? Could she conceive and bear children with the body they had left her, or would she be like him? And her mind, her mind?

. . . He had been dreaming now. He had felt his child warm in his hands, warm and soft and round. Now he woke to find it small, excessively small. It was the bird, the pigeon he was nursing in his coat. His grasp must have hurt it. He opened his coat and tilted it towards the moon. The eyes were closed, this time they did not open.

Then all of a sudden he began to long for the village, for the people, for Ella. He had been a bad husband to her tonight, to leave her to go out first-footing without him. She had her son; but her son was her son, only he was her husband. He had broken his promise to her.

The little town was quiet when he got down to their street, and dark. But his house was not dark. For when he inserted his key and opened the door, a shaft of light came from the sittingroom illuminating the cheerful disorder of the hall. Ella sat by the dying fire under the standard lamp. She had kicked off her shoes and was warming her feet.

She jumped up to meet him. There was a stirring in the bedroom; she called softly, so as not to wake the children, "Papa's in, Rob." Robert's voice came from inside, "Happy New Year, Papa!" Then there was a creaking of the bed as he turned over to sleep.

"You're the latest of us all," Ella said. "You didn't come first-footing with us. You must have been going your mile, Jan! Where have you been?"

"Up on the hill." It was all he could tell her.

"Well, are you wanting anything before bed?"

He put his hand into his coat and drew out the pigeon and held it out to her. "It goes not well with it. It was too sick."

He was ashamed to lift his head, because the hot tears burnt his eyes. "I think it is dead."

If she felt surprise to see the pigeon she did not show it. She took it from him gently. "Yes, it is dead. Poor thing. I think it must have had a rough time before it came here. — You're not going to grieve for it, Jan, are you? It's only a bird."

He said, "I would not grieve so long as it is safely dead."

Another woman might have asked him, "What do you mean?" But not Ella. She said, "It's quite dead. Its troubles are all over." Then she said briskly, "I think we should bury it, right now, in the garden. It's lucky there's no frost, the ground's nice and open." She was in her nightdress and dressinggown, yet she bustled into the scullery. "I've got just the thing." She pulled down a shoe-box — she had given him slippers for Christmas. There were pieces of tissue paper still in it. In those she wrapped the pigeon, covering from his view the soft grey and iridescent plumage, the rounded head, the round closed eyes. "Now you come out and dig its grave," she said.

When he had dug the hole and laid the box in it and filled in the soil again, he stood unable to move. But Ella linked her arm in his and drew him indoors, to their makeshift bed in the sittingroom, and lay beside him with her arms round him till he had found oblivion in sleep.

JANET CAIRD

The Deprived

I remember the very first time I saw The Roses thinking what a wonderful exercise in camouflage it was. On that beautiful June day with the sun blazing, and the famous rose-beds in their first outburst of bloom, it looked wonderful.

The long low house with its old grey sandstone walls covered with Gloire de Dijon roses was charming, and the extensions had been skilfully added at the back so as not to spoil the effect when one emerged from the shady drive into the open ground before the house. The entrance hall prolonged the effect; low-ceilinged, with a wide shallow beautiful wooden staircase leading from it. Everywhere gleaming wood, beautiful rugs, and a huge silver rose-bowl filled with flowers reflected in an antique mahogany table. If it wasn't a fine old country house, it must be a very good hotel: and even though one knew it wasn't, it was a shock when the crisp white uniform of a nurse appeared to ask your business. I got used to the set-up, of course, but the first impression was always at the back of my mind through all the long months when I visited my Aunt Sophia there.

Aunt Sophia was the last member of my mother's family. With the exception of a brother drowned at sea, they had all lived well into their eighties. My mother had reached eighty-nine. Aunt Sophia was ninety-two. She, alone of the family, was extremely wealthy, having been left what seemed to the rest of the family a vast fortune by a doting husband. She was childless and had been a wonderful aunt to all her nieces and nephews. When at last it became clear that she must have skilled nursing, and it being impossible to find private help, it was only natural that she should move into The Roses: The Roses being, in the geriatric world, the equivalent of Claridge's or the Savoy in the normal world. I don't know what the fees were at The Roses, all that being handled by Sophia's lawyers, but they were certainly vast.

Not that the inmates didn't get value for money. They did. The furnishings, food, nursing were all of the highest standard. Everywhere the emphasis was on immaculate freshness, cleanliness, perfection. The roses in the flower-vases always seemed newly-picked. I never saw a fallen petal or a faded flower all the time I visited there. It was the acme of discreet good taste. No effort, no detail, was spared to veil the reality of the slow drifting from life of the patients.

And this was more than an elaborate exercise in public relations. When I came down from Aunt Sophia's room on that first day, I was met by a discreet and charming secretary who asked me to call in at Dr Mactaggart-Thom's office. Dr Mactaggart-Thom was medical director and part-owner of The Roses. I must admit that I went in with some prejudice. He would, I was sure, be large, smooth, smell of expensive after-shave and have soft white hands. Not at all. Dr Mactaggart-Thom was certainly tall but very lean, brown (he was a keen fisherman and commuted to Scotland whenever possible), with a firm grasp and a faint tang of snuff. It was all rather reassuring after the smooth perfection outside his office. Dr Mactaggart-Thom was, among other things, an astute businessman. He was also, and with absolute sincerity, passionately interested in and concerned about his patients.

He greeted me courteously, motioned me to a chair and said:

'I always like to have a little chat with our guests' nearest relatives. I understand you are in the position of being Mrs Hope's next-of-kin.'

'Yes, I am.'

'I like to explain just what the principle is on which we run The Roses, so that friends and relations can play their part in the therapeutic arrangements.'

'"Therapeutic"?' I said. 'I should have thought any curative procedures were not on . . .'

'Ah, there you are mistaken. Mrs Grant. Some of our guests *do* go back home. But I agree, for the majority, that is not possible. So our aim must be to keep them happy. You may have noticed that we do our best to make their surroundings here as far removed from a hospital atmosphere as possible . . . .'

I made affirmatory noises.

'But we go further. We never, I repeat never, mention the possibility of — ah — their final departure. Our nurses are instructed never to hint at such a thing, or even discuss it among themselves. And we earnestly ask relatives and friends to do the same.'

'You mean,' I said, 'that we must never use the word —.'

He raised a hand.

'Please. It is never uttered in here. Except perhaps by a guest who has newly arrived. But they soon stop using it, and indeed, I am convinced, even thinking of it, surrounded as they are by so many of the pleasant things of life. And if they ever do show signs of —ah — restiveness, we calm them down.'

'With drugs?'

'Various ways and means. A little hypnotic treatment, a glass of good wine . . . The thing is, they are kept cheerful, happy, and do not think of the future . . . We protect them from it.'

He paused. I was silent, thinking of my mother's last illness and the year she had spent in the local geriatric hospital, a place supplied with all the necessities and none of the luxuries; a place of humour and sadness and steady indestructible human courage, where, as my mother had remarked casually one day, 'the wings are always hovering' and no one had any illusions about the outcome . . .

'You don't approve?' Dr Mactaggart-Thom had a penetrating eye. I had been silent too long.

'oI shouldn't dream,' I said, 'of in any way interfering with the principles on which you run The Roses. I'll co-operate to the best of my ability.'

'Thank you, Mrs Grant. I was sure you would understand.'

I could certainly undertake to co-operate: but I couldn't answer for Aunt Sophia, who was a strong-minded woman and still remarkably alert mentally. But to my surprise she slipped into the atmosphere of The Roses from the start. The day was skilfully broken up by mealtimes, elevenses and so on. There were cosy little sessions of physiotherapy and occupational therapy — if patients wanted to weave bags, embroider tapestry, they could. Aunt Sophia declined. 'I've always hated sewing and I won't begin now.' There was a library of light novels, which she read with relish. And a small colour TV by each bed provided some contact with the outside world. The TVs surprised me. Meeting

Dr Mactaggart-Thom one day as he admired a splendid bed of roses, I said:

'Doesn't the TV distress the patients? I mean the violence and sudden —'

He raised a deprecating hand.

'Please, not that word. And "guests" rather than "patients". Hmm? No. TV does not disturb them. To them, it is something quite outside them and not quite real . . . and it fills the day. The great thing is to avoid blank spaces; otherwise they may begin to have unpleasant thoughts. Ah! Here's the car. Excuse me. One of our guests is going back home — a proud moment for us. He was quite convinced that he — that life held nothing more for him when he came. Now he is returning home.'

From beside the rose-bed I watched while an old man, walking with a tripod, was packed into a large and shiny car and driven off beside an anxious-faced middle-aged woman. Then I made my way to Sophia's room. Perhaps what I had just seen did justify all the luxury, the cocooning against reality. Perhaps ignoring the facts could be therapeutic. That afternoon I saw Sister.

'Is there any likelihood that Mrs Hope will ever be able to go home? I saw a p—, a guest leaving today.'

Sister shook her head.

'Not a chance. And Mr Penhurst will be back in a month. They all come back.'

I had to admit to myself that Sophia was as happy — if one could use the word about a totally negative absence of unpleasantness — as was possible for a person in her condition. She lived, apparently, from moment to moment, never thinking of the future but lingering among the pleasanter memories of the past. She rapidly built up a strong attachment to her room-mate (there were no single rooms at The Roses; they encouraged 'undesirable introspection', I was told). I never knew Miss Shivas's first name; following the convention of their time they were always 'Mrs Hope' and 'Miss Shivas' to each other. She was perhaps not as mentally alert as Sophia — at times she seemed to slip into another time-stream — but physically she was in better shape, did quite a lot of physiotherapy, and could make her way up and down the corridor with the help of a zimmer. She also, I gathered, had a niece who visited her at intervals but our paths never crossed. Aunt Sophia and she seemed to spend a lot of time exchanging reminiscences; occasionally, to their vast content, finding they had common acquaintances at some remote connection. Altogether, I began to feel that Sophia was probably in as satisfactory circumstances as the situation allowed.

Time passed. The rose-beds declined into winter austerity — not shabby, as my roses always looked in winter; it was clear these roses enjoyed every advantage, and were being tended with all the horticultural skill available, to mitigate the disadvantages imposed by the routine of nature. Christmas was celebrated at The Roses with exactly the right note of good taste — a beautiful Christmas tree, holly and evergreens, a suitable present for each guest. Sophia got an amazing number of cards; Miss Shivas very few; I sent her one myself. I learnt with surprise that she was even older than Sophia and must have had few friends left. Her niece sent a magnificent bouquet of out-of-season flowers, which, to my amusement, rather roused the envy of Sophia, who ordered me to send her a similar display at her own expense.

On the other hand, Easter went by unnoticed; not surprisingly, it being difficult to celebrate Easter if you've put a taboo on Good Friday.

One day at the end of May, when I went to Sophia's room, she was not in her bed. Miss Shivas told me she was having her hairddone —a hairdresser came regularly to the little hairdressing-room at the end of the corridor — and would be back soon. I sat down to wait and made conversation.

'You're fortunate here in having a hairdresser coming.'

'Yes indeed. We are very well looked after.' She raised her head from the heaped-up pillows. 'Not only all this —' waving a thin hand latticed with the prominent veins of old age round the room — 'but in other ways.'

She beckoned me to lean closer.

'Before I came here, I was afraid, *very* afraid. But not any more.' Her voice, surprisingly clear for one of her age, dropped; her glance shifted sideways, and she said, softly and clearly but not addressing me:

'It happened to the others, but it won't to me, no, never, never to me.'

I had seen her have one of these lapses, when it was as if a cog missed and her mental grip on things slipped, and I was going to take her hand and draw her back to reality when

Sophia was wheeled in, splendidly blue-rinsed and very cheerful. Sister followed behind; she gave a sharp glance at Miss Shivas, nodded to me and said brightly:

'Miss Shivas! Time for your walk,' and at once the cog slipped back and the old lady was herself again.

A fortnight later, when I came to see Sophia before going off on holiday, Miss Shivas was progressing down the corridor with two tripods, helped by a physiotherapist and watched by Sister. I paused to watch too.

'Will Miss Shivas be going home soon? I asked.

Sister looked startled.

'"Going home"?'

'She seems so much more active.'

'Oh, I see. Well, there are problems'

'I suppose it depends on her niece.'

'Well, yes, it does rather. And relatives aren't always willing . . .'

Aunt Sophia was in an unusually morose mood, due entirely to the fact that I was going away for a fortnight.

'Shan't have any visitors,' she said. 'I've got used to you coming in.'

'Oh but you will have visitors,' I said, and mentioned a few names. 'Besides you've got your television to look at.'

'I never do look at it. All the plays are full of fighting and nasty things. Just put it on and you'll see.'

I switched on. It was a news bulletin and the little screen was filled with soldiers with guns at the ready running down a street towards a column of smoke billowing up with slow menace. In the foreground two ambulance men knelt by a woman lying in an ominous sprawl.

'You see,' said Sophia petulantly, 'that's what I mean. Always something nasty. They shouldn't put on plays like that.'

'It isn't a play.' But I said no more, switched off, and talked of other things. As I went out into the sunlight I thought that Dr Mactaggart-Thom would probably be highly delighted with Miss Shivas and Aunt Sophia. The one didn't believe it would happen to her and the other didn't believe it happened to other people. It might be highly satisfactory to the good doctor, but for myself . . . But I was off on a fortnight's holiday and I was firmly resolved to put The Roses and all it implied behind me.

When I entered Aunt Sophia's room on my first visit after

returning, Miss Shivas's bed was empty. After greeting Sophia and handing over the small present I had brought, I said:

'Where's Miss Shivas?'

'She's gone home.'

'"Gone home"?'

At first I wondered, but Sophia went on:

'Yes, her niece came for her. Quite suddenly, and we didn't have a chance to say goodbye. They had wheeled me into the sun balcony, and when I came back she was gone. But I've had a letter from her. There it is. You can read it.'

A sheet of notepaper lay on her locker. I lifted it. It was a grey-blue colour, oddly stiff and with a faint musty smell as if it had been kept for a long time in a damp cupboard. The writing was faint and spidery but legible enough, and the contents were brief. Miss Shivas was sorry she hadn't had time to say goodbye and was missing their nice talks.

'It was nice of her to write,' I said.

'Yes it was, and when I feel like it, I'll answer.'

Miss Shivas's bed remained unoccupied. I made unobtrusive enquiries and Sister said they found it harder to fill beds owing to having to put charges up. Aunt Sophia certainly seemed to miss the company and I began to see a deterioration in her condition; she was less alert, less cheerful. So I was quite glad when after about a week she greeted me with more animation than she'd shown for some time and said:

'I've had another letter from Miss Shivas. There it is.'

I took the letter from the envelope. The paper still smelt damp and musty; the writing was even frailer. It was a sad little letter. Miss Shivas didn't feel at home; she had nothing in common with the other people, looked back with regret on her pleasant conversations with Mrs Hope, and would like to think they could meet again. She remained hers affectionately.

'She doesn't seem very happy,' I said, as I put the letter back into the envelope. For a moment I wondered what was odd about it.

'The letter isn't stamped, Aunt Sophia. How did it get here?'

'How do I know?' She was unusually querulous. 'It was there when I woke up. I expect her niece handed it in.'

'Probably. I see she uses the same notepaper as you do, but it must have been in a cupboard for a long time.'

'What does it matter? I'm tired. I think you'd better go.'

It was then I realized how quickly she was failing. Three days later I got word that she had passed away.

All the arrangements were, of course, made with the utmost tact. When everything was over, I paid a last visit to The Roses to pick up her personal effects. When I arrived there was no one about; the whole place was quite silent with an early-afternoon hush. The guests were all asleep, all lapped in a vast make-believe, carefully cocooned against the last experience available to them ... I went up to Sophia's room. The two beds were made up, immaculate; the room a model of airy freshness. Sophia's travelling clock, her silver-backed brushes, her writing case were nearly arranged on her locker. And on top of the writing case, an envelope.

Yes. Another letter from Miss Shivas; unstamped. Her niece couldn't have heard ...

I forced myself to open it. The mustiness was even more marked; it was almost an earthy smell: the writing was fainter, in places illegible, but one phrase stood out:

'I feel quite lost here.'

Some little sound made me look up. Sister stood in the doorway.

'Oh, good afternoon, Sister. There was no one about, so I just came up.'

'That's all right. I think everything is in order.'

'Yes indeed. And I'd like to thank you for all the care my aunt enjoyed.'

'Well, it's our job, you know. We try to make our guests happy.'

'I know. Poor Miss Shivas doesn't seem too happy, now she's gone.'

'Miss Shivas?'

I hadn't realized before that Sister must be much older than she appeared. And why was she so white?

'She's written two or three times to my aunt, but they're rather sad letters.'

'But she can't have.'

'But she has. Here's a letter I found today.'

I held it out to her. The earthy smell lingered between us. Sister backed against the locker, her hands raised in rejection.

'She can't have. Miss Shivas is dead; she died when you were away. She's dead; dead and buried.'

The forbidden words hung in the air and into their aftermath came a sharp order.

'Sister, you had better go to my office.'

Dr Mactaggart-Thom stood aside to let her pass. Then he turned to me. 'I'm sorry about that. Sister forgot herself — perhaps she has been doing too much.'

I was bundling Sophia's things into the case and didn't answer.

'I am sorry,' he repeated.

I looked at him. All I could see were the bones of his skull sharp beneath the skin and the rigid rictus of his smile. I brushed past him and ran down the stairs, through the gleaming silent hall, past the rose-beds, down the drive and back into my world of life and death.

CATHERINE LUCY CZERKAWSKA

A Bad Year for Trees

It had been a bad year for trees. The elms in the deer park were the first to go. They were diseased and there was no help for it. Martin mourned them like old friends, stooping over their fallen carcases and cursing under his breath so that the forestry workers called in to do the felling should not hear him and think him foolish. In late spring there came freak gales from the wrong direction. The prevailing winds here were Easterly and the trees had long ago learned which way they ought to bend. The sudden change, this onslaught from the West, brought many casualties: a tangle of fallen hazel and beech in the plantation that sheltered garden from shore. Now, looking up at the birch grove that divided precise terraces from conifers striding in serrated ranks up the hill above the house, he saw that the birches too were growing old and could not be expected to last for much longer.

Martin was the head gardener in this small country park where visitors came to walk and picnic each summer. But it was already late October and the gardeners could go about their business in peace. He did not like summer visitors, seeing them as a necessary evil. They parked their cars where they should not. The dropped litter and picked flowers and etched their initials into tree trunks. Earlier that year he had come across a hedgehog staggering blindly along a gravel path with its head firmly jammed into a tin can, cutting a ludicrous little figure. Anger rose in him as he caught the terrified animal and freed it from its encumbrance.

He had moved to a small cottage on this estate some twenty years before while his daughter Rosemary was a baby and his wife still alive. But she had died young and suddenly, and after her death, his work in the small enclosed world of the park had begun to intrude upon him to an intolerable degree. He saw the growing and dying, the preying of parasitic plant upon plant or bird upon small animal

275

with a searing clarity. If so much as a rose tree in the walled garden withered he felt something wither and die in him also. Last winter he had found birds on the beach, unfamiliar birds that he learned later were cormorants, staggering ashore their wings black with oil. At the time he had raged around the cottage that seemed too small to contain his passion. He frightened his daughter and was sorry for it later. But the tragedies of land and sea ate into him and there was nothing he could do to remedy them.

On this fine autumn morning he was working with a group of men, combing the lawns with strong, long handled rakes to rid them of loose grass. He paused to rest his back which was often painful these days, and saw his daughter walking up the terraces towards him, shading her eyes against the sun. She raised a hand in greeting, smiling.

'What are you doing here at this time?' he asked accusingly. 'I woke you before I went out. You should be at work.'

'You forgot your flask. I brought it.'

She was a big girl, standing awkwardly, holding out his flask over the fence. He saw that her dress was too small for her, clinging to heavy breasts and thighs. That it was too thin for the day. She embarrassed him.

'Put it down. Leave it there,' he said, quickly. 'I can't take it now, can I?'

'No. I'm sorry.'

She was always sorry. He felt impelled to say 'Thanks for bringing it.'

'No trouble.'

'Why aren't you at work?' He looked at her suspiciously.

'I was sick.'

'Were you?' She seemed very robust and healthy: an outdoor girl with apples in her cheeks, her mother would have said. She was a tree in bloom, sturdy and handsome. All unconscious of the cold, she stood, rubbing one foot up and down her leg, leaving a smear of mud. Mouse shy, she was afraid to go, afraid to stay.

He turned back to his raking and in doing so, noticed the other men watching Rosemary with sidelong, covetous glances.

'Dad?'

'Well?' He looked over his shoulder and she was reminded of a horse, eyes wild, ears laid back. 'Go away. Go away' he thought desperately.

'Nothing,' she said. 'I'll get off to work then.'

He watched her go down the hill and shrugged in exasperation. He was not a bad man. The men who worked for him thought him very calm and quiet. He aroused no antagonism in them. His speech was usually gentle with the occasional glimpse of an oblique, wry humour which they appreciated. He was always tactful with strangers. Only with his daughter could he allow the mask of his customary civility to slip. Consequently it was at once a relief and an irritation to be with her.

She went down the track to the cottage. Looking in her purse to see if she had change for the bus, she was irresistibly drawn to the photograph in the card compartment. At least once a day she found herself staring at it. It was a cheap one taken in a station booth. There had been four for twenty pence. Her own face seemed large and vacant to her, like a full and witless moon. Her companion was a good-looking boy with a clever, beaky face. He was screwing up his mouth and crossing his eyes for the camera. She remembered the sensation of his arm around her, fingers deftly squirming up inside her nylon blouse, his too-long nails catching at the fabric, catching at her flesh. 'A nice warm girl' he had said, chuckling in her ear. What was his name? Johnnie? Bobby? She had met him at a dance. Later he had taken her to a pub, a city pub with carpets and soft music and little tablets of pink soap in the ladies. She remembered all that but she could not remember his name. In his small flat with its debris of wet towels, cigarette ends, dirty clothes, her mind had been fuzzy with unaccustomed alcohol; too happy, overwhelmed by his welcome attention. Her body, hungry for affection, had clung much too closely to this stranger. She almost smiled at the memory. Then the cool ascetic face of her father came into her mind. 'Why aren't you at work?'

'Because I'm sick. Because I think I'm pregnant.'

How could one say such things? How could such things be? They must not be. She began to walk blindly around the little kitchen, her hands pressed to her temples as though something were hurting her there. He had carried her on his shoulders when she was small, showing her birds and trees and flowers. He had walked with his hands holding her small feet, firmly. Her mother had been alive. She had been safe. How could she ever tell him? She stumbled against the table and banged her legs. Then she sat down and resting her face in her hands, began to cry. Presently she dried her eyes, washed her hot cheeks at the sink and went out to catch her bus. She was embarrassed. The conductor would see that she had been crying.

In the park, Martin raised his eyes to the birches. They were his favourite tree with their white paper bark, their drooping twigs that fashioned the spring-time leaves into veils of coined light, a dazzling gold. And now they were golden again but with the deeper nostalgic yellow of autumn.

Rosemary had been a gentle child. But adolescence had not favoured her. She had become clumsy, heavy, diffident. Even her name seemed too light and pretty for her solid, reproachful presence. 'I'm sorry' she told him all the time. He had no sympathy for her. He no longer knew how to speak to her.

'These birches' he said, 'They'll have to come down sometime. Getting past it.' The trees were so old that their bark had grown very dark, gnarled and irregular.

'Not much you can do with birches' said one of his companions. 'They make good kindling. No heartwood though. One way and another it's been a bad year for trees.'

A Change of Face

I was five pounds short of the two hundred I needed by Thursday, and I had only two days to make it up.

"Why do you need two hundred pounds?" asked Ingrid, my room-mate.

"Let's say I promised myself that amount."

"That explains everything," she said. "I once promised myself a holiday in Majorca, but things don't always work out."

"In your case things never work out."

"I think you're crazy," said Ingrid. "What good is money to you anyway?" Her fatuity was maddening, but I kept calm.

"Lend me a fiver. You won't regret it."

Her tiny laugh pierced my ear. "What me — with scarcely a bean!"

"Get out," I said, "before I cripple you."

She folded down her tartan skirt and walked out the door with a hoity-toity air, ludicrous, I thought, in a down and out whore. I waited a good five minutes to make sure she was gone before I fetched the briefcase from under my bed. I never failed to be impressed by the look of it. Good quality leather was more in my line than the trash Ingrid flaunted. The briefcase had originally belonged to one of her clients. I remembered his piggish stamp of respectability. Mind you that was ten years before when Ingrid was in better condition. He had left it by the side of the bed, complete with lock and key and containing two stale sandwiches, while Ingrid slept off her labours. I explained later I had found it in a dustbin. Once again I counted the money acquired in pounds and pence but it still totalled only one hundred and ninety-five.

In Joe's Eats Café I leaned over the counter. "Joe," I asked, "how's about lending me a couple of quid — five to be exact. Until the Giro comes on Saturday."

Joe kept his eyes on the trickle of heavy tea he was pouring. He breathed hard. "What for?"

"Oh I don't know. Who needs money."

"It don't pay to lend money. I should know."

"Of course, never a borrower or lender be," I said, fishing for ten pence.

"I've been done before. No reflection on you."

I looked round, then leaned over and whispered. "You can have a free shot and I'll still owe you the fiver."

He recoiled then hooted with laughter. "You must be joking — not even with a bag over your head."

I shrugged and put on what passed for a smile. "It's your loss. I know some new tricks."

Joe patted my shoulder. "I know you mean well, Lolly, but you're not my taste — nothing personal."

We brooded together for a bit. Finally Joe said, "Ingrid might lend it to you."

"Not her."

"Oh well . . ." He turned to pour water into the pot.

"I've got one hundred and ninety-five pounds," I threw at him. His back stiffened.

"What's the problem then?"

I knew I was wasting my time but I explained. "I need two hundred by Thursday. It would alter my whole life."

He chortled. "You paying for a face lift or something?"

"Better than that."

He shook his head. "Sorry kid, you see —"

I took my cup of tea over to the table without listening. Ten minutes later I was strolling along a quiet part of the city occupied mainly by decaying mansions.

"I'm short of a fiver," I explained to the tall man in the black suit.

His eyes glowed with regret. "I'm sorry. Two hundred is the price. I can't accept less."

"Will it be too late after Thursday?"

"I'm afraid so." He could not have been more sympathetic.

"What should I do — steal?"

"I can give you no advice."

He closed the door gently in my face and left me staring at the peeling paint. A cat leapt on to the step and wound itself round my legs. I picked it up and forced it to look at my face. "Stupid animal,"

I said as it purred its pleasure. I threw it away from me and returned home.

I walked into the bedroom and grabbed Ingrid by her sparse hair as she lay splayed over Jimmy Font, identifiable by his dirty boots.

"Out," I shouted.

She pulled on her grey vest screaming, "I'll kill you."

Jimmy thrashed about like a tortoise on its back clutching his privates as if they were gold.

I towered above him. "Hurry!" He gained his feet, made the sign of the cross, grabbed his trousers and ran.

"May you burn in hell," moaned Ingrid, rubbing a bald patch on her head.

I tossed over a handful of hair. "Before you go, take that filth with you."

"Where can I go?" she sobbed.

"The gutter, the river, the madhouse. Take your choice."

She pulled on her dress. "I don't feel well." I didn't answer. "Anyway," she added, "if you had let Jimmy stay I might have earned a fiver to lend you."

I was not swayed by her logic. A drink from Jimmy's bottle would have been the price. I walked out of the room to escape from her staleness.

At one time they told me in the hospital, plastic surgery could eventually work wonders. I did not like the word 'eventually'. Civilly I had requested that they terminate my breath, but they merely pointed out how lucky I was to be given the opportunity. Suspecting they would only transform me into a different kind of monster I had left them studying diagrams. That happened a long time ago, but I still had my dreams of strolling along an avenue of trees holding up a perfect profile to the sun.

"Are you listening," said Ingrid, breaking through my thoughts with some outrageous arrangement she would fix for me to get five pounds. She backed away when I headed towards her. As she ran through the door and down the stairs I threw out her flea-ridden fur coat, which landed on her shoulders like the mottled skin of a hyena.

The Salvation Army Band on the street corner blared out its brassy music of hope. I settled down on the bench beside Teddy the tramp and spun thoughts of fine wire in my head.

"Nice?" commented Teddy from the depths of an abandoned army coat. He offered me a pale-green sandwich from a bread paper, which I declined.

"We have much to be thankful for," he said as he bit into the piece.

A body of people gathered on the far side. The music stopped. Everyone applauded. I joined the group, who courteously stood their ground when I brushed close. My eyes were on the Sally Ann coming towards us with trusting goodwill and the collection box in her hand. I slipped my hand beneath the other hands holding out donations, then tugged the string loosely held by the good lady, and ran.

Six pounds and forty-seven pence lay strewn over my bed in pence and silver. I blessed the kindness of the common people and the compassion of the Salvation Army who would never persecute or prosecute a sorry person like me. Tomorrow was Thursday and I had the two hundred pounds, with one pound forty-seven to the good. With a mixture of joy and fear I poured five pounds into the briefcase. Then I studied a single sheet of parchment, the words on which I knew by heart. The message was direct and unfanciful, and unaccountably I believed it, perhaps because of its simplicity, and also the power which emanated from the black handwriting. Even the mercenary demand for two hundred pounds strengthened my belief in a force much deeper than plastic surgery. I calculated there must always be a price to pay, which for effort's sake should go beyond one's means, to accomplish results.

All evening Ingrid did not return. I wasn't surprised or sorry. In my mind's eye I could see her tossing against dank alley walls in drunken confusion — her wispy hair falling like damp thistledown over her forehead, her eyes rolling around like those of an old mare about to be serviced. Not that I wished her to be any different. Her degradation had afforded me stature, though after tomorrow. I hoped never to see her again. Fancying a bout of self-torture to pass the time, I began searching for a mirror, suspecting it would be useless since I had forbidden them in the flat. I peered at my reflection in the window. Like a creature from outer space it stared back without pity. Satisfactorily sickened I raised two fingers, then turned away.

"See your pal Ingrid," declared Maidy Storr when I passed her stall of old hats, shoes and rusty brooches.

"Not recently."

"She stole a bundle of money from Dan Riley when he dozed off in Maitland's bar last night."

"Never."

"Well she did. I sat on one side of him and she was on the other. I remember she left quickly without finishing her drink. Next thing he woke up shouting he'd been robbed."

"How much?" I asked.

"Fifty quid," she said. "Mind you I was surprised he had that much." She added winking. "You'll be all right for a tap."

"Haven't seen her since yesterday morning."

"Done a bunk has she?"

"Couldn't say."

"Well she would, wouldn't she. The law will be out for her."

"For stealing from a pickpocket. I don't see Dan complaining."

Maidy frowned. "I see what you mean. It makes you sick to think she'll get away with it."

"Couldn't care less whether she gets away with it or not." I picked up a single earring. "Have you many one-eared customers?"

"Leave that stuff and get going."

I walked away quickly when Maidy threw a shoe at me, and headed towards Joe's for breakfast.

"I'd think I'd like something special today," I informed him.

"How about some weedkiller," he suggested.

"I said something special, not the usual." I considered his confined choices.

"Be quick and move to your seat before the joint gets busy." Being a liberal-minded fellow Joe allowed me in his place when it was quiet, provided I sat in the alcove behind the huge spider plant. I chose a pizza and a glass of tomato juice.

"Living it up," he sneered.

"Might as well. Anyway I'm tired of the little creatures in your meat pies."

I could see Joe looking anxiously at a neatly dressed old lady approaching. Hastily I moved to the alcove with my pizza and tomato juice. The old lady was having an intense conversation with Joe. I suspected she was complaining about me. I finished my pizza and deliberately took my tomato juice over to a centre table. At a table near by a couple with a child looked at me, aghast. The child wailed. I smiled at them, or in my case, grimaced. The child's wails increased in volume. Joe charged over and signalled for me to get out. The neat old lady appeared out of the steam.

"Don't you know this is a friend of mine," she said, looking hard at Joe then bestowing a loving smile on me. Joe look unconvinced, but he was stumped.

"If you say so." He moved the couple and the child behind the spider plant.

The old lady sat down beside me and said, "I'm sorry you have to put up with this sort of thing."

I shrugged. "That's all right."

"Such a lack of kindness is terrible," she continued.

"I suppose so."

"Can I get you something?" she asked.

"A pizza, if you don't mind."

She attended to me smartly. I could feel her eyes boring through me as I ate. She cleared her throat and asked, "Are you often exposed to such er — abuse?"

"Don't worry about it," I said. "You'll only upset yourself." Her eyes were brimming over by this time and I couldn't concentrate on eating.

"Is there nothing that can be done?" she asked just as I had the fork half-way up to my mouth.

"About what?" I was really fed up with her. I find it impossible to talk and eat at the same time.

"I mean, my dear — what about plastic surgery — or something."

I threw down my fork. "Listen, if you don't like the way I look, bugger off." I paid her no further attention when she left.

"That's another customer you've lost me," Joe called over. I told him to bugger off too, then hastily departed.

For the remainder of the day I kept checking on the time, which meant I had to keep searching for the odd clock in shop windows. I half expected to bump into Ingrid. In a way I would have been glad to see her, because even if she was completely uninteresting, in her vapid manner she used to converse with me. She was still out when I returned home, no doubt holed up somewhere, frightened to stir in case she met Riley. I washed my face, combed my hair, put on a fresh jumper, and looked no better than before, but at least it was a gesture. Then I checked the money in the briefcase and left without a backward glance. I headed slowly to my destination so that I would arrive on the exact minute of the hour of my appointment. Normally I don't get excited easily, for seldom is there anything to get excited about, but I must admit my heart was pounding when I stood on the steps of the shabby mansion. The tall man in the black suit received my briefcase solemnly. He bowed, then beckoned me to follow him.

Agnes Owens

"Are you not going to count thee money?" I asked.

His sepulchral voice resounded down the corridor, "If you have faith in me I know the money will be correct."

I wanted to ask questions but I could scarcely keep pace as he passed smoothly ahead of me. Abruptly he stopped outside a door and turned. The questions died on my lips as I met his opaque glance. It was too late to have doubts so I allowed him to usher me into the room. I can give no explanation for what followed because once inside I was dazzled by a translucent orange glow so powerful that all my senses ceased to function. I knew nothing until I woke up outside the corridor holding on to the tall man. Even in that state of mesmerism I knew I was different. My lips felt rubbery and my eyes larger. Tears were running down my cheeks, which in itself was a strange thing, since I had not cried for years. The man carefully escorted me into another room and placed before a mirror, saying, "Don't be afraid. You will be pleased."

I breathed deep, and looked. I didn't say anything for a time because the image that faced me was that of Ingrid. I leaned forward to touch her, but it was only the glass of a mirror.

"You are much nicer now?" the man asked in an ingratiating manner.

What could I say? I didn't want to complain, but I had been definitely altered to be the double of Ingrid. Certainly the face was the same, and we had been of similar build anyway.

"Very nice," I croaked. "Thank you very much."

His lips curled into what could have been a smile, then he tapped me on the shoulder to get going. I shook hands with him when I stood on the step outside, clutching my empty briefcase.

"It's a funny thing — " I began to say, but he had vanished behind the closed door.

It might have been a coincidence but Ingrid never showed up. This was convenient because everyone assumed I was Ingrid, so I settled into her way of life and discovered it wasn't too bad. Certainly it has its ups and downs but I get a lot of laughs with her clients and it doesn't hurt my face either. The only snag is, now and again I worry about bumping into Dan Riley. Sometimes I consider saving up for a different face, but that might be tempting fate. Who knows what face I would get. Besides, I have acquired a taste for the good things in life, like cigarettes and vodka. So I take my chances and confront the world professionally equipped in a fur jacket and high black boots, trailing my boa feathers behind me.

NOTES ON CONTRIBUTORS

MARY BRUNTON (1778-1818, b. Orkney) published two novels, *Self-Control* (1811) and *Discipline* (1814) before her death in childbirth. *Emmeline* appeared posthumously in 1819. 'A Civilized Kind of Game' is taken from chapter 28 of *Self-Control*, which was republished in 1986 by Pandora Press.

JANET CAIRD, b. 1913 in Malawi, has published thrillers, poetry, a children's book, and a historical novel, *The Umbrella-Maker's Daughter* (Macmillan, 1980). 'The Deprived' is taken from *Scottish Short Stories 1976* (Collins, 1976).

CATHERINE CARSWELL (1879-1946, b. Glasgow) was a literary critic, biographer of Burns, D.H. Lawrence and Boccaccio, and author of two novels, *Open the Door!* (Andrew Melrose, 1920; Virago, 1986) and *The Camomile* (Chatto and Windus, 1922). 'The Zoo: The Dream' is a fragment from her unfinished autobiography *Lying Awake* (Secker and Warburg, 1950).

CATHERINE LUCY CZERKAWSKA, b. 1950 in Leeds, has written poetry, short stories and plays, notably the radio plays *O Flower of Scotland* and *Bonnie Blue Hen*. 'A Bad Year for Trees' appeared in *Chapman* 27-28, Summer 1980.

ELSPETH DAVIE, b. 1919 in Kilmarnock, is a novelist and short story writer who received the Katherine Mansfield short story prize in 1978. She has published three novels: *Providings* (Calder and Boyars, 1965), *Creating a Scene* (Calder and Boyars, 1971), and *Climbers on a Stair* (Hamish Hamilton, 1978); and four collections of short stories: *The Spark* (Calder and Boyars, 1968), *The High Tide Talker* (Hamish Hamilton, 1976), *The Night of the Funny Hats* (Hamish Hamilton, 1980), and *A Traveller's Room* (Hamish Hamilton, 1985). 'Pedestrian' is taken from *The Night of the Funny Hats*.

WINIFRED DUKE (1896-1962, b. Liverpool) published many historical novels, such as *Scotland's Heir* (Chambers, 1925), as well as works of history and biography, and edited several volumes of the Notable British Trials series. 'Captain Pert' is taken from her short story collection *Tales of Hate* (William Hodge, 1927).

SUSAN FERRIER (1782-1854, b. Edinburgh) wrote three novels: *Marriage* (1818; Virago, 1986), *The Inheritance* (1824), and *Destiny* (1831). Her work was admired by Sir Walter Scott. 'By Express Invitation' is taken from chapter 16 of *Marriage*.

JANE HELEN FINDLATER (1866-1946, b. Lochearnhead) wrote five novels, including *The Green Graves of Balgowrie* (Methuen, 1896), and two volumes of short stories: *Seven Scots Stories* (Smith, Elder, 1912) and *A Green-Grass Widow* (John Murray, 1921). With her sister Mary (q.v.) she produced two further collections of short stories: *Tales that are Told* (Methuen, 1901) and *Seen and Heard before and after 1914* (Smith, Elder, 1916); and three novels, notably *Crossriggs* (Smith, Elder, 1908; Virago, 1986). 'The Pictures' is taken from *A Green-Grass Widow*.

MARY FINDLATER (1865-1963, b. Lochearnhead) collaborated with her sister Jane (q.v.) in writing several novels and collections of short stories. On her own Mary Findlater wrote six novels, of which *The Rose of Joy* (Methuen, 1903) is generally considered the best. 'Void of Understanding' is taken from the collection *Tales that are Told* (Methuen, 1901).

ELIZABETH HAMILTON (1758-1816, b. Belfast) wrote essays, memoirs and works on education. 'A Sensible Effect on the Nerves' is taken from chapter 8 of her novel *The Cottagers of Glenburnie* (1808).

MARGARET HAMILTON (1915-1972, b. Glasgow) wrote many short stories, which have not so far been collected in book form. She also wrote poems in Glasgow dialect, and a novel, *Bull's Penny* (MacGibbon and Kee, 1950). 'Bung' is taken from *Modern Scottish Short Stories*, edited by Fred Urquhart and Giles Gordon (Hamish Hamilton, 1978; Faber and Faber, 1982).

DOROTHY K. HAYNES, b. 1918 in Lanark, has written two novels, *Winter's Traces* (Methuen, 1947) and *Robin Ritchie* (Methuen, 1949). Some of her many short stories have been published in two collections, *Thou shalt not suffer a witch* (Methuen, 1949) and *Peacocks and Pagodas* (Paul Harris, 1981), from which 'Dorothy Dean' is taken.

VIOLET JACOB (1863-1946, b. Montrose) is best known as a poet, though she also wrote historical novels such as *The Sheep-Stealers*

Heinemann, 1902) and *The Interloper* (Heinemann, 1904). Her short stories were collected in *Stories Told by the Miller* (John Murray, 1909), *The Fortune Hunters* (John Murray, 1910), and *Tales of my Own Country* (John Murray, 1922), from which 'Thievie' is taken. *The Lum Hat* (Aberdeen University Press, 1982) contains recently discovered novellas and short stories.

JESSIE KESSON, b. 1916 Inverness, has written several novels set in north-east Scotland: *The White Bird Passes* (Chatto and Windus, 1958; Paul Harris, 1980), *Glitter of Mica* (Chatto and Windus, 1963; Paul Harris, 1982), and *Another Time, Another Place* (Chatto and Windus, 1983). A number of her short stories are collected in *Where the Apple Ripens* (Chatto and Windus, 1985), from which 'The Gowk' is taken.

JOAN LINGARD, b. 1932 in Edinburgh, has written both for adults and for adolescent readers. Her adult novels include *The Prevailing Wind* (Hodder and Stoughton, 1964; Paul Harris, 1978), *The Headmaster* (Hodder and Stoughton, 1967), *The Second Flowering of Emily Mountjoy* (Paul Harris, 1979), *Sisters by Rite* (Hamish Hamilton, 1984), and *Reasonable Doubts* (Hamish Hamilton, 1986). 'An Edinburgh Lady' is taken from chapter 8 of *The Prevailing Wind*.

EONA MACNICOL, b. 1910 in Inverness, has published two historical novels, *Colum of Derry* (Sheed and Ward, 1954) and *Lamp in the Night Wind* (William Maclellan, 1965); and three collections of short stories: *The Hallowe'en Hero* (Blackwood, 1969), *The Jail Dancing* (Albyn Press, 1978), and *A Carver of Coal* (Ramsay Head Press, 1979), from which 'The Pigeon' is taken.

NAOMI MITCHISON, b. 1897 in Edinburgh, has written over 70 books which reflect her wide range of interests, including mythology, history, socialism, the West Highlands and Africa. Of her many novels, particularly notable are *The Corn King and the Spring Queen* (Cape, 1931; Virago, 1983) and *The Bull Calves* (Cape, 1947; Richard Drew, 1985). Her short stories have been published in several collections, including *Five Men and a Swan* (Allen and Unwin, 1958), *Images of Africa* (Canongate, 1980), *What do you think yourself?* (Paul Harris, 1982), and *Beyond This Limit* (Scottish Academic Press, 1986). 'The Teeth' is taken from *Five Men and a Swan*.

LORNA MOON (1886-1930, b. Strichen, Aberdeenshire) became a scriptwiter in Hollywood before her early death from tubercolosis. Her two books, a short story collection *Doorways in Drumorty* (Cape, 1926) and a novel *Dark Star* (Gollancz, 1929) were virtually forgotten until their reissue, in 1981 and 1980 respectively, by Gourdas House, Aberdeen. 'Wantin' a Hand' is taken from *Doorways in Drumorty*.

NANCY BRYSSON MORRISON, born in Glasgow, has written a number of novels, notably *The Gowk Storm* (Collins, 1933) and *The Following Wind* (Hogarth Press, 1954), and also biographical works on the Brontes, The Carlyles and others. 'No Letters, Please' is taken from *Casual Columns: the Glasgow Herald miscellany* (George Outram, 1955).

WILLA MUIR (1890-1970, b. Shetland) was the wife of the poet and critic Edwin Muir, with whom she translated works by Kafka, Feuchtwanger and other European writers. She wrote two novels, *Imagined Corners* (Martin Secker, 1931) and *Mrs Ritchie* (Martin Secker, 1933). 'Clock-a-doodle-do' was published in *The Modern Scot*, vol. 5, 1934.

MARGARET OLIPHANT (1828-1897, b. Wallyford, East Lothian) wrote almost 100 novels, together with short stories and non-fiction. Several of her novels have been republished in recent years, including *Salem Chapel* (1863; Virago, 1986); *The Doctor's Family* (1863; with *The Executor* and *The Rector*, Oxford, 1986; with *The Rector*, Virago, 1986); *Miss Marjoribanks* (1866; Zodiac Press, 1969); *Hester* (1883; Virago, 1984); and *Kirsteen* (1890; Dent, 1984). Her short stories were collected in *The Ways of Life* (1897), *A Widow's Tale* (1898), and *Stories of the Seen and the Unseen* (1902). 'Mrs Merridew's Fortune' appeared in *Cornhill Magazine*, September 1869. 'The Library Window' first appeared in *Blackwood's Edinburgh Magazine*, January 1896, and has been frequently reprinted, most recently in Margaret Oliphant: *Selected short stories of the supernatural* (Scottish Academic Press, 1985).

AGNES OWENS, b. 1926 in Milngavie, has published one novel, *Gentlemen of the West* (Polygon, 1984),. Nine of her short stories, including 'A Change of Face', appear with stories by James Kelman and Alasdair Gray in *Lean Tales* (Cape, 1985).

MURIEL SPARK, b. 1918 in Edinburgh, has acknowledged the influence of her Scottish birth and upbringing on her work though most of her novels are set outside Scotland; an exception is *The Prime of Miss Jean Brodie* (Macmillan, 1961; Penguin, 1965). Her short stories have been collected in *The Go-Away Bird* (Macmillan, 1958; Penguin, 1963), *Voices at Play* (Macmillan, 1961), *Collected Stories I* (Macmillan, 1967) and *Bang-Bang You're Dead* (Granada, 1982). *The Stories of Muriel Spark* is to be published by The Bodley Head in 1987. 'The Black Madonna' is taken from *The Go-Away Bird*.

SARAH TYTLER (1827-1914, b. Cupar) was a prolific writer of novels, short stories and non-fiction, both under this pseudonym and as Henrietta Keddie, her real name. Much of her work lacks literary quality, but she wrote two interesting novels, *St Mungo's City* (1884) and *Logie Town* (1887). The extract 'A Harmonious Little Arrangement' comes from chapter 27 of *St. Mungo's City*.

JOAN URE (1919-1978, b. near Newcastle) is best known as a playwright: *Five Short Plays* (Scottish Society of Playwrights, 1979) is the only collection of her work so far published. She also wrote poems, essays and short stories. 'It's My Day for Leaving Home' appeared in *Scottish International*, April 1969.